MILO AND MARCOS AT THE END OF THE WORLD

Milo AND Marcos AT THE End OF THE World

KEVIN CHRISTOPHER SNIPES

HARPER TEEN
An Imprint of HarperCollinsPublishers

HarperTeen is an imprint of HarperCollins Publishers.

Milo and Marcos at the End of the World
Copyright © 2022 by Kevin Christopher Snipes
All rights reserved. Printed in the United States of America.
No part of this book may be used or reproduced in any manner whatsoever without written permission except in the case of brief quotations embodied in critical articles and reviews. For information address HarperCollins Children's Books, a division of HarperCollins Publishers, 195 Broadway, New York, NY 10007.
www.epicreads.com

Library of Congress Control Number: 2021950882
ISBN 978-0-06-306256-6

Typography by Chris Kwon
22 23 24 25 26   PC/LSCH   10 9 8 7 6 5 4 3 2 1
❖
First Edition

FOR TWERPETTE

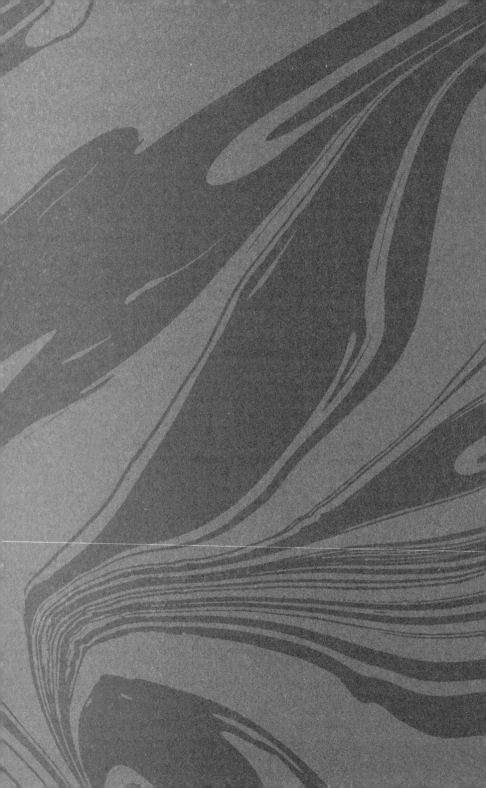

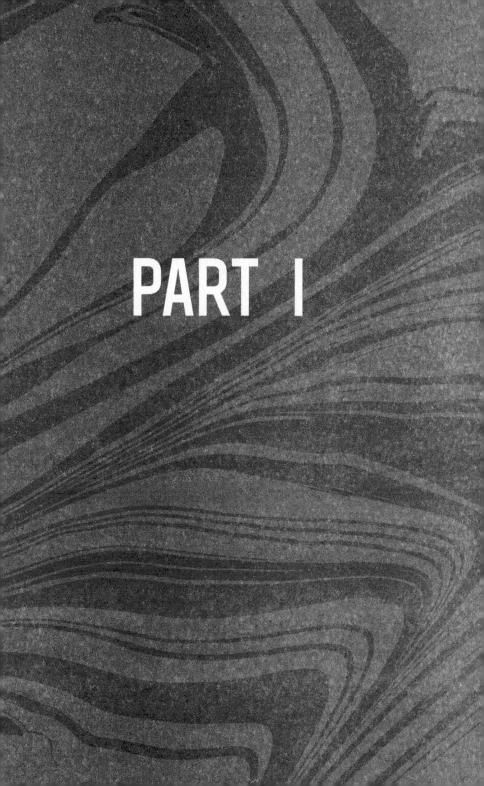

PART I

1

One Month, Three Days, and Eleven and a Half Hours until the End of the World

The first sign that the world is going to end occurs on Monday, August 15, at 12:13 p.m.

I know the exact time because I'm looking at my phone, wondering where the heck Van is. Because if there's one thing I know about my best friend, it's that Van Silvera is never late.

I *hate* when people are late. If I'm waiting for someone and it's been more than fifteen minutes, I start worrying that (a) I've missed them, (b) they're not coming, or (c) they've secretly hated me all my life and this is how they've finally decided to let me know.

In my defense, I *know* that's an overreaction. But Van was supposed to meet me here in the school parking lot at noon so we could grab lunch off campus. The fact that I've been pacing next to her empty Jeep for thirteen minutes—that's right, *thirteen*—can only mean one thing: she's dead.

Or our friendship is.

Or both.

Where on earth is she? If today were any other day I might not be freaking out, but it's the *first* day of our *senior* year, which means I'm already wound tighter than the restraints on a straitjacket.

Somehow, miraculously, I've managed to coast through the last three years of high school without any major disasters. No failed tests. No major bullying. No awkward erections in class. So by my calculations, I'm pretty much due for some sort of Epic Teenage Catastrophe because, let's get real, no one gets through high school unscathed. No one. That's just a fact.

Van calls me paranoid, but I basically operate under the principle that if something can go wrong, it will. The way I see it, if you don't watch your step and keep your head down, the universe will make you a target. And I can't think of anything more horrifying than being the center of attention.

I've certainly never sought any sort of spotlight. In fact, if someone were to ask my classmates at Spruce Crick to describe me, their first response would probably be, "Who's Milo Connolly?"

As for the small subset of people who do actually remember my name, they'd probably say I'm that super-religious, super-shy nerd who only does "church stuff." Which is only *half* accurate. Technically, it's my diehard Presbyterian parents who are super religious. I'm more religious by proxy.

That said, I do spend most of my free time doing "church stuff." I'm a *big* fan of rules. And church is all about rules—very specific rules that are very clear about what you can and cannot do. And if you follow the rules, you're all set. No surprises. No confusion. No problem. It's like having an instruction manual for life.

Most people are surprised to learn that a rule-loving and painfully introverted Christian like me has a best friend like Van, a self-proclaimed agnostic who is both the star player on the girls' soccer team *and* the lead of every fall musical. But what people forget is that Van also used to be a quiet, well-behaved little Presbyterian. Back before she scandalized my parents by "taking a break from Jesus," Van regularly attended our church. That's how we met.

One December, when we were six, Van and I were cast as Mary and Joseph in our Sunday school's nativity play. I was painfully shy even then and pretty much refused to say any of my lines. Van on the other hand thrived in the spotlight and wanted to say everybody's lines: the wise men's, the angel's, even the sheep's. Somehow our Silent Joseph and Chatty Mary routine was the unexpected hit of the Christmas season, and we've been inseparable ever since.

Which is why I'm freaking out that it's now 12:13—no, 12:*14*— and Van is *literally nowhere to be seen*. I've texted her *five* times and she hasn't responded. Which means today just might be the day that my one and only friend has finally and irrevocably realized that I—Milo Connolly—am a Lost Cause.

I shouldn't be surprised. I knew this day would come. There's no way someone as special as Van could stay friends with someone as embarrassingly lame as me.

I just thought we had more time.

"Milo!" a voice yells out as the school doors bang open.

Oh, thank goodness . . .

Van waves at me across the parking lot, and the sigh of relief that escapes my lungs practically blows me over.

I'm so relieved by the sight of her smiling face and bouncing mane of auburn hair that it takes me a moment to realize she's not alone. A boy is with her. I don't recognize his face, so I assume he must be some clueless underclassman who doesn't understand the valuable time he's wasting by trapping Van in whatever inane conversation he wants to have. But as they get closer, I notice the boy is smiling.

At me.

"Look who I found!" Van shouts with a flourish.

My brain is still struggling to make sense of what I'm seeing when the boy sticks out a hand and winks.

"Hey, Connolly. Long time no see."

Oh. My. God.

Marcos.

I can't believe I didn't recognize him. It's been three years since we were all together, so of course he looks older, but everything I remember about him—everything *I can't help* but remember about him—is still the same. His jet-black hair still perfectly coiffed to look intentionally messy. His lean face still ending in that ridiculously sharp jawline, like the hero in an action movie.

As for his eyes . . . they haven't changed a bit. Dark and penetrating, they still look as if they're taking in everything *and* everyone around him. As if they could peer straight into your soul.

I never wanted to see those eyes again for as long as I live.

Before I know what I'm doing, though, I start to reach for him.

Our hands touch.

And the Earth trembles.

2

All Shook Up

"Whoa!" Van shouts as she stumbles sideways, falling against her Jeep.

A second later Marcos staggers backward, his hand pulling out of mine, and I realize that I'm not the only one having trouble staying vertical as the ground of the Spruce Crick parking lot shifts and rumbles beneath our feet.

Marcos and Van are shaking. As is every car around us. As is the whole, entire high school. Everyone and everything is literally shaking down to its foundation.

And then, just as suddenly as it began, it stops.

"What the heck?" Van gasps, trying to catch her breath. "Was that an *earthquake*?"

"Can't be," Marcos says. "Florida doesn't get earthquakes."

"Then what was *that*?" she asks.

"Maybe there was an explosion?"

"I didn't hear any explosion. The ground *literally* moved. That was definitely an earthquake."

"Weird."

"So weird."

Then they both look at me. Because I still haven't said a word. Because I'm speechless. Not because of the earthquake, which, yeah, is *pretty freakin' weird*, but SO WHAT?

Marcos Price is STANDING IN FRONT OF ME!

Every atom of my body is quivering. I feel like I'm still shaking apart at the seams even though the ground has settled.

How is this possible? What is he doing here? More importantly, *What do I do?* Because right now all I can think is *DO. NOT. FAINT.* Which is easier said than done considering my legs won't stop wobbling.

"Are you okay?" he asks.

I have no idea how to answer that. Thankfully, I don't have to.

"Holy crap!" Van exclaims, staring at her phone.

"What's the matter?" Marcos asks, turning his attention back to her. "Is there something online about what just happened?"

"What? Oh. No," Van clarifies. "I was about to look, but I just saw the time. We need to get a move on if we want to get to Holloway's and back before fourth period."

"Are you sure it's safe to drive?" Marcos asks, squinting skeptically at the road leading away from Crick. "What if there's another earthquake?"

"Trust me, dude, you'd rather take your chances with an earthquake than with the slop they serve in our cafeteria *any day.*"

"Well, if you put it like that," Marcos chuckles.

"Oh, it's definitely like that," Van says, unlocking her Jeep. "Now let's go. Everyone, inside!"

I'm too numb to argue. I slide into the front passenger seat next to

Van as Marcos climbs into the back like it's the most natural thing in the world. Like he's been doing it all his life.

"Hold on," Van commands as she keys the ignition.

She barely stops at the parking guard station so Mr. Kirby can check our student IDs before peeling out of the lot like she's competing in the Daytona 500. Normally, I'd be screaming at her to slow down, but right now I'm far too distracted with the thoughts racing through my brain.

Marcos is here.

Marcos Price is *here*, and he goes to my school.

Since when?

Well, since today apparently. He must have transferred over the summer. Did Van know and not tell me? She certainly seems happy to see him.

Am I happy to see him?

I don't know.

It's been three years since I've seen his face so a part of me is obviously *curious*. Especially as I made a vow to never—*ever*—look him up on social media. But happy? No. Why would I be? It's not like we were *friends*. Friends don't treat one another the way he treated me. Friends don't turn each other's lives upside down and then completely abandon each other without a word of explanation. Not unless one of those "friends" is a sociopath.

I mean, *look* at him. You'd think he'd have the decency to at least pretend to look guilty after everything that went down between us. But no! If he's feeling any awkwardness about our reunion, he's certainly not letting on.

"Seriously, I feel so bad," Marcos says, leaning forward.

For a second, I think he's read my mind—that maybe I've judged him too harshly—until I realize his apology isn't aimed at me. It's for Van. For making us late. Something to do with picking up his student ID from the front office.

"I didn't think it would take so long."

"Welcome to Port Orange," Van sighs, "where everything takes twice as long and is half as interesting."

"Is that the town motto?"

"Surprisingly, the mayor shot it down when I recommended it."

"For real, though," Marcos insists, "I'm sorry. I know you two had this whole back-to-school lunch plan and I've totally crashed it."

"Dude, don't worry about it. It's fine. Seriously, we're cool, *bro*."

"Thanks, *bro*."

A second later Van and Marcos are cracking up, and I am more confused than ever. "*Bro?*" It's only been only a couple of hours and they already have weird in-jokes? Typical. It's like camp all over again.

"Sorry," Van apologizes, clocking my baffled expression. "We're making fun of Mr. Henderson. He spent the summer doing 'youth outreach theater' in Miami, and now he thinks he's super woke and calls everyone 'bro.' It is deeply problematic but also deeply hysterical."

"Oh," I say.

"'Oh'? That's it? That's your only reaction?"

"White people." I shrug.

It's a purely automatic response—something I've picked up from years of hanging out with Van and witnessing firsthand some of the cringeworthy behavior she's had to endure from people with my complexion—but the way it makes Marcos laugh catches me off guard. I feel warm all over. Like I've inadvertently won a prize.

"Did you just say 'white people'?"

"I've trained him well," Van brags. "I mean, he's still got some work to do when it comes to understanding the intersectionality of race and gender, but he is vastly superior to the Milo that you first met."

"Aww . . . Don't tell me you've changed him too much," Marcos says, shooting me a grin in the rearview mirror. "I kind of liked him the way he was."

He clasps my shoulder, and the whole back of my neck feels warm. I don't dare turn around. Or speak. All I can do is stare out the window and force myself to breathe as my face turns bright red.

I can't believe this is happening. I can't believe that after all this time he still has the ability to turn my own body against me with a touch. I thought I was done with these feelings. I thought I was safe! But from the way my skin is practically burning up under my clothes, I know I am far from immune.

"Isn't that right, Milo?"

Oh no. Van just asked me a question, and I have no idea what it is. Are we still talking about Mr. Henderson?

"Uh . . . sure," I say. As a rule, it's always safer to agree with Van.

"Sure? *Sure?* So you *admit* it?" she asks, raising an eyebrow in surprise.

Oh crap! Did Marcos tell her something? About us?

"Wait, wait, wait, what was the question?"

"No, no, no!" Van cackles with glee. "No take-backs. You admitted it. Marcos is my witness. *I'm* the one who discovered Holloway's

BBQ. Not *you*. Me!" Then to Marcos she adds, "Milo and I have been arguing about this for *years*. I can't believe he finally admitted the truth!"

Oh, thank goodness. She's talking about lunch. I'm so relieved I don't even bother to contradict her, even though I know for a fact that I was the one who first discovered Holloway's. It's one of my few sources of pride.

After all, Holloway's has the distinction of serving what can only be described as the Greatest Curly Fries in the Universe. Simultaneously spicy, sweet, and tangy, Holloway's fries contain twenty-seven secret ingredients that make each bite so deliciously addictive, they're the closest things to culinary heaven a person can experience in the suburban wasteland that is Port Orange, Florida.

Seriously, Van's earlier joke about our city wasn't far from the truth. Port Orange basically has the unremarkable distinction of being the completely forgettable neighbor of Daytona Beach, a place most people recognize as either (a) the former Spring Break Capital of the World, (b) the birthplace of NASCAR, or (c) the setting for the Aileen Wuornos movie *Monster*. Port Orange, on the other hand, isn't fancy enough for speed racing, killer prostitutes, or anything else for that matter. It's basically a quiet town full of quiet people where nothing out of the ordinary ever happens.

Except today. Today apparently Port Orange has decided to become the effing Twilight Zone.

"My ex took me to Holloway's on one of our first dates," Van explains to Marcos. "It was the *only* good thing to come out of that relationship. That's how I know *I'm* the one who discovered the curly fries. Besides, I'm literally the only person Milo hangs out with, so it's not like he could've gone there with anyone other than me."

"Oh, come on," Marcos half-heartedly protests on my behalf. "Maybe Connolly's had a date or two you don't know about."

Oh. My. God. If I threw myself out of this moving Jeep, it would honestly be less *excruciating* than hearing Van and Marcos discuss my love life. It's bad enough she's painting me as the school pariah, but the unmistakable *pity* in Marcos's voice makes me want to curl up in my seat and *die.*

"Okay, we're here!" Van shouts, as we pull into Holloway's parking lot. Somehow, we've made the journey in under ten minutes—which is *criminally* irresponsible—but I don't have time to chide Van with statistics about teen driving fatalities because she's already out of the Jeep, hurrying us inside.

"Does everyone know what they want?" she asks as we step up to the counter to place our order.

"Um . . . ," says Marcos, which is the *wrong* answer. Van doesn't truck with indecision.

"Can we get three extra-large curly fries, three chocolate shakes, and three fried chicken sandwiches with extra barbecue sauce?" she orders on our behalf.

"Marcos is a vegetarian," I remind her, the words slipping out of my mouth before I can stop myself.

Ugh! Why do I remember that? And why does Marcos look so pleased that I remember?

"Really, Marcos?" Van groans. "Still?"

"Afraid so."

"Ugh, *fine*. Can we get *two* chicken sandwiches and whatever the vegetarian option is for my weird friend who doesn't eat animals because he hates all things tasty and delicious?"

Marcos catches my eye and chuckles at Van's disdain. I can't help smiling back. It's like old times.

Old times that did not end well, I remind myself before quickly turning away.

The cashier hands Van our order number, and we grab a seat while we wait for our food. I can feel Van relentlessly tapping her foot against the table, which is how I know she's worried about making it back to school in time. With good reason.

Lunch at Crick is strictly observed from 12:00 p.m. to 1:00 p.m. Freshmen, sophomores, and juniors are required to eat what passes for food in the school's windowless dungeon of a cafeteria, while seniors are permitted to dine off campus—provided they're back in time for fourth period. Anyone who returns late from lunch automatically loses their off-campus privileges *for the year*.

Van explains all this to Marcos, but the whole time he's listening to her, his eyes keep darting over to me.

Why? What does he expect me to say? Does he really think I have any interest in reconnecting with him? After everything that happened?

Thank goodness Van is here to keep him distracted. As long as she can keep the conversation going, I have time to figure out what I'm going to do about this whole Marcos Situation.

Option one: I could go with the "Polite but Aloof Approach," so he knows I don't care one way or the other that he's back in my life. *Which I don't.* But if I'm too distant, he might suspect I'm still resentful about what happened, which might imply that I've been secretly obsessing about him for the last three years. *Which I haven't.*

Option two: I could go with the "Exceedingly Friendly Approach." That way he sees how *more than okay* I am with his sudden reappearance. But the risk there is that if I'm too nice, he might think I'm still "desperate" to be his friend. *Which I'm not.*

Option three: I could—

"You okay, Connolly?"

Crap! He's talking to me. And I don't have a plan. *Okay, I can do this. I just need to keep my answers short and simple.*

"Yeah, I'm okay," I say. "Just hungry."

Marcos nods, still looking at me with those stupid, inescapable eyes of his. I turn to Van, hoping she'll launch into a new topic (Van's always good for a passionate diatribe against something), but for some reason she seems perfectly content to just stare at her phone.

"So . . . you go to Crick now?" It's the safest question I can think to ask. Bland and noncommittal. But Marcos smiles like he's been waiting for me to ask.

Don't look so smug, I want to snap. *I don't actually care if you do. I'm being polite!*

"Yeah," he says. "My dad was working at the Salvation Army—not the thrift store, but the central office in Orlando—and they ended up having to lay off half the staff, so he and my mom decided we'd give Port Orange a try. Well, *he* decided. My mom and I basically got dragged here against our will."

Against his will? So Marcos doesn't want to be here any more than I want him here. That's good to know. Maybe it won't be so hard to avoid him after all.

15

"Sorry you got dragged here. And that your dad lost his job. That's rough."

"It's all good. He got a job at Port Orange Presbyterian, so it all worked out."

"Your dad works at POP?" I gasp.

"POP?"

Port Orange Presbyterian. POP. Our old pastor, Pastor Fields, used to shake his head in exasperation when congregants referred to his church as POP. He said it was borderline blasphemous and made him feel like he was a soda jerk, not a minister. After Pastor Fields retired, though, Pastor Foley became our minister. And in an effort to make the church more "accessible" and "fun," Foley embraced a more progressive view on certain subjects, including abbreviations.

"Oh, yeah, POP." Marcos nods. "My dad's the new treasurer."

"Great," Van says, still not looking up from her phone. "Milo will finally have someone to keep him company."

Yeah. *Great.* Now in addition to having to see Marcos five days a week at school, I can also look forward to him ruining my weekends. Super-*effing*-awesome.

Before I can wallow in my misery, though, the cashier calls out our order number, and Van springs back into action. In sixty seconds flat, we're in her Jeep, out of the parking lot, and tearing down the road on our way back to Crick.

It's 12:45 p.m. The part of my brain still focused on not losing our lunch privileges knows we're cutting it close even with Van running every yellow light and treating the speed limit like a mere suggestion. But somehow that threat pales in comparison to the threat that's sitting behind me. It's too much. I honestly think I might faint. Between Marcos and the "earthquake," my mind is drowning in a sea of anxiety, and all I want is to go home and crawl into bed before life has the chance to throw any more curveballs my way.

"What the hell?" Van shouts, slamming on the brakes.

I grip the dashboard as the Jeep screeches to a halt—just in time to avoid plowing into the car ahead of us.

"What's going on?" Marcos asks, leaning forward to stare at the impenetrable gridlock of bumper-to-bumper traffic stretching down the road as far as the eye can see.

"I have no friggin' clue."

From the honking and shouting in the cars ahead of us, I can tell that most of the drivers are our fellow classmates. What I can't see is the cause of the congestion. There doesn't appear to be an accident or an alligator sunning itself in the middle of the road (which, believe it or not, is one of the most common causes of traffic delays in Florida).

Whatever the reason, though, one thing is painfully certain.

We. Are. Screwed.

There's no way we'll make it back to Crick before fourth period. Sure, Marcos and I could make a run for it. The school's only a couple of blocks away. But I'd never abandon Van. And apparently neither would Marcos. Though God knows I wouldn't be surprised if he did. Marcos is good at disappearing.

"I can't believe this," Van mutters as she lays on the horn in one last futile gesture of exasperation. Then we stare at our phones in silence as the passing minutes condemn us.

12:58, 12:59, 1:00 . . .

My stomach lurches.

1:05 . . . 1:11 . . . 1:18 . . .

"Give me the bag," Van orders when my phone reads 1:30 and the line of cars in front of us still hasn't moved an inch. She angrily distributes our lunches, but the food's gone cold, and even the Greatest Curly Fries in the Universe can't cheer us up.

As I suck the seasoning off my fingers, I sneak a look at Marcos in the rearview mirror. I know there are supposed to be twenty-seven distinct ingredients but right now, in this impossible moment, there are only two things I can taste.

Salt and regret.

3

Sinkholes and Other Affairs of the Heart

Turns out it's a sinkhole.

That's what triggered all the shaking earlier. And the traffic jam. They're both the result of an enormous, gaping chasm that chose today of all days to rise up from the depths of the Earth and swallow fifty feet of the Spruce Crick parking lot.

I guess God didn't think this day was weird enough.

I guess He thought, *Milo has had it too easy these last few years. I know! Let's trap him in a car with the one person most likely to induce a panic attack and make him wait ninety minutes for the fire and rescue department to arrive. That way his first day back will be a real soul crusher!*

Not that it had to be soul crushing. I suppose a less neurotic person (i.e., not me) could've used the time to reconnect with Marcos instead of nursing a three-year grudge. But no way am I putting myself out there for him. Not again.

Fire and rescue cordons off the perimeter of the sinkhole with orange traffic cones, then begins directing cars back into the school parking lot. Apparently, they've determined there's no further risk of it expanding, though Van for once is a cautious driver, giving it a wide berth.

"Whoa," she exclaims as her Jeep creeps past the massive chasm. "We seriously dodged a bullet."

I assume she's being sarcastic—until I follow her gaze and realize that the sinkhole has formed in the exact spot where her Jeep was parked before lunch. If we hadn't left when we did, her reliable old Cherokee would currently be sitting at the bottom of a very deep pit—probably in pieces.

My parents would say it's a miracle. They'd also say I should thank God for looking out for us. But considering everything that's happened today, I think God has a lot of explaining to do.

In total, twenty-seven seniors lose their right to dine off campus for the rest of the year—including Van, Marcos, and me. If you think that's wildly unfair given the extenuating circumstances, you're not alone.

By the end of the day, my outraged classmates are already banding together and calling themselves the Sinkhole 27. Their self-appointed leader—and senior class president—Ashleigh Audrey Woods spearheads the campaign to protest the administration's "draconian policy" (her words). As the school's inevitable valedictorian, Ashleigh's worked harder than anyone to achieve a perfect academic record, and she's not about to see it tarnished by a flagrantly unfair disciplinary citation. Especially when her tardiness is clearly the result of "an Act of God" (again, her words).

By the time school lets out, she's badgered Vice Principal Holland to the point where he agrees to at least *consider* restoring our lunch privileges. But on the off chance he refuses to change his mind,

Ashleigh is already planning a protest meeting at her house for Friday night where the Sinkhole 27 will organize the next steps of their resistance. Yes, Ashleigh used the word "resistance." It's bit intense, but then so is Ashleigh.

In the fifteen minutes between the time that I pull out of the Crick parking lot and the time I pull into my driveway, I've already received three DMs and six texts demanding to know whether I'll be attending her "Freedom Rally."

I'm not. As much as I hate the thought of spending my senior year in the culinary Siberia of our cafeteria with its gray pizza and ice-cold tater tots, the thought of hanging out with twenty-six outraged, indignant, and *unchaperoned* teenagers is even more horrifying.

Besides, I've got enough on my plate right now with Marcos.

Ugh, Marcos . . .

My hands are literally shaking as I unlock my front door. If I don't stop thinking about him soon, I'm going to give myself a panic attack. I need a distraction—anything—to keep my mind off this disaster, so as soon as I'm inside my house I turn on the TV.

Channel 7 news has a story about the sinkhole. A very sweaty man from the school board is standing in the Crick parking lot trying to sound as reassuring as possible while dabbing the perspiration from his forehead.

"What can I say?" he says with a shrug. "Sinkholes happen. The important thing is that no one was hurt and that we're working as quickly as possible to repair the parking lot so our children can continue to learn in a safe and secure environment."

The story goes on like that for a few more minutes, but it's clear from the reporter's vacant expression that there's not much else to say on the subject. Nobody seems to know why the sinkhole appeared out of nowhere or why it was able to spread so quickly. Apparently, it's just "one of those things." Like hurricanes, jellyfish, and palmetto bugs, if you live in Florida long enough, sooner or later you're going to come face-to-face with one.

Part of me has a nagging suspicion that I ought to be more concerned about the fact that holes are just opening up in the earth, but I'm finding it difficult to keep my eyes open. Anxiety does that to me. Too much unwanted stimulus and I go down. It's like having a stress-activated off switch.

In fact, I don't even realize I've drifted off until the bang of the garage door startles me awake, and I realize my parents are home.

My mom and dad are reasonably curious about the sinkhole, but by dinner it's old news. Which is good because I'm still too exhausted for a protracted conversation. I answer their questions by repeating what the sweaty man from the school board said on TV and leave it at that.

I *don't* tell them I've lost my lunch privileges because I missed two classes my first day back. Such news would not go over well with Bruce and Dana Connolly.

My dad works in construction, which tends to make him an exhausted grump on the best of days, and my mom is a bank teller, which is about as straitlaced a profession as one can get. They're both deeply religious and devoutly Republican. They also don't believe in divorce or single parenting or any other "social disease" that couldn't be depicted in a Norman Rockwell painting. In fact, my father once told me, "The problem with the world today is that everyone has *too* much freedom." So I'm pretty sure he won't have much sympathy for someone who got in trouble for choosing curly fries over his education.

Besides, I'm not sure how to mention my lost lunch privileges without mentioning Van. And Van is always a touchy subject.

When she left POP, the news of her newfound secularism did not go over well with my parents, who basically reacted as if Van had announced she was going to burn all her bras and join a cult. She hasn't been allowed inside our house since.

Of course, my parents know I still hang out with her, but the less I mention Van, the less chance there is I'll have to sit through one of my father's impromptu lectures on the "Dangers of Straying from the Fold."

"Oh, I almost forgot," my mom says brightly, setting down her fork in excitement. "Patty Reynolds came into the bank this afternoon, and she told me that Reverend Foley *finally* hired a new treasurer."

My stomach does a somersault. I can feel my chicken cutlet working its way back up my throat at the mention of Marcos's father, but I force myself to swallow it down. After all, there's no reason to freak out. Obviously, everyone is going to be talking about the Prices. A new family moving to town and joining the church is always a noteworthy event. But it has nothing to do with me.

"It's about time," my dad says approvingly as he wipes a bit of marinara sauce from his beard. "I don't know how the church has lasted this long without one."

"I know. But Patty got to meet him today and she says he is more than worth the wait. Also, his last name is Price, which is a pretty good name for a treasurer, don't you think? Conrad or Connor Price."

For someone who works in a bank and is a legit ace with numbers, my mom is shockingly bad with names. Case in point: there is no one named Patty at our church. She means Patsy. Patsy Reynolds. Who's been POP's administrative assistant for the last ten years.

"Anyway, Patty says he's very charming and apparently quite good-looking."

"Is he married?" My dad has an innate distrust of charming, single men. Especially if they're good-looking. In his book, a man without a family is a man looking for trouble.

"Yes, he's married. I think the wife's name is Jacinta—or something like that. She's Mexican. Though Patty says she speaks perfect English. And they have a teenage son who started at Crick today."

There are so many things wrong with what my mom just said that I have to bite my tongue to stop myself from correcting her. Mrs. Price's family is from Cuba, not Mexico. More importantly, she was born and raised in Miami, so she's just as American as the rest of us and nobody should be surprised that she can speak English.

I know I should say something, but as far as my parents are concerned, I've never heard of the Prices. And that's *exactly* how I need to keep things.

"Anyway," my mom says, turning to me with a smile, "you'll have to look for their son at school tomorrow. Introduce yourself. Make him feel welcome. I'm sure he could use a friend."

What my mom actually means is that she's sure I could use a friend who's *not* Van Silvera. Which is pretty ironic considering that if she knew everything I do about Marcos, the last thing she'd do is encourage our friendship.

For that reason alone, for a split second, I'm almost tempted to tell my parents all about the new treasurer's son. I mean, all I'd have to do is let slip that I know him from camp and that he's a bad influence—which strictly speaking is 100 percent true—and then Marcos Price will be persona non grata in the Connolly household.

But all I say is, "Okay."

My mom prides herself on being an upright Christian woman, but like most upright Christian women, she's a bit of a gossip. Anything I tell her about Marcos will be disseminated to the rest of the congregation before the end of the week. So if it gets back to Marcos that I've started spreading rumors about him, he might just decide to spread a few rumors about me.

And God knows there's a lot he could say.

PART 1½

4

"I can't believe you talked me into this," Van grumbles as she heaves her battered old suitcase out from the trunk of my mom's Volvo.

I cast a quick glance over my shoulder to make my sure my mom didn't hear. She's not a fan of Van's recent forays into sass and sarcasm, but thankfully she's still on her phone complaining to my dad about the insane amount of traffic we hit on our way to Gainesville this morning.

"I didn't talk you into anything," I remind her, lowering my voice. "You *wanted* to come." And it's true. She did. She was all gung ho about coming to camp with me when I first brought up the idea last month.

"I feel like I accepted the invitation *before* I had all the relevant information," she shoots back, slamming the trunk shut with a satisfying thud.

"I told you it was a Bible camp."

"Yeah, but I was picturing cabins in the woods. Sing-alongs by a campfire. A lake."

I was too if I'm being honest. When my parents initially suggested I spend the first three weeks of my summer break at the Gainesville

Presbyterian Youth Retreat, I had visions of Van and me having out-doorsy adventures involving long, invigorating hikes and s'mores. In reality, though, the Gainesville Presbyterian Youth Retreat is more like summer school for Protestants. During the day, campers take various seminars on how to be better Presbyterians, and at night they sleep in dorms rented from a local community college.

I did tell Van all this when I become aware of my misconception, and while she was (obviously) disappointed, she still said she wanted to come.

Now that we're here, though, looking out at the cluster of beige cinder-block buildings giving off a sad industrial park vibe, I can tell she's already regretting her decision.

"Do you want my mom to take you back to home?" I ask, a lump of fear rising in my throat. It would totally suck if Van went back to Port Orange and left me here to fend for myself. It would, in fact, be utter misery. But I wouldn't blame her. I can't think of many people other than me who'd want to kick off summer vacation with three weeks of Bible study and prayer circles.

"Dude, *relax*," Van sighs. "I'm not going anywhere."

"You sure?" I ask, still slightly holding my breath.

"Yes, I'm sure. I'm just giving you a hard time. I'm sure this'll be fun. Or fun-adjacent. And if not, at least it beats hearing my mom curse my dad as she cries herself to sleep every night."

She laughs like that last part is a joke, but I know her well enough to see she means it. Between her parents' very bitter divorce and her dad abruptly moving back to Puerto Rico, these last couple of months have been rough for Van. It's one of the reasons I wanted her to come away with me this summer. To give her a break from all the family drama. In fact, now that I think about it, *that's* probably the reason Van decided to come to this retreat even after she found out there was zero chance of canoeing.

"Don't worry," I say, trying to rally her spirits. "We're going to have fun. We're about to have three weeks of uninterrupted Quality Van and Milo Time. QVMT!"

Van raises her eyebrow skeptically. "QVMT, huh?"

"All the QVMT in the world!" I reassure her.

"But you're also going to find time to make some *new* friends, right, sweetie?" my mom's voice calls out behind me.

Oops.

I turn around and see her slip her phone back into her purse while she stares at me with a mixture of maternal concern and exasperation. "I know it's difficult being in a strange place and meeting new people," she says, coming to my side and launching into the same pep talk/motivational speech she's used on me since I was six, "but if you are kind and open with others, then nine times out of ten, people will be kind and open with you. You just need to have confidence and be yourself."

Have confidence *and* be myself? That's an oxymoron.

But what I say is, "I know, Mom."

"Good. So you promise to try one hundred percent?"

"I promise."

Strictly speaking, it'll probably be closer to 10 percent, but the last thing I want right now is for my mom to make a scene. She's already a little on edge from waking up at 6:00 a.m. on a Saturday to drive Van and me to the middle of Florida during a heat wave—and that was before we sat in traffic for two hours. I can tell she's in no mood for my antisocial tendencies. It's the whole not-so-secret reason she and my dad pushed me to come to this camp in the first place. Like Van, my parents have been on a mission for years to get me "out of my shell."

Which, frankly, is a phrase I've never understood. I mean, do you know what happens when you take a turtle out of its shell?

It *dies*.

"Don't worry, Mrs. Connolly," Van jumps in. "I'll make sure Milo isn't a hermit. He's going to be a social butterfly and make new friends if it kills him."

My mom purses her lips, but I can tell she doesn't want to have to lecture me in public any more than I want to be lectured, so eventually she just smiles and says, "Thank you, Vanessa, I'd appreciate that. Though let's try not to kill Milo if at all possible."

I flash Van a grateful smile and she shoots me a wink. What would I do without her?

"All right," my mom says, turning toward the campus. "Let's get you kids checked in. I have a good feeling about this place. I think you're both going to have a really special time."

"You do?"

"I do indeed," she chuckles as she hands me my suitcase. "In fact, I think it might just be the best three weeks of your entire summer."

I am 99.9 percent convinced this is *not* going to be the best three weeks my entire summer, but as I lug my suitcase up the stairwell to the third and final floor of the boys' dorm, I tell myself to keep an open mind. Who knows? Maybe if my nerves don't get the best of me and I keep the sulking to a minimum, I might actually make a friend or two. It's not impossible.

I unlock my door and step inside the room that will be my home away from home for the rest of June. It's smaller than I expected but the east-facing window bathes the room in light. There are two twin beds, two desks, and a closet where my roommate—a tall boy with jet-black hair—currently seems to be trying to force a suit onto a flimsy but defiant wire hanger.

The boy doesn't turn around when I enter. I'm not sure if it's because he didn't hear me or if he's just too preoccupied waging war on that hanger. I don't want to startle him, but as the seconds crawl by, I start to feel like a total creeper just staring at him from the doorway.

"Umm . . . hello," I finally blurt out.

"Hi," the boy grumbles back, still not turning around.

Okay, not the most promising introduction. My heart is thumping in my chest and my palms are starting to sweat. But before I decide to have a full-on freak-out and race out of the room screaming for Van, I take a deep breath and remember what my mother said. *Have confidence. Be yourself. If you're open and kind with others, people will be open and kind with you.*

"I'm Milo," I say, forcing myself to take a step forward and extend my hand.

The boy sighs in exasperation and turns around, pushing a tuft of unruly hair out of his face and revealing two eyes so dark and so intense they look like the sea during a thunderstorm.

"Marcos," the boy grunts, ignoring my hand.

"It's nice to meet you, Marcos. Are you excited for camp?"

"I don't believe in God."

Umm . . . *What?*

I must have misheard him. For a second it almost sounded like he said—

"I don't believe in God," Marcos repeats even more adamantly. "I'm an atheist, and I'm here against my will because my father is a fascist jerk who hates that I'm smarter than him and this is his way of punishing me. So, no, I'm not 'excited' for camp. And if you think I'm going to spend the next three weeks making small talk about my favorite Bible verse or about how awesome Jesus is, you have another thing coming because to me Christianity is total nonsense, and I refuse to pretend it's not."

"Oh," I say, the blood draining from my face.

So much for the Best Three Weeks of My Summer. At this point I'll settle for the Summer I Don't Get Murdered.

Maybe it's the deer-in-headlights look of horror in my eyes, but Marcos suddenly takes a step back. His eyes soften and a second later he flashes me what I can only describe as the World's Most Dazzling Smile.

"Other than that, I'm like totally cool."

Which makes me laugh! Because what else can I do? *Of course* Bible camp is already a disaster. *Of course* my roommate is an atheist. It's the Number One Rule of the Universe: if anything can go wrong, it *will*.

"What's so funny?" Marcos asks.

"Nothing," I manage to gasp as my whole body convulses with hysterical laughter.

And then I faint.

5

Milo and Marcos at the Beginning of the World

"Do you do that a lot?" Marcos asks, pressing a cup of water into my hands.

"Not really," I say, looking up at his confused face from my place on the floor. I've decided it's safer to stay down here on the maroon threadbare carpet. At least, until I can trust my legs again.

I can't believe I fainted. Not that I haven't fainted before, but I was sort of hoping I'd outgrown that phase. Thankfully I didn't hurt anything. Except my pride.

"But you're *okay*?" Marcos asks skeptically. One benefit of fainting is that he's no longer glaring at me like I'm some sworn enemy he's vowed to challenge to the death. Instead, he just looks like someone who got tossed a rare tropical fish without any instructions on how to keep it alive.

"I'm fine," I reassure him. Though a part of me does enjoy seeing *him* on the defensive. Maybe that'll teach him not to terrify harmless if skittish Presbyterians. "I just get a little overwhelmed sometimes and when I do—"

"Boom?"

"More like *splat*, but yeah."

Marcos nods, letting out a slight chuckle. "You sure you don't need to see someone? Like the nurse?"

"What? No!" I shout a little too quickly, causing Marcos to step back. The last thing I need is for my parents to get a phone call telling them their son fainted on his first day of camp. "I don't need to see anyone. I'm fine. *Really*."

"Okay," Marcos says, throwing up his hands in surrender. "That works for me. It's not like I want to have to explain to everyone that I almost killed my roommate."

"Yeah, I bet the camp probably frowns on that kind of thing."

Marcos smiles, and for some strange reason I find myself smiling back.

A second later, though, he catches himself. The smile fades and his guard is up.

"Look, I'm sorry if I freaked you out," he says, not sounding particularly sorry at all. "I've just found when it comes to religion that if I don't put my foot down people like you tend to take it as an open invitation to try to convert me, and I'm sick of it. I might not be able to do anything about the fact that I'm stuck at this camp, but I refuse to spend the next three weeks pretending to be someone I'm not or letting anyone try to change me. I'm good *exactly* as I am. Understand?"

"Yeah." I swallow. "Understood."

I've never met anyone who claimed to like himself exactly as he was. Most days I'd be hard-pressed to name *one* thing I liked about myself. But I imagine if I was the sort of person who thought they were perfect *as is*, I'd probably want to stay that way too and not let anyone else mess me up.

"Okay." Marcos nods, his shoulders relaxing slightly. "So, are we good or do you have any questions?"

I actually have a million questions. *How does a hard-core atheist wind up at Bible camp? Is he going to give that "I don't believe in God" speech to everyone he meets today? How does one even become an atheist?* But these all sound like conversational land mines, so instead I ask the first safe question that pops into my head.

"Do you like *The Golden Girls*?"

It's my all-time favorite show and a generally good barometer for gauging someone's personality. And, yes, I know it's a bit "unusual" (my dad's word) for a teenage boy to be obsessed with a show from the late eighties about "four postmenopausal women living in Miami" (again, Dad). But from the moment Van introduced me and I heard Betty White tell her first St. Olaf story, it was pretty much love at first cheesecake.

Marcos, though, just stares at me like I've grown two heads. "Do I like *what*?"

"*The Golden Girls*."

"Oh. Umm . . . yeah, I guess." He shrugs. "Sometimes I watch the reruns with my mom if there's nothing better on. That's the show about the women who run a decorating business in Atlanta, right?"

Oh.

My.

God.

Marcos is a monster. Not believing in God is one thing. But *this*? This is sacrilege.

Oddly enough, the fact that I'm more scandalized by his inability to distinguish *The Golden Girls* from *Designing Women* (which are TOTALLY and COMPLETELY different shows) than by his atheism seems to endear me to Marcos. Okay, technically what he says is, "You're a weird one, aren't you, Connolly?" But at some point between leaving our room and arriving at afternoon orientation, he must have decided he can trust me not to narc on him to the counselors or convert him against his will, because for the rest of the day he pretty much sticks by my side.

Not that he has a lot of choice in the matter. Most of the first day activities require us to pair up with a partner, and since these exercises are annoyingly segregated by gender (something, I'm sure, Van will have plenty to say about later tonight), Marcos ends up kind of stuck with me by default. To his credit, though, not once does he try to ditch me for someone (a) more athletic, (b) more outgoing, or (c) less fainty.

I guess he's figured I'm as good a Presbyterian as any to be stuck with. And despite my initial hesitations, I have to say that as atheists go, he's not half bad. Especially if you're looking for one who loves to talk.

Which Marcos does.

A lot.

Over the next few hours I'm treated to his unedited thoughts about religion ("You know there's no historical evidence outside the Bible that someone named Jesus ever existed, right?"), Florida history ("You know ninety-five percent of the Native Americans on this land were wiped out by diseases brought over by Europeans, right?"), and the moral superiority of vegetarianism ("You know the beef industry is responsible for fifteen percent of the total carbon emissions that are causing climate change, right?").

He's basically a walking TED Talk. But I have to confess, I find Marcos's tirades kind of fascinating. I've never met anyone so sure of his own opinions before. Or himself.

Of course, not everyone at camp is impressed with Marcos's brand of total forthrightness and unshakable convictions. To my dismay, he does indeed give his "I don't believe in God" speech to almost everyone who tries to befriend us, and it goes over about as well as a flag burning on the Fourth of July.

By dinner, news of Marcos's bad attitude has spread across the entire camp. I hear the phrase "wolf in the fold" whispered like a warning among my fellow campers, and even the counselors seem at a loss as to what to do about him.

If I'm honest, I'm not sure what to do either. As his roommate, I'm already getting suspicious glances myself, as if Marcos's atheism might somehow be contagious.

I don't want to spend the next three weeks as a social pariah—especially since for once in my life I didn't actually do anything wrong. At the same time, though, I feel a strange obligation to defend Marcos. Maybe it's because he's my roommate. Or maybe it's because if the situation was reversed and I was the odd man out, I'd want someone to stick by me. I honestly don't know why I feel so protective of him.

What I do know is that this day has been overwhelming and confusing, and all I want right now is to get some dinner and find Van. If anyone will know what to do about Marcos, it's her.

I finish taking my tray through the hot buffet, then scan the crowded cafeteria. On the far side of the room, Van is seated at a table of girls who are cheerfully chatting at her in a *very* animated manner. Aggressive glee has never been Van's thing, so when she catches me watching, she waves and gestures frantically toward the empty chair beside her.

I can't help smiling. I know that wave. That's not her "so great to see you" wave. That is very much her "rescue me right now or I will kill you" wave.

Poor Van. This seems to be her lot in life. People always like her way more than she likes them. She calls it her Burden.

I start to head to her table when out of the corner of my eye I spot Marcos. He's seated in the center of the room at a table big enough for eight but which, at present, is painfully empty. All around him tables are overcrowding with boisterous kids, but Marcos is by himself. An island of lonesomeness.

I catch him looking at me, and he immediately looks away, staring down at his salad as if it's the most fascinating plate of vegetables in the world.

Crap. I really want to sit with Van. It's my fault she's here with a bunch of overly peppy Presbyterians; the least I can do is spend what limited time we have together. But I saw the look in Marcos's eye before he turned away. It's the look of every lonesome kid in a lunch-room who's desperate for someone—anyone—to sit with him.

I practically invented that look.

Van is doing semaphore with her napkins, desperately trying to get my attention. I can also feel the eyes of everyone in the cafeteria watching me, waiting to see what I'll do. But the truth is, I know what I have to do. I mouth "I'm sorry" to Van in what I hope is my most forgivable and least punchable face. Then I set my tray down in front of Marcos.

"How's the salad?" I ask.

Marcos looks surprised—then instantly dubious. He turns around in his seat and glances across the room at Van.

"Aren't you going to sit with your friend?"

"Van seems kind of busy."

Van grabs her tray of lasagna and starts to rise, but before she's out of her chair, one of the girls at her table grabs her wrist and pulls her back down into the conversation. Oh, the Burden, indeed.

"You can sit with her if you want," Marcos says nonchalantly, still not looking at me. He fiddles with a tomato wedge, and it occurs to me that despite his confidence and bluster, or maybe *because* of those things, he might be the Loneliest Person in the World.

And I thought I had that title locked down.

"I'm good," I say, sliding into a chair. Then, changing the subject before he can tell me to get lost, I add, "Did you see the schedule for tomorrow? We're doing something called Biblical Theater."

"Kill me now."

"Yeah, I know, right? I think Van will be into it, though. She actually founded our church's drama club a few years ago. Well, sort of. It wasn't a real drama club. Mostly it was just her and me putting on weekly plays inspired by stories from the Bible."

"Sounds scintillating."

"It was actually pretty cool while it lasted."

"You don't do it anymore?"

"No. Van and our pastor had artistic differences."

"What does that mean?"

"Well, Van kind of has a thing for the gorier books of the Bible. She loves anything with a beheading. Salome and John the Baptist, Judith and Holofernes, David and Goliath. Our pastor tried to get her to do more 'family friendly' stories that we could perform for the kids in Sunday school, but then Van asked him to buy us a tub of stage blood, and that was pretty much the end of our club. Though I still have some of the severed heads we made out of papier-mâché in my closet."

Marcos stares at me like he's debating whether eating alone might not have been the better option, and I feel my entire face flush.

Ugh! Why did I tell him all that? This is why I stay inside my shell. Because I am incapable of talking to people without coming off like a total weirdo who *literally has severed heads in his closet*!

"Huh." Marcos snickers unexpectedly, once again flashing me his dazzling grin. "You really *are* a strange one, aren't you, Connolly?"

I'm about to protest, but looking at the confidence of his smile, I realize maybe "strange" isn't such a bad thing. After all, Marcos is strange. Probably the strangest person I've ever met. And if he can own it, well . . .

"Yeah," I say, sitting up as tall as I can and taking a satisfying bite of my burger. "I guess I am."

6

The Gospel According to Marcos

"So do you maybe want to rethink that whole There's No God thing?"

It's my first attempt at a joke about his atheism, and I'm actually quite proud of it. Not that Marcos looks very amused. Though that's probably because we've just come back to our room after dinner on our third night of camp to find that the thunderstorm that's been battering Gainesville all day has caused our roof to spring a leak.

Directly over Marcos's bed.

Of course, I know God doesn't play with the weather to mess with "unbelieving heathens," and Marcos hasn't ruined any group activities with withering sarcasm or made any of the counselors doubt their life choices in the last forty-eight hours; still, the irony is kind of delicious.

"You've got to be kidding me," he groans.

"Look on the bright side. Now you've got a waterbed."

Marcos punches me in the shoulder, which makes me laugh even harder.

"Stop enjoying this so much and help me move this thing," he orders, grabbing one end of the bed frame as I grab the other. Together we pull his bed out from under the falling rainwater. At which point, almost on cue, the dripping stops.

"Oh, come on!"

"Looks like the rain has a sense of humor."

"The rain is friggin' *hilarious.*"

"Don't worry," I say, helping him wring out his pillows. "You can sleep in my bed tonight."

For the first time since I've known him, Marcos looks unsure what to say.

"Oh . . ."

"I'll sleep on the floor," I clarify.

"What? No, that's okay."

"Don't worry. I'm used to it. Whenever I spend the night at Van's, I always sleep on the floor next to her bed. I'm good with floors."

"I'm not going to make you sleep on the floor, Connolly. I'll sleep on the floor. It's *my* bed that's soaked."

"Yeah, but *I'm* the good Christian. I basically have to offer you my bed, or I lose points with Jesus."

Marcos chuckles. "Well, I wouldn't want to get you in trouble with Jesus. I know you guys are close."

"Totally."

"But as a Rational Humanist—"

"I thought you were an atheist."

"I'm both."

"Got it."

"I can't let you use your religion to gain the moral high ground in this situation. So I'm taking the floor."

"Don't be stubborn," I groan. "The floor is gross. I mean, neither of us should sleep on it. Who knows what's down there? Besides, my bed is big enough for the both of us."

Actually, "big enough for the both of us" might be a bit of an exaggeration. In fact, now that I look at it, it barely seems big enough for one person let alone two. Unless they're on top of each other.

"I mean, it'll be tight," I clarify. "But if you sleep with your head on one end, and I sleep on the other, it should be okay."

Right? That wouldn't be weird. Why does this whole situation suddenly feel awkward? *I'm just trying to be nice.*

"Um, sure," Marcos agrees. "If you don't mind?"

"I don't mind." Then, to break the tension, I add, "I can put up with your disgusting heathen feet in my face for one night."

Marcos smirks and kicks off his shoes.

"Oh, you think you can handle me?"

"Yeah," I say, smirking back, "I can handle you."

Having two people crammed together in a twin-sized bed ends up being about as awkward as I thought it would. But only for the first hour. Once I get accustomed to (a) the limited range of movement, and (b) the total lack of privacy, it's actually kind of fun having a bed buddy.

It's certainly gotten Marcos to open up. Not that he has a problem speaking his mind. But for once, instead of railing against the various sociopolitical problems of the world, he's actually talking about himself. In fact, for the last hour, we've been swapping stories about our lives, our friends—our parents.

"*Ugh,* don't get me started," Marcos groans dramatically before giving me the rundown on his home life back in Orlando. "They're the worst."

"The worst" seems like a bit of an exaggeration.

His mother, whose family came over from Cuba in the fifties, sounds like a pleasant enough woman. She teaches piano and spends most of her free time volunteering at their church. In fact, from what I can tell, the only real obstacle to familial bliss is Marcos's dad, who's white and something of a control freak. Apparently, there have been some epic dustups between him and his wife, especially when it comes to raising Marcos. And most of the time, Mr. Price seems to get his way.

"He's the reason I had to come to this stupid camp," Marcos gripes. "My mom was all set to let me go to this art program in Miami. They only take a hundred students each summer, and you have to apply with a portfolio to get in, and I did."

"That's cool. Congratulations."

"Yeah, except as soon as my father found out there would be life-study classes, he totally flipped out."

"Life study?"

"Drawing naked people."

"Oh."

"Which is ridiculous. I mean, I don't know what he thinks he's protecting me from. Has he heard of the internet? I can see naked people whenever I want."

"Yeah." Although personally I've never had the guts to do that. I'm pretty sure that's how your computer gets a virus.

"He's totally unreasonable," Marcos grumbles. "And he's like that *all* the time. About *everything*. You should have seen how he lost it when I told him I didn't want to go to church anymore. He threatened to send me off to military school."

"He *what?*"

"It's not a big deal. He threatens to send me off to military school at least once a month. It's like his thing."

"Still, I can't believe you actually told your parents."

"Yeah, talk about shooting myself in the foot. That'll teach me to never have an honest conversation with them again."

"But do you really . . . ?"

"Really what?"

"Do you *really* not believe in God? Like at all?" I hope I'm not setting off a conversational grenade. I've seen enough casual inquiries snowball into accusatory screaming matches to know what a mine-field religion can be.

"Nope," he calls out gleefully. "Don't believe in God. Not even a little."

"But how can you be so sure?" I'm not trying to pick a fight. I genuinely want to know. It's never once occurred to me to question whether God exists. How could He not? It'd be like doubting gravity.

Marcos rolls over and sighs like someone who's had this conversation a thousand times. Which he probably has. Probably with his parents. Which is why he's been banished to Bible camp.

"Yeah, sure, I guess from a purely statistical perspective, I can't *one hundred percent* rule out some sort of higher power. It's *possible* God exists. But if He or She or They do exist, and that's a *big* if, then I don't think God can be what we're taught. It just wouldn't make sense."

"Why wouldn't it make sense?"

"Well, for one, doesn't it ever seem like God is a little narrow-minded for the most powerful deity in the universe? I mean, He's supposedly got all these rules about what people can and can't do. And some of them make sense, like 'Thou shalt not kill.' But some of the others? If we're actually supposed to obey them, then I think it makes God come off really controlling and petty and—*cruel*. I mean, there are some things people should be allowed to do and it shouldn't be a big deal, and everyone should just get over it."

"What things?"

The air feels tense and I don't know why. Maybe because the room feels way too quiet. Even the frogs outside our windows have stopped croaking, as if they're also waiting to hear Marcos's answer.

"Just . . . things."

Something warns me not to push. Because I'm not sure the answer is something I'm ready to hear. In fact, something deep inside me tells me the smartest thing I can do right now is change the subject.

"How are my feet?" I blurt out. "They not bothering you, are they?"

"Uh. No. You're good." He sounds taken aback by the abrupt shift in conversation, but he must also be relieved, because a second later he adds, "How are mine? Still the best thing you've smelled all day?"

"Actually, Marcos, I didn't want to say anything before, but your feet are kind of disgusting. It's basically like chemical warfare up here."

"Yikes. Well, if that's true and you really are the decent Christian you claim to be, maybe you should wash them?"

"Excuse me?"

"You know, like in the Bible? You Christians are always washing each other's feet. You're like *obsessed* with it."

"I wouldn't say we're obsessed with it."

"Isn't there a whole story about Mary Magdalene washing Jesus's feet *with her hair*?"

"Okay, well, *you're* not Jesus. You're actually kind of the opposite of Jesus."

"Aww, come on, Church Boy," Marcos pleads. "Don't we heathens deserve clean feet?"

Something caresses my cheek, and it takes me a moment to realize that it's Marcos's big toe.

"Oh gross!" I laugh, pushing his foot away.

"Wash the foot, Connolly. Wash. The. *Foot.*"

"Tell you what, if you're so obsessed with feet, why don't you wash mine?"

I kick back the covers and swing my foot toward Marcos's face. I must misjudge the distance, though, because suddenly there's a warm wetness, and I yank my foot back.

"Oh. My. God," Marcos gasps.

"That was an accident."

"Your toe . . . was *in* my mouth."

"I know." I practically felt it go down his throat.

"Your TOE. Was IN. My MOUTH."

Before I can move, Marcos is on top of me, pinning me to the bed.

"It's your fault," I laugh, trying to wrestle him off me. "I told you to stop!"

"You. Little. Freak!" Using his weight to hold me down, Marcos grabs my flailing limbs one by one and folds them into my body, almost like he's rolling me up.

"What are you doing?"

"This is your punishment. Since you can't share the bed without

49

launching a *crusade*, you are going to sleep scrunched up in a ball so none of your violent, Christian limbs can inflict any more damage on my gentle, peace-loving body!"

And just like that he folds me up into a tight little ball of Milo.

"You realize," I gasp beneath his weight, "that if you want to keep me rolled up like this, you're going to have to sleep on top of me *all* night?"

"Damn," he sighs in defeat, rolling off me. And for some reason I can't quite explain, I wish I hadn't said anything.

Still, lying side by side, his face next to mine, I can just make out his smile in the moonlight. It really is the most dazzling thing I've ever seen.

In fact, it takes my breath away.

7

Daddy Dearest/Mother Tongue

"So, do I need to kick your dad's butt? Because I *will* kick it," Van declares as she plops her tray of scrambled eggs down across from Marcos and me at breakfast.

Initially, I was a little nervous about introducing the two of them. Van and Marcos can both be kind of opinionated when it comes to other people—especially people who strike them as being (ironically) too opinionated. But after choosing to sit with Marcos at dinner that first night of camp, I got a *very* stern talking-to, during which time Van made it painfully clear that she did not appreciate being "cruelly and deliberately ignored" after being "dragged across this swamp of a state" by her "fickle and ungrateful supposed best friend." Henceforth, she expects to be included in *all* our meals, otherwise there will be "serious repercussions."

Thankfully, Marcos and Van hit it off almost immediately. In fact, I'm actually a little jealous of how quickly they've bonded. It's only been a week and they're already finishing each other's sentences, sharing private jokes, and threatening bodily harm to anyone who crosses their newest BFF.

Case in point: when we were in line at the hot breakfast buffet, Marcos happened to mention that he doesn't speak Spanish. Van didn't give it much thought until Marcos explained that the reason he doesn't speak Spanish, despite his mom being fluent, is because his dad prohibited Mrs. Price from teaching him. At which point Van suggested the aforementioned butt kicking.

"I don't understand," I say. "Why doesn't your dad want you speaking Spanish?"

"Because he's a fascist, and because he thinks Americans should speak English."

"That is literally one of the most offensive things I have ever heard," Van scoffs.

"Welcome to my life."

"How is your mom okay with that?"

"She's not 'okay with it,'" Marcos says, his shoulders tensing defensively. "They've argued about it more times than I can count. But my dad can be a real baby when he doesn't get his way—like if he's not happy then *no one* gets to be happy—so sometimes it's just easier for her to pick her battles."

"Still, that is some seriously patriarchal—not to mention *racist*— bullshit."

"I *know*," Marcos huffs, shifting uncomfortably in his seat. As much as he might enjoy eviscerating his father in front of his friends, he clearly has no desire to see his mom caught up in the crossfire. "But when I start high school in the fall, I'll have to take a foreign language, so I'll learn Spanish then. My dad can't object if it's literally a requirement for me to graduate. It's *fine*."

It's obviously not fine. But from the curtness of his tone, I can tell Marcos is ready for this conversation to be over.

Van must also clock his discomfort because, without missing a beat, she shrugs off her outrage and says, "Yeah, you're right, dude. If you learn Spanish, you learn it, and if you don't, that's cool too. It's not, like, mandatory. I mean, I'm *barely* proficient. Half the time when I call my grandma back in Mayagüez, I only catch about sixty percent of what she's saying, So, it's all good. No judgment."

Marcos nods in appreciation and his shoulders relax. But just to dispel any lingering tension, I decide a change of subject might be in order.

"So!" I exclaim, looking at our daily itinerary. "Who's excited to make some puppets?"

"What?"

"Our next workshop. Ten a.m. Biblical Puppetry. Is everyone ready?"

Van gets the hint. At least, I assume she does because, very slowly and very deliberately, she sets down her toast, leans across the table, and says, "Dude, I was born ready for puppets."

Unfortunately for Van, her supposed love of puppets will have to wait as the workshop, like all the other workshops at camp, are segregated by the sexes. A fact we remember almost as soon as breakfast is over. While Van reluctantly heads off to a seminar called "Maintaining a Christian Household," Marcos and I make a quick detour back to our room.

"Van's pretty hilarious," Marcos says as he fixes his hair in the mirror for the fifth time this morning. "How long have you known each other?"

Despite this being a perfectly natural question, something about it makes the hairs on the back of my neck stand on end.

"Since we were six," I mumble as I brush my teeth over the sink.

"Nice. You can tell you guys are really close."

"Yeah. We are. I mean, she's my best friend."

"Have you guys ever thought about being *more* than friends?"

My throat chokes mid-swallow, and toothpaste sprays from my mouth, splattering Marcos.

"Whoa! Are you okay?" he asks, wiping away the flecks of white foam from his face.

"Yeah, sorry." I don't know what's going on with me this morning. It's like my whole body has decided to malfunction.

"No, my bad," Marcos laughs. "I didn't mean to put you on the spot."

"You didn't," I lie. "It's just a weird question."

"Why is it weird?"

"I don't know," I say, trying to sound more casual than I feel. "Van's like my sister. The idea of us being anything more than friends would be . . ."

"Weird?"

"Exactly." And it's true. I've never once had any desire to date Van. And as far as I know she's never thought of me as anything other than a brother. "I mean, once when we were eight, Van went through this phase where she was obsessed with brides, so we got all dressed up and had a fake wedding in front of her stuffed animals. But a week later she said the marriage wasn't working, so we got a divorce. Also in front of her stuffed animals."

Marcos nods, seemingly satisfied with my answer. But a second later he asks, "So you're not interested at all?"

"Nope," I say, trying to swallow down my mounting sense of dread. "Are you?"

Strangely, the idea of Marcos and Van being *more* than friends fills me with a very real panic.

"What? No!" he laughs, shaking his head. "Don't get me wrong, she's awesome. But, no, she's definitely not my type."

"Oh," I say, savoring the sense of relief that floods my body. "What is your type?"

Marcos looks at me, blushes, then looks at his phone. "We're going to be late. Those puppets aren't going to shove their own hands up themselves."

"Hey, no fair!" I shout a little too shrilly. "I answered all your deeply personal questions. You have to answer mine."

"Is that a fact?"

"Yes. So, come on, what's your type?" I don't know why, but for some reason I really, really, *really* need to know.

"Actually?" Marcos chuckles, "I think I'm a lot like my mother."

"What do you mean?"

"I mean, I always seem to go for people who are completely wrong for me."

8

Thank You for Being a "Friend"

For someone who once claimed he was unable to distinguish *The Golden Girls* from lesser female-driven sitcoms, Marcos Price has become quite a devotee of the show over the last two weeks. I'm not joking. Tonight, like every night after dinner, he flops down on my bed with an eager grin and waits for me to pull out my iPad so we can watch as many episodes as we can before falling asleep.

I've got to say I'm kind of proud of myself for converting Marcos to my one and only obsession so easily. It makes me wonder what else I could change his mind about if I really wanted. Not that I'd ever ignore his boundaries and go all "missionary" on him. I like Marcos too much to try to change him.

More selfishly I like who *I* am around Marcos. I'm not Shy Milo or Super-Religious Milo or Socially Awkward Milo. I'm just Milo. The Real Milo. More relaxed. More sure of myself. More (dare I say) out of my shell?

And I like that Milo almost as much as I like Marcos. Actually, if I'm being honest, I like Marcos so much it's starting to make me a little uncomfortable.

Like now. We've been lying together huddled over my iPad for the last three hours in bed—a bed we're *still* sharing after two weeks even though we've had plenty of opportunities to inform a counselor about Marcos's mattress being ruined. I don't know why we haven't. I guess I've just gotten used to having him beside me. The warmth of his body, the sound of his little snores, the smell of him in the sheets: it's comforting.

And maybe something *more* than comforting.

Every time his arm brushes against me, or his leg presses into mine, my whole body comes alive. Like a wave of electricity is dancing over my skin. It's almost addictive, this rush of euphoria whenever our bodies touch.

It scares me.

"What time is it?" Marcos yawns, struggling to keep his eyes open beside me. He's been fighting a losing battle against sleep for the last half hour.

"It's a little after midnight," I answer. "You want to stop for the night?"

"No, I'm good."

This is also part of our routine. Him insisting he's awake and ready for more when really he's one yawn away from oblivion.

The next episode starts to play on my iPad, but as the theme song fills the silence of our room, I watch as Marcos's eyelids grow heavier and heavier until he finally nods off, his head slumping down and coming to a rest against my shoulder.

This is the final part of our routine. My favorite part. The part I find myself hoping will happen every night even though I don't know why.

I turn off the iPad and rest my head against his. In the dark, I listen to his gentle breathing, our faces so close I can sometimes feel his lashes brush against my cheek. And I feel whole.

Which is okay, right? I mean, these are just feelings. We're not *doing* anything wrong. We're just two boys sharing a bed—which is a completely normal teenage thing to do. Friends fall asleep together all the time.

Except . . .

I don't think "friends" are supposed to enjoy it as much as I do. In fact, I can feel a Very Predictable Reaction happening in my pajama bottoms right now—a reaction that is deeply mortifying not to mention super problematic. There's nothing I can do to stop it, though, so as nonchalantly as possible I pull away from Marcos and roll onto my side so that both me *and* my "reaction" are facing the wall.

I try not to panic. But it's hard to ignore my body.

As much as I want to deny it, as much as I'd like to pretend otherwise, I know what I've been feeling for Marcos over the last few days is more than friendship. There are, in fact, *very specific* words for it. Words my parents and my pastor would be horrified to utter. But maybe if I don't think them or say them or *act* on them, then everything will be okay.

After all, lots of kids go through a "phase," right? Isn't that what people say? I just have to get through mine without embarrassing my family or shaming my church or damning my immortal soul to the everlasting fires of Hell.

What could be easier?

Except . . .

What if Marcos feels the same way?

We only have one more week together. If he's going through a similar "phase," maybe the best thing we could do is get it out of our system. Together. I mean, it's not like I'll ever see him again after next Friday. He'll go back to Orlando; I'll go back to Port Orange; and whatever happens at the Gainesville Presbyterian Youth Retreat stays at the Gainesville Presbyterian Youth Retreat.

I mean, let's be logical. *If* something happens between us, there's a pretty strong chance I won't even enjoy it, and I'll realize that everything I've been feeling for the last two weeks is just a combination of hormones and an overactive imagination. Basically, I'll be curing myself of these feelings for the rest of my life.

But if I don't take advantage of this opportunity, then there's a real chance I could spend the rest of my existence obsessing over "what could've been" and blowing the whole thing out of proportion to the point that it ends up stunting my emotional growth and haunting me until the day I die.

So really, the scientific *and* Christian thing to do is just give it a try. Just once. Just so I never have to think about it ever again.

Right?

9

Scared Straight

"Are you okay?" Marcos asks. "You've been kind of quiet today."

We're back in our room after another long day of prayer circles, Bible lessons, and mandatory crafting—activities meant to instill a sense of faith and decency in us as Righteous Children of God, but which instead have only succeeded in making me feel *incredibly* guilty on account of all the very impure thoughts I've been having about Marcos.

In fact, I don't think I said a single word to him at breakfast, lunch, or dinner. I've been too busy freaking about the decision I've made. Which is that tonight, against all my better judgment, I am going to confess my feelings to Marcos.

Okay, well, not "confess." I'm not that bold.

I can't just sit him down and say, "Hey, Marcos, want to make out for an hour and see if it awakens any particular desires that could ultimately damn us for all eternity?" For all I know, I've completely misread this situation and his feelings for me are strictly platonic. So before I make a total fool of myself, I need a little more certainty. I need to "test the waters."

Thankfully I've concocted the perfect water tester. The only trouble is I'm not sure tonight's the best night to implement my plan. Marcos has been pretty standoffish all day. I don't know if it's just one of his random moods or if maybe he's starting to suspect I have not-so-innocent feelings for him, but whatever the case he's been unusually withdrawn ever since lunch.

Typical. The day I finally work up the courage to make my move is the one day he decides to become a grouchy brick wall.

Why is nothing ever easy?

"I'm fine," I tell Marcos, answering his question and trying to muster as much nonchalance as I can while I slip on my pajamas. "It's just been a long day."

It actually *hasn't*. I mean, it's not like I've been down a coal mine for the last eight hours. So I'm surprised when Marcos nods rather solemnly and says, "Yeah. It has."

"Are *you* okay?" I ask. "You seemed a little 'off' today."

"Yeah. Sorry. It's just . . . family drama."

"Oh." That explains the moodiness.

"My dad called. Right before lunch. We had a fight."

"Is everything okay?"

"No. Yeah. Everything's . . ."

I wait for Marcos to finish, but it soon becomes clear he doesn't know how.

"It's whatever." He shrugs. "Really. Not worth talking about."

"Are you sure?"

"Yep. Definitely. So . . . do you want to put on the *Girls*?"

There's something a bit forced about his smile as he plops down onto our bed. Part of me wants to make sure he's actually okay, but his question is just about as perfect a segue into Operation: Test the Waters as I could hope. I don't dare waste it.

"Sure," I say, grabbing my iPad and lying down beside him.

"What episode do you want to watch tonight?"

I shrug, pretending to think it over. "I don't know. How about something from season four? It feels like a season four kind of night."

Of course, I know *exactly* what episode I want us to watch, but I also know I need to lead up to it so as not to be too freakin' obvious. Thankfully, we've already seen the first few shows of this season, so we only have to sit through a couple more until the one I want begins to play.

Episode 9. "Scared Straight."

It's the one where Blanche's brother Clayton comes to visit and reveals he's gay. And, *yes*, as a way of testing the waters, it's a little *on the nose*. But I didn't say my plan was subtle. And, honestly, so far, there's been a bit too much subtlety in our relationship.

I figure if Marcos hates the episode or makes fun of Clayton, I can call off my plan and avoid making a colossal fool of myself. And if he likes it . . .

Well, we'll burn that bridge when we get to it.

As the episode unfolds, I try to clock Marcos's reactions without making it too obvious I'm watching him instead of the iPad. I'm so nervous I'm shaking to the point that Marcos asks if I'm cold. I force myself to be calm, and not long after we're both (mercifully) laughing at all the right places. More encouragingly, Marcos doesn't bat an eye when Clayton reveals his preference for men.

So far, so good.

As the episode continues, though, and Blanche struggles to accept her brother, I can feel the energy in our room change. It's subtle at first but definite. The air seems charged, as if one false move might send the whole dorm up in flames.

Also, for the first time since we've started sharing a bed, I'm very much aware that not a single inch of Marcos's body is touching mine. Is that deliberate? Is he keeping his distance on purpose? Is *this* my answer?

The episode ends, and my heart is pounding so hard I'm afraid I'm going to have a heart attack. Marcos, though, is oddly quiet. And way too still.

Why isn't he saying anything?

"I liked that one."

Oh, thank God . . .

He says it simply. Calmly. Like it's a matter of fact. Only he's not looking at me. He's staring straight ahead at the screen and watching the credits flash by like they hold some secret to the universe.

"Yeah?" I ask.

"Yeah. It was funny but . . . but it was also about something important."

"Yeah." I swallow. "I agree."

Marcos looks at me, as if surprised, and our eyes lock. "You do?"

I feel like I've just taken off all my clothes. Like Marcos can see every secret part of me. But I can't chicken out now. I want him to see me. All of me.

I nod.

The faintest of smiles curls across Marcos's lips. He understands.

A wave of relief washes across my body and, in that moment, I am struck by how devastatingly beautiful he is. I mean, I've known he was attractive since the first day I saw him. Even Van (who doesn't believe in giving boys compliments because she says they already have big enough egos) has taken to referring to him as my "hot roommate." But sitting with him now, his gentle eyes gazing into mine, I'm more aware than ever that his face is the most perfect thing that I have ever seen.

I could look at him forever.

Marcos clears his throat. He looks away nervously, his smile vanishing, and with a rising horror I realize that, even though it hasn't been "forever," I've still been staring at him in total silence for way longer than it is ever appropriate for one boy to stare at another. Especially when said boys are in bed together.

"Do you want to watch another episode?" I ask, flustering. The air suddenly feels too thin, and Marcos's shoulders have gone tense. Why does he look so uncomfortable?

"Do you mind if we don't watch any more tonight?"

"Oh. Um. Sure. Okay," I say, trying not to panic. We've never deviated from our nightly routine before, and I'm not sure why it's happening now. Is Marcos upset? Have I totally misread our situation? I have no friggin' clue. Thirty seconds ago, I was certain we were on the same page, but now . . . ?

I turn off my iPad, and we settle down onto our pillows, neither of us saying a word. Despite the darkness I can feel him looking at me, but I keep my eyes glued to the ceiling. More than anything I want to turn to him and tell him everything I've kept buried in my chest for the last two weeks. But I can't find the words. I've completely lost my nerve. Which means if something is going to happen between us, then Marcos needs to be the one to make it happen.

I mean, he's the confident one, right? The rule breaker? The one who's not afraid of anything? So why does the burden of this moment feel like it's entirely on me?

If he likes me, if he likes me in the way that I need him to like me, then he has to make the first move. I can't do this on my own. He has to meet me halfway.

"Milo?" he whispers.

"Yeah?"

He hesitates and the room is so quiet I want to scream.

"Good night."

I stare at the ceiling. I stare at the ceiling for the rest of the night, listening to Marcos sleep and hating myself. Because I have my answer. I finally know exactly what I am.

A coward.

10

East of Eden

The next day the camp organizes a rare off-site and surprisingly secular field trip to the Kanapaha Botanical Gardens. For the first time since coming to Gainesville, Van is genuinely excited because apparently there's (a) a special greenhouse devoted to carnivorous plants and (b) wild alligators wandering the park. This sounds like a lawsuit waiting to happen, but sitting on our chartered bus as it rumbles down the interstate, I don't have the energy to worry about my potential death by gator. I'm still kicking myself about last night.

Marcos barely said a word at breakfast this morning. Then when it came time to get ready for the field trip, he announced he had a headache and wasn't going to join us.

I think I really screwed things up.

I know he doesn't have a headache. That's obviously an excuse to avoid spending time with me. But what I don't know is whether he's mad at me because I tried to make something happen between us or *because* nothing happened. Which is it?

And what do I do now?

"Hey, you okay?" Van asks, bumping her shoulder against mine. "You seem painfully uninterested in me or my thoughts on gators."

"Yeah," I lie. "I just wish Marcos was coming. It stinks he's not feeling well."

"Oh, come on!" Van groans. "I've barely gotten any QVMT in two weeks. We can have one day of fun without Marcos."

"Yeah. Totally," I say, forcing myself to smile.

But if I'm being honest, I don't think I *can* have fun without Marcos. I literally feel empty without him. Which is kind of disturbing. I mean, if I miss him this much and we've only been apart for half an hour, what am I going to be like in a week when we have to say goodbye forever?

True to its reputation, the Kanapaha Gardens do indeed feature freely roaming gators, though most of them seem content to sun themselves around the large pond at the center of the park far away from the public footpaths.

"Hmph," Van snorts in disappointment as we plop down on a bench to eat our gator-shaped souvenir popsicles. "I thought we'd be able to get closer."

"There's no barricade. You can walk right up to them if you want."

"You trying to get me eaten, Connolly?"

I don't know when it started, but Van's picked up Marcos's habit of referring to me by my last name. Normally I'd find it endearing, but today it just makes me miss him all the more.

"Oh, I spoke to my mom this morning," Van says excitedly, licking the melted popsicle juice off her fingers. "Have you heard about the drama at church?"

"No." I've been so obsessed with Marcos these last couple of weeks I'd pretty much forgotten there was a world outside our camp. "What's going on?"

"Brace yourself. Pastor Fields? He's retiring."

"Oh. Wow. Really?"

"Yeah. Apparently, he's stepping down after Christmas."

"Wow."

"I know, right? About time. That dude is a dinosaur."

I've never actually felt one way or another about Pastor Fields. In fact, until Van started griping about him a few months ago, it never occurred to me that someone could approve or disapprove of their minister. It'd be like approving or disapproving of math. You can love it or hate it all you want, but in the end the rules are still the same.

"Your mom must be happy," I say. "I know she's never been his biggest fan." Which is the Understatement of the Century.

When Ms. Silvera's marriage was falling apart earlier this year, Pastor Fields kept telling her to have "more patience," even though everyone knew Mr. Silvera was cheating on his wife while they were still in couples counseling. Finally, Ms. Silvera got so sick of Pastor Fields defending Mr. Silvera that she told him (rather publicly) that if he loved her husband so much, *he* should marry him. It's been pretty frosty between them ever since.

"My mom is thrilled," Van gloats. "This is *long* overdue. And who knows, maybe whoever takes over won't be such a misogynist fossil."

"Totally. And now you don't have to switch to a new church."

"What?"

"You mentioned last month that your mom was thinking of finding a new church."

"Oh. Right."

"Yeah, so, now she doesn't have to. You can both stay." Which is definitely one aspect of this development that I can totally get behind.

Only instead of echoing my enthusiasm, Van takes a deep breath and scrunches up her face in the way she does when she's about to deliver a piece of news that she knows I'm not going to like.

"So . . . here's the thing. My mom is kind of done with church for a while. She told me she needs a break from the whole organized religion thing. And honestly? I think I do too."

And just like that this already terrible day has managed to get a million times worse.

"I'm not going full-blown Marcos and saying I don't believe in God," she assures me, clearly trying to stave off the emotional freak-out that she suspects I'm about ten seconds away from having. "I just know that for me personally, organized religion isn't a good fit any-more. I mean, I don't know what the boys have been learning in their seminars these last couple weeks, but some of the classes I've had to sit through? They're a little too *Handmaid's Tale* for my taste.

"And I know there are really good Christians out there—*you're* a really good Christian. But given everything that went down at church with my dad and how people having been treating us, I just don't think *this* is for me anymore. Honestly, *this* hasn't been me for a really long time. I mean, in a few months we're going to be starting high school. It's going to be a brand-new chapter in our lives, and I don't want to start that chapter by pretending I'm someone I'm not. I want to be me. The real me. Whoever that turns out to be. Does that make sense?"

I nod because what else can I do? It's not like I didn't see this coming. When it comes to religion, Van and I have been going our separate ways for a while now. In fact, I'm pretty sure the only reason she stuck with it for as long as she did was for my sake.

"Hey," she says, taking my hand. "This doesn't change anything between us, okay? You're still my best friend. The Rose to my Sophia. We're still going to see each other every day at school and hang out on weekends. This isn't a big deal."

"Okay," I say.

"Okay?" From the skepticism in her eyes, it's clear Van was expecting me to put up a much bigger fight and/or shed a few thousand tears. "You're cool with all this?"

I'm not actually cool with *anything*. I mean, church is what brought Van and me together. It's the one thing we share—the one connection she doesn't have with any of her other friends. And she can say that leaving won't change things between us, but how can she be sure? How can she know that the "Real Van Silvera" who doesn't need church won't wake up someday and realize she doesn't need me?

"Milo?"

Still, as shattering as that thought may be, I also know it's selfish. Van has always been there for me. She's fought off bullies, nursed me through panic attacks, and generally made the world feel like a safer, better place. Whenever I've needed her, she's never let me down. And now here she is, telling me what *she* needs, and I can't let her down.

"It's cool," I say, swallowing down my fear and looking in her eyes. "I know you've had some issues with Pastor Fields—and religion— for a while. And I'm *definitely* going to miss seeing you at church every Sunday. But I think it's good you're trying to figure stuff out for yourself—to find yourself."

"Yeah?"

"Yeah." I smile. "It's brave."

"Wow," she says, looking genuinely relieved. And it dawns on me that maybe I wasn't the only one worried about losing our friendship. "I was *not* expecting you to take it so well. Thank you."

"Thank *you* for being honest with me. I know that must have been scary. Especially considering how—"

"How you overreact to literally every situation with no concept of moderation?"

"Yeah. That."

Van nudges my shoulder with hers and then wraps an arm around mine. "Well, look at us being all adult and crap. I'm proud of us."

"Me too."

"Seriously, though, how did we get so mature?"

"I don't know."

Except maybe I do. I mean, a month, or even a week ago, I might have been so devastated by Van's announcement that I would've run straight into the open jaws of the nearest gator. But after everything that's happened—that *is* happening—with Marcos, maybe I understand Van's need to figure out her "real self" more than she knows.

And right then and there I know exactly what I have to do.

When I get back to camp, the second I see Marcos, I have to tell him how I feel. No matter the consequences. No matter the fear.

I have to tell him *everything*.

Except when I get back to my room Marcos is gone.

His dresser is empty, his suit isn't hanging in the closet, and his mother's floral suitcase is gone from under the bed.

No note. No goodbye. No Marcos.

A sickening sense of dread creeps across my body. Panic floods my veins, and my hands begin to shake. I don't understand what's happening. My only instinct is to find the nearest counselor and demand they tell me *what is going on?*

But I can't. I can't because I'm terrified the answer will be, "I think you know very well what's been going on, Mr. Connolly. We're *all* aware of what's been *going on.*"

It's the only explanation that makes any sense. Marcos wouldn't just disappear. Not without telling me. Something *must* have happened. Either someone suspected something and reported us, or Marcos himself was feeling guilty about our relationship and confessed. Either way the result is the same. They've sent Marcos away. And it's only a matter of time before they send me away too.

I can't believe I've been so stupid. Worse than stupid, I've been *reckless.* I've put my entire life—not to mention my soul—in jeopardy. And why? *Over a boy?*

I want to throw up.

Any second now my parents are going to get a call telling them their son is a dirty, filthy degenerate. Any second they're going to know the horrible, disgusting truth about me. And they are going to hate me.

Why wouldn't they? I hate myself.

I know what I was doing with Marcos—what I *wanted* to do with Marcos—is a sin. If it wasn't, I wouldn't feel so ashamed. I wouldn't loathe myself with every fiber of my being. I wouldn't wish I was dead.

Oh God, what have I done?

I don't know if it's day or night.

Between the crying and hyperventilating and vomiting, I lose track of time. The waiting is torture. Every pair of footsteps outside my door sends me dry heaving into my trash can.

I'm not sure how much more of this I can take. I can't stop sweating. My sheets are soaked. I'm exhausted.

All I want is for this nightmare to be over. For things to go back to the way they were before I ever set foot in this stupid camp. Before I ever laid eyes on Marcos.

I know that's not possible. I know time doesn't work that way. But maybe—maybe there's a chance I can still fix all this. Maybe if I try hard enough, I can change. Like Paul on the Road to Damascus. He went from sinner to saint in a single night. Why can't I? I can't be worse than Paul. And God knows I want it more than he did. I at least have to *try*.

I crawl out of bed, my face wet with tears, and fall to my knees.

Please, God, help me. Please don't let my parents find out. I promise I can change. I promise I won't look at another boy for as long as I live. I swear. I'll do whatever You want. I'll be whoever You want! Just please, please, please HELP ME!

I don't know how long I pray. At some point I fall asleep on the threadbare floor. That's where one of the counselors finds me the next morning.

"Oh, Milo," he says, tenderly placing the back of his hand against my forehead. "I'd no idea you were so sick, kiddo. I wish you'd told someone."

The counselor helps me into bed then pulls the covers up over my chest. "Don't worry. I'm going to get the nurse, and we're going to get you feeling better in no time. Just try to rest. Everything's going to be okay."

I spend my final week of camp in the infirmary. Everyone is kind to me. My parents call every day to check up on me, and their love makes me cry. Because I don't deserve it. Because I know what I am even if they don't.

No, correction: I know what I *was*.

Because somehow, miraculously, God has answered my prayers. He's given me the clean start I asked for. Marcos might have abandoned me, but he didn't rat me out. As far as I can tell, no one knows the truth about us or about how close I came to throwing my whole life away.

I've got my second chance. And this time I'm not going to waste it. This time I'm going to be the person that God wants me to be—and that my parents want me to be—and that *I* want to be.

I have to try.

I will try.

I do.

11

Except

Except that was three years ago.

Back when I thought I was safe from these feelings. When I thought I would never see Marcos Price ever again.

And now he's back.

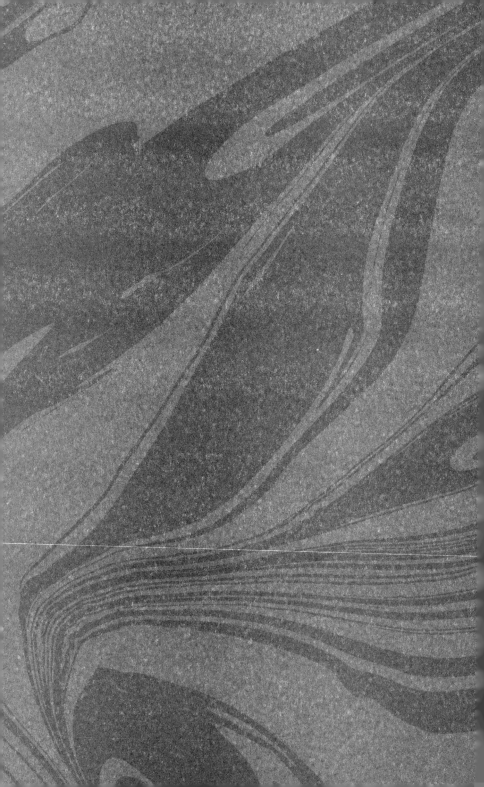

PART II

12

We Now Return to Our Regularly Scheduled Apocalypse

"Earth to Milo."

"Earth to *Milo*."

"*Earth* to *Milo*."

I look up from my laptop and from the shaggy throw rug I'm sitting on to see Van peering down at me from her bed with a look of resigned exasperation. I think she's been trying to get my attention for a while, but I've been so caught up in my thoughts about Marcos and his sudden return that I must have spaced out. Again.

I've been doing that a lot this week, and it's seriously starting to become a problem. In fact, the whole reason I came over to Van's after school today was to force myself to focus on something other than the unfolding disaster that is my life right now, and yet I'm pretty sure I've just spent the last half hour staring at a blank computer screen.

"What?" I ask, a little too defensively.

"Don't *what* me. I said it's cool having Marcos around."

"Oh. Yeah." I shrug then quickly turn back to the welcome distraction of my homework.

"You don't agree?"

"I literally just said 'yeah.'"

"In *literally* the most unenthusiastic tone ever."

"Oh my gosh, Van, what do you want me to say?" I groan, no longer able to hide my frustration. "You've done nothing but talk about how great it is having Marcos back every day for the last *three* days and I've agreed every time. I'm all agreed-out. I literally have nothing more to say on the subject."

"Okay. *Sheesh*. My bad."

I know I shouldn't be so short with Van, but from the way she's been going on and on *and on* about how "miraculous" it is that Marcos transferred to our school, you'd think she was the one who obsessively thought about hooking up with him during a two-week *Golden Girls* marathon. Honestly, her enthusiasm is driving me a little insane. Especially as I still have no idea what to do about Marcos.

So far, he's joined Van and me for lunch in the cafeteria for the past two days. And from the way he's already acting like Van's bestie, it's pretty clear he plans to become a permanent fixture in our social circle—which doesn't make me want to tear my hair out and run screaming into the ocean at all.

Thankfully, we only have two classes together—fourth period World Lit and fifth period American History. But for some reason that baffles all understanding, Marcos has decided to sit *directly* in front of me—in *both* classes—which means I have no choice but to stare at the back of his stupid head for two straight hours *every* day.

Why would he do that?

I mean, what does he even *want* from me? Every day he's like, "Hey, Connolly." "How's it going, Connolly?" "What are you and Van doing after school, Connolly?" This afternoon he even cornered me in the parking lot and suggested we "hang out sometime" because "it's been a while."

What kind of mind games is he playing?

I might—*might*—be less of a mess if just once he acknowledged our past. But nope! So far, he's told me about his favorite coffee shops in Orlando, the graphic artists he follows on Instagram, *and* the latest developments in his parents' "endlessly dysfunctional marriage," but what we *don't* discuss or even come close to alluding to is our two weeks together at Bible camp. Or our late-night *Golden Girls* viewing parties. Or his sudden disappearing act.

That might be the worst part about this whole impossible situation.

Here's a boy who once made me feel things I have *never* felt before—things I didn't even know I was capable of feeling—and now he's walking around, acting like we were nothing more than *roommates?*

Unless . . . maybe . . . that's all we were?

I suppose it's possible that for all these years I've been completely mistaken about why he vanished. Maybe he didn't disappear because he was having feelings he couldn't handle. Maybe I only *imagined* there was something between us, and the reality is that I was just some Jesus Freak he got saddled with for the summer and couldn't wait to escape.

Maybe he left without a word because I simply wasn't worth saying goodbye to.

Could that be true? Was I so wrapped up in my obsession with him that I misread our entire relationship? Did I really almost throw my life away for someone who never even cared if I existed?

If so, I'm the Biggest Fool in the Whole Entire Universe.

Thank God Van invited me to come over to her house today. Right now, more than anything, I need routine and familiarity and *order*. I need to focus on my academics, reaffirm my commitment to God, and (most importantly) *stop thinking about Marcos.*

"We should invite Marcos over to study with us," Van says, looking up from her laptop and taking a sip of her peppermint tea.

OH. MY. GOD.

Absolutely not. I cannot have Marcos in my life any more than he already is. We are already at critical danger levels.

"What's the matter?" Van asks when I continue to stare at my laptop in silence. "You don't want to invite him over?"

"What? Oh, sorry," I cover, trying to sound as if I'd been lost in thought and not totally freaking out. "Yeah, we can invite him. If you want. Although I think Marcos prefers to be on his own. He's kind of a loner."

"A loner? You think *Marcos* is a loner?"

"I don't know. That's just the vibe I get."

I realize how hollow my excuse sounds, so I decide it's time to deploy my trump card. I hate to do it because I know how much it annoys Van, but she's left me no choice.

"Besides," I say, casually sipping my own tea, "I'm not sure my parents will approve of me hanging out with a full-blown atheist."

Van rolls her eyes and sucks her teeth, but she doesn't contradict me. She knows how hard it was for me to stand up to my parents when they wanted me to stop hanging out with her. Actually, no, standing up for Van was surprisingly easy because she's my best friend and I knew my parents were wrong to try to cut her out of my life. It was, however, the most stressful and unpleasant conversation I ever had to have with my mom and dad. And while I'd do it again in a heartbeat for Van, there's no way I'll risk it for Marcos.

Of course, my parents have no idea about Marcos's atheism, so before Van has a chance to realize the flaw in my logic, I decide to keep the conversation moving forward and away from all things Marcos.

"How are you doing with your chart?" I ask, hoping she takes the bait.

"Ugh!" Van groans, tossing aside her laptop in disgust. "This assignment is so frustrating!"

Bingo.

Our first assignment in our Critical Thinking class is to construct a Life Goal Chart. We're supposed to pick a career we want and then break down that goal into a series of smaller achievable goals, so we have a better idea of the steps we'll need to take in order to achieve success. It's actually a pretty practical and helpful assignment, and I completed mine before I left school today, but I know it's *exactly* the kind of exercise designed to drive Van up a wall.

"What if I don't have just *one* goal?" she huffs as she jumps off her bed and begins pacing the room. "What if I don't want to decide my entire future right *now*? What if I want to keep my options open? What if I want to be both an Academy Award–winning actor *and* compete on the women's Olympic soccer team?"

"Then you could play yourself in the movie they make about you leading America to gold."

"Exactly!" she exclaims without a hint of irony.

I sit back and take a long, indulgent sip of my tea. Van's about to have one of her epic tirades and I know it's going to be glorious.

"It's so *reductive*! Making us focus on *one* thing? I mean, we're young, we have all this potential, we could literally do *anything*, but they want us to put on blinders and just shut off entire aspects of our personalities, just so we can fit into some easily definable box that is all about *limiting* potential instead of celebrating it."

"Totally." I don't know what's more delicious. This tea or Van's outrage.

"Why aren't they teaching us to think *holistically*? This is supposed to be a *critical* thinking class, right? Why aren't they teaching us to think synergistically?"

"I don't know what that means."

"It means instead of teaching us that life is linear, that it's either/or, why don't they teach us how to incorporate all the potential paths of our lives into a mutually reinforcing system that allows them to build on and support each other instead of canceling each other out? Why can't they teach us to aim for *everything*?"

"Right . . . ," I say, choosing my next words carefully. "But in the end, you kind of have to choose either acting school or sport school."

"Okay, first off, there's no such thing as 'sport school,' and I am *deeply* disturbed that you think there is. Second, would you tell Leonardo da Vinci, 'Hey, you can either paint the *Mona Lisa or* try to invent the helicopter'? Would you tell Stacey Abrams, 'You can either write romance novels *or* crusade for voting rights'?"

"Yeah, but those are, like, extraordinary people."

"Maybe. Or maybe *everyone* has the potential to be Stacey Abrams or Leonardo da Vinci. Maybe people just have to have the courage to want *all* their dreams and not listen to anyone who asks them to choose. Maybe Stacey Abrams and Leonard da Vinci are who they are precisely because *no one* ever made them fill out a friggin' Life Goal Chart. Boom!"

Van drops an imaginary mic like she's just solved the oldest mystery of the universe. She's so darn proud of herself, I give her a standing ovation even if I don't 100 percent agree with her theory.

This is exactly what I needed to take my mind off everything: QVMT and passionate tirades and peppermint tea. In fact, I'm having such a good time I'm not even *thinking* about Marcos.

Unless "not thinking about Marcos" counts as thinking about Marcos . . .

Thankfully, I'm spared having to spiral down that metaphysical rabbit hole when Van's phone bursts into song. She scrambles to silence it, and I can't help but smirk because I know *exactly* who's calling even before the look of guilt flashes across her face. Van has very specific ringtones for the important people in her life. Mine is *The Golden Girls* theme song (obviously). Her mother, for some reason I've never understood, is Pat Benatar's "Love Is a Battlefield." And Lady Gaga's "Bad Romance" is reserved for Caleb Yates.

"I'll be right back," she says a little too quickly as she slides off her bed and out of the room.

Van and Caleb met in detention freshman year (him for repeated tardiness; her for staging an unsuccessful sit-in to protest the school's continued use of the outdated term "freshman" instead of the more gender-inclusive "first-year student"). They've been dating on and off ever since.

Mostly off.

In fact, the first time they broke up, Van gave me an exhaustingly detailed list of all Caleb's many, *many*, MANY faults—some of which Van was pretty sure amounted to Crimes Against Humanity. It was an epic, rage-filled conversation that lasted all weekend, buoyed by bouts of self-loathing and indignation, and resulting in the resolution that Caleb Yates was the most immature, irrational, unreliable boy in the universe and that neither of us would ever speak of him again.

A week later he and Van were dating.

A week after that they were broken up.

And a week after that . . . Well, you get the picture.

I'm never sure on any given week if Caleb is "deep down a really good person who has *definitely* matured this year" or "a goddamn child who is never—NEVER—going to grow up," so I've learned the safest opinion to hold about Caleb is no opinion. Van, in turn, has learned to leave me out of their drama.

I'm actually a little surprised he's calling. After their last breakup, I was under the impression they might be done for good. Especially since Van didn't mention him all summer. But from the way she's whispering in the other room, I suspect seeing each other at school this week has started the cycle all over again.

I guess some things never change.

I can tell it's going to be a while before Van returns, and I don't want to start spiraling about Marcos again, so I try to keep myself busy by looking over my own Life Goal Chart. Unlike Van, who's always been torn between multiple career paths, I've always known exactly what I wanted to be.

A teacher.

Well, not *any* teacher. I would *never* want to teach high school.

Speaking as a teenager, we're all pretty much monsters. But teaching at an elementary school and working with children who *weren't* secretly sexting while I was trying to instill in them a love of history or literature? I could handle that.

At least I think I could.

I already volunteer at POP's day care center, and I truly enjoy that. Unlike the teenagers at Crick, the kids at POP are genuinely fun to be around and actually seem to respect me. Probably because they're not old enough to realize that if they ever challenged my authority, I would crumble in a heartbeat, and the day care would descend into free cookies and chaos.

Then again, to my credit, there's never been a problem I couldn't solve with a time-out and a hug. Miss Lindsey, who runs the day care, says it's because I'm so patient. I never lose my temper or shout. And I've made it a goal never to make a child feel bad about anything. They know if they accidentally glue their hands together or misplace the caps to all the markers or wet themselves, I'm not going to be upset.

Because, hey, we've all been there.

Also, Van *is* right about the whole potential thing. When we're young we really do have all this unlimited promise. For kids anything is possible. Life hasn't crushed their dreams or told them No. And I like the idea that, as a teacher, I can help my students hold on to that excitement by being the adult in their life who tells them Yes.

Yes, they can grow up to be whatever they want. Yes, they should follow their dreams. Yes, I believe in them.

Even if I don't always believe in myself.

"Sorry about that," Van mumbles as she slides back into the room, pocketing her phone like it's a dirty secret. Then she flops down on her bed and studies her Life Goal Chart with such a level of mannered concentration it makes Sherlock Holmes seem like a slacker.

If she thinks she's off the hook, though, she has another thing coming. It's not often in our relationship that I get to be the cocky one and she gets to be the awkward one, and I am not about to let this opportunity pass.

"How's Caleb?" I ask as innocently as I can muster.

"Fine."

"Did he have a nice summer?"

"I guess."

"That's nice."

"Yep."

"So why was he calling?"

Van groans and slams her laptop shut.

"He asked if I wanted to see the new Alfonso Cuarón movie this weekend and I said yes, *okay?*"

Ha! I knew it. Her face is so red right now.

"Cool."

"Don't look at me like that."

"I'm not looking at you—"

"Milo."

"Vanessa."

This is our usual stalemate. As fun as it is to see her squirm, I know not to push any further because (a) despite her tough exterior Van can be incredibly sensitive when it comes to the Caleb Situation and (b) if she wanted to turn the tables on me, she could very easily eviscerate my upper hand by bringing up my own general awkwardness in any and all social situations. And that's without having any clue about Marcos.

Ugh. Marcos. God knows what Van would have to say about that.

Part of me wishes I had the guts to tell her about camp. She's probably the one person in my life who wouldn't care that I like Marcos—I mean *liked* Marcos. But saying the words out loud would just make everything too real, and I need whatever I felt for Marcos to stay in the past. It's the only way I'll have any sort of future.

Then again, if there's anyone who knows what it's like to have feelings for someone they'd probably rather forget, it's Van. It might not be the worst thing in the world to pick her brain. If nothing else she might confirm that I'm absolutely right to keep someone like Marcos at a distance.

"Hey, Van? Can I ask you a question? About Caleb?"

Van narrows her eyes. "What about Caleb?"

"Do you ever, you know, regret dating him?"

"*Dude.* So rude."

"No, I don't mean it like *that.* I'm not making fun of him. Or saying you *should* regret it."

"Good."

"But do you?"

"*Wow.* WTF?"

"Sorry! It's just that you and Caleb are always breaking up and getting back together and then breaking up—which is totally fine—but it just seems like that would be really painful, you know? To be with someone and have it *not* work out? And then to have to see them every day and know they knew stuff about you that no one else knows. Stuff you'd never *want* anyone else to know."

"What stuff?"

"I don't know. Bad stuff."

"Caleb's *never* talked shit about me behind my back once."

"No, I know. But he could, right? Or he could make stuff up."

"Dude, what you are even talking about?" Van snaps, looking at me like I've just run over a puppy for kicks. "Did you hear a rumor about me or something?"

"No, of course not."

"Then why am I suddenly getting the third degree about Caleb?"

"You're not!"

"Really? Because right now I'm feeling a lot of Presbyterian judgment?"

"Oh my gosh, no! No one is judging you. I'd never do that. You *know* I'd never do that!" At least, I *hope* she knows that. Van once said if I started using religion as a weapon instead of a tool, our friendship would be over. She made me promise I would never do that, and I meant it.

"Then what is going on, dude?"

Ugh! How did this conversation get so out of control so quickly?

"I'm sorry," I apologize, "I didn't mean to upset you. Or make you feel judged. It just seems like it would be a really big risk to date someone you're not a hundred percent sure about, and I wanted to know how you have the courage to do something like that."

"Like what?"

"To trust someone. How do you trust someone knowing they might hurt you?"

"Oh," Van says, her shoulders slightly relaxing. "Is that all?"

"That's *all*."

"Well, why didn't you say *that*?"

"Because I'm me and everything has to be ten times harder than it needs to be?"

Van chuckles and lies back on her bed, shaking her head in baffled amusement.

"I really didn't mean to make you feel bad," I tell her, just in case she needs to hear it again.

"I know, dude, it's fine. Seriously. I shouldn't have gotten so defensive. Your question just hit a little too close to home, you know?"

"Forget I asked it."

"No, it's *fine*," she says. "We should be able to have honest conversations about the people we're dating. It's actually kind of weird we never do."

"Well, I wouldn't go that far. I think a healthy respect for privacy is the bedrock to any lifelong friendship."

"I know you do, weirdo."

This time we both chuckle, and Van slides her laptop off her bed and motions for me to sit beside her.

"Okay, well, to answer your question: *yes*, there are times I'm annoyed with Caleb because he can be immature. And sometimes dating him makes me feel like a bad feminist. But, no, I don't regret dating him."

"What about . . . sleeping with him?" I'm almost too embarrassed to ask, but I know Caleb was Van's first. She might not regret dating him, but she might regret that her first time was with someone who's managed to break her heart on more than one occasion.

"No," Van says quietly. "I don't regret sleeping with Caleb."

"Okay. In a completely judgment-free way, can I ask why not?"

"Well, at the time, I really liked him. I thought I was, you know, *in love*. And I think he did too. And just because things didn't work out between us and we're no longer together, I don't think that means we were wrong to—*Ugh!*—I don't know how to put this in a way that doesn't sound totally cliché, so just know that I'm mentally vomiting as I say this. But I don't think it was wrong for us to have taken a chance on love. I mean, what's the alternative? Never trust anyone? Live your life *not* doing things because you *think* someday you *might* regret them? You'd never do anything. And who wants a life like that?"

Whether she knows it or not, Van is literally describing my entire MO. So in answer to her question: *I* want a life like that.

Sure, everything she's saying about "taking a chance" and "following your heart" sounds good *in theory*. It's literally the premise of every romantic comedy. But it still seems like too much of a risk. I mean, Van makes falling in love sound like buying a sweater. If you outgrow it, no big deal, no one judges you for getting a new one that fits better.

With Marcos, though, the situation is totally different. If anything happened with him, if I let myself "regress," it wouldn't be like buying a sweater. It'd be like getting a tattoo—on my face. Even if I outgrew it, I'd be stuck with the consequences for life.

There's also the not-so-insignificant matter of his disappearance. I know I should just come out and ask him what happened. Even if we were only roommates and nothing more, he still owes me some sort of explanation. But the truth is I'm terrified of what he might say. If he honestly didn't think it was a big deal to just run off without a word, then what does that say about the kind of person he is? And how could I trust him not to do something like that again?

"I don't think I could do that," I say.

"Do what?" Van asks.

"I don't think I could be with someone if I didn't know for certain everything would work out in the end."

"Well," Van sighs, "then it's a good thing you're not in love."

13

Not in Love

Okay, Executive Decision Time. If my conversation with Van has clarified anything, it's that I need to nip this Marcos Situation in the bud.

Maybe insinuating himself into my social circle is purely innocent. Maybe all he wants after all these years is just to be my friend. But his presence is an intolerable distraction. More than that, it's a reminder of the Milo I don't want to be.

The Milo I *can't* be.

For the sake of my family, and my sanity, and my *soul*, I have to put some distance between us. Of course, given that he goes to my school and my church, that's not exactly feasible. If I suddenly stop talking to him or start avoiding him, he'll know something's up. So will Van. Which means I need to find a way to get *him* to start avoiding *me*.

Thankfully, I have a plan.

"What are the Glorious Peccadillos?" Van asks at lunch on Thursday.

The three of us are sitting in what has become "our" booth in the corner of the cafeteria, and Van is reading the name printed across

Marcos's T-shirt. A shirt, I might add, that is way too tight for someone who isn't deliberately trying to show off his body.

"It's my uncle's band," he explains with a proud grin. Then to me he adds, "I told you about him at camp. My uncle Eddie, remember?"

I remember everything Marcos has ever told me. "Vaguely."

"A band?" Van says. "Cool."

"Yeah, he's not famous or anything, but the band's really good. They're sort of modern punk/alternative with a bit of Afro-Caribbean influence thrown in. They mostly play local gigs in Miami, though they did do a set at Joe's Pub in New York last year."

"Awesome." Van sounds genuinely impressed, and I make a mental note to google whatever "Joe's Pub" is when I get home. Then I delete that note because obviously I don't care about Marcos's uncle's band or anything Marcos-related.

"I wish I got to see him more," Marcos sighs as pokes at his tater tots that are somehow both ice-cold and burned black. "He's basically the *only* person on my mom's side of the family who isn't a total a-hole. For real. When my parents got married, he was literally the only member of the Alvarez clan who deigned to attend the wedding."

Oh. I didn't know that. "Why didn't your grandparents come to the wedding?" I ask before I can stop myself.

"They didn't think my dad was good enough for my mom. And they weren't wrong. But they were mostly furious that my mom converted just so she could marry my dad. We've got a couple priests on the Alvarez family tree, so my mom turning her back on the Catholic Church was kind of a huge scandal. Her family basically disowned her. Eddie's the only one who's kept in touch."

"Dude, that sucks."

"Yep. Yet another reason why religion is the absolute worst and ruins everything."

Marcos tosses a tater tot into the air and catches it in his mouth, and the nonchalance with which he writes off my entire belief system stings like a slap in the face. Of course, he hasn't said anything that he hasn't said a million times before, but then I wasn't looking for a fight.

"Religion doesn't ruin everything," I snap.

My pulse is racing, and I can tell my face is beginning to flush. This must be what moral outrage feels like. I don't like it.

"What?"

"I said religion doesn't ruin everything." I'm trying to keep calm though I can feel my blood boiling. "You keep saying that but it's not true. I mean, look at Hitler. He was an atheist. And Stalin. And Mao. There have been lots of terrible people who did terrible things *without* religion. But I don't go around saying atheists are the cause of all the world's genocides because I know it's more complicated than that. I know bad people can corrupt any belief system no matter how good its intentions. And maybe you should remember that before you make blanket statements about people's faith that are really, *really* offensive."

Van and Marcos are silent. They're both staring at me like they don't recognize the person in front of them, and I don't blame them. I don't recognize me.

"I'm sorry," Marcos says. "I didn't mean to offend you."

"Whatever." I shrug. "It's fine."

I've made my point. He's apologized. There's nothing more to be gained by making a bigger scene. Besides, I've accomplished what I set out to accomplish. I've drawn the first line in the sand between us. A line he now knows he can't cross. A line that will hopefully grow wider and wider every day until there's no common ground between us. Until he doesn't know the person standing on the other side of it. Or until he doesn't *want* to know that person.

But just to hammer home the point that I am no longer the Milo he once knew, I turn to Van as nonchalantly as I can and say, "You're friends with Margot Chen, right?"

"Um, yeah?" she says, visibly caught off guard by the abrupt shift in conversation. "I'm friends with Margot. I mean, friendly."

"But you like her?"

"Yeah. I like her. She's a bit Jesus-y. Like you. But she's cool."

"Cool." I'm trying to work up the nerve to ask what I'm about to ask. It's not going to be easy, but I have to do it. My future depends on it.

"I'm thinking of asking her out," I say.

The stunned silence that greets my announcement isn't unexpected but that doesn't make it any less awkward. Both Van and Marcos stare at me in unconcealed horror—as if instead of saying I wanted to ask Margot out, I'd said I wanted to wear her like a suit.

"I'm sorry . . . *What?*" Van asks.

"I said I'm thinking of asking her out."

Because let's be practical. If I date a nice, sweet girl, then maybe—very probably—all these confusing feelings I have for Marcos will go away. In fact, maybe the only reason I have these feelings for a boy in the first place is because I haven't been dating girls, and my body has had to direct all my teenage hormones and longing *somewhere*.

Also, I really do like Margot. She's not some random choice. I didn't just flip open my yearbook last night and throw a dart at a page. I made a very *precise* and *logical* determination as to which of my female classmates I would be the most compatible with based on a variety of factors, and hands down the right person for me is Margot.

Factor one: she's SO nice. Like maybe the nicest girl at Crick. And only someone with an unlimited reserve of patience and kindness could deal with someone like me.

Factor two: she goes to POP, so my parents will approve.

Factor three: she's friends (or "friendly") with Van. And obviously my best friend would need to approve of my girlfriend.

Factor four: she once overheard Van and me discussing *The Golden Girls* and said—and I quote—"Oh my gosh, I love that show!"

Factor five: her name goes really well with mine. Milo and Margot. I can already picture it on our wedding invitations. "You and a guest are cordially invited to the wedding of Milo and Marcos."

Margot! The wedding of Milo and *Margot*. Oh my god. I need to *focus*.

Also, why aren't Van and Marcos saying anything? They're both still looking at me like nervous parents who don't have the heart to tell their kid the truth about Santa. I mean, it's not inconceivable that I, Milo Connolly, would be interested in a girl. I might never have expressed an interest *before*, but people change. And I plan to be one of those people.

"I wasn't aware you liked Margot in that way," Van says, visibly shaking off the shock of my announcement.

"Well, we've been hanging out a lot. At church." Which is *technically* true in the sense that Margot and I are both in the same building together for several hours every Sunday.

"And you want to ask her out?"

"Yes."

Marcos still hasn't said a word, but Van's brow furrows. "Is that why you were asking me all that stuff about sex and relationships the other day?"

"No!" I shout, my face burning scarlet.

Oh. My. God. Is she trying to kill me? How could she mention that conversation in front of Marcos? What if he thinks I was asking because of him?

Wait a minute . . .

On second thought, maybe this is actually a good thing. If Marcos thinks I was asking Van for relationship advice about Margot then that would kind of be perfect for my plan!

"Well," I hedge, pretending to backtrack. "Maybe a little."

Marcos looks genuinely confused, but Van just takes a bite of her corn dog and shrugs. "Well, dude, I don't know what to tell you. I think Margot's waiting for marriage."

Good. I mean—it's good she's waiting for marriage. I'm also waiting for marriage. It's yet another thing we have in common. #PerfectCouple.

"That's okay," I say. "I'm in no rush."

"No kidding."

"Right now, I'm more focused on getting to know her better."

"Great."

"Yeah. So . . . maybe you could put in a good word for me?"

Van pulls the corn dog from her teeth and gives me a withering look that she's perfected from the countless times she's watched Bea Arthur.

"You want *me* to put in a good word for *you* with *Margot*?"

"Yeah," I reply. Mainly because I know I certainly don't have the guts to make the first move and someone's got to get this ball rolling if I ever hope to be a normal teenage boy.

"Why can't you ask her out yourself?"

"Oh . . . Well, you know, I don't want to be forward. I feel like in dating there's a process. You can't just walk up to someone and ask them out."

"Yeah, I'm pretty sure you can."

"Okay, yeah, most people can. But you know me. I'm awkward." She can't argue with that.

"Uh-huh. And what exactly would you like me to say to Margot?"

Huh. That's actually a really good question. I mean, as a potential suitor for her friend, I'm not giving Van a lot to work with.

"Umm . . ."

"Hold that thought," Van says. Then, waving across the cafeteria, she shouts, "Margot!"

Oh God. What is she doing?

Margot looks up from her table of friends, not twenty feet away, and smiles.

"Can you come here a sec?" Van shouts.

"What are you doing?" I hiss.

"You want to ask her out? Ask her out."

"I didn't mean I wanted to do it *right now*."

But it's too late. Margot is already coming our way.

"Hey, Van. What's up?" she asks in her trademark chipper tone that has endeared her to every student, teacher, and parent who's ever met her.

"Milo has something he'd like to ask you."

Yeah, do you know the number for a good lawyer? Because I'm going to need one after I murder my best friend.

"Um . . . ," I begin in what is not the most articulate start of our courtship.

Okay. Calm down. I can do this. There's *nothing* to be nervous about. Margot is a nice Christian girl. I'm a nice Christian boy. We're perfect for each other. I've done the math and Milo + Margot is an equation that works. It has to.

"I was just wondering if maybe you wanted to go out sometime? With me? On a date?" I add that last part in case there's any confusion. Which apparently there is.

"Oh," Margot says. "A date?"

"Yeah."

"With you?"

"Yeah."

I can feel Van's and Marcos's eyes burning into the back of my head, and I want to tear my skin off.

"Oh, Milo . . ."

She doesn't need to finish that sentence. I know that tone. It's the same tone my mom uses when she says, "Oh, Milo, let me get you some Pepto Bismol for your tummy."

"That's *so* sweet. I'm really, *really* flattered," Margot gushes. "But I'm just so busy with church, and the youth ministry, and with applying for colleges. But it's *so* flattering you'd even ask. You've really made my day. Thank you."

Then with a wave and a smile, Margot is gone.

Van and Marcos are silent. When I finally work up the courage to turn around and face them, Marcos is staring at his wilted salad like he wishes he was anywhere else in the world, and Van is cringing into her pudding cup.

"Excuse me," I say, pushing aside my tray and rising from the table. I can feel a lump rising in my throat and I know I have about ten seconds to get out of here before I start crying in the middle of the cafeteria.

"Are you okay?" Marcos asks.

"Yeah. Fine. I just need the bathroom."

"Milo—"

"I'm fine."

I'm not fine, but thankfully the boys' bathroom is empty because the tears are rolling down my face before I can cram myself into one of the claustrophobic stalls.

Stupid Milo! Stupid, stupid Milo!

How could I possibly think that would work? Did I really think I could just ask a girl out and she'd miraculously be into me? That we'd fall in love and all my problems would go away? Who did I think I was fooling?

Certainly not Marcos. The look of *pity* on his face was almost too much to bear. He saw through me—*right through me*—and I have no idea how I'll face him ever again.

14

Mixed Signals

"Hey, Connolly."

Crap. Marcos is leaning against the hood of his dark blue Subaru when I step into the parking lot after school. Despite having two classes together after lunch, I managed to avoid speaking with him all afternoon thanks to a combination of precisely timed lateness and incredibly lame excuses. Now, however, there's no getting past him. He's parked right next to me.

"Hey."

"I'm just waiting for Van," he adds.

"Oh. Okay."

Waiting for Van? Why? Are they hanging out?

My stomach ties itself into a knot at the thought. Van has been so insistent about spending time with Marcos these last few days. I assumed she was just being her typical friendly self, but maybe there's something more going on?

"Are you okay?" he asks when I continue to stare at my feet in confusion.

"What? Oh. Yeah. I'm fine," I cover. "I just thought Van would be hanging out with Caleb." I have no reason for thinking this, let alone repeating it to Marcos, but for some reason I can't quite explain, I double down with, "He called her yesterday, and I kind of got the impression they might be getting back together so . . ."

"Oh. Cool. I wasn't sure what the deal was there."

"Yeah, well, I don't know for sure. It's kind of an on-again, off-again thing. They've been like that for the last three years."

"Three years?"

"Yeah."

"*Wow.*"

"Wow what?"

"Nothing. You'd just think after three years they'd know whether or not they want to be together."

"I don't know about that," I snort, coming to Van's defense. "It's not always easy to know if someone's right for you. Sometimes there are a lot of mixed signals."

Marcos looks at me, surprised by the sudden bitterness in my voice. It surprises me too. I don't know why I'm taking what he said so personally. We're talking about Van and Caleb, not *me*. Aren't we?

"Anyway, I should . . ." I motion to my car and start to reach for my keys.

"I really am sorry, you know?" The sincerity in his voice catches me off guard and stops me in my tracks. "For what I said at lunch. I didn't mean to insult your beliefs. Or you. It wasn't cool and I genuinely apologize if I hurt your feelings."

"Oh." The last thing in the world I expected from Marcos is another apology. Especially after the way I've been acting today. "It's okay."

"No, it wasn't. I mean, I totally stand by the *substance* of what I said. I think religion is deeply problematic and helps perpetuate fascism and white supremacy. But the way I said it? I should know by now not to be so glib when it comes to people's beliefs. Especially people I like and respect."

People he likes and respects? Does that mean me?

"I shouldn't have snapped at you," I say, looking down at my shoes so I don't have to meet his eyes. "I know you weren't trying to hurt me. It was a total overreaction. And I'm . . . I'm sorry too."

What am I doing? *Why* am I apologizing? *This isn't part of the plan!* I mean, I'm deliberately erasing the line in the sand—the line I specifically drew to keep us *apart*—but I can't help myself. I need to make things right between us. Even if I don't know why.

"No worries," Marcos says. "I guess we're both a little off our game these days."

"Well, it has been a while."

"Yeah. I guess a lot changes in three years."

Marcos holds my gaze, and I feel a chill run down my spine.

I guess a lot changes in three years?

Is this his way of finally acknowledging what happened between us at camp? Of letting me know it wasn't all in my head but that he's also not looking to repeat the past? What else could it be? You don't tell someone how much you've "changed" if you're hoping to pick things up where you left off. Why else would he have waited until we're alone to finally bring it up? Why else would he be staring at me with such intensity?

"Yeah, I guess you're right," I say, forcing myself not to look away from his piercing gaze. I need him to know that we're on the same page. That the past needs to stay in the past. "But change is good, right? Who wants to be the person they were three years ago? I cringe when I think about the person I used to be. I'm sure you do too."

Marcos doesn't say anything. He just nods, almost imperceptibly, and for a split second I'd swear he looks . . . *disappointed*. Then he turns away and dismisses me with a curt, "Well, see you 'round, Connolly."

"Yeah," I mumble, taken aback by his sudden indifference. "See you around."

I don't know why but my hands are shaking. They don't stop until I'm home, and even then, I can't stop my heart from racing. It's like there's a panicked bird trapped inside my chest.

Everything feels wrong.

Why? I should be relieved. I should be celebrating. If Marcos isn't interested in picking up where we left off, then there's nothing for me to worry about. My secret is safe. And there's no risk of future temptation.

If he's moved on, and I've moved on, then . . .

Then . . .

Then . . .

Then this year is going to be *unbearable*.

15

Things Get Better, Things Get Worse (Not Necessarily in That Order)

"You guys going to Ashleigh's party?" Caleb asks, downing a bag of Cheetos as he follows Van, Marcos, and me to the parking lot after school on Friday. He's been by Van's side for most of the day and his presence has honestly been a godsend. Things have been kind of tense between Marcos, Van, and me ever since yesterday. I'm pretty sure we barely said three words to each other at lunch. So having someone as oblivious and distracting as Caleb as a buffer has been an unexpected stroke of luck.

"I'll be there," Van says as she tosses her backpack into her Jeep. She and Ashleigh have been friends ever since they were cast as cousins in *The Crucible* sophomore year, so it's a no-brainer she'd be going to her party.

Tonight was supposed to be the night of the Sinkhole 27's "Freedom Rally," but shortly before sixth period the school sent out an email reinstating everyone's lunch privileges. Apparently, Ashleigh's around-the-clock hounding of Vice Principal Holland proved too much for the man, so now her protest has been rechristened as a victory celebration. To quote Ashleigh's revised evite, "It's going to be *epic*."

"What about you, M-Lo?" Caleb asks.

"Milo doesn't do parties," Van says with a smirk. Which *totally* pisses me off. I mean, yes, *technically* it's true. Power-drunk teenagers with unfettered access to alcohol is literally my idea of Hell. But Van is already on *very* thin ice with me after the whole Margot Chen fiasco. I don't need her making me feel like even more of a complete and total *loser*.

"I do so go to parties," I shoot back.

"Since when?"

"Since . . . *always*."

I'm lying through my teeth, and she knows it. But I'm not backing down. I'm tired of being the brunt of everyone's joke.

Van, though, just shrugs like it's not worth her time to argue. "Okay. I guess I'll see you there then?"

"Why don't you pick me up?" I suggest—then instantly regret it.

"Sure," she agrees, calling my bluff. "Pick you up at seven thirty?"

"Great."

"Great."

"Great!" Caleb says, still clueless to the war of passive-aggression raging between Van and me. "See you there too, Marcos?"

"Uh. Yeah." Marcos shrugs. "I'll be there."

"Great. So, we'll all be there!"

Yeah . . . great . . .

Convincing my parents to let me attend Ashleigh's unchaperoned party with zero advance notice is shockingly easier than I expected. I drop the word "valedictorian" into the conversation about fifty times, as if Ashleigh's throwing some intimate, academic soiree for Crick's most intellectually elite students, but I'm not sure my parents buy it. They do, however, seem genuinely relieved that for once in my life I'm making an effort to "get out of my shell."

I don't know whether to be thankful or mortified.

Either way, I excuse myself early from dinner and spend the next hour trying to decide what to wear. After three whole years at Crick, this will technically be my first high school party, and I have no idea how to dress.

I put on the gray suit I wear to church on the Sundays I help collect the offering, but it only takes one glance in the mirror to realize I look like I'm heading to a funeral. Then I try going in the opposite extreme: flip-flops and a Bible camp T-shirt. But this makes me look like I'm twelve, and I'm pretty sure Ashleigh has a really nice house, so flip-flops feel kind of disrespectful.

After turning my closet inside out, I finally decide to wear the same cuffed shorts I wore to school but with a somewhat preppy-looking polo that my aunt gave me last Christmas. I'm just about to tackle my hair (its normally bland caramel color has picked up a surprisingly nice golden sheen from being outdoors so much this summer, but it *definitely* needs a cut) when Van texts that she's in my driveway.

Before my parents have time to clock that she's here and make any of the disapproving comments and/or faces that they do whenever they see us together, I rush downstairs and hop inside her Jeep. Instead of keying the ignition, though, and putting some immediate distance between us and my parents, Van just looks me over, her eyes carefully studying me.

"What?" I ask, ready for something snarky.

"Nothing," she says. "You look nice."

I'm a bundle of nerves by the time we pull up to Ashleigh's house. Ashleigh is a supremely grounded and responsible student, so I'm not anticipating anything too crazy tonight. Then again, if teen movies are any indication, it's always the grounded and responsible student who ends up spiraling out of control after a couple drinks.

Ashleigh, though, seems sober and genuinely thrilled to see us when we arrive. She gives Van a big hug then turns to me with a welcoming smile that instantly puts me at ease. That is, until she follows it up with, "Milo! I can't believe you came. You never come to *anything!*"

Which is the exact moment I notice Marcos hovering a few feet away. He exchanges a knowing smile with Van, and my blood boils.

How dare he act like he knows me? Like he's in on the whole "Poor Milo" joke? He didn't think I was such a pathetic loser when I was literally the only person at camp who would talk to him.

I need to show Marcos *and* Van *and* everyone else at this party that I'm not the total sad sack they all think I am. That contrary to popular opinion I, Milo Connolly, am actually quite "cool" and "with it" or *whatever* people say these days. So when Ashleigh asks if anyone wants a drink, I'm the first to respond with a way too enthusiastic "Sure!" before Van has the opportunity to embarrass me further by announcing I don't believe in (a) underage drinking, (b) alcohol, or (c) fun.

Ashleigh leads us into the kitchen where a couple of my fellow seniors are milling around the snacks. Off in the living room I can see about ten students hanging out on the sofas, and through the glass patio doors, I spy ten more mingling by the pool. No one seems drunk or out of control, despite the celebratory atmosphere, so that's a good sign.

"What do you guys want to drink?" Ashleigh asks, standing over an assortment of various wine, beer, and liquor bottles. "Milo?"

"I'll have whatever you're having." I figure that's as safe a way as any to cover for the fact that I have absolutely no idea what I want as I've never had alcohol before.

Ashleigh, though, looks skeptically at the red plastic cup in her hand. "I'm drinking a vodka cranberry. Are you sure you want that?"

"Sounds great."

It's not. The second I take a sip I almost gag. It's simultaneously too sweet and too strong. But everyone is staring at me like a rat in a lab experiment, so I just smack my lips and say, "That's perfect."

An hour later my stomach is doing somersaults. In fairness to Ashleigh, though, I'm not sure if that's from (a) the vodka, (b) skipping dinner, or (c) the stress of my first party. Actually, I'm pretty sure it's that last one. Yes, I've known most of these kids for years, but I'm not close to any of them. Van and Marcos are the only two people I feel remotely comfortable talking to, but a few minutes ago they wandered off to chat with some of Van's friends from the drama club about the "big audition" next week. Guess who got left behind to stare at the living room carpet?

"Need a refill?"

Ugh. Ashleigh.

I've finally managed to choke down the last drops of my disgusting drink but somehow, like a psychic butler with X-ray vision, Ashleigh's spotted my empty cup from across the room and zeroed in to make sure no guest gets left behind. No wonder she's a shoo-in for valedictorian. She's *relentless*.

"Um, sure," I say, because maybe if I drink enough, I'll work up the courage to talk to someone. Or if not, at least I won't mind so much that I'm utterly alone.

Ashleigh takes my cup and is about to head into the kitchen when she stops, turns back to me, and leans in confidentially.

"Hey, quick question. What's the deal with Marcos?"

My shoulders instantly tense. "Marcos?"

"Yeah, do you know if he's seeing anyone?"

"Uh . . . No. I don't know."

"I think someone overheard him say he has a girlfriend back in Orlando. Do you know if that's true?"

My stomach does another somersault. *A girlfriend?*

I want to tell Ashleigh that's absurd. But then it occurs to me that I actually don't know much about Marcos's life back in Orlando. Sure, he's told Van and me about his favorite restaurants and bookstores. But he's never mentioned any friends. And certainly no one "special."

Which now strikes me as a very ominous omission.

"I don't know if Marcos has a girlfriend," I grumble, hoping Ashleigh will go away and never come back. My stomach feels like it's trying to twist itself inside out. I can tell something's wrong even before a wave of nausea rises in my throat and I'm forced to clasp my hand over my mouth.

"Whoa! Are you okay?" Ashleigh asks, jumping back nervously.

I nod. But another wave hits me, and I almost double over.

"I think I need your bathroom."

Ashleigh grabs my hand and hurries me down a hallway. I'm afraid she's going to be upset, but when I risk a glance at her face, she only looks concerned.

"I'll be right outside if you need anything," she says as she shuts the bathroom door behind me.

For a minute I just stand over the expensive marble sink and force myself to breathe. My insides seem to settle, and I'm briefly convinced that all I needed was a little peace and privacy. But then I think about what Ashleigh said, about Marcos possibly having a secret girlfriend, and my stomach does a backflip. Before I know it, I'm kneeling in front of the toilet saying goodbye to the first (and hopefully last) vodka cranberry of my life.

When it's over I wash my face and rinse out my mouth, praying nobody heard me. I feel drained—both physically and emotionally—and in this moment I'd love nothing more than to fall asleep on the bathroom floor. But I know that if I stay in here any longer people will start to talk. Assuming they haven't already.

"Milo, are you okay?" Van calls through the door. Without waiting for a response, she slips inside, her face twisting in concern when she sees how pale and spent I am.

"I'm fine," I lie.

"Do you want me to take you home?"

"What? No!" I screech a little too loudly. "Why would I want to go home?"

"Ashleigh said you looked really sick."

"Well, Ashleigh makes really disgusting drinks."

"I don't mind driving you."

"Oh my gosh, Van, stop acting like I'm the first person to ever throw up at a party. *You've* thrown up lots of times."

"Yeah, I have. And I know what it feels like, which is why I want to make sure you're okay."

I know she just wants to help. But the thought of her feeling sorry for me—of her *always* feeling sorry for me—only makes me feel worse. It makes me feel like a freak. And I'm so *tired* of feeling this way.

"Really?" I scoff. "You want to make sure I'm okay? Because you're such a *good* friend?"

"Um, *yeah*, I am."

"Is that why you completely embarrassed me in front of Margot?"

"What?"

"You heard me." I know I'm lashing out. I know I'm being completely unreasonable. But I don't care. Because right here, right now, I'd rather be a jerk than a freak.

"Dude, you have *no* interest in Margot. That whole thing was super awkward, and honestly it was really shitty of *you* to try to rope me into whatever weird game you were playing with her."

"It wasn't a game."

"Then what was it? Huh? Seriously, dude, what is going on with you?"

My entire body tenses. "What do you mean?"

"You have been a mess ever since school started. You're picking fights with Marcos. You're asking me to pimp out my friends. You're getting wasted at parties. *What is going on?*"

I want to tell her. *Oh God, I want to tell her.*

But I can't. If I told her about Marcos, I know she'd be nothing but 100 percent supportive and understanding. She'd probably tell me there's nothing wrong with having feelings for another boy and that I owe it to myself to see where these feelings go. But that's *exactly* the opposite of what I need to hear right now. I need to stay strong and keep in control of my emotions. I've made my decision about who I am, and who I'm going to be, and I have to stick to it.

I don't have a choice.

"Dude, I asked you a question," Van snaps. "What is going on with you?"

"I don't know," I lie, staring at the tiled floor so I don't have to meet her disappointed eyes.

"You don't know?" she scoffs. "Well, do me a favor and figure it out. Because whatever *this* is, it needs to stop. Now."

I hear the bathroom door slam behind her. And I'm alone.

16

Things Get Worse, Things Get Better (Not Necessarily in That Order)

I wander back to the living room and plop down in an armchair. I know I should find Van and apologize, but I don't trust myself not to make things worse. If I can't tell her the truth about why I've been acting the way I've been acting, then how do I even begin to explain my behavior to her?

I've really screwed up. And given how thin the bathroom walls are, I'm pretty sure everyone at this party knows I'm a screwup. For the next ten minutes, nobody says a word to me. Then again, the chances of anyone talking to me even before I puked up my guts and got chewed out by my best friend were pretty infinitesimal. I've spent my entire life trying to make myself invisible. I can't really complain now that all my hard work is finally paying off.

I pull out my phone and consider ordering an Uber to take me home, but just when I'm about to confirm the pickup, a hand shoves a red plastic cup in front of my face.

"Here," Marcos says. He's standing over me, his expression inscrutable. When I don't take the cup, he gives me a slight smile and clarifies, "It's water."

The first sip feels so cool and refreshing that I drain the entire cup in one gulp.

"Thanks," I sigh.

"No problem. You looked like you needed it."

He settles down on a nearby sofa and sips his drink. A full minute passes as I wait for him to say something, but for once he seems totally content to simply enjoy the silence. At which point I realize just how silent the room is. And empty. Everyone else is either outside by the pool or in the kitchen with the liquor.

Marcos and I are alone. Which is both oddly comforting and terrifying.

"Are you having a good time?" I ask when I'm no longer able to bear the silence.

"Sure."

"Ashleigh's really nice."

"Yeah."

"Thanks again for the water."

"'Course."

Typical. Three years ago, he couldn't stop talking if his life depended on it. Now, when I'm desperately in need of some genuine human interaction, all I'm getting are one-syllable answers. Because everything always has to be difficult with Marcos.

Then again, it's not like I have anyone to blame but myself. I've been deliberately pushing him away all week. Maybe his stingy conversational responses are just his way of respecting my need for space. But right now, I *need* him to talk to me.

"This week has been a disaster," I say, more to myself than Marcos. But it seems to get his attention.

"Yeah," he agrees with a sad laugh. "I guess it has been kind of rough."

"I feel like I keep screwing up."

"I'm sure you and Van will patch things up," he says, confirming my fear that everyone did indeed overhear our argument.

"It's not just Van," I tell him. Though that's certainly a big part of it.

"Margot?" he asks.

"I never should have asked her out," I snort, my cheeks burning at the memory of my misguided attempt to prove my supposed straightness.

"Hey, you took a chance. So what if it didn't work out? There's no shame in putting yourself out there. Sometimes we like someone and, for whatever reason, that person just can't like us back. And it hurts. Sometimes it hurts *a lot*. But believe me, it's always better to tell someone how you feel and find out the truth than to keep everything bottled up inside and spend your whole life wondering . . ."

Marcos doesn't finish his sentence. He just shakes his head and stares down at his plastic cup, and I have the distinct impression we're no longer talking about Margot.

In fact, from the way he can't meet my eyes, I'm almost certain he's talking about us. But he can't be, can he? I mean, didn't we just agree the other day that neither of us was interested in revisiting the past? I *thought* that's what we decided.

Maybe I was wrong. If so, I need to know. And I need to know now.

Maybe it's the alcohol or the exhaustion or Van's instruction to figure my stuff out, but I need to know what Marcos wants from me. I'm tired of guessing and making assumptions and thinking I have us all figured out when I don't even have a clue.

I need answers.

"I never liked Margot," I say, my voice coming out in a whisper.

Marcos looks up from his drink, his face furrowed in confusion. "You didn't?"

"No."

"Then why did you ask her out?"

Why do you think? I want to shout. *Use some of that logic and reason you're always going on about and read between the lines.*

Instead, I simply shrug my shoulders.

Marcos nods but he doesn't say anything. Why isn't he saying anything? True, I'm not giving him a lot to work with but I'm doing the best I can!

I guess I'm going to have to try a different approach.

"I bet the parties are a lot more fun in Orlando," I say when a burst of shrill laughter on the patio catches Marcos's attention.

"Not really." He shrugs. "Parties are parties."

"Do you miss your friends?"

"I was never really that close to anyone."

"What about your girlfriend?"

Marcos turns back to look at me, his eyes wide with bewilderment. "My *what?*"

"Your girlfriend," I repeat. "In Orlando."

Marcos stares into my eyes like he's trying to see into my soul. Then very slowly, very deliberately, he says, "Why would *I* have a *girlfriend?*"

My heart stops. There's *no* misconstruing his meaning. I wanted an answer and Marcos just gave me one. The only trouble is I have no idea what to do with it.

"That's the rumor," I say, pretending not to catch his meaning.

Marcos sighs then slowly shakes his head in disappointment.

Great. Good job, Milo. Marcos can't even look at me now. He's being so honest, so *vulnerable*, and I'm still playing dumb. *What is wrong with me?* Any second now he's going to realize there's no point in trying to talk to a lost cause like me. Then he's going to get up, walk away, and *never* speak to me again.

Which is what I want. Or what I *thought* I wanted.

I don't know anymore. Everything is so *confusing*. All I know is I don't want this conversation to end. Not like this.

"Do you still watch *The Golden Girls*?" I ask, blurting out the question like my life depended on it.

"*The Golden Girls*?"

"I was just thinking about how we binged all those episodes at camp." I'm grasping at straws, trying to find some way to keep him from walking out of my life. I know it's not the kind of response his confession deserves, but at the very least I hope he can see I'm *trying*. "Do you remember?"

A reluctant smile spreads across his lips. "Of course I remember. You were obsessed with that show."

"Okay, well, as I recall *you* were pretty obsessed with it too."

"Not really."

"Yes, you were. You couldn't wait to get back to our room every night and watch it."

"I just liked the company."

Oh.

"I liked the company too," I say. Which is okay, right? There's nothing wrong with one boy telling another he enjoys spending time with him. That's just good manners.

"Yeah?" he asks, and for the first time his eyes are alive with something close to hope.

"Yeah."

"I wasn't always sure."

"Well, now that you've told me you *don't* actually like *The Golden Girls*, I'm not sure anymore either."

Marcos chuckles. "Hey, don't get me wrong, it's a good show. But most of the time while we were watching it, I was just working up the courage to kiss you."

And just like that all the oxygen rushes out of the room. I can't move or speak. My mind is spinning so quickly it feels like it's about to catch fire.

I was just working up the courage to kiss you. Who says something like that? And in *public*?

I scan the room to make sure no one overheard us, and thankfully everyone is still outside or in the kitchen.

What do I do now?

Every instinct I have is telling me to change the subject before anyone says anything they can't take back. Though I'm pretty sure that line's been crossed, double-crossed, and utterly obliterated.

Unless I turn what he said into a joke!

Yeah, that's it. A joke. To show I have a sense of humor and that I'm the kind of "modern boy" who doesn't get weirded out when another boy says he wants to kiss him—even though that's clearly something I'd never do.

When I open my mouth, though, all that comes out is, "Why didn't you?"

"I didn't know if you wanted me to."

I'm not answering that.

I *can't*.

Yes, I finally have proof that all those years ago I wasn't crazy. That I wasn't just imagining some special connection between Marcos and me. But instead of feeling relieved or grateful or vindicated, I feel *angry*.

I mean, it's been *three* years! Three years of silence and wondering why he abandoned me and trying to bury this part of myself. And *now* he just strolls back into my life to ask if I'd be up for a kiss? How dare he? How dare he turn my life upside down all over again?

He had his chance. He broke my heart, and I *will not* let him break it again. No matter what I might have felt for him.

It's too late.

"There you guys are!" Ashleigh exclaims, swooping into the room and smiling triumphantly like she's just discovered the lost city of Atlantis. She's clearly still got her sights set on Marcos as potential boyfriend material but, even so, I've never been so glad to see her perfect head of golden hair in all my life.

"We're all about to do some Jell-O shots out on the patio if you guys want to join us," she announces, perching on the sofa and resting a perfectly manicured hand on Marcos's shoulder. Then to me she adds, "We've also got just plain Jell-O."

Marcos shifts uncomfortably in his seat. I can tell he's about to decline the invitation, but I need this conversation to be over.

"Great!" I exclaim, jumping up from my armchair. "Let's do it."

And I'm out onto the patio before anyone can say a word.

When we down our collective Jell-O shots in honor of the Sinkhole 27, I pretend to swallow the contents of my cup, then spit it out into the grass when no one is looking. If nothing else, I'm going to get through this party without puking again.

I then spend the rest of the evening floating from group to group, forcing myself to make small talk with people I barely know, while desperately trying to avoid Van and Marcos. Although given how they both look away whenever I happen to catch their eyes, it might be more accurate to say that they're the ones avoiding me.

For a while I try glomming on to various conversations, but I have a hard time emotionally investing in whether Crick's football team will finally "go all the way" this year or ranking the relative hotness of the Hemsworth brothers.

Mercifully, after what seems like an eternity, the party starts to wind down, and Van makes her way over to collect me.

"Hey," she says, barely deigning to look at me. Which is 100 percent fair. I wouldn't blame her if she never spoke to me again.

"Hey."

"Enjoy the party?"

"Not really." I'm too exhausted to lie. There have been enough lies this evening.

A flicker of concern flashes across Van's eyes, and I feel even worse for how I've treated her. These last couple days I've been a total jerk to the one person who has always been there for me, and yet here she is, still unable to stop herself from worrying.

"Are you feeling sick again?" she asks, pulling me into the empty kitchen for some privacy.

"No, I'm okay."

"You sure?" she asks again. Because that's what a good friend does. Just like a good friend calls you out when you're acting like the number one a-hole of the universe.

"I'm sure," I say. "And I'm sorry. I know I've been a jerk tonight. And I know I shouldn't have asked you to help get me a date with Margot. That was weird. *I've* been weird. And I'm *really* sorry."

Van nods, but she doesn't say anything.

"I've just been trying to figure some stuff out this week—personal stuff—and it's been kind of hard for me. But that doesn't give me the right to take it out on you. Or Marcos. Or anyone else. And I'm going to do better. I promise."

"Okay. *Good*," Van says. "Apology accepted." She smiles, and my body feels twenty pounds lighter. "But just so *you* know, if there's something going on, you can talk to me. That's, like, literally what best friends are for."

"I know."

"*Is* there something going on?"

I want to tell her about Marcos. I really do. But I'm just not there yet.

"No, I'm fine," I say. "It's just . . . stuff with my parents."

Van nods again but doesn't look convinced. "Okay, well, if you ever want to talk about *anything*—"

"I know," I say a bit too quickly. "Thanks. Are you ready to go?"

"Actually, Caleb and I and a couple other people are thinking of heading over to the beach for a midnight swim."

Oh no. I cannot go to the beach. I need this night to be over. Also, my parents will have a meltdown if I miss curfew.

"Don't worry," Van sighs, reading the panic on my face. "Marcos said he can drive you home."

My stomach lurches like I've been punched in the gut.

"Marcos?"

"Yeah. He volunteered. Is that a problem?"

A problem? Why would it be a problem? It's only the Worst Possible Ending to the Worst Possible Evening. *Ever.*

"No," I mumble. "No problem."

The car ride home takes place in almost total silence. Other than giving Marcos the occasional direction, we don't exchange more than six words. It's excruciatingly awkward, but I prefer this general awkwardness to the very specific awkwardness we could be experiencing if we continued our earlier conversation.

Besides, what's there to say? Nothing can happen between us. And pretending otherwise is just *reckless.*

We pull into my driveway, and Marcos kills the lights and engine. From the way his body tenses, I know he's gearing up to say something—something I *don't* want to hear—but if I can just get out of the car before he opens his mouth—

"We don't have to talk about it ever again."

My hand freezes as I reach for the door.

This is my chance. All I have to do is say "okay" and go inside and this whole impossible situation goes away forever. Marcos will leave me alone, and I'll never have to see the disappointment in my parents' eyes when they learn their son likes boys. It's literally the moment I've been praying for.

So why can't I do it?

"Well?" he asks.

"If that's what you want," I whisper.

"It's not."

Something touches my hand in the dark, and I look down to see Marcos lacing his fingers through mine. It's the smallest gesture but, in this moment, it means everything.

I look up into Marcos's eyes and, for the first time since I've known him, I'm taken aback by what I see. Marcos looks scared. Truly and properly scared. It doesn't seem possible that someone as bold and confident as Marcos could ever look that frightened of anything—of *me*. But he is. And it breaks my heart.

I squeeze Marcos's hand and his palm feels so good against mine. It's like our hands were made for this. Like they belong together.

I feel like such a fool for getting angry with him at Ashleigh's party. Yes, he hurt me when he disappeared from camp, but looking into his frightened eyes, I know he's been hurt too. And whatever pain or confusion we've caused each other in the last week—or three years ago—it is nothing compared to the joy of this moment. This simple, little moment that is somehow everything I've ever wanted.

"I thought about you," I whisper, the words escaping from my mouth before I know what I'm saying. "Every day. For the last three years."

"I thought about you too. Every day."

Marcos smiles, the fear evaporating from his eyes, and for a brief second, I can't help but smile back. I mean, look at us. After all these years, here we are. Sitting in the moonlight. Staring into each other's eyes. Holding hands.

Oh crap . . .

Oh crap, oh crap!

WHAT AM I DOING?

I'm parked in my driveway *holding hands with* a *BOY.* Anyone could see me. My neighbors. My parents. God.

What am I going to do if—?

But I don't have time to finish that thought. Because at that exact moment, every streetlamp in my cul-de-sac explodes. And the world goes dark.

17

Things Get Complicated

It's a blackout.

As Marcos and I stand at the edge of my driveway and stare out into the endless darkness, we can't see a single light for miles. Streetlamps, porch lights, even the neon sign of the Exxon station that's normally visible in the distance: they're all dead.

"What do you think is going on?" Marcos asks.

"I don't know."

Normally the only time we lose power like this is when a storm blows down a power line. Tonight, though, there's barely a breeze, and the sky above us is clear and open. I'd almost call it romantic. Except "romance" is precisely what had me freaking out two minutes ago in Marcos's car, and I've only just now gotten my heart to stop beating like it was going to burst out of my chest, so it's probably better if I don't dwell too much on how amazing it is to be standing under the stars with Marcos.

"Milo, is that you?" my dad's voice calls out through the darkness.

I hear a screen door open behind me, and I immediately step away from Marcos. We're not doing anything inappropriate (at least, not anymore), but where my parents are concerned, I don't want to take any chances.

"Yeah, it's me, Dad."

My parents emerge from the house dressed in their bathrobes and carrying flashlights. They cautiously navigate their away across our pitch-black yard and join Marcos and me at the end of the driveway.

"Hi, Mr. Connolly. Hi, Mrs. Connolly," Marcos says, extending his hand.

"This is Marcos," I explain. "He gave me a ride home. His dad is Mr. Price, our new treasurer."

That's probably the most calculated statement I have ever said to my parents, and it works exactly as I intend it.

"Oh, of course!" my mom says, shaking Marcos's hand with genuine enthusiasm. Decent churchgoing boys are few and far between, so if anyone can keep her son from heading down the dark path of apostasy like Van Silvera, a wholesome treasurer's son is as safe a bet as any. "It's *so* nice to meet you."

"Looks like we've got ourselves a blackout," my dad states rather obviously.

"Yes, sir. We'd just pulled up when all the lights went out," Marcos explains, strategically omitting what we were actually doing when the lights went out.

"I'm just glad you weren't driving," my mom says. "The roads must be a mess with all the traffic lights out. I wonder if it's just our neighborhood or the whole city?"

We instinctively look out at the horizon. There's not a single light as far as the eye can see.

"Marcos, honey, do you want to spend the night?" my mom asks. "I don't think it's safe for anyone to be on the roads right now."

Marcos spend the night?

I'm not sure I can handle being in such close proximity and not completely explode. Both metaphorically and . . . *you know.*

Thankfully, Marcos shakes his head. "That's really kind of you to offer, Mrs. Connolly. But I don't live far. Plus, my mom will be worried."

"Of course." My mom doesn't sound persuaded, but she can't argue with another mother's fear. She knows she'd want me home if the situation was reversed. "Just be sure to drive slow. And text Milo when you get home, so we know you made it safely."

"We'll see you at church on Sunday," my father says, shaking Marcos's hand goodbye.

"Yes, sir. See you then."

Marcos gives me a nod, which I return as casually as I can, hoping my parents can't see the crimson blush that I know is creeping across my face.

As his car pulls out of the driveway, Marcos's headlights illuminate our street, and for the first time I notice that my family isn't the only one milling about on their lawns. Neighbors are emerging from their homes to peer curiously into the dark, some suspicious and frightened, others faintly amused.

My parents decide to go check on the elderly couple next door. I should probably lend a hand or see if anyone else needs assistance, but I'm so exhausted after the night I've had that as soon as my parents are out of sight, I slip inside my house and collapse into bed.

I'm aching for sleep, but I also can't take my eyes off my phone. Marcos and I didn't get to finish our conversation in the car, and part of me is worried that maybe it's going to be another three years before I hear from him.

I swear to God if he ghosts me again . . .

My phone beeps. A text.

Marcos: Safe at home. You can stop worrying. 😌

I sink down into my pillow as the stupidest grin spreads over my face and my whole body relaxes. Given how utterly bizarre this night has been, I don't know why I feel so good. But then I realize it's because he's right. I *can* stop worrying. Because for once I know exactly how Marcos feels about me. And he knows how I feel about him.

And whatever happens next, at least we know the truth.

Sunday is the Price family's first official day at POP. Before service I spot Marcos in the lobby with his parents, and I can already tell how much he resents having to be in a house of worship. He's not exactly sulking as Reverend Foley introduces him and his parents to their fellow congregants, but his smile is definitely wearing thin.

At least until he sees me. Then his whole face brightens, and I have to pinch myself to stop from blushing.

"Oh, there are the Prices," my mom says cheerfully, putting her hand on my back and steering me toward them. "Let's go say hello."

True to Patsy Reynolds's description, Mr. Price is quite handsome with his chiseled cheekbones and salt-and-pepper hair. There's no doubt where Marcos gets his good looks. Mrs. Price is beautiful too, though there's something a little reserved about her demeanor. While her husband enthusiastically shakes my parents' hands, Mrs. Price simply nods and smiles. It's a polite smile, but there's something a bit practiced about it. If I had to guess, I'd say it's the smile of a woman all too accustomed to living with a husband who loves the spotlight but hates having to share it.

"It's nice to meet you both," I say, wondering if they have any clue who I am. From the way their eyes pass over me, though, it seems pretty safe to assume that Marcos has been just as secretive about our past with his parents as I've been with mine.

I receive a cursory "Nice to meet you too" before Mr. Price and my dad start swapping stories about Friday night's blackout. Not that either has a particularly scintillating tale to tell.

Power was restored to the city around noon yesterday, so in total we were only without electricity for about fourteen hours, which isn't even enough time for food to spoil. The power company is still investigating the cause of the outage. They say it was something to do with an unexpected surge that overloaded the power grid, which seems both vague and disturbing. But with temperatures in the low nineties, most people are just relieved to have their AC back.

While our parents commiserate about the heat, Marcos shoots me a series of surreptitious winks, and pretty soon I'm blushing so hard I'm afraid my face is going to match my father's maroon tie. Thankfully, the tuning of the organ is our cue that service is about to start. My parents say goodbye to the Prices, and we make our way to our usual pew on the far right of the auditorium where my dad claims (without evidence) the acoustics are better. The Prices sit on the left side of the auditorium, but since the pews are angled toward the altar in an ever-expanding V-shaped pattern, Marcos and I end up having a surprisingly clear view of each other.

I try to force myself to focus on Reverend Foley's sermon, but for the next hour, every time I glance across the room, I find Marcos's eyes waiting for mine. It's both incredibly distracting and insanely intoxicating.

It also raises a very real question that I've been putting off all weekend: *What do we do now?*

I mean, yes, I might finally be able to admit to myself that I like Marcos. *A lot.* But there's no way I'm ever going to be able to tell anyone how I feel about him. I know myself, and there's no way I could handle something that monumentally *public.* Mainly because I'm pretty sure my parents would disown me, and his parents would definitely disown him, so it's not like Marcos and I can "date." He's never going to be my "boyfriend."

So where does that leave us?

Yesterday, after the power came back on, he called to check up on me and to tell me we could take things as slow as I needed to go. "I'm not exactly ready to come out to the world either," he confided to me as I hid (unironically) in the back of my bedroom closet in case my parents overheard us.

It was the nicest thing he could've said. He clearly understands how difficult this situation is for me. But his thoughtfulness only ended up making me feel more guilty because I'm pretty sure that even if Marcos gave me all the time in the world to get comfortable with our newly acknowledged feelings, I'd still be stuck in this endless cycle of desire, shame, and regret.

At one point he asked if I wanted to come over after school next week "to study," but I turned him down before he'd even finished the question. I know his dad will be at work and his mom recently signed up for an afternoon yoga class, so we'd have the whole house to ourselves. But for some reason the thought of being alone together in his bedroom—unsupervised—terrifies me.

Actually, that's a lie. I know the exact reason. Even though we've admitted our feelings for each other, Marcos and I haven't acted on them—hand-holding aside—and as long as we don't act on them, then technically I can tell myself we haven't done anything wrong. By which I mean "anything God or my parents could object to or which could jeopardize my immortal soul."

And that's true. So far, we haven't crossed any uncrossable lines. And maybe we don't have to. Maybe just *knowing* how we feel—without acting on it—is enough. I mean, who says things have to get physical? Maybe we can just be really, *really*, REALLY good friends.

That, at least, is what I tell myself—until I see Marcos in nothing but a swimsuit.

18

Life's a Beach

I blame Van.

I was just figuring out how to have a normal, healthy, platonic-if-slightly-crushy relationship with Marcos when she had to go and text me—right in the middle of Pastor Foley's sermon—that it was "too glorious a day to be cooped up inside" and she was dragging my butt to the beach whether I wanted it or not. What she didn't mention is that she'd also be dragging Marcos's butt—a fact I only discovered when my parents were saying goodbye to the Prices in the church parking lot, and Marcos asked what time he and Van should pick me up. I thought about making up some excuse to get out of going, but my mom was so overjoyed at the thought of me hanging out with the new treasurer's son, I didn't dare back out.

Now the surf is pounding in my ears and Marcos is rubbing sunscreen into my shoulders while I desperately try *not* to get an erection.

"You're so tense, Connolly. Don't you ever relax?" he laughs, massaging the lotion into my shoulders. He's taking *way* more time than he needs, but if he never stops, that's fine with me. His touch is paradise.

It also doesn't hurt that it's about as perfect a beach day as any

Floridian could wish for. Nothing but blue skies above and white sand under our feet. Van's packed snacks, folding chairs, and a cooler full of soda, so it's clear she's planning to make a day of it. That would normally be fun in theory, except for the fact that I can't help but worry how I'm going to get through the next few hours without salivating over Marcos's body. Which is in ridiculously good shape.

Ri-dic-u-lous.

"All done," he says, giving my neck an extra squeeze for emphasis.

"Want me to do you?" I ask a little too eagerly.

"I'm good. I actually put some lotion on before we left."

Darn. Oh well. That's probably for the best. If I start rubbing him down, I don't honestly think I could stop. Shirtless Marcos is definitely bringing out feelings I did not think a Good Presbyterian Boy was capable of.

"Um, one of you losers can do *my* back if it wouldn't be too much trouble?" Van snipes, tossing me her special hypoallergenic lotion.

Oops. I was so busy drooling over Marcos I totally forgot Van was here. *Get it together, Milo.*

I finish Van's back, making sure to take just as much time with her as Marcos did with me. Then the three of us are racing down to the water and throwing ourselves into the cool, salty surf of the Atlantic. The water's a little choppy for my taste. I prefer my oceans to be more like lakes (i.e., boring), but Van and Marcos are having a blast, diving into the waves and trying to ride them to shore.

Marcos, in particular, looks like he's in his element, striding through the water like some Greek sea god. It's getting increasingly hard not to stare, especially as his suit is riding loose and low around his hips. Every time a wave hits, the trunks sag ever lower, revealing more of his backside as well as the muscular V leading down to his groin.

"Enjoying the view, Connolly?"

Marcos winks at me and yanks up his suit. I blush before I can stop myself, and the only thing I can think to do to hide my embarrassment is dive underwater. With all the other horny little fishies.

An hour later the three of us are tanning in Van's beach chairs, our exhausted bodies drunk on the sun. I've never been much of a beach person, but after today you can sign me up for a lifetime membership. This, right here, is heaven. I've got my best friend to the left, my secret crush to the right, and nothing but blue skies above us for as far as the eye can see.

How could anything be better?

In fact, I'm so lost in this seductive lethargy that I don't even open my eyes when something soft brushes my hand. When it happens again, I loll my head to the side, expecting to see a fly circling my fingers.

Instead, I see the back of Marcos's hand resting imperceptibly against mine. Anybody passing by wouldn't notice, but it's enough to send shivers down my spine.

I close my eyes and pretend to stretch, as if I'm settling down for a nap, which gives me the convenient excuse to "accidentally" run my fingers against the length of Marcos's arm before once again settling back into the same position as before, our knuckles gently grazing.

I can't believe only a few hours ago I thought I could be happy with being "just friends." I am truly and utterly incompetent when it comes to knowing what's good for me. Because I definitely, absolutely,

100 percent want *this*. Secret glances, and private touches, and skin against skin . . .

There's an embarrassing stirring in my shorts (again), and I realize this is getting to be a regular occurrence around Marcos. I'm definitely going to need to "cool down" before I can get out of this chair. But from the way my skin ignites whenever Marcos rubs the back of his hand against mine, I don't know how I'll ever be cool again.

I mean it. Maybe I've been in the sun too long, but my body is practically on fire. Every pore feels like a furnace burning with the heat of a raging supernova. It's almost too much to bear.

And then it hails.

That's not a metaphor. It *literally* hails. A clump of ice falls from the sky and hits my big toe. At first, I think I've been stung by a horsefly, but as the temperature plummets, I look up to see massive storm clouds blanketing the sky.

"Jesus Christ . . . ," Van gasps.

The pummeling comes out of nowhere. Across the beach, swimmers are hurrying out of the water and families are gathering up their children and racing to the safety of their vehicles. I've always thought it was pretty gross—not to mention environmentally unfriendly—that people in Daytona are allowed to park their cars directly on the beach. As we scramble into our Jeep, though, for once I'm thankful.

Van slides into the front seat and rolls up the windows while Marcos and I squeeze into the back. Hail rains down like machine gun fire, banging against the windows so violently I'm worried they might shatter.

"This is wild," Marcos exclaims. "You guys didn't tell me you had hailstorms."

"We don't," Van grumbles. "Like ever."

But Mother Nature seems determined to prove her wrong. In every direction, as far as we can see, families are staring out from their cars, faces pressed against their windows in shock, as the beach is battered and blanketed with ice.

19

A Leap of Faith

"Crazy day, huh?" Marcos asks in what may be the Understatement of the Year.

"You can say that again."

"Crazy day, huh?"

"*Really*, Marcos?"

"What?"

"Are you proud of that?"

"You're not impressed with my wit?"

"Let's just say it's a good thing you're pretty."

For some reason it's a lot easier for me to flirt with someone when it's over the phone like this. Even if it is getting a little claustrophobic here in the back of my closet.

"So you think I'm pretty? Good to know."

"I mean, you're *okay*."

"Be specific, Connolly. How pretty would you say I am? On a scale of one to ten?"

"I'd say you're a seven."

"*Seven?*"

"On a good day."

"You were staring pretty hard at me today for someone who's *only* a seven."

I can't help smiling. Despite the impromptu "blizzard," our beach trip was the most fun I've had in a very long time.

Besides, the hail only lasted a few minutes. After that the clouds evaporated, the sun came out, and the temperature shot back up to the eighties. Pretty soon there wasn't a single piece of ice left on the sand. In fact, if it weren't for the tiny dings and scrapes on Van's Jeep, we'd probably have assumed we'd hallucinated the whole thing.

"For real, though, Connolly. Is this city of yours, like, cursed?"

"What do you mean?"

"I mean, I've only been here a week and so far, there's been a sink-hole, a blackout, and a hailstorm. Is this normal?"

"No," I laugh. "Not at all."

"Really?"

"I swear. None of this stuff started happening until you showed up."

"Oh, so *I'm* the jinx?"

"I mean, if you want to be technical about it? Yeah, you're a jinx."

"Wow. Okay. You know what, Connolly?"

"What?"

"It's lucky *you're* cute."

I blush so hard I think my face might catch fire. When did this become my life? Flirting and compliments and late-night phone calls with a boy I can't stop thinking about and who can't stop thinking about me? Only a few days ago my life was a living nightmare. Now, almost overnight, I can honestly say things are . . . *good*.

"So, listen," Marcos says, his voice changing gears in a way that brings me up short. "There's something I want to ask you."

Uh-oh. I know that tone. That is not the tone of small talk. That is the tone people reserve for difficult and/or serious conversations. That is the tone of bad news.

Ugh! Of course, something's wrong. I should've seen this coming. Bad things always happen when you drop your guard. That's Rule Number #1. How did I think—

"I want to take you out on a date."

Wait. What?

"Connolly? Did you hear me?"

"Uh-huh."

"I said I want to take you out. On a *date*."

"Okay."

Marcos must be as surprised by my answer as I am because he immediately starts to clarify.

"I mean a date. A Real Date. No Van. Just you and me."

"Yeah, I get it," I laugh, suddenly giddy. "Just you and me. A date-date."

Marcos laughs too. "Yeah. A date-date."

"Okay."

"Okay. Great."

"Why are you laughing?"

"Why are *you* laughing?"

"I didn't think it'd be that easy."

He's right. Agreeing to something as momentous and life-altering as a date *with a boy* is normally something I would've hemmed and hawed over for days before eventually talking myself out of it. Tonight, though, I'm reckless with joy. Or maybe I just know a date means more chances to touch and be touched by Marcos, which after today are two things very high on my to-do list.

"I was thinking next Friday," he continues. "After school. We could get dinner and maybe see a movie or something?"

"Sounds great," I say. "I'd really like that."

"Cool."

"Cool."

We both fall silent, but I swear I can hear him grinning. I'm pretty sure he can hear me too. Neither of us knows what to say for a full minute, but eventually he thinks of the perfect thing.

"I really like you, Connolly."

"I really like you too."

20

Drama (Onstage and Off)

The next few days of school are both paradise and torture. They're paradise because every time Marcos and I glance at each other, we can't help but smile thinking about our impending date-date. It's torture because every day that isn't Friday feels like eternity.

Classes are mostly a blur. I'm too excited to focus on anything my teachers are saying, and I'm pretty sure I bombed my history quiz, but I don't care. I have a *date*.

In fact, I'm in such a good mood, I don't even mind sitting through Van and Caleb's latest public squabble. As I predicted, the "honeymoon period" of their latest attempt at courtship lasted exactly one weekend. That was followed by two days of increasingly passive-aggressive bickering and has now entered what I like to call their pre-breakup fireworks.

"You are *not* joining the football team," Van practically shouts at Caleb as we loiter outside the school auditorium. We're waiting, along with a dozen other hopeful drama students, for Mr. Henderson to post the cast list for the fall musical. Which is something called *Chicago*. Which Van is *very* excited about.

Some might even say too excited.

She's been a bundle of nerves all week leading up to yesterday's audition, so her patience for Caleb and his antics is already wearing dangerously thin. She certainly doesn't need any added stress now that she's a few minutes away from learning if she has once again landed the lead and maintained her domination over the Spruce Crick drama program.

"I just said I'm *thinking* of trying out," Caleb groans, letting out an exasperated sigh.

"Well, you can stop thinking it. Because it's not happening."

Officially, our school's football team is the Spruce Crick Falcons, but Van has always referred to them as the Spruce Crick Neanderthals. A name that is sadly all too appropriate given their extreme entitlement, utter lack of self-awareness, and general bro-ness.

"What's the big deal?" Caleb protests. "You're always on me about doing more extracurriculars. Well, I found one!"

"Absolutely *not*. You are not going to start spending all your afternoons with those Stone Age knuckle-draggers. Every guy on that team is like a date rapist in training."

"Whoa. Come on. That is not fair."

"They're jerks, Caleb! They barely ever win a game, and yet they walk around this school like they own the place, constantly talking shit about the girls' soccer team, which actually *has* gone on to compete at State. And don't even get me started on all the shit they spew about the girls they've slept with. Or the girls that *won't* sleep with them. They are like the *literal* embodiment of toxic masculinity—in shoulder pads."

"Jesus, V, you've always got to exaggerate *everything*."

"Is that why you shaved your head?" Van pivots, narrowing her eyes at Caleb's new buzz cut.

"What? *No!*" Caleb scoffs, though from the way he can't meet her eyes, I suspect Van knows it is. "I mean, it's not *the* reason. But, yeah, when I was at Supercuts the other day, Jared Resnick and a couple of the other guys from the team happened to be there too, and we got to talking—"

"*Jared Resnick?*" Van practically spits the name. If the Falcons are a bunch of Neanderthals, then Jared Resnick is the King of the Knuckle-Draggers.

"Yo, calm down. Jared's actually a pretty chill dude."

"Jared Resnick is one roofied drink away from being the next Brett Kavanaugh."

"Oh my god, seriously? I can't talk to you when you get like this!"

"Like what? Like when I use reason and *facts* to point out that you are hanging out with some deeply problematic people and that your association with said people might lead some to question whether you are also a problematic person."

"You know what? Eff this. I'm done. I can't!" Caleb exclaims, throwing his hands up in exasperation as he storms off down the hallway.

"Wow! Really?" Van calls after him. "Okay! Nice! Way to leave me all *alone* in my hour of need!"

I clear my throat to remind Van that I'm actually standing right next to her.

"Oh, dude, sorry!"

"No worries. But let the record show that I am here in your hour of need."

"Thanks." Van smiles, though a second later her face clouds over as she looks down the hall. "Seriously, though, can you *believe* Caleb?"

Can I believe that Caleb Yates, who once declared his greatest ambition in life was to become a professional taste tester for Doritos, would become friends with Jared Resnick and eventually claim his rightful place among the knuckle-draggers? *One hundred percent.*

But what I say is, "Crazy."

Van clocks my not-so-subtle sarcasm and glares at me but, a second later, she just shakes her head and starts to laugh.

"Oh my god, why do I keep doing this to myself?"

"For the sex?" I tease.

"Dude, you joke, but Caleb is shockingly good in that department."

"Ew."

"Seriously. Like, I don't know if he spends a lot of time on Wikipedia studying human anatomy or watching how-to tutorials, but he knows where *everything* is *and* how to use it."

"Oh my gosh, Van, stop!" I shout, throwing my hands over my ears as she cackles with glee.

"Okay, okay, I'm done," she says, catching her breath. "I promise. No more sex talk. I know you're an innocent virgin who's never had an impure thought in his entire life."

If I wasn't still blushing from my unsolicited peek into Van's sex life, I'm pretty sure I'd be turning beet red right now recalling all the *very* impure things I've been fantasizing about doing with Marcos. I mean, the two of us haven't even kissed yet. But in my mind? Let's just say we have done oh-so-much more. And I have enjoyed every second of it.

"What's with that face?" Van asks when I continue to stare down at my shoes in hormone-fueled embarrassment.

It's the strangest impulse, but part of me actually wants to tell her about my date with Marcos. About *everything*. It's kind of the perfect opportunity. We're already talking about her complicated love life; it wouldn't be too hard to segue into mine. Plus, just the other day, Marcos told me that he'd be down with telling Van about "us" whenever I felt comfortable enough to take that next step.

Maybe it's time.

"Ah! Mr. Henderson's posting the cast list!"

Van squeezes my arm then dashes over to the bulletin board outside the stage door where Mr. Henderson has just pinned up a sheet of paper before quickly ducking back into the auditorium. No doubt to avoid the sudden swarm of students who are now crowding around the casting sheet to learn their fates.

"Yes! Yes! Yes!" Van shouts. "I'm Roxie Hart!"

"Congrats!" I holler, even though I have no idea what that means. Not that it matters. Van's too busy being showered in praise and envy by her fellow thespians to even hear me.

I guess my coming-out will have to wait. Which is totally fine. Today is Van's day, and that's how it should stay.

And that's *not* me chickening out. I will tell her about Marcos and me. Soon. Right after our date.

Probably.

Definitely.

Maybe.

21

The Date-Date

"How did you hear about this place?" I ask as Marcos and I slide into a booth in the back of a funky little Mexican cantina on Beach Street. There's a smell of cilantro and sizzling chorizo in the air, and festive colored lights hang from the rafters. I'm not sure if Marcos picked this place because it's out of the way and not a chain, so the likelihood of any of our classmates showing up is slim, or because he's just in the mood for tacos.

"You told me about it, remember? You said it was your favorite place to get Mexican food with Van."

I have zero memory of this conversation. "When did I tell you that?"

"At camp."

The fact that he remembers such an obscure conversation makes me swoon in my seat. Unfortunately, what comes out of my mouth is, "The only thing I remember about camp is you completely abandoning me."

WTF? Seriously, Milo, where the hell did that come from?

The words are out before I know what I'm saying, and I instantly regret them. Yes, I still have questions about Marcos's Disappearing

Act. And, yes, we need to talk about it. But the last thing I want to do is pick a fight in the first five minutes of my very first—and now probably last—date.

"It's okay," Marcos says, reading the horror on my face. "I deserve that."

"No, ignore me. I don't know why I said that."

Except I do. Marcos hurt me—he *really* hurt me. And sitting here across from him, I need to know why. Especially if we're going to have any sort of future.

"I guess it has been on my mind," I confess. "I mean, it just seemed like we were getting really close at camp. And even if we weren't ready to admit how much we liked each other, we were still friends. And then you just—"

"Bailed. I know. I should've told you I was leaving camp early. It was really shitty of me. But the short explanation is my grandfather died, and I had to go home for the funeral."

"Oh my gosh," I gasp, practically choking on my water. "That's awful. I had no idea."

Of course, Marcos has a perfectly reasonable excuse for why he disappeared. I feel terrible now for even thinking he might've had some sinister or selfish motive.

"It's actually fine," he assures me. "I wasn't close with my grandfather. He basically treated my mom like 'the help' and me like an embarrassment. Like in all our family portraits, he'd put my blond cousins front and center and stick me in the back. One time he even cropped my head off."

"For real?"

"Yeah. Basically, he was a bigot who never got over the fact that his son disobeyed him by marrying my mom."

"I thought it was your mother's family who didn't approve of the marriage."

"Nope. Everyone in my family hates everyone else. It's like *Romeo and Juliet* if nobody learned their lesson."

"Wow."

"Yeah. Though I think that's why my mom has put up with my dad for as long as she has. At one point he was apparently, like, a semi-decent guy who actually loved her so much he chose her over his own family. I have no idea where *that* guy has been my entire life—it's like he did a complete one-eighty after I was born—but that doesn't stop my mom from hoping he'll come back."

The waitress arrives to take our order. Three chicken tacos for me. Three cactus tacos for Marcos.

"Anyway," he continues, "when my dad called me at camp and told me I had to come home for my racist grandfather's funeral, I *begged* him to let me stay and finish the last week. But he told me I was being 'disrespectful' and that I needed to be packed and ready to go in twenty-four hours. No excuses."

"Oh," I say as my brain processes this new piece of information. "Twenty-four hours? So you knew you were leaving for an entire day?"

I don't mean to put Marcos on the spot, but from the way he avoids my eyes I can tell that's exactly what I've done. "I *wanted* to tell you. I really did. Not just that I was leaving but also, you know, that I *liked* you. But then . . ."

"Then what?" I ask when he continues to stare at the bowl of complimentary salsa in silence. He's debating something. Something he isn't sure how to say. I'm actually starting to get nervous, but eventually he just shrugs and says, "I got scared."

I'm pretty sure that's *not* what he was going to say—that's there's something he's leaving out—but I nod. Because I know what he's telling me is true. Even if it's not the Truth.

"I liked you," he continues. "A lot. But I was afraid if I told you and you didn't feel the same, you might freak out and tell someone. Like the counselors. Who'd tell my parents. And then I'd have that whole disaster to deal with. And if you *did* feel the same, it's not like it would've mattered because I'd still have to leave the next day, and then you might end up hating me for *that*.

"Eventually I figured everything would be simpler if I just left without saying anything. I did think about calling you when I got home, just to make sure you were all right, but every time I picked up the phone, I lost my nerve."

"I thought I'd done something wrong," I say, my voice barely a whisper as I recall the terror I felt the day Marcos vanished.

"What?"

"When you disappeared. I thought it was because of me. Because I did something to make you run away."

"No," he says, reaching across the table and taking my hand. I flinch and cast a quick glance around the restaurant to make sure no one's watching. Marcos clocks my unease and retracts his hand. "Sorry."

"It's okay."

"And, no, of course you didn't do anything. I should've said good-bye. You deserved a goodbye. I just wasn't brave enough to tell you the truth."

It's hard to imagine Marcos lacking bravery. Aside from Van, he's the most courageous person I know. But I should know by now that just because he's not a total coward like me, that doesn't mean he doesn't have his own troubles and insecurities. All I have to do is remember the terrified look on his face that night in his car when he told me how he felt to know he's no stranger to fear.

"You're not the only one who was too scared to make a move," I confess. "I wasn't exactly brave either."

"Maybe not. But you didn't run away."

True. But if Marcos can take responsibility for his part in the confusion that occurred at camp, I can take responsibility for the Emotional Dumpster Fire that was our first week at Crick.

"I've been running from you ever since school started," I say. "I mean, literally from the second I saw you in the parking lot with Van, I've been trying to push you away and get myself as far away from you as possible."

Marcos smirks. "Yeah. I noticed."

"I'm sorry about that. And about everything else. I know I've sent some really mixed messages. And I've been a little erratic. And distant. And moody."

"A little?"

"Okay, *a lot*. But you didn't exactly make things easy," I exclaim, completely forgetting I'm in the middle of an apology.

"Me? What did *I* do?"

"You acted like you'd completely forgotten what happened between us. You *never* mentioned camp. And then there was that whole 'it's been three years, people change' speech."

"What about it?"

"I thought you were telling me you didn't like me anymore."

"*What?* No, I said that because I thought *you* didn't like *me*. I was trying to let you know I'd gotten the message and you didn't have to worry that I was going to out you or mess up your life."

"Well, obviously I know that *now*."

"Seriously, Connolly, the only reason I didn't immediately start reminiscing about the past the second I saw you is because *you* seemed totally freaked out. That first day, when we sat in traffic for two hours and you barely said a word to me? I was convinced you hated me."

"Oh." That's actually a pretty accurate read of the situation.

"I'm sorry if you interpreted that as me trying to forget the past," Marcos laughs, "but I was genuinely trying *not* to scare you off."

"I *know*," I assure him, feeling like a total monster for every unkind thought I had during our first rocky week of being reunited. "And you don't have to apologize. This is *my* apology."

"Oh. Right," Marcos chuckles, tossing a corn chip into his mouth. "Carry on then."

"Well . . . I think I've actually already told you everything I needed to tell you," I say rather anticlimactically. "Except, I know I've been really unfair to you, and I'm sorry. We should've had this conversation a week ago. It definitely would've cleared up a lot of things, but I was too busy freaking out."

"About me?"

I shake my head. "About *me*. And what I was feeling. I didn't want . . ."

"*Want* what?"

"I didn't want to be gay."

It's an ugly confession. I hate how it sounds coming out of my mouth, but it's the truth.

"Is that why you suddenly got interested in Margot Chen?"

"Yeah," I sigh. "I thought if I had a girlfriend that I could push away these feelings. That I could be normal—"

"You *are* normal," Marcos interrupts, his hand once again reaching out for mine. This time I don't pull back and he doesn't let go. And I don't want him to.

"Thanks," I whisper. I'm not sure I believe him. I've honestly never felt "normal" a single day in my entire life. But I appreciate him believing I could be.

"I mean it," he says, flashing me his dazzling smile. But a second later, a hint of worry creeps into his voice. "You don't still feel that way, do you?"

"What way?"

"You don't still want these feeling to go away?"

It's a question I've been asking myself every day. And every day I have a different answer. But sitting here with Marcos, holding his hand, I know I feel the most like "myself" than I have in a long time.

"No," I say, squeezing his hand. "I don't want these feelings to go away."

Marcos beams like he's won the lottery. I can practically see him doing a happy dance in his head. "Good. Okay then. *Right* answer."

"Glad I passed the test."

"Me too," he laughs. "Now, is the interrogation and apology portion of this date over? Or do you have anything else we need to clear up before we move on to the fun and flirty part of the evening?"

"Just one thing."

"Seriously?"

"Yes, but it's a good segue into the fun and flirty part of this evening. I promise."

"Okay. Shoot."

"Were you really working up the courage to kiss me?" I ask.

"What?"

"At Ashleigh's party you said that all that time we were watching *The Golden Girls* at camp, you were actually working up the courage to kiss me."

"Oh, right." Marcos blushes and it's the most adorable thing I've ever seen. "Yeah, that was the plan."

"But you didn't."

"Like I said, I wasn't sure you wanted me to."

"Well," I say, trying to keep my own cheeks from turning scarlet, "just in case it comes up in the future? The answer is yes."

We spend the next hour catching each other up on our lives as well as all the things we can't discuss in front of Van. I'm particularly curious if Marcos has dated anyone or been in a relationship. Orlando is way more cosmopolitan than Port Orange, so he must have had some opportunities.

"I tried dating a couple different girls when I first started high school," he says as he polishes off his last taco. "You know, in case the whole liking boys thing was a phase."

"What happened?"

"Nothing. That was the problem. I really liked some of the girls—as friends—but eventually they'd want to do more than hold hands and hear me pontificate on whatever topic I was currently obsessing over. Then they'd dump me."

"Good for them."

"Right?"

"What about guys?" I almost don't want to know. If there's been someone else or multiple someone elses, I'm afraid of how I'll measure up.

"There were a couple of openly gay and bi guys at my school, but I tended to keep my distance."

"Why?"

"I wasn't ready for people to know about me, so it just felt safer to avoid them."

I know what he means. My sophomore year there was a rumor going around that one of the seniors on the basketball team was gay. One day he came to school with a black eye, and after that I avoided him like my life depended on it.

"There was one guy who was very out that I started to become friends with. Maybe it could have been something more," Marcos says, looking down at his empty plate. "But when I brought him home to study, my dad made it abundantly clear what he thought about me bringing 'someone like that' into his house."

"Oh."

"Yeah."

I squeeze his hand, but he just shrugs. I suspect Marcos is used to shrugging off a lot of his dad's behavior, otherwise he'd spend most of his life feeling like crap.

"What about you, Connolly? Have you dated anyone?"

I'm almost too embarrassed to tell him. "I joined the abstinence club."

"You what?"

"Well, it's not called the abstinence club. It's called Promise Keepers. We all basically promise not to have sex before marriage. And even then, I think we're supposed to keep it to a minimum."

"Wow," Marcos laughs, and I don't blame him. Looking back, it was a pretty obvious move on my part.

"Yeah, everyone at school thinks I'm super religious."

"You kind of are, aren't you?"

"Well, yeah, that's why it's the perfect cover."

Marcos laughs even harder, and I think to myself that if I devote the rest of my life to making him as happy as he is right now, it will be a life well spent.

Marcos insists on paying for dinner. When I protest, he tells me not to worry. "You can pick up the tab next time."

Next time?

Yes! Yes! Yes! I've already got my next date confirmed before the first date is even over! I, Milo Connolly, am a dating prodigy!

My euphoria, though, is short-lived. As we head to his car, I ask

Marcos what movie he wants to see, and from the way he avoids eye contact, I know I'm not going to like whatever comes out of his mouth next.

"So here's the thing . . ."

Oh no. Now what?

"We can totally go to a movie if you want."

"Okay . . . ?"

"But Atlantis is hosting a dance tonight."

Atlantis is Port Orange's *other* high school. It's located, as the aquatic name suggests, right across the street from the ocean. Yep, a school on the beach. And unlike Crick, which was built in the seventies and looks like a Communist prison complex, Atlantis was built at the turn of the millennium by an architect who clearly drew his inspiration from nineties teen dramas set in California. With sleek glass exteriors, modern architecture, and lush green quads, it's a school straight out of *Beverly Hills, 90210*. Rumor even has it that instead of a cafeteria, they have a food court with an actual Panera.

Despite all that, I'm still not sure why Marcos wants to go there. I'm definitely not a dancer, but even if I were, why would we go to a rival high school full of rich brats with beach houses?

"It's not just a dance for Atlantis students," Marcos explains. "It's open to all the students of Volusia County. There will be kids there from Ormond and Holly Hill and Daytona."

I don't say anything because I know something else is coming.

"It's sponsored by the Gay-Straight Alliance."

Oh. My. God.

Marcos must see me mentally rocketing back into the closet because he plows forward with his pitch before I can run screaming into the night.

"I know, *I know*! It sounds like a lot, but there's no reason to be nervous. It's just a dance. It's an opportunity for all sorts of students to get together and have a good time without having to worry about who they are and who they're attracted to."

I take a deep breath and try to stop my heart from exploding out of my chest. This is the craziest thing Marcos has ever said. There's no way I'm ready for people to know about us. Especially not a room full of strangers.

"I don't think I can do that."

But Marcos isn't giving up.

"Don't you want to go someplace where you won't have to be scared of what other people are thinking? Where everyone will just assume it's totally normal for us to be together? Besides, no one we know will be there. Or if we do run into anyone from Crick, we'll just say we're the straight part of the Gay-Straight Alliance."

I give him what I hope is my most withering look, and he sighs because even he knows how stupid that sounds.

"Look," he says. "I know this is a lot, especially for a first date, but I've been waiting three years to do something like this with someone I care about. With *you*. And I'm tired of wasting time. Aren't you?"

I don't know. Am I?

A month ago, I assumed I was going to go through life completely alone and celibate. A week ago, I assumed I was going to spend my senior year panicking over and/or longing for a boy who didn't want me back. Now that boy is standing in front of me saying that the *one thing* he wants more than anything in the world is to take me to a dance. How do I say no to that?

So instead I say, "I don't know how to dance."

And he says, "I'll teach you."

22

It's Starting to Feel Personal

I don't know quite what I'm expecting when I step into the Atlantis gym, but it's not a scant twenty-five students bopping around the near-empty dance floor to the new Lady Gaga single. Actually, no, the Lady Gaga single I expected. But for some reason I thought this dance was going to be a lot more . . . I don't know. Decadent? Hedonistic? Sodom and Gomorrah–ish? I was totally picturing "New York City Pride Parade meets *Game of Thrones* orgy."

In my defense, I *know* that's ridiculous, but that's pretty much the messaging that I've been receiving about "gay people" from my parents for most of my life. Not that they know—or claim to know—any gay people personally. They just repeat what they hear from their friends or from the conservative talk shows they watch. And somewhere along the way, I guess I started repeating it to myself.

Thankfully, this dance is a much-needed reality check. In addition to the kids on the dance floor, some other students are clustered in small groups around the periphery eating snacks while a DJ who looks old enough to be someone's dad spins some tunes on a makeshift stage. It's all very basic and blissfully tame.

In fact, the only thing that sets this dance apart from any other school event I've attended is the decorations.

"That's a lot of rainbows," I say, clocking the plethora of flags and streamers blanketing the walls in all their Technicolor glory.

"Yeah." Marcos nods, grinning with approval.

"Some might say *too* many rainbows?"

Marcos gives me a look.

"What? I'm more into neutrals," I say. "Or pastels."

"You said you'd *try*, remember?"

"I am," I protest. Though what I want to say is, "*Now can we leave?*"

I *barely* made it the short distance from the parking lot to the gym without having a full-blown panic attack. Every time Marcos and I passed someone in the hallway, all I could think was: they *know*.

They know why we're here.

They know where we're going.

They know *what we are*.

Of course, no one said anything. And the few people we have interacted with (like the peppy girl who sold us our tickets at the door) have been perfectly pleasant. But that doesn't mean I'm letting my guard down.

Marcos wanted to come to this dance, so we're here. But if he expects me to loosen up and enjoy myself, he's got another thing coming. My neurosis and me are a package deal, and the sooner he accepts that, the better.

"I love that guy's outfit," Marcos says, pointing to a very skinny boy on the dance floor wearing a silver-sequined blazer that makes him shimmer like a mirror ball. It's a pretty snazzy ensemble, and

I can't help but feel woefully underdressed in my jeans and polo, especially after I notice another boy with platinum-blond hair in pink floral pants dancing next to a girl with a shaved head and wearing a purple velvet jumpsuit. Thankfully, though, it just takes a cursory scan of the gym to see that everyone else looks pretty much normal.

I mean straight.

I mean—UGH!

"What's the matter?" Marcos asks when he sees me cringe.

I'm worried I'm going to say something even more problematic than that last sequence of thoughts, so I just mumble a quick "Nothing."

"You okay?"

I want you to douse me in gasoline and then set me on fire because that would be less excruciating than trying to grapple with a lifetime of self-loathing and internalized homophobia while Lady Gaga blasts in my ear.

"Yeah. I'm fine."

"You sure?"

"I'm sure."

"Okay. Good. I'm going to get us some punch."

"No!" I yelp, grabbing his arm.

"What?"

"I mean, I'll come with you."

Marcos extracts himself from my grasp with a weary sigh. "You know nothing bad is going to happen if I leave you alone for two minutes?"

I absolutely do not know that. All I know is that I am so far outside of my comfort zone that if the world ended right now, I would consider it a mercy.

"Yeah. I know."

"Do you?"

"*Yes*," I lie, a little too emphatically.

"Great. So . . . I'll be right back."

Marcos heads off to the refreshments table, and I try to convince myself he's right. There's *nothing* to worry about.

Except I don't believe that. Not for a second. How could I?

I've spent my entire life trying to conceal who I am. Now I'm deliberately undoing all my hard work just by stepping into this rainbow-strewn wonderland and consorting with these people.

Ugh. "These people"?

I sound like my father. Or the guys on his construction crew.

"The trouble with liberals is *these people* have no respect for family values."

"The trouble with feminists is *these people* don't know how to take a joke."

"The trouble with the gays is *these people* want to shove their lifestyle in everyone's face."

These people . . .

I've always known thinking about people this way is wrong, but I never said anything. I never defended them—any of them—and I certainly never dared to admit I was one of them. Me? Milo Connolly? One of These People?

How could I say that out loud? If I did, my parents would *never* look at me the same way ever again. Instead of being their son, I'd just be yet another "freak." Someone to fear and ridicule and condemn.

I've kept my mouth shut and made myself invisible my entire life so my parents would never know who I am—so *no one* would ever know who I am—because I thought that was my only option. To make myself as small as I can be. To hide.

I thought it was the only way to survive. But looking around this room, I know how utterly and spectacularly wrong I've been. Because there's always been another way. And every kid at this dance knows it.

These kids—"these people"—they're not content with just surviving. They're actually owning who they are and claiming their place in the world just by being here tonight and demanding to be seen. They're not apologizing or hiding or letting anyone else define who they are. They're making their own rules and following their own paths and living their own lives. And more than anything I want to be a part of that.

No, correction: I *need* to be a part of it.

The Lady Gaga song ends and the skinny boy in the silver blazer struts off the dance floor. He's about to pass right in front of me so, swallowing down my fear of human interaction, I take a deep breath and do what I promised Marcos I would do.

I try.

"I like your jacket," I say. Except I'm still so nervous that my voice comes out way too fast and way too high, making it sound more like, "*Ilikeyourjacket!*"

"Excuse me?" the boy asks, turning back to me with a piercing look that would make Dorothy Zbornak proud. Oddly enough, it kind of puts me at ease.

"I said I like your jacket," I repeat, forcing myself to enunciate.

"Oh, thank you," he says, his face breaking into a smile. "It's like they say, glitter and be gay."

I don't know anyone who says that, but I extend my hand and introduce myself. "I'm Milo."

"Orion. And before you ask, yes, that's my real name. My mama named me after the star because someday that's what I'm going to be."

"Oh. Cool." His confidence makes me smile. It reminds me of Marcos. Although the pedantic part of my brain can't help reminding me that technically Orion *isn't* a star. It's a constellation. But I don't think Orion (or his mama) will appreciate me ruining the metaphor, so instead I just ask, "Are you enjoying the dance?"

"I am indeed. How 'bout yourself?"

"Yeah. It's nice. Really nice."

I expect Orion to say something back, but he just looks at me, politely waiting for me to ask my next question. Which under normal circumstances would be a perfectly reasonable thing to expect. I mean, *I* stopped *him*. And there are literally a million follow-up questions I could ask. Unfortunately, in the panic of the moment, my mind does what it always does. It shuts down.

"Um . . ."

"Are you okay?"

"I'm sorry. I don't know what else to say right now."

Orion laughs. Not in a mean way, but like he's genuinely amused.

"Is this your first dance? I mean, a dance like this?" he asks.

"Is it obvious?"

"Obvious? Boy, you look about as jumpy as a virgin at a prison rodeo."

Now it's my turn to laugh because I absolutely get that reference.

It's one of my favorite lines from *The Golden Girls*.

"I take it you're Team Blanche?" I ask.

"Always and forever, newbie. And given your whole little lost sheep vibe, I'm going to say you're Team Rose?"

"Guilty," I laugh. And it occurs me that not only am I having an actual honest-to-God conversation with a complete stranger at a dance, I'm actually *enjoying* it.

"You here all by yourself?" Orion asks.

"No, I'm here with Marcos."

"Is Marcos by any chance that cute boy with amazing hair over at the punch bowl who keeps looking this way?"

I follow Orion's gaze to the refreshments table to find that Marcos is indeed watching me—a proud smile plastered over his face.

"Yeah. That's him."

"Damn."

"What?"

"I thought for a second he was looking at me. Turns out he's only got eyes for you."

I can't help blushing. Now that Orion mentions it, it does seem almost inconceivable that the cutest boy in the room—if not the world—is here with me.

"Well, Team Rose, for someone who's at his first dance, you seem to be doing all right for yourself."

"Yeah, I guess I am."

"Now, if you'll excuse me, I'm going to go join my friends to try to console myself from this devastating loss."

"It was nice meeting you, Orion."

"You too, newbie. And if you ever get tired of that cute boy drooling all over you, feel free to send him my way."

Orion slips into the crowd just as Marcos returns with our punch.

"New friend?" he asks, handing me my drink.

"His name's Orion. He's Team Blanche. And he's named after the star because someday he's going to be one."

"Cool."

"Yeah."

"Although, you know, Orion's not actually a star. It's a constellation."

Oh. My. God. Just when I think Marcos couldn't be more perfect . . .

"What?" he asks when I grin at him like a smitten idiot. "What did I say?"

"Nothing."

"Are you feeling better?"

"Yeah," I say, somewhat surprised by my answer. "I am."

My heart has stopped beating like it's trying to break a world record, and I'm not sweating through my shirt anymore. All in all, I'm doing much better than I was five minutes ago when I was pretty sure Marcos would have to carry me out of here on a stretcher.

"Thanks for suggesting we come here," I say. "I'm glad we came."

"Thanks for giving it a chance."

"Thanks for giving *me* a chance. Several chances actually."

"No problem." Then, reaching out for my hand, he asks, "Shall we dance?"

Part of me wants to protest, but his hand feels so good in mine, I don't want to let go. Besides, who am I trying to fool? At this point I know I'd follow Marcos to the moon.

We make our way to the dance floor and, for probably the first time in my life, I make the futile attempt to "shake what my mama gave me" (as Van likes to say). Unfortunately, my mama didn't give me much. I wasn't kidding about being a lousy dancer. In fact, as soon as Marcos sees me jerking my shoulders back and forth like a short-circuiting robot, he breaks out laughing.

"You're so stiff!" he says, grabbing my shoulders and trying to loosen me up. "Relax!"

A new track starts to play, and I immediately recognize it as Van's favorite Panic! At the Disco song. Actually, it must be everyone's favorite Panic! At the Disco song because a horde of teenagers flock to the dance floor. Which is honestly a relief. In the anonymity of the crowd, I feel way less awkward.

"That's it!" Marcos shouts over the music.

He puts his hands on my hips and tries to get me to move in sync with the music. It works, but the proximity of our pelvises grinding against each other causes a Very Predictable Reaction. I'm almost relieved when the song ends, and DJ Dad (as I've decided to call him) segues the music into a buzz-killing slow dance. Half the teenagers abandon the dance floor, and I start to follow until Marcos stops me with a gentle tug on my arm.

"Where do you think you're going?"

I'm about to explain that a *quick* dance in a crowd of people is one thing, but a *slow* dance to a melancholy Taylor Swift ballad during which time we'll be one of the *only* couples on the dance floor is way too far outside my comfort zone. But Marcos doesn't give me the chance. He pulls me into his embrace, and before I know what's happening, we're swaying to the music.

My mind, which is very much aware that we are making ourselves the center of attention and therefore a *target*, is desperately trying to think of a way to extract me from this situation without hurting Marcos's feelings. But my body isn't listening. In fact, at this point it's pretty much safe to say that my body is *only* listening to Marcos. His hands caress the small of my back, and I can't help wondering what they would feel like all over my body. . . .

"Did anyone ever tell you you're a very strange boy, Connolly?"

Marcos's breath against my cheek sends shivers down my spine. I nuzzle my face into his neck, drinking in the scent of him.

"Good thing you like strange."

"I don't like strange," he whispers. "I love it."

As if on instinct, I tilt my head back and his mouth finds mine. We kiss and it's like a tiny miracle—like my lips have finally found their purpose—and I don't care who sees us. Because kissing Marcos is the most incredible sensation in the whole entire universe, and in this moment all I want is *more*.

More kisses. More touching. More Marcos.

My body is in heaven. The closer he holds me, the closer I want to be to him. Space becomes our enemy. Even the clothes between us feel like an impossible barrier. Every inch of my skin is burning—so much so that I'm afraid I might burst into flames.

Seriously, I'm not exaggerating. I can't tell if this gym has exceptionally weak AC or if I've started running a fever, but I swear I'm burning up.

Even so, I don't care. I don't care because all I want—all I'll ever want from this day forward—is Marcos. And he wants me. And we are finally going to be together.

At least, that's the plan.

What isn't part of the plan is the earthshaking KA-BOOM that rocks the gym, knocking Marcos and me out of our reverie and almost off our feet.

At first, I think I might have imagined it, until I notice that everyone in the gym is looking around, nervously trying to figure out what happened. My second thought is that there's been an explosion. Or maybe another sinkhole.

DJ Dad turns off the music, which isn't an encouraging sign, and the students instinctively start edging toward the exits. Part of me wonders if Marcos and I should do the same when a middle-aged woman in a pantsuit enters the gym and wanders up to the stage almost catatonically.

"Um . . . excuse me, everyone," she says, her oddly halting voice amplified over the speakers as she borrows the DJ's microphone. "This is a bit . . . unusual . . . but will the owner of the dark blue Subaru with the Orlando license plate please come out to the parking lot?"

Marcos's face falls.

He slowly raises his hand, and the woman motions for him to follow. As we exit the gym, he tries to ask what's going on, but the woman isn't giving anything away. All she says is, "You're going to want to see this for yourself."

A crowd of curious teens follows us outside, and as we step into the parking lot, the first thing that hits us is the smell. It's autumnal—like leaves burning. Like fire. And then I see why.

It takes my brain a full minute to process the sight in front of us. Mainly because what we're seeing doesn't make any sense. In fact, it's like something out of a bad 1950s sci-fi film.

Marcos's car is on fire. And the reason it's on fire is because it's been demolished. By a meteor.

PART III

23

Heavenly Signs

Fun Science Fact #1: During any given year, the surface of the Earth is struck by hundreds of meteorites. According to my sixth-grade science teacher, Mr. Nguyen, most of these meteorites are minuscule, often weighing less than a pound, and tend to fall into the ocean. That's why you never hear about them on the news. As a natural phenomenon, meteorites are publicity shy.

Fun Science Fact #2: Occasionally larger, heavier rocks do manage to survive their fiery descent through the Earth's atmosphere and cause damage. For example, a Chevy Malibu in New York and an SUV in Ontario were hit by meteorites in 1992 and 2009, respectively. No one was hurt in either of these incidents, but in 2013 over a thousand people in Russia were injured when one of the largest meteors on record exploded over the city of Chelyabinsk. So while meteor strikes are rare, they are by no means impossible. Which is to say, if you happen to witness one, there's absolutely no reason to freak out.

Fun Science Fact #3: I am TOTALLY freaking out.

Marcos and I are standing in the Atlantis parking lot watching what's left of his Subaru burn to a cinder after being decimated by a meteor the size of a watermelon. You can shove all the scientific statistics that you want down my throat; it won't change the fact that what we're witnessing is INSANE. All we can do is stare in shock, which seems to be the reaction of pretty much everyone around us.

Orion, DJ Dad, the kids from the dance: they're all standing in stunned silence, mesmerized by the smoldering wreckage. I don't blame them. I mean, what *is* the appropriate response after you witness the Impossible?

"You need to call Van."

A chill creeps down my spine. I've never heard Marcos so frightened.

"Milo, listen to me," he repeats, his voice growing urgent. "Call Van and tell her she needs to come pick you up *right now*. Do you understand?"

I don't. My brain can't even begin to process what he's telling me. All I can do is stare at him like he's speaking a foreign language and hope the world starts to make sense again.

"Milo, my car was just incinerated by a meteor! There's no way my parents aren't going to hear about this. It's going to be all over the news. You need to get out of here *now*, so your parents don't find out you were with me."

Marcos isn't exaggerating. He *is* going to be all over the news. Because a *meteor* fell from outer space and *crushed* his car—*at a gay dance.*

Oh God. After tonight the whole world is going to know about Marcos. And anyone who's with him.

"No," I protest. "I'm not going to leave you."

"You have to. There's no reason for both of us to get caught."

"Your parents are going to kill you when they find out."

"Your parents are going to kill *you*."

Sirens wail in the distance. A handful of teachers have sprung into action and are doing their best to keep the awestruck students back from the smoke and fire. We're running out of time.

"Listen," Marcos says, "if my parents know we were here together, they will *never* let me see you again. Please don't argue. Just call Van before it's too late."

He's trying to save me. He's literally going down in flames and yet all he cares about in this moment is protecting me. I'm so overcome all I want to do is throw my arms around him and hold him until this nightmare is over.

But he's right. If we're caught together, then that's the end of us. Best-case scenario: we end up grounded for life. Worst case: I don't even want to *think* about worst case.

My hands tremble as I dial Van. Thankfully, she picks up on the second ring.

"Hey, loser, what's up?"

"I need you to come to Atlantis and pick me up. Right now. It's an emergency."

"Are you all right?"

"Yes, but only if you get here in, like, the next five minutes."

"Tell her you'll meet her across the street at the Catholic church," Marcos interjects.

"I heard Marcos," Van says. "I'm on my way."

I hang up and slide my phone into my pocket just as a screeching fire truck barrels into the parking lot.

"You better go," Marcos says, staring at the flashing lights.

"I can't believe this is happening."

"At least we'll never forget our first date."

"Yeah." First and *last*.

I want to kiss Marcos goodbye—it may be the last time we get to do that for a very long time—but there are too many people around. Most have their phones out now and are taking videos. It's only a matter of time before this story is everywhere.

"Go," Marcos pleads. And even though I hate myself for being such a coward, I do.

The Church of Our Lady of Perpetual Sorrow seems an aptly named place to wait for Van as the world falls apart. I pace the deserted parking lot, thinking about Marcos and the impossible phone call he's probably making at this moment. God knows what he's going to say to his parents. What *can* he say?

"Hey, Mom, hey, Dad, I need you to stop whatever you're doing and come pick me up because a meteor fell from space and totaled my car while I was getting my groove on at a gay dance. Also, spoiler alert, I'm gay."

Somehow I doubt even he could be that nonchalant. In fact, I'm pretty sure he'll be terrified. Terrified and alone.

How could this happen?

I'm so *angry* at the universe right now. All we wanted was to go out on a normal date like two normal teenagers, and now Marcos's car *and* his life are in ruins.

Why?

I mean, of all the places for a meteor to strike, why did it have to be Port Orange? Why the Atlantis parking lot? Why Marcos's car?

It's almost like the universe is conspiring against us. Like we're deliberately being singled out and punished.

No. Correction: *we're* not being punished.

Marcos is the only one whose life is going to be blown apart after tonight. Marcos—who's the best thing in my life. Who's throwing himself on a grenade to protect me. Who'd never abandon me the way I'm abandoning him.

"Jesus Christ," Van exclaims as she pulls into the church parking lot. "What the heck is going on over there?"

The Channel 7 news chopper is circling Atlantis, its massive spotlight illuminating half a dozen emergency vehicles parked below as they put out the last of the smoldering fire. The media circus has begun. And Marcos is trapped in the center ring.

"Hey, Earth to Milo," Van repeats. "What's going on? Where's Marcos? What's happening at Atlantis?"

I know Marcos told me to go. I know the most logical thing in the world would be to jump into Van's Jeep and drive away as fast as we can. But I can't do it. I can't abandon Marcos. I have to help him.

But I can't do it alone. I'll need Van's help. Which means I need to tell her everything.

24

The Performance of a Lifetime

"Wow," Van says. Then, just in case her shock and surprise aren't apparent enough, she says it ten more times. I've just told her my entire history with Marcos, including the events of tonight, in under five minutes, and I think I may have broken her brain.

"I know. It's a lot."

"Yeah. I mean . . . *Wow.*"

I knew it was only a matter of time before I'd tell Van about my relationship with Marcos. I'd have preferred slightly different circumstances (more peppermint tea, fewer meteors) but, unfortunately, I don't have the luxury of curating my "coming out" experience. Marcos is in trouble. And that, more than anything, is my priority right now.

"So, just to recap," Van says tentatively. "You're gay. Marcos is gay. You've had a thing for each other for three years. And tonight you went on a secret date to a queer dance party and a meteor fell on his car?"

"Pretty much."

"That's *insane.*"

She says it with such vehemence, the bottom drops out from under me and my legs start to tremble. I'd taken it for granted that Van would be cool with everything I had to tell her. After all, she's the most progressive person I know. But now that I've spilled my guts and shown her the real me, I'm terrified she might not like what she sees.

"The meteor!" she clarifies. "*That's* insane. Not you and Marcos being gay. That's awesome!"

I let out a sigh of relief and only then do I realize I've been holding my breath. It's only been for a few seconds, yet somehow it feels like I've been doing it my whole life.

"For real?" I ask, barely trusting myself to speak.

"For real," she says, pulling me into a hug. "That's great news. I'm so glad you finally told me."

I'm glad too. Even with everything that's happened tonight, I somehow feel lighter. Like I've been carrying a massive weight on my shoulders and—

Wait. Did she say *finally?*

I'm so glad you finally *told me.* What does that mean?

Actually, it doesn't matter. What matters now is Marcos. And he's running out of time.

"What are we going to do?" I ask, extracting myself from the hug and looking over at the ever-increasing media spectacle filling the Atlantis parking lot.

"I don't know, dude. We've probably got five minutes before Marcos's parents show up. If they're not there already."

"There has to be something. Marcos is going to be in so much trouble if his parents find out he's gay."

"I know. I want to help Marcos too, but our hands are totally tied.

It's not like we can lie our way out of this and say Marcos wasn't at the dance. His car is *right there*. I mean, what are we going to say? 'Yes, Mr. Price, that's your son's car in the school parking lot, but he had no idea there was a gay dance going on inside. It's totally a coincidence that . . .'"

Van trails off, and for the first time since she arrived, I feel a faint stirring of hope. She's got that look on her face: one-half excitement, one-half wonder. I call it her Inspiration Look.

"What is it?" I ask.

"Dude, I can't believe I'm saying this. But I think I have a plan."

As Van and I make our way into the Atlantis parking lot, I can see Marcos sitting on the front steps of the school, head in his hands, a portrait of teenage despair. Thankfully, there's no sign of his parents, which means there's still time to implement Van's plan.

Okay, "plan" might be an exaggeration. What Van has come up with is more like half a plan—*at best*. But it's all we've got and at this point I'm desperate enough to try anything.

I just hope that when Marcos called his parents, he wasn't too honest over the phone; otherwise, what Van and I are about to do is utterly pointless and we're walking straight into a trap of our own design.

"Marc?"

Oh crap. I was wrong. Marcos's parents are here. Or at least his dad is. Across the commotion of the parking lot, Mr. Price slams shut the door of his minivan, scowling at the noise and lights and chaos as if they were somehow a personal affront to him.

"We're too late," I say, stopping in my tracks.

"Don't worry," Van says. "I've got this. Follow my lead."

"But Marcos's dad is already here."

"Dude, I'm an actress, remember?"

"So?"

"So I'm going to improvise."

Before I can stop her, Van rushes across the parking lot, like the heroine in some teen melodrama, and lets out a fear-stricken wail of "Marcos!"

Marcos looks up from the steps in confusion. I suspect he's even more confused five seconds later when Van throws her arms around him and shouts loud enough for everyone to hear, "Oh baby, I'm so glad you're okay!"

I steal a quick glance at Mr. Price, who stops in his tracks when he sees his son being swept into the arms of an attractive young woman. *So far so good.*

"Uh, hi, Van . . . ," Marcos manages to stammer when she finally releases him. "What are you—?"

But Van doesn't let him finish that sentence. Instead, she shuts his mouth with a kiss. A kiss that was definitely *not* part of the plan. But I guess that's what she meant by "improvise."

"Marc?" Mr. Price practically barks when he finally reaches his son. "What's going on?"

Van breaks the kiss, and from the utter bafflement on Marcos's face, it's a safe bet that he too would like an answer to that question.

"Oh my goodness, you must be Mr. Price," Van gushes. "It's *so* nice to finally meet you. I'm Vanessa. Isn't this *insane?*"

Marcos's dad looks thoroughly confused, but not so much that he forgets his manners. "Uh, hello, Vanessa," he says, tentatively extending his hand.

Van shakes it, and before Mr. Price can get another word in, she immediately plows forward with the story we've rehearsed.

"Marcos was just on his way to meet us at the movie theater when he got a flat tire. Thank God he wasn't sitting in his car when he called to tell me he was going to be late, or I don't know *what* would've happened."

Van shivers as the thought of that potential horror washes over her, then pulls Marcos into another all-consuming hug. She's always been a good actress, but tonight she's on fire. I mean, for someone who has never been a scared, lovesick girl, she plays one like she was born for the role.

Mr. Price looks from Vanessa to the mangled rubble of Marcos's car then back to Marcos. For the first time, it seems to dawn on him how close his son came to being reduced to a smoldering pancake.

"Are you all right, Marc?"

"Yeah, Dad, I'm fine." He still looks a little bewildered but from the way he puts his arm around Van, I can tell he's pieced together our strategy.

Mr. Price nods, though he still seems unsure what to make of Van. In fact, he almost seems more surprised that his son has a girlfriend than by the fact that his son's car was just demolished by space debris.

At least, I hope that he buys that Van and Marcos are dating. I also hope that in all the confusion he hasn't had time to notice any of the very prominent rainbow signs plastered all around the school's entrance.

I'm pretty sure we're in the clear—that is until Orion walks by, his mirror ball blazer sparkling in the beam of the chopper's spotlight like a fabulous gay beacon. I catch Mr. Price wrinkle his nose in disgust and am shocked at how such an attractive man can suddenly look so ugly.

"Why are there so many kids here at night?" he asks, taking in the rest of the well-dressed teenagers.

"I think there was some kind of dance," Marcos says vaguely. "I don't know. I was on my way to meet Van to see—"

"The new Cuarón movie," she interjects.

"Yeah. I'd only just gotten out of the car to call her when the meteor hit."

Mr. Price nods. Then his eyes land on one of the rainbow signs and a hint of suspicion returns to his voice. "I thought you were meeting that boy from church tonight?"

This is my cue to spring into action.

"I'm here," I say, stepping forward, my hand extended. "Hello, sir."

"Oh. Hello . . . ?"

"Milo, sir."

"Milo," he repeats, as if this time he's going to make sure to remember it. "So you're here too?"

"Yes, sir. I came with Van." Then I repeat her version of events almost word for word.

In fact, my version might be a little too "word for word" because after I finish Mr. Price is silent for what seems like ages. I'm hoping, though, that with Van, Marcos, and me all feeding him the exact same story, he'll have no choice but to believe us. I mean, from a purely logical standpoint, why would a Good Presbyterian Boy like me and an obviously heterosexual couple like Van and Marcos be at a gay dance? It doesn't make sense.

Then again, neither does the meteor that flattened Marcos's car. So maybe logic isn't exactly something I should be relying on tonight.

"Have you talked to the police yet? Filled out a report?" Mr. Price asks, turning back to his son.

"Um . . . no. Not yet. I was waiting for you."

"Okay. Let's go take care of that. We're going to need some sort of police report in order to file a claim with our insurance. Assuming this is even covered."

Marcos breathes a sigh of relief, and every muscle in my body relaxes. If Mr. Price is grumbling about something as banal as insurance, then we must be in the clear.

"Do you kids need a ride home?" Mr. Price asks, turning to Van and me as if he's just remembered we're still here.

"No, sir, I have my Jeep."

"Right. Well, drive safely, Vanessa." Again, the way he says her name, it's like he's making a mental note not to forget her. Like she's a clue in an unfolding mystery that might be important in the future. "Marc, say good night to your—err—friends."

Marcos takes Van aside like he wants a little privacy, but in a voice loud enough for his father to hear he says, "Sorry our night was ruined."

"No worries. I'm just glad you're okay, babe. Besides, we'll have plenty more movie nights in the future."

"Yeah, although maybe next time it can just be the two of us."

Ouch. That stings. I mean, I know Marcos is *acting.* I know this is all technically part of a plan that I very much agreed to, but it's still an unpleasant thing to hear—even if it is exactly the right thing to say in front of Mr. Price.

"Later, Connolly," Marcos shouts over his shoulder as he joins his dad. Together they walk over to the nearest police officer, and Van and I are all but forgotten.

"I can't believe that worked," she sighs, practically collapsing against me.

I'm not sure I believe it either. On the one hand, the story we concocted sounds plausible enough. But on the other, it does require a person to swallow an awful lot of coincidences. Maybe too many. In the end, it's all going to come down to whether Mr. Price *wants* to believe his son. For Marcos's sake, I really hope he does.

"Thank you," I say, pulling Van into a hug and holding her tight. "I don't know what we would've done without you."

"Yeah, you two *totally* owe me," she laughs, giddy from the adrenaline coursing through her veins. "God, I'm a good actress! I mean, I *knew* I was good, but tonight was next level. I should get an Oscar for that performance."

"I don't know," I chuckle. "I thought the kiss was a bit much."

"Um, that kiss sold the performance."

"Eh. Just seemed a little inauthentic."

"Well, I guess you'd know what an *authentic* kiss with Marcos looks like."

My entire body blushes, and for a second, I think I'm going to need the fire department to turn their hose on me.

"Oh my god, you do! You dirty, *dirty* Presbyterian."

"We should get home," I say, heading back toward the church.

"Oh, no you don't. You don't get to come out of the closet and then *not* give me all the juicy details about your sexual awakening. I just saved your ass—*and* Marcos's ass—and I want to know everything that's been going on between you two from the very beginning. And don't leave out the R-rated bits."

"There haven't been any R-rated bits."

"*Yet.*"

I blush again. But as embarrassed as I am that my private life is no longer quite so private, part of me is excited to finally talk to Van about everything that's been happening.

"Fine," I sigh in faux exasperation. "I'll give you all the juicy details."

"Yes!"

"But first can we stop at Holloway's and get some curly fries for the drive home? I'm starving."

"Dude, don't ask stupid questions, *of course* we're getting curly fries."

My parents are glued to the TV when I get home. "Oh, Milo, come and see this!" my mom says in unconcealed excitement as she waves me over. "You're never going to believe what happened."

I suspected that news of the meteor would've reached my parents by now and I'm prepared. Van spent most of the ride home helping me rehearse everything I'd need to say, though I'd be fooling myself if I said I wasn't still nervous. I've never directly lied to my parents before and part of me is worried I won't be able to go through with it. But for Van's plan to work, I need to get everyone on the same page—including my parents.

"What do you think of that?" my dad asks, shaking his head in disbelief at the TV.

"Well, funny you should ask . . ."

Then I take a deep breath and tell them about the Weirdest Night of My Life.

Thankfully, once they both get over their initial shock, my parents accept my version of events without question. I guess one of the perks of being a Good Presbyterian Boy is that people tend to take you at your word. Even when your word is nothing but a total fabrication.

"I'm just so relieved you and your friends are okay," my mom says, pulling me into a hug.

"Yeah," I say. "Me too."

Then, before I can help myself, I start crying. Like *really* crying. I'm not sure if it's because I'm just so relieved to be out of danger or if it's guilt from lying to my parents or if I'm just exhausted from this utterly impossible day, but once my tears start, I can't stop them.

"Why don't you go upstairs and get some rest?" my dad says, putting a comforting hand on my shoulder. "You've had a tough day. You're beat. Best thing in the world for you right now is a good night's sleep."

I nod, thankful for the chance to get some privacy, then hurry upstairs.

I don't know if I've just been in shock for the last couple hours or if I haven't had time to process everything that's happened, but the second I collapse into bed, the incredible truth of what happened tonight hits me with the force of an atom bomb.

I almost died.

If Marcos and I had left the dance earlier or if we'd arrived a little later, we might have actually been in his car when that meteor hit. We could have been crushed to death. Or incinerated. It's inconceivable and yet it almost happened.

I went on my first date ever with another boy and *we almost died.*

I want to believe it's a coincidence. Just a random freak occurrence that could've happened to anyone. Like the sinkhole. Or the blackout. Or the hailstorm. But what happened tonight feels different. *Deliberate.* As if someone or something was trying to send us a message.

I try to shake off the feeling, but as I lie in bed, a single thought keeps running through my brain—over and over and over.

We've been warned.

25

Web of Lies

The meteor dominates the news. All day Saturday, on every channel and every program, a slew of astronomers, experts, and government officials weigh in on the utter randomness of what happened, while simultaneously assuaging viewers there's no need for alarm. The general theme coming from Those in the Know is, "It's crazy but what can you do?" Which doesn't surprise me.

That's basically Florida's state motto.

Thankfully, none of the news stories have identified Marcos as the owner of the unlucky Subaru. According to Van (and Google), reporters aren't legally allowed to release Marcos's name to the public on account of him being a minor, which is a huge relief. But I can't help worrying that some less-than-scrupulous news outlet will leak the information.

I mean, the Prices and my parents *might* have swallowed our story, but if the general population of Crick found out that Marcos and I were both at the Atlantis dance—or even just in the parking lot—there'd be no escaping the rumors. Our story would totally crumble under the scrutiny.

And so would I.

I don't hear from Marcos, which I sort of expected. The smartest thing we can do right now is lie low. But knowing that doesn't help with my anxiety. I desperately want to make sure he's okay—to make sure our plan is still working and he's not in any trouble—but Marcos warned me once that his dad has a habit of randomly checking his phone, and I don't want to inadvertently make things worse by calling twenty times or sending any sort of message that might give us away.

I consider texting something innocuous like, "See you at church tomorrow." That way he'll know I'm thinking about him, but it won't look suspicious if his dad really is intercepting his messages. But I don't want to risk it.

Sunday morning, though, I've never been more eager to get to POP. I rush my parents through breakfast because I want to be ready and waiting in the church lobby when the Prices arrive. My parents, I'm sure, will want to talk to about the meteor, which means I can use the opportunity to get a few seconds alone with Marcos.

Except when I spot the Prices in the church atrium, Marcos shakes his head in warning. I'm not sure if it's because his parents have figured out the truth or if he just doesn't want to risk being seen in public with me so soon after the dance, but I make a quick about-face and usher my parents to our pew before they have the chance to clock what I'm doing.

The rest of Sunday is a blur. I spend most of it trying not to panic—telling myself there are plenty of reasons Marcos could've wanted me to keep my distance. Maybe his parents were just in a lousy mood. Or maybe Mr. Price found out his car insurance doesn't cover meteors. But I can't shake the feeling that something has gone horribly wrong.

I barely sleep that night and by Monday morning I've worked myself into such a panic I'm shaking as I eat my cereal. The only thing giving me a sliver of hope is the fact that my parents are still behaving as if everything is perfectly normal. If Van's plan *had* somehow collapsed, then the consequences would surely have come knocking at the Connolly house by now. Wouldn't they?

I consider driving to school early and waiting for Marcos in the parking lot. That way we can talk before class, and I can get some answers. But without a car, Marcos will be relying on his mom or dad to drop him off. And seeing me waiting for their son like a desperate puppy isn't going to help matters if the Prices really do have suspicions.

Which means I'll have to wait until lunch.

Which means the next three hours are torture.

I check my phone every two minutes, hoping Van will text me. She has second and third period with Marcos, but as usual I can't get a stupid signal because the stupid architect who designed this concrete cavern of an educational complex decided to reinforce the walls with lead or Adamantium or Kryptonite or some other teenage-hating, cell-phone-blocking element.

By the time the lunch bell rings, my nerves are so frayed I'm almost sick with apprehension. I bolt to the parking lot, practically shoving my classmates out of the way.

Please let everything be okay, please let everything be okay, please let everything be okay . . .

I emerge into the blinding light of the Florida sun and almost faint with joy when I see Marcos waiting with Van next to her Jeep.

It takes all my self-control not to let out a squeal of happiness and run into his arms, but (a) the parking lot is swarming with seniors and (b) I'm way too out of breath for squealing.

"Hey," I say, forcing myself to sound as casual as possible. As if we didn't just share the most life-altering weekend imaginable.

"Hey," he sighs, trying equally hard to muster a smile.

"So, change of plans," Van says. "We're eating in the cafeteria."

This strikes me as the most pointless thing anyone could say in this moment. But then Marcos clarifies.

"My parents don't want me going off campus for lunch anymore. They want to know exactly where I am at all times, so they called the school and revoked my lunch privileges."

"Oh," I say.

That's not good. That's not good at all.

"My dad's grounding me because he thinks I've been lying to him about who I've been hanging out with," Marcos sighs as he picks at his plate of tater tots. "He thinks I've been secretly running around town and hooking up with Van. That's why he called the school and canceled my lunch privileges. He wants to make sure I'm not sneaking off in the middle of the day to have wild heterosexual sex."

"I don't understand," I say. "I get that your dad is upset because he thinks you lied. But is he really that upset you're dating Van?" If anything, I would've thought finding out his son had a girlfriend would've put Mr. Price's mind at ease. Especially after finding said son at a gay dance.

Marcos opens his mouth to answer, then hesitates.

"It's okay," Van groans, rolling her eyes. "Tell him."

"My dad kind of asked around about Van. At church."

"Oh." *Oh no.*

"Yeah. He wasn't exactly thrilled to find out I'm dating the one girl in town who's as big an atheist as me."

"Agnostic, not atheist," Van corrects him. "And screw your father. I was *so* nice to him. I was polite, charming, compassionate. Your dad should feel *honored* that I'm dating his son. I'm a catch!"

"No argument there," Marcos agrees.

"Also, I know this isn't about me, but can we just acknowledge for a second how messed up it is that you two were the ones sneaking around having a secret romance, yet somehow *I'm* the one whose reputation is now being called into question. I mean, this is some seriously patriarchal BS."

"If it makes you feel any better, my mom wants to meet you," Marcos chuckles. "She got kind of excited when I told her your last name was Silvera. She always wanted me to meet a 'nice Latina girl.'"

"Great, I can't wait to meet my pretend boyfriend's mother."

"But this is good, right?" I interject, grasping at any silver lining I can find. "I mean, your parents think that you and Van are a couple. They might have some reservations about Van—no offense—"

"Offense taken."

"But at least it's better than them knowing the truth."

Marcos stares at his hands and sighs. "Yeah, I guess."

From the way he avoids my eyes, though, I don't get the impression he means it. In fact, I can't help feeling that I've messed things up. Again.

"What's the matter?"

"Nothing. Really. It's just . . ."

"Just what?"

"That night, when I was in the parking lot waiting for my dad, all I could think was: *This is it. I'm about to come out to my parents.* And I was terrified. Like really, properly terrified. But also . . ."

"Also?"

"I was kind of relieved. I knew they'd freak out, especially my dad. And I knew there'd be consequences. But at least everything would've been out in the open. I wasn't going to have to walk around with this secret anymore."

"Oh." I hadn't thought about that. At the time I was so focused on trying to rescue Marcos from certain doom it never occurred to me that maybe a part of him didn't want to be rescued.

"I didn't know you felt that way," I say. "I just thought, because of the meteor, you were being *forced* to come out. I thought we were helping."

"You did," he reassures me with a smile. "You *both* did. If you guys hadn't come back and lied for me, there's no way I'd only be grounded for the month. So, thank you. For real. You two seriously saved my ass."

"That's Milo and me: Professional Ass Savers."

"Ew," I wince. "Can we please have a different name?"

"No. I've already ordered the T-shirts."

Marcos lets out a laugh then slides his hand under the table and squeezes mine. He does it so naturally, so instinctively, I almost faint from shock. Not that I'm complaining. In fact, for the first time in days, I'm almost starting to believe that—despite Marcos's grounding—everything might just turn out okay.

It's a nice feeling. But like most nice feelings, it doesn't last.

"Just so you know, my parents might be calling yours," Marcos tells me on the way to World Lit. I'm not sure why he's waited until we're in the middle of a crowded hallway to drop this bombshell. Probably so I won't freak out. Although Marcos should know by now that I am quite capable of freaking out anywhere.

"They *what*?"

"Don't worry! You're not in trouble."

"Then why would your parents call mine?"

"Apparently, when my dad was asking around about Van, he also asked around about you."

"And?" I'm not sure I want to know where this is going.

"And—surprise, surprise—everyone at POP told him you were basically a saint."

Whew. That's a relief.

"I guess it's nice to know my reputation as a rule-abiding goody-goody has finally come in handy," I say.

"Yeah, *except* my dad doesn't understand why his devil spawn of a son would be hanging out with such a perfect angel unless I was using you for some nefarious purpose."

"Like what?"

"Like as cover so I can hook up with Van. He thinks every time I told him I was hanging out with you—like at the beach or Ashleigh's party—I was out with Van. He thinks I've been asking you to lie for me."

"Did you tell him that's not true?"

"Yes, but after the way Van kissed me in the parking lot, my dad's totally convinced we've been hooking up regularly."

Crap. I knew that kiss was too much.

"I just wanted to give you a heads-up that my dad might call and tell your parents to keep an eye on us. You know, to make sure I'm not unduly taking advantage of their angel child or corrupting him."

"It's a little late for that."

"Hey, *you're* the freaky little Presbyterian who invited me into *his* bed, remember?"

My face goes pink at the memory of camp, and Marcos bursts out laughing. He casts a glance down the hallway and, when the coast is clear, pulls me into an empty science lab, locking the door behind us.

"What are you doing? We're going to be late for class."

"I know. But we just spent all of lunch talking about me and my problems. I want to make sure you're okay. It was a pretty insane weekend."

"Understatement of the Year."

"Exactly. That's why I want to make sure you're not freaking out or . . ."

"Or what?"

"Or having second thoughts? About us?"

Marcos says this nonchalantly, almost breezily, but I can see in his eyes that now-familiar look he gets whenever he's nervous. I hate that look. But I also understand why it's back. If ever a skittish closet case like me needed a reason to end things, nearly getting outed and/or killed by a meteor would be it.

If I'm being 100 percent honest, there was definitely a dark hour or two over the weekend when I found myself wondering if all this lying, sneaking around, and *nearly dying* was worth it. But now, looking up into Marcos's eyes—eyes that are staring down at me with so much tenderness and hope—I know it is.

"I'm okay if you're okay."

The smile of relief that spreads across Marcos's face is the most amazing thing I've seen all day. I could look at it for the rest of time.

"You're sure?" he asks.

"I'm sure."

"Good. Because I was just getting used to kissing you and I'd really hate it if we had to stop."

"You don't have to stop," I say, grabbing his shirt collar and pulling him close.

Marcos leans in and kisses me. And we are very, *very* late for class.

26

¿Adivina quién viene a cenar?

When I get home from school, I remember Marcos's warning about his dad calling my parents and do my best to prepare. But as the evening progresses, it seems that my fear (for once) is unwarranted. Mom makes pork chops and green beans for dinner. Dad complains about his new electrician. At no point are there any new questions about the events of Friday night or the nature of my friendship with Marcos.

I should feel relieved but, staring at my half-eaten pork chop, all I can feel is guilt. It's my fault Marcos is grounded. Yes, the lie that Van and I concocted might have spared him from being outed to his parents, but it still managed to get him in hot water. Meanwhile my sterling reputation is as spotless as ever.

Then again . . . Maybe I can use that reputation to my advantage.

I mean, maybe if the Prices *saw* Marcos and me together—if they saw he wasn't taking advantage of me to sneak around with Van and that our friendship was genuine—then maybe they might go easier on their son.

Even if they don't initially buy the idea of us as friends, they'll have to concede it would be in their best interest to let Marcos spend time with me. After all, if they think I'm a Good Presbyterian Boy—and other than being totally hot for their son, I *am* a Good Presbyterian Boy—then who else could be better suited to bring their wayward child back into the fold?

As far as the Prices know, I could be *exactly* what Marcos needs.

At lunch the next day I run my idea by Marcos. I'll find some reason to come over to his house so his parents can observe us hanging out in a purely platonic, completely innocent manner that will prove to them that our friendship hasn't been some giant ruse to cover Marcos's amorous exploits. They'll see they've misjudged their son, that he's a decent kid, and—who knows?—maybe they'll even restore his lunch privileges.

"That's never going to work," Marcos sighs when I finish laying out my plan.

"Why not?"

"Because."

"Because *why*? Give me one good reason."

"Because I'm *grounded* and there's no way my parents will let me invite anyone over."

Huh. That's a pretty good reason.

An hour later, though, a solution to that particular problem comes our way courtesy of Ms. Snook and our World Lit class. Everyone is instructed to partner up and then given a random scene from a Shakespeare play that we're asked to rewrite in contemporary dialogue and then perform at the end of the week.

I for one can barely contain my excitement. Not that I'm looking forward to acting in front of my peers. That'll be hell. But as a legitimate excuse to spend time with Marcos, it's *perfect*.

"Your parents will have to let me come over now," I whisper. "It's fate! *And* homework!"

And I'm right. After some initial hesitation, the Prices relent, and I'm benevolently granted permission to come over the following afternoon to *work on our assignment*. That last part, according to Marcos, is emphatically stressed by his father. I'm coming over to *work*. Not to hang out, not to goof around, not to watch TV. To work.

Which isn't a problem. After all, there's no rule that says I can't work *and* charm the socks off someone's parents at the same time. It's called multitasking.

When I pull up to Marcos's house after school on Wednesday, I'm both excited and nervous. Especially as I have no idea what sort of greeting I'll receive. To my immense relief, Mr. Price is still at work, so the only parent I have to worry about impressing for the moment is Marcos's mom.

Mrs. Price is her usual self when she greets me at the door: polite but withdrawn. She seems neither pleased nor displeased to see me— like a judge awaiting evidence before delivering a verdict.

"Make yourself at home," she says as she welcomes me inside. Though from the way Marcos's laptop and books are already laid out on the dining room table, it seems pretty clear that any "home making" is expected to be confined to this room and this room alone.

"Ready to get our Shakespeare on?" Marcos asks as I sit beside him at the table.

"I was born ready."

Over the next couple hours, we then proceed to get most of our adaptation of *Twelfth Night* completed, modernizing dialogue like "I cannot be so answer'd" into "I'm not trying to hear that." Mrs. Price occasionally wanders into the room, ostensibly to see how our assignment is progressing, though it's pretty obvious these interruptions are just an excuse to keep an eye on us.

In fact, whenever Marcos or I say or do something that cracks the other one up, it's only a matter of seconds before Mrs. Price sticks her head into the room to see what's so funny. When she does, I always smile and repeat the joke, so she feels included. After all, there are no secrets here. Just pure, educational fun.

As for my plan, it definitely seems to be working. In the last hour alone, Mrs. Price's interruptions have grown less abrupt and inquisitorial and more causally curious. She asks how my parents are doing and what my plans are for college. At one point she even offers her own suggestion on how to update some of Shakespeare's dialogue when Marcos and I get stuck on a particularly tricky monologue.

I can tell she's letting down her guard, but even I'm a little surprised when, three hours into our assignment, she breezes into the room with a pitcher of freshly squeezed lemonade and says, "I thought you boys could use a break. You've been working so hard. You should give your brains a rest."

I risk a quick smile at Marcos—one that I hope conveys my none-too-subtle pride that, when it comes to winning over parents, I am *crushing* it. After all, mothers don't chop and squeeze lemons for boys they don't trust. That's a fact.

"This is delicious," I say, taking a long, satisfying sip. "Thank you so much, Mrs. Price."

"Please, it was nothing," she says, waving away my compliment. "I had a bunch of lemons that were about to go bad, so I needed to use them up."

"Really?" Marcos asks, his voice tinged with playful sarcasm. "You just happened to have twenty lemons lying around about to go bad?"

"Watch it, smart aleck," Mrs. Price chuckles as she tousles her son's hair.

"Hey!" Marcos protests. Then he grumbles something in Spanish and immediately fixes his hair. Mrs. Price laughs and teases him back. I can't understand what they're saying, but for the next minute, they go back and forth—teasing and arguing in Spanish—until Marcos catches the surprised look on my face and says, "Okay, Mom, enough, we're being rude."

"Pardon us, Milo," Mrs. Price says with a smirk. "My son is very serious about his hair."

"*Mom.*"

Before they can get into it again, the phone rings and Mrs. Price excuses herself to the kitchen.

"You speak Spanish!" I practically shout as soon as we're alone, unable to stop the grin that spreads across my face.

"What? Oh. Yeah. So?"

"So? That's great! When we were at camp, you said your father wouldn't let you learn because he was a fascist."

"I'm pretty sure I didn't say *fascist*."

"No, you did. You said it a lot actually."

"Okay, yeah, probably," Marcos laughs. "I've been taking Spanish for the last three years. It was a requirement at my school in Orlando, so my dad couldn't object."

Even so, I'm impressed with how quickly he's picked it up. I mean, I've also been taking Spanish for three years, and I'm nowhere near proficient. A fact Van loves to tease me about whenever I insist that we put on the subtitles when we watch anything by Almodóvar.

"I'm glad you finally got to learn," I tell him. "I know it was important to you."

"Thanks. I still don't speak it when my dad's around, though. He gets annoyed. Thinks my mom and I are conspiring against him."

"Are you?"

"Sometimes."

As if on cue, Mrs. Price returns looking more relaxed than I've seen her all afternoon. "That was your father," she announces. "He has to work late, so he won't be home for dinner."

"Oh no," Marcos groans sarcastically.

"Tone," his mother warns, her entire body stiffening.

"Sorry."

Having laid down the law, Mrs. Price once again relaxes. Then she turns to me and says the words I've been hoping to hear since I arrived.

"Milo, would you like to stay for dinner?"

"You have a beautiful home," I say as I help Mrs. Price set the table. Marcos has run to the store to get some sweet potatoes after convincing his mother to cook something called boniato con mojo, which apparently is a vegetarian dish he loves but never gets to eat on account of Mr. Price's insistence that "real dinners contain meat." He invited me to go with him, but I figured it would be better to remain behind and continue my charm offensive.

"Thank you," she says, humming to herself as she sets out the silverware. "Our house in Orlando got more sunlight but what can you do?"

Initially, I was a little nervous to be left alone with Mrs. Price. I halfway expected her to start grilling me about Marcos and Van the second he was out the door, but the news of her husband's absence seems to have put her in a surprisingly good mood. In fact, she's already uncorked a bottle of wine and is halfway through her first glass.

"I really like that painting," I say, nodding toward the picture over the piano in the living room. I want to keep the compliments coming. I know from experience that my own mother tends to feel slighted if she doesn't receive at least three distinct compliments about our home whenever guests visit.

"Oh? That old thing?" Mrs. Price sets down the silverware and walks over to the painting. It's a sunrise over an ocean, though the colors are darker and more somber than you'd expect from a typical beach scene. The shoreline is deserted and windswept, as if a storm has passed through and scattered all the people. It's peaceful but also, somehow, lonely.

"I painted this many, *many* years ago," she says. "Back when I still lived in Miami."

"You're a painter?"

"Oh no. No, no, no. When I was in school, I dabbled. Who didn't?

But now . . . ?" She waves her hand like she's waving away the past.

"It's really good," I persist. "Like *museum* good."

"Marcos is better. He's the real artist in the family. Has he shown you his sketches?"

"No. He hasn't." I've seen him doodling in class, but I've never seen anything I'd call art. I wonder why.

"Ask him. Marcos is very good. But he's shy."

"Shy" is probably the last word in the world I'd use to describe Marcos. Then again, seeing him with his mother today, I'm starting to realize that there are sides to him I'm still discovering.

"Oh, look at this," Mrs. Price says, plucking a framed photo off the piano. It's of a baby with a dazzling grin and a full head of thick black hair, and I can't help smiling because I know exactly who he is.

"Marcos?"

"Of course," Mrs. Price chuckles. "Wasn't he a handsome baby? The doctors, the nurses, even people on the street, they would all stop and tell me what a beautiful son I had. Everyone said he could be a model."

"He still could," I say without thinking—then instantly want to die.

Oh. My. God. Am I trying to out myself?

Thankfully, instead of reeling back in disgust from the sex-crazed degenerate she's let into her home, Mrs. Price just chuckles harder.

"Oh, don't tell *him* that. His head is big enough."

Dinner with Marcos and his mother ends up being more fun than I could've imagined. Mrs. Price is a good cook, though if I'm being 100 percent honest, boniato con mojo is a little too sweet for my taste.

Marcos, though, relishes every bite, which seems to make his mom happy. In fact, the whole evening couldn't be going smoother.

That is until Mrs. Price turns to me at the end of the meal without warning and says, "So, Milo, tell me about this Vanessa Silvera my son is dating but whom he can't be bothered to introduce to his mother."

My heart stops. I should've known the subject of Van would come up sooner or later, and I kick myself for not being more prepared. Then I notice the mischievous twinkle in Mrs. Price's eye, and I relax. This isn't an interrogation. She's not trying to put me on the spot or catch me in a lie. She's just a mom who wants to know about her son.

"Marcos tells me you and this girl are good friends?" she continues.

"Yes," I say after a quick glance at Marcos to make sure he's okay with us wading into this territory. "She's my best friend."

"Best friend?" She sounds impressed. "You've known her a long time then?"

"Almost twelve years."

"That is long."

"Yeah. Van's great. She's funny and smart and super ambitious— in a good way. She's always joining different clubs and trying new things and expanding her mind."

"But she doesn't go to church?"

Oops. Guess I walked into that.

"Mom," Marcos groans.

"I'm just asking."

"And you know the answer. We've discussed this. No, Vanessa doesn't go to church."

"Yes, but your friend here does. And he's best friends with this girl. So I'm curious what he thinks about that?"

"You're putting him on the spot."

"No, it's okay," I say, swallowing the last bite of my citrusy sweet potatoes. I want to answer Mrs. Price's question. After all Van's done for us, I need to have her back. She might not actually be dating Marcos, and she probably couldn't care less what the Prices think about her, but she's my best friend and a great person, and the Prices should know how lucky Marcos and I are to have her in our lives.

"I know you and Mr. Price have some concerns about Van," I begin. "And I get it. My parents had the same concerns. Well, *have*, actually. But that's because they believe there's only one way someone can be a good person, and that's if they go to church."

"You don't agree?"

It's not an accusation, just a question. Still, I choose my next words carefully.

"I think just because someone goes to church every Sunday that doesn't automatically make them a good person. I mean, there are certain people at POP you probably wouldn't want to run into the other six days of the week, if you know what I mean?"

Mrs. Price chuckles, which makes me suspect she does.

"But then there are people like Van who don't go to church or believe in organized religion but who are some of the best people I know," I continue, risking a quick glance at Marcos so he knows I'm including him in this group. "I guess for me a person's actions are more important than what they claim to believe. Someone can say they're a Christian all they want, but if they're not living their life in a way that puts other people first or makes the world a better place, then what good are their beliefs?

"But Van? I've never met anyone with such a big heart. She's looked out for me, and protected me, and been a better friend to me than I have ever been to her. And that's how she is with everyone she cares about. She always puts other people first. She always tries to help. Because that's who she is. She's not the kind of person who can be happy if other people are hurting."

"That's very admirable."

"Yeah. It is. Van once told me that her idea of a perfect world is a world where everyone succeeds. Where everyone is living their best life. So every day she tries to make the world a better place. She wants that as much as anyone who goes to POP or any other church. She might even want it *more* because when Van helps someone, she doesn't do it because it's what's expected of her. She doesn't do it for any sort of reward or because she's trying to get into Heaven or because it's what she was told God wants. She does it because doing the right thing is *right*. And that's enough for her."

"I see," Mrs. Price says, her expression inscrutable. "Anything else?"

I'm not sure if she's encouraging me to wrap things up because I've sufficiently made my point or because she's tired of listening to my teenage nonsense, but I take the hint.

"No, that's pretty much it. Except to say that Van might not have faith in the traditional sense, but she does have it. It's just a *different* kind of faith. And if you ask me, the world would be a much better place if more people had her faith."

Mrs. Price nods. I'm pretty sure I've said too much, but I also know what I've said is the truth. Hopefully that counts for something.

"Well," Mrs. Price says, taking a sip of her wine, "I look forward to meeting this exceptional young lady someday." Then with the twinkle returning to her eye, she turns to Marcos and adds, "I knew when my son started dating, he'd find someone special."

Marcos blushes, his face turning the exact same color as his sweet potatoes. Then he shoots me a quick smile and says, "Yeah, I have."

"Thanks for that," Marcos says, walking me out to my car.

Mrs. Price offered to make us something for dessert, but I figured I ought to quit while I was ahead and go home before I inadvertently say or do anything that burns down any of the bridges I've managed to build tonight. Plus, Mr. Price is due home any minute, and I doubt things would remain as carefree with him around.

"Thanks for what?" I ask.

"All that stuff you said about Van—about someone being a good person even if they don't go to church. I know deep down my mom believes the same thing—or *wants* to believe the same thing—but every time she tries to bring it up with my dad, it always ends in him making the same old, tired argument. You either go to church or you go to Hell, and there is no room for debate."

"I'm pretty sure my parents think the same thing."

"That's why I think it actually meant a lot to her to hear someone like you—you know, an actual Christian who was raised by Christians—say what you said. Most of the time, she just has my dad or some busybody from church telling her all the things that are wrong with me. So hearing you defend people like Van and me,

I think it made her happy to know she's not totally alone. To know there's someone else—besides her—sticking up for me."

"I'll always stick up for you," I say with a smile, though it saddens me to think of Mrs. Price never hearing a kind word about her son. If it were up to me, I'd tell her how amazing Marcos is every single day. "And for what it's worth, I really liked your mom. I wasn't expecting her to be so cool."

"Yeah. She's *a lot* more easygoing when my dad's not around. Everyone is."

That's true. As charming as I've seen Mr. Price be in public with people he's trying to impress, I can't say I've ever been at ease around him. There's something about the way he studies people that gives me the impression he's always keeping score.

"She liked you too, by the way."

"Your mom?"

"Yeah," he chuckles. "She said you remind her of my uncle."

"Oh." I'm glad I made a good impression. Though I don't quite understand the comparison. "How am I like your uncle?"

"Well, you're really skinny like him. And polite. And . . . *you know*."

I don't.

"My uncle's gay," Marcos laughs when he sees the confusion on my face. "Did you not know that?"

"Umm . . . *No.*" I think I'd remember Marcos telling me about a gay uncle. I mean, that's kind of noteworthy given our present circumstance. Then again, now that I think back on everything that he's told me about Eddie and his relationship with the rest of his family, it does kind of make sense. Like *a lot* of sense. Like "I can't believe I didn't piece the clues together sooner" sense.

"It's okay," Marcos chuckles, "it's not like it's anything my family discusses. *Ever.* My mom still refers to Eddie's boyfriend as his 'roommate,' even though they've been together for, like, ten years."

I laugh, but a second later an unsettling thought creeps across my brain.

"Wait, if I remind your mom of your uncle, does that mean she knows about me?" Because that's exactly the opposite impression I wanted to make tonight. I'm supposed to be Milo the Good Friend. Not Milo the—

"Don't worry. I don't think she meant anything by it. I think she was just letting me know she liked you and that she approved of my choice in friends."

"Oh. Okay." Though I'm not 100 percent convinced.

Through the window of the house, I can see Mrs. Price moving about the kitchen, cleaning up the remains of our dinner. Marcos follows my gaze, and a moment later I know we're thinking the exact same thing because he whispers, "I wish I could kiss you good night."

"Well, if I keep coming over and impressing your parents, maybe in ten years they'll let me be your roommate."

Marcos laughs and opens my door for me. "Get out of here, Connolly, before I wipe that smug grin off your face."

"I'd like to see you try."

"I bet you would, you naughty little Bible Thumper."

I slide into my car, closing the door, and Marcos hovers outside my window, smiling under the streetlamp. I can tell he isn't quite ready for the night to end. Neither am I.

"Hey, so, speaking of boyfriends," he says. "I was wondering . . ."

"Wondering what?" I ask when he trails off and stares down at his shoes. Maybe Mrs. Price is right. When it comes to certain things, Marcos is very shy.

"I was just wondering how you'd feel about me calling you my . . . boyfriend?"

If I wasn't already sitting down, I'm pretty sure I'd be a puddle on the ground because my whole body just melted.

Boyfriend? He wants to be *my* boyfriend?

"Obviously, I don't mean publicly. I just mean in terms of defining what this is—"

"Yes!" I shout, before he can finish the sentence, and I'm suddenly very glad the sun's gone down because I am definitely blushing from head to foot. "I mean, yeah, that'd be all right."

"Okay, cool," he says, slowly backing away from my car like a very pleased peacock. "I'll see you tomorrow then, boyfriend."

27

Saint Bruce and Our Lady of the Salt-Rimmed Margaritas

"Your father is a saint, Milo."

This is a phrase I've grown up hearing most of my life and which I've already heard three times in the last hour. Which isn't the worst way to spend a Saturday.

My dad is the construction site manager for the Port Orange branch of Habitat for Humanity. In layman's terms, he's the person in charge of building all the houses for the low-income families who apply to the organization, and he's really good at his job. In fact, he once finished three homes in a year, which is some kind of record. He's basically able to construct, refurbish, or rebuild literally anything—a skill he has definitely *not* passed along to his one and only son. And not from want of trying.

This week the latest home he completed was certified "habitable" by the city, so today Habitat is hosting the official House Dedication Ceremony. Which is a pretty cool event where the mayor makes a speech and Reverend Foley offers a blessing before the family who's moving in is finally presented with the keys to their new home.

I've been to about fifteen of these dedications over the years, and

I never get tired of them. I still tear up every time the mayor hands the family their brand-new keys to their brand-new home so they can embark on their brand-new life.

What can I say? I'm a softie. I mean, people's dreams are coming true. I defy anyone not to get a little misty-eyed. I've even seen my dad choke up on occasion, and he once told the guys on his crew, "If you're not dying, you shouldn't be crying." Even so, days like today tend to bring out the best in him.

I try not to be too effusive, though, because I know excessive praise and/or emotion make him uncomfortable, but I can't help being proud. So far at least twenty different people have stopped to shake my hand and tell me what a fantastic job my father did, including Ms. Daniels, the single mother of two who's moving into the house.

"Your father has forever changed my life, Milo," she tells me, tears of pride welling up in her eyes. "You are so lucky to have a man like that for a father."

"I know," I say. And I mean it.

That's actually one of the reasons I volunteered at Habitat over the summer. Well, *technically* I volunteered to avoid being conscripted into any of the team sports that my dad was eyeing on my behalf down at the rec center. But paternal pride and a general sense of goodwill definitely played a part.

I'd actually never worked with my father on a house before this year. There was a pretty steep learning curve—and a lot of blisters—but I'm proud of the work I did. Although, if I'm being honest, I think my primary accomplishment was not sawing off any of my limbs or inadvertently nailing myself to a wall. In fact, I'd say a good 90 percent of my volunteering generally consisted of me narrowly avoiding death.

I'm still surprised my dad allowed me to volunteer for as long as he did, considering how prone I am to what his crew affectionately dubbed "Milo Mishaps." I think he was secretly hoping that after a few weeks of physical labor, I'd magically develop an aptitude for carpentry and reveal myself to be an engineering prodigy.

Unfortunately, that dream, like most of my father's dreams for me (Little League champion, Boy Scout leader, human capable of sustained eye contact), never materialized. Still, in my own small way I helped. I made a tangible difference in Ms. Daniels's life, so I'm feeling pretty good right now.

As Ms. Daniels heads off to thank Reverend Foley for his benediction, my phone buzzes in my pocket. I check it and see I have a text from Marcos asking about the ceremony.

I can't help but smile. We've been texting a lot this week. Pretty much constantly. Not that anyone would ever know it if they were to scroll through my phone. At least once a day I delete anything remotely incriminating in case my parents see it. Not that I'm particularly worried. As strict as they are, my parents have never been the kind of people who'd demand to read my texts or search my browser history. That's more Mr. Price's MO. Still, it never hurts to be careful.

I text Marcos back, telling him, *Wish you were here.* A moment later he texts, *No, I wish YOU were HERE.* I'm about to ask where "here" is when he sends me a photo of himself in bed (with his shirt off) along with the text, *Golden Girls marathon soon?*

My heart flutters and I find myself smiling so hard I think my face is going to crack in half.

"What are you grinning about?" my mom asks, coming up behind me and almost scaring my soul out of my body.

"Nothing," I say, sliding my phone in my pocket and trying not to look as guilty as I feel. "No reason."

My mom gives me a playful smirk and tousles my hair. "You've sure been smiling *a lot* these last couple of days for someone with 'no reason.'"

I have? Crap! I didn't even notice.

"It's just been a good week," I lie. "Marcos and I aced our Shakespeare project. And Van is loving rehearsals. Did I tell you she got the lead?"

My mom flinches slightly at Van's name, but a moment later her smile is back.

"Well, that's good."

"Yeah."

"And there's no other reason you've been in such a good mood?"

No other reason?

"Like what?" I ask, my entire body tensing.

"I don't know. Maybe you've met someone special?"

"What? No!" I sputter. *Oh my gosh, how obvious have I been?*

I know I've been in a good mood ever since Marcos asked me to be his boyfriend, but I didn't know I was walking around with a huge sign on my forehead announcing that fact to the world.

"I'm just asking," my mom laughs. "You don't need to get defensive."

"Mom, there's no one special. I swear. It's just been a good week. *That's all.*"

"Okay," my mom relents. "My mistake."

I can tell she doesn't believe me, but she knows if she keeps pushing then her turtle of a son will retreat into his shell and stay there until Christmas. Not that that stops her from leaning in conspiratorially and whispering, "For the record, I think any girl would be lucky to date you." Then she kisses my cheek and wanders off to find my dad.

Whew... That was *way* too close.

I'm going to have to be way more careful in the future. I mean, it's not going to do me any good to delete all my texts if my stupid face is going to be an open effing book and blab all my secrets to the world. I need to get some self-control. And fast.

"Welcome to Ay Caramba," our sombrero-clad waitress exclaims as she hands my parents and me our comically oversized menus that proudly boast, "The revolution will have nachos!" I'm never been able to decide if this restaurant's excessive kitsch and rampant cultural appropriation is knowingly ironic or just bad taste, but over the years dining here after a house dedication has kind of become a Connolly family tradition.

My mom stumbled upon the place a few years ago when she and some of her coworkers from the bank had a rare girls' night out. She claims she loves the "fun family atmosphere" and the Che Guevara taco cheesecake (don't ask), but I know the real reason.

"Oh, this takes me back," she sighs contentedly as she sips her freshly made, salt-rimmed margarita. This is something she says whenever she orders her beverage of choice, though to date I've never gotten her to elaborate on what *exactly* "this" takes her back "to." It's pretty hilarious, though, to see her enjoy a drink so openly. Especially considering how my mom, for all intents and purposes, does not drink. In her own words she is strictly "an iced tea kind of woman."

"I think I'm going to get another," she croons before she's even halfway through her first.

"Oh, so I'll be carrying you home?" my dad teases.

My mom scrunches up her face into an exaggerated smirk and "boops" my dad on the nose like she's pressing his off button.

"Oh, boop yourself," my dad groans before shooting her a wink.

I love when they get like this. My parents are good parents, but they're not always fun parents. Not that I blame them. I mean, my dad might have a rewarding job building homes for those in need, but it's also exhausting. I get that after a long day at a site, he doesn't want to come home to exuberance, noise, or whimsy.

As for my mom, well, she's never gone into much detail about her childhood, but from the hints my dad has dropped, I'm pretty sure both her parents (whom I've only ever seen in photographs) were the kind of people who liked to party way too hard and not very responsibly. It's what led her to find Jesus and why, most days, her only true cravings are for order and decorum.

Then there are nights like tonight. They're few and far between, and they don't last long, but for whatever reason, on these magical nights my parents basically throw all the rules out the window and let their walls down. They practically become different people. Or maybe they just become the people they used to be long before work and stress and life forced them to grow up.

Tomorrow my mom will be back to iced teas, and my dad will be back to monosyllabic grunts in response to any and all questions, but tonight anything's possible.

"You want a sip of my beer?" my dad asks, extending his bottle to me.

My mom's eyes instinctively narrow, and I can see her walls rising up.

"Just a sip," he reassures her. "It's a special occasion. Besides, he's earned it."

I don't know if narrowly avoiding the emergency room twice a week for three months straight qualifies as "earning it," but I appreciate the gesture.

"I know it wasn't easy for you working on-site all summer," my dad continues. "It was a lot of hard work, and I know you would've preferred to spend your vacation doing something indoors. But you stuck with it. You showed up every day, you put in the hours, and you didn't quit. And *that* is commendable. I'm proud of you."

Oh. Wow.

I'd always assumed my father viewed my hours on his construction site as an unavoidable burden if not outright embarrassment. It never occurred to me that he might actually be glad I was there.

"Thanks," I manage to whisper, feeling my cheeks blush.

I glance at my mom, who still looks hesitant about the bottle of Miller that my dad is holding out to me. I'm about to refuse for her sake when she sighs dramatically and throws her hands up into the air in a show of moral surrender.

"Okay, *one* sip."

My dad presses the bottle into my hands, and I do my best to look grateful even though a quick sniff of the contents makes me think of fermented swamp water. But my dad is right. It is a special occasion.

I take a quick sip, trying to ignore the sting of flavor that hits the back of my throat. *Yep, definitely swamp water.* Then I return the bottle while trying not to make a face.

"Thanks."

My dad slaps my shoulder, which over the years I've learned is his own version of the boop. Unlike my mother's boops, though, my father's shoulder slaps are much harder to come by. I guess tonight's my lucky night. In fact, tonight is pretty much perfect. The only thing that could make it more perfect is if Marcos were here.

He's not though. And as much as I'd like to be able to conceive of a world where he could be, I know it's not possible.

I mean, a world where I'm out to dinner with my parents *and* my boyfriend? Maybe on some parallel Earth in another universe that *might* be a possibility, but in this universe? No way. In this universe Marcos is always going to be the part of my life that I can never share with my parents. He'll always be the secret I have to hide.

I look at my mom and dad across the table, huddling behind their oversized menus and pretending to argue about what appetizers to order, and I wonder how many more times we'll be sitting at a table like this. Just the three of us. My mom asking if I'm dating "anyone special." My dad being proud of me but only because he doesn't really know me. Me denying the existence of the person I claim to care about more than anyone in the world.

It's not a very appealing future. And it's certainly not sustainable.

At some point Marcos and I will have to choose between our families and each other. And when that day comes, I realize I have no idea what I'll do.

28

Two Steps Forward, Three Steps Back

On Sunday afternoon I volunteer to babysit at POP while most of the staff and congregation are busy with the fall rummage sale happening out in the church parking lot. Normally Miss Lindsey, who runs POP's daycare, would watch the kids. But today she asked me to fill in for her so she could go to Fort Myers to deal with a small family emergency. Her sixty-year-old father just got out of the hospital after injuring himself on a Jet Ski (#OnlyInFlorida), and her usual full-time assistant, Miss Grace, has the flu, so for the next few hours I, Milo Connolly, will be solely responsible for the safety and well-being of the children of POP.

God help us all.

We've already had one bumped noggin, two tantrums, and three time-outs—and that's only been the first hour. On the plus side, though, the kids are 100 percent on board with my snack selection for the day, and as any good child care provider will tell you, that's 90 percent of the battle.

In fact, right now my only major obstacle is Maxwell MacMillan, POP's resident trouble tot, who's currently trying to suck the ink out of all the scented markers. You'd think it wouldn't be too difficult keeping a kid from deliberately poisoning himself, but just when I think I've gotten through to his six-year-old brain that just because something *smells* like a blueberry that doesn't necessarily mean it *is* a blueberry, Maxwell moves on to a new color/flavor combo and we have to start the explanation all over again.

"Everything under control, Connolly?" a voice calls out behind me.

I turn around from prying yet another marker out of Maxwell's mouth to see Marcos leaning in the doorway and I'm instantly overjoyed *and* racked with guilt. Dinner with my parents last night left me feeling kind of depressed and uncertain about our future, so I never got around to responding to his text about a *Golden Girls* marathon— or to any of the other fifteen flirty texts he sent after that. Which is definitely not Acceptable Boyfriend Behavior.

"What are you doing here?" I ask, hoping he's not too annoyed with me for ghosting him last night or avoiding him at service this morning.

"I figured you could use a hand," he says, strutting into the room and flashing me his dazzling smile.

"You did?"

"You sound shocked."

"I didn't think extracurricular church activities were exactly your thing." Also, as much as I'd like to see him right now, this isn't *exactly* the best timing. I mean, his presence here is going to be really hard to explain if Pastor Foley or Mr. Price or anyone else sees us together.

"Don't worry," Marcos laughs, clocking my unease. "It's *okay*. I was helping my dad with the rummage sale. You know, as part of my continued punishment? And I overheard Pastor Foley mention that you were short-staffed in the day care, so I asked if he wanted me to come over and lend a hand."

"And Foley agreed?"

"He said he was sure you'd be happy for the help and that I was a 'very considerate young man.'"

I can't help but laugh at Marcos's ingenuity, especially now that I know we're in no immediate danger.

"And what did your dad say?"

"What could he say? It's not like he can contradict his own pastor."

"Wow. You can be really devious when you want to be."

"Anything to spend time with you."

Marcos winks and once again I find myself wondering how I ended up with such an incredible boyfriend. I really don't deserve him or his thoughtfulness. Especially not after ignoring him all evening.

"I'm sorry I didn't get back to you last night," I whisper so the kids won't overhear. "Things got kind of busy with my parents."

"No worries. I figured you were tired and just needed to crash after your dad's big day."

"Yeah. Exactly," I lie.

Marcos nods, but his smile falters a bit. "Although part of me wondered if maybe I freaked you out with that bed pic? I didn't come on too strong, did I?"

"What? *No.* I like when you come on too strong."

Marcos chuckles, but I can still see a flicker of concern in his eyes. "Right. And you'd obviously tell me if anything was wrong?"

"Obviously." And I would. If something was really, *really* wrong. Or if the something was something I thought he could fix. Somehow, though, it doesn't seem fair to burden him with my constant low-grade panic about where this relationship is headed. Mainly because if I did, we'd never talk about anything else.

"So we're good?" he asks.

"We're good."

Marcos nods, his face once again breaking into that dazzling smile. Then looking around the day care, he claps his hands together like a man ready to get down to business and says, "Okay, then, what can I do to help?"

"Well, right now I'm trying to convince Maxwell here not to eat the scented markers," I tell him, grateful for the change of topic.

"And how's that going?"

"Not good."

Marcos turns to Maxwell, who (as if to prove my point) shoves an oversized orange marker down his throat.

"Hey, Maxwell!" Marcos barks, causing both me and every child in the room to jump. "Stop eating those markers *right now* or your head will *explode*."

Maxwell removes the marker from his orange-tinged lips but stares at Marcos skeptically. "No, it won't."

"Yes, it will. Do you see that stain?"

Both Maxwell and I follow Marcos's gaze up to an old water stain on the ceiling. It's been there since last October when Tropical Storm Velma damaged the roof.

"Yeah?"

"That stain is all that's left of a little boy named Wellington. He wouldn't stop sucking on markers and one day the ink seeped inside his brain and made his head explode. Do you want your head to explode?"

"No."

"Do you want to be a stain on the wall?"

"No."

"Then what are you going to do about it?"

To my surprise, Maxwell puts the cap back on the marker, carefully sets it down, then backs away from the offending object as if it were a stick of dynamite.

"Good choice," Marcos says. "I like your survival instincts." Then he turns to me and grins. "All right, Connolly, solved that problem for you. What's next?"

The rest of the afternoon is a pleasant blur of activity. Marcos and I cut jokes during story hour. We tease each other while playing dress-up. We even manage to get in some discreet flirting during a vigorous round of hide-and-seek. It's almost like being back at camp. In fact, given what a terror Marcos was with our fellow campers, I'm a little surprised at how good he is with the POP kids. Despite the Exploding Child Story (which Maxwell seems to have recovered from), he's kind of a natural. Probably because when Marcos lets down his guard, he's nothing more than a big kid himself.

"All right, who's ready for arts and crafts?" he announces, and the whole room explodes in cheers.

Normally, Miss Lindsey asks the kids to draw pictures of whatever

Bible story they learned in Sunday school that week. But Marcos, in typical Marcos fashion, has other plans. "Use your imagination!" he encourages them as he passes out the supplies. "Go wild. I want you to draw whatever makes you happiest. Whatever your favorite thing is in the whole entire world, I want you to draw *that*."

The kids don't need to be told twice. For the next half hour, they are focused little machines, churning out pictures made with markers, paint, stencils, stickers, watercolors, and whatever else we can find in the art cupboard. Marcos even convinces me to let him break out Miss Lindsey's most coveted possession: the glitter.

It's a bold move considering we'll be the ones cleaning it out of the carpet when the kids inevitably spill it all over the floor. I'm also pretty sure we've burned through the day care's entire art budget in one afternoon. But the kids are having a blast, so it's hard to say it's not worth it.

For the rest of the afternoon, Marcos drifts from child to child, praising their work but also giving them genuinely helpful suggestions on how they might improve their pictures. The artist inside him is clearly relishing the chance to shine. In fact, when I look up from helping Maxwell with his self-portrait, I'm pleasantly surprised to see Marcos feverishly drawing something on one of Miss Lindsey's oversized sketch pads. He stops when he catches me staring, but a few minutes later, when he thinks I'm too distracted to notice, he's at it again.

What is he up to?

None-too-subtly, I make my way over to where he's sitting, hoping to get a glimpse. The second I get within view, though, Marcos deftly covers up his sketch and pretends to be busy helping Sophie Prescott, who can't decide what color to paint her unicorn's hair.

I guess Mrs. Price is right. Marcos really is shy about sharing his art.

Given how nervous I was when this afternoon began, I'm shocked at how disappointed I feel when the rummage sale ends and the parents start collecting their kids. Most of the children can't wait to show off their glitter-covered masterpieces, and most of the parents are horrified by how much of that glitter is actually in their children's hair.

Still, you can't argue with happiness.

Soon enough it's just Marcos and me and a handful of stragglers. So while the three remaining children keep working on their drawings, Marcos and I decide to kick back and relax over a couple of juice boxes. After all, we've earned them.

"Thanks for all your help today," I say, hoisting my tired feet up onto a nearby chair. "I really appreciate it."

"Don't mention it."

"Seriously, you were a real lifesaver. I don't know how I would've survived if you hadn't shown up."

"What are you talking about? You had the situation completely under control. The kids love you."

"No, the kids *like* me. They *love* you. You're like some sort of Child Whisperer. I honestly wasn't expecting you to be so good with them."

"Why? Because I'm generally an insufferable know-it-all who hates humanity?"

"Basically."

"Yeah, but that's just adults. You've got to hate adults. Kids are all right."

As if on cue, Sophie waddles over to Marcos to show him her finished masterpiece.

"Oh wow," Marcos coos. "That is amazing, Sophie. I love that you gave your unicorn a rainbow mane. That's really creative. High five."

Sophie tries to high-five Marcos and misses. Mainly because she's six and also because hand-eye coordination has never been Sophie's strong suit.

"No worries, Soph. Try again."

A swing and a miss.

"Third time's the charm!"

Marcos lowers his palm so it's practically in Sophie's face and this time she makes contact. She cheers and races back to her table leaving a trail of glitter in her wake.

I shoot Marcos a proud smile and without thinking I say, "You're going to be a really amazing dad someday."

"Jeez, Connolly, buy a guy dinner first," Marcos whispers as his entire face blushes.

"Oh! No, I didn't mean—that's not—Sorry! I wasn't suggesting we—I'm just saying you're good with kids!" I stammer, my face turning bright red. "Not that you have to have one. Obviously. You probably don't even *want* kids—"

"Of course I want kids."

"You do?"

"Yeah. I mean, *someday*. Don't you?"

That's a really good question.

"I don't know." I shrug. "I never really pictured myself getting married, you know? So kids never seemed like an option."

"You don't have to be married to have kids. There are other ways. Like adoption. I mean, do you know how many kids are out there who need good homes? Thousands. Maybe millions. It'd basically be socially irresponsible *not* to adopt. Besides, people like you and me? We need to have kids. It's the only way the world is ever going to stop being such a colossal dumpster fire."

"What do you mean?" I laugh.

"Think about it. There are so many terrible, close-minded parents out there—like my dad—who are probably screwing up their kids for *life* while simultaneously creating an entirely new generation of terrible, close-minded people, who are going to go on and make their *own* generation of terrible, close-minded people. Etcetera, etcetera."

"So?"

"*So*, if sane, amazing, rational people *like us* don't have kids and teach them to be sane, amazing, rational human beings, then the terrible people are going to keep making the world a terrible place, and things will never get better."

"Okay . . . So you're saying we need to have children in order to save the world?"

"Basically."

"Wow."

"Plus, I'd just be an amazing dad."

Marcos leans forward to kiss me, which under any other circumstance would be the most adorable way to end this conversation. Unfortunately, there are three children sitting ten feet away, and the thought of even one of them telling their parents that they saw me sucking face with Marcos fills me with so much terror that, before I even know what I'm doing, I shove Marcos away—knocking him to the floor.

"Ow!"

Oh. My. God. What is wrong with me? That is not the appropriate response when your boyfriend tries to kiss you!

I jump to my feet to help Marcos up, but he won't take my hand. Mainly because he's too preoccupied moaning and rubbing his right elbow.

"Seriously, Connolly?" Marcos shakes his head then stares at me with a look that can only be described as 50 percent confusion, 50 percent anger, and 100 percent disappointment.

"Sorry!" I whisper, kneeling down beside him. "But the kids could've seen us!"

"So what if they had?"

So what if they had? Has he forgotten how much trouble we'll be in if *anyone* finds out about us? Flirtatious smiles and saucy winks might be one thing, but kissing in front of anyone who could expose us to our parents is absolutely out of the question. Does he really not see that?

"Is everything all right in here?"

Oh. Crap. A chill runs down my spine even before I turn around and see Reverend Foley and Mr. Price standing in the doorway. Foley's face is a mixture of confusion and concern, but Marcos's dad radiates suspicion.

Not that I blame him. I'm kneeling over his prostrate son, who's cradling a bruised arm while lying on the floor and staring at me like he doesn't even recognize me.

"We're fine!" I say, scrambling to my feet. "We were just horsing around."

"Yeah," Marcos agrees, though he barely looks at me. "We just got a little carried away."

"I hope you didn't hurt yourself," Foley says, stepping forward to look at Marcos's arm.

"No. I'm fine. It's nothing."

Foley nods, but Mr. Price looks even more annoyed than usual. "You were supposed to be looking after these kids, Marc, not goofing off."

"Sorry," he grumbles.

"Get your things," Mr. Price huffs. "Your mother is waiting in the car."

"I'm not done here." Marcos's voice is laced with defiance. He stares at his father with such barely concealed animosity that I swear the temperature drops twenty degrees. Even Foley looks uncomfortable.

"That's okay!" I blurt out. "I can handle these last couple of kids. You can go."

Marcos shoots me a look like I've just stabbed him in the back, but his father nods. "Thank you, Milo. Come on, Marc."

Marcos hesitates, like he's preparing to stand his ground. Then he shakes his head and storms out the door without a backward glance.

I spend the next half hour scrubbing marker stains out of the tables and vacuuming glitter out of the carpet while desperately trying *not* to think about how badly I messed up with Marcos. Not that that's even remotely possible. I'm literally the Worst Boyfriend in the World. I mean, somehow, in less than five minutes, I managed to betray Marcos not once but twice. First with the kiss, then with his dad.

But what choice did I have?

If we're going to have *any* sort of relationship, we have to be careful. That means keeping our parents *happy* and our romance *invisible*. And, yes, that sucks, but it's the truth. And there's nothing we can do about it.

I gather up a stack of discarded scrap paper and carry it over to the recycle bin. I'm just about to toss it when something in the pile catches my eye.

It's Marcos's sketch. The one he wouldn't let me see.

It's a portrait in pencil of a teenage boy with unruly hair and a quiet smile. The likeness is spot-on, but even so it still takes my brain a moment to fully understand what I'm seeing.

Draw your favorite thing in the whole entire world. That's what Marcos told the children. And he drew me.

29

Trouble in Paradise

"Hey."

"Hey."

Marcos and I are in the Crick parking lot. I got here early so I could talk to him before class and apologize for yesterday. Which is easier said than done given that he'll barely look at me.

"How's your elbow?"

"It's fine."

"Do you have a bruise?"

"No, it's just a little sore."

"I'm sorry."

Marcos shrugs.

"How are things with you dad? I hope I didn't get you into trouble."

"When it comes to my dad, I'm always in trouble."

"Was he angry?"

"He wasn't exactly pleased I was 'goofing off' at church."

"I'm sorry."

He shrugs again.

"No, Marcos, really. I'm really, *really* sorry."

Marcos sighs. And for the first time I hear myself the way he must. The endless, repetitive apologies that mean nothing because after three years I still have to make them.

"It's okay," he says.

But it's not. I can tell he's disappointed. *I'm* disappointed. I mean, I basically agreed to be his boyfriend, then the first moment he tried to act like said boyfriend, I shoved him away like he disgusted me.

I have to do better. Marcos *deserves* better. I just wish I knew how to give him that.

"I really liked the picture," I say.

"What picture?"

"The one you drew. Of me."

Marcos seems taken aback. "Oh. I completely forgot about that."

"I have it in my car. If you want it."

"No. That's okay. You can keep it."

A chill goes down my spine. What does *that* mean? Does he genuinely want me to have it, or does he really not care what happens to it? His tone is so curt and his face so expressionless, I honestly can't tell.

"Are you . . . Are you breaking up with me?"

For the first time, he looks at me. "What? *No.*"

"Are you sure?"

"Yes, Connolly, I'm sure. I'm not breaking up with you."

His words are reassuring even if his exasperated tone isn't exactly comforting. Still, I let out a huge sigh of relief. That is until he says, "I just . . ."

"Just what?" I ask, my body tensing.

Marcos looks torn. Like even he doesn't know what he's going to say.

"Look, I understand why you reacted the way you did. I'm not upset that you pushed me. I know you were scared. And I know you like me. I just wish sometimes you liked yourself."

"I like myself," I protest.

"Do you?"

I open my mouth to say yes, but the answer gets stuck in my throat.

"From what I've seen these last couple weeks, and from the way you talk about yourself in general, I don't think you do. I think you still think there's something wrong with you. And I think that 'something' is your feelings toward guys. Toward me."

"That's not true," I whisper. "I know I like boys."

"There's knowing it and there's accepting it. And I don't think you've accepted it."

"Yes, I have."

"Really?"

"*Yes.*"

"So if tomorrow some scientist said they'd invented a pill that could make you straight, you wouldn't take it?"

I'm about to say, "Of course not." But then I think about my parents and about how much easier my life would be and, in that hesitation, Marcos has his answer.

"You see?"

"Marcos, I want to be with *you*," I insist. My heart is racing. I need to fix this. I need to get through to him before things get any worse. "You have to believe me. I want to be with you more than anything in the world."

"I know you do. And I want to be with you. I just don't know what kind of future we have if I'm always going to be the part of your life that you're ashamed of."

I spend the rest of the week trying to remind myself that Marcos and I are *not* broken up. That I still have a boyfriend. A boyfriend I've massively disappointed to the point that he's questioning whether we have a future together. Which somehow feels worse than if we'd broken up.

I hate that I've let Marcos down. I hate that I've made him feel like a dirty secret. I hate that despite knowing exactly what the problem is I have no idea how to make things better. I mean, coming out isn't an option. For either of us. So what can I do? How do I prove to Marcos we have any sort of a future when most mornings I wake up barely knowing how to get through the day?

As for "liking myself," let's get real. That ship sailed long ago. It's currently at the bottom of the Atlantic. With the *Titanic*.

"Are you okay, sweetie?"

My mother's voice snaps me out of my funk, and I sit up in my bed to find her hovering in my doorway. I wonder how long she's been standing there, watching me mope in the dark. I don't even remember the sun going down.

"Yeah. I'm fine," I say as she flips on the lights.

"Well, dinner will be ready in a few minutes if you want to come downstairs and set the table?"

"Okay."

I don't get up and she doesn't leave.

"Everything okay at school today?"

"Yeah," I lie. "It was good. I'm just a little tired. Lots of homework."

"You're not feeling under the weather, are you?" She takes a step forward, her hand instinctively reaching out to touch my forehead.

"No, I'm fine. Really. I just needed a rest before dinner."

I've actually needed a rest before *and* after dinner for the last four days. My inability to fix my relationship with Marcos has basically left me with the desire to do nothing more than stare at the ceiling and feel sorry for myself.

"Okay. Well, if you feel yourself getting a cold, let me know. Flu season is starting soon. I don't want you getting sick."

"I will. I promise."

I force myself to smile, trying to look like the picture of teenage health. My mom smiles back, but just as she turns to go, her eyes catch on something on the far side of my room. I follow her gaze and realize with horror that sitting on my desk in open view is the portrait Marcos drew of me. Normally, I keep it rolled up in my closet, but today I was so depressed after school, I needed something to remind me of happier times. I must have forgotten to put it away.

"What's that?" my mom asks, walking over to my desk to get a closer look.

I force myself to stay calm. After all, there's nothing inherently suspicious about one boy drawing another.

"Just a picture."

"Oh, Milo, this is wonderful. We should get it framed. Who did it?"

"Just a friend."

"Vanessa?"

I consider lying, but there have been too many lies lately. And keeping track of them is exhausting.

"No," I say, trying to keep my voice even. "Marcos."

"Oh."

My mother stares at the picture in silence. I wait for her to say something. Anything. But she doesn't. She doesn't speak and she doesn't take her eyes off the portrait. Finally, after what feels like an eternity, she rolls up the paper and sets it down on my desk.

"I need to check on dinner."

30

How (Not) to Talk to Girls

By Friday the awkwardness between Marcos and me is palpable. He's never rude, but he's definitely a lot more reserved around me. I wouldn't call it cold so much as distant. Neither of us seems to have much to say to the other, and the one time I tried to hold his hand under the table at lunch, he found an excuse to pull away after a few seconds.

I haven't mentioned our fight to Van, but I can tell she knows something is wrong. She's been extra chipper all week, and ever since we sat down for lunch today, she's been peppering us with questions, trying to draw us out.

"You guys got any exciting plans this weekend?" she asks, clearly grasping at conversational straws. She must know we don't. I mean, Marcos is still grounded, and I'm boring.

I'm genuinely surprised, then, when Marcos turns to her with a slight shrug and says, "Yeah, actually, I do."

For a second my heart stops. Did my plan to win over Mrs. Price actually work? Is Marcos no longer grounded?

"I don't know if it qualifies as *exciting*," he clarifies with a sharp snort, "but tomorrow night my parents are taking me to the Reverend Rapture Revival."

Van's mouth drops. As does mine. *The Reverend Rapture Revival?* Is he joking?

Reverend Rapture (real name: Ernest Eugene Gallop) is one of those evangelical, fire-and-brimstone preachers who are always predicting the End of the World. Years ago, he started off with nothing more than twenty bucks and a soapbox on a street corner in Dallas. Then with a little showbiz pizzazz and an unprecedented willingness to exploit a national tragedy, his soapbox became a church, which in turn became Dallas/Fort Worth's largest megachurch, complete with stadium seating, jumbotrons, and pyrotechnics. This lasted until a few years ago when some sort of scandal with the IRS brought everything crashing down on Eugene's head. The Reverend lost his church and his millions, but not his need to perform or his desire for applause. Now he tours the country, booking the Reverend Rapture Revival into midsized sporting venues, community theaters, and civic centers as he carries on with his self-proclaimed mission to "Save America's Soul" before the impending Armageddon—which for fifty dollars a ticket he assures his followers is very, *very* near.

"That's insane," Van exclaims. "Why are your parents making you go to that? Everyone knows that guy's a total fraud. Even normal Christians know he's a fake. Right, Milo?"

I nod. All the Reverend does is spew hate, peddle doomsday predictions, and rant about the "homosexual menace." It makes me physically sick that anyone should be subjected to that kind of bigotry and vitriol. Especially someone like Marcos.

"Guess my dad hasn't given up on trying to put the fear of God in me," Marcos sighs, looking more miserable than I've ever seen him.

"Dude, that's rough," Van says, pulling him into a hug that only manages to make me feel worse.

Marcos is *my* boyfriend. It's *my* job to comfort him. And I can't even give him that because I'm still terrified of touching him in public lest anyone suspect we're an item. All I can do is sit here like a useless sack of regret and let him down over and over and over again. Because that's all I'm fit for. Because after all these years I, Milo Connolly, am still a coward.

"What the hell is going on here?" a voice suddenly barks beside me.

I look up to see Caleb standing over our table and staring at Van and Marcos in a bewilderment bordering on outrage.

Crap. I should've seen this coming.

Caleb has been giving Van and Marcos side-eye all week, and I can't say I'm surprised. Anyone watching the two them at lunch recently would totally assume Van and Marcos are dating. And that's kind of by design.

After the meteor incident, Van figured that if news did get out about Marcos being at the Atlantis dance, it'd be easier to convince our classmates of the story we'd concocted (i.e., Marcos got a flat tire on his way to meet Van for a normal heterosexual date) if the two of them were seen together as much as possible—especially at lunch. Marcos tried to tell Van that wasn't necessary—that he didn't care if people gossiped about him and that she'd already gone above and beyond the call of duty—but Van didn't want to take any chances. And, frankly, neither did I.

I mean, does it suck that most of the school has started to assume that my boyfriend and my best friend are dating? Totally. But if it keeps our classmates from suspecting the truth about Marcos and me, I figured it'd be worth the price. And in all fairness, up until ten seconds ago, the plan was working without a hitch.

"Well?" Caleb demands, huffing down at us.

"Well, *what*?" Van snaps. "I'm talking to my friend."

"Oh, is that what this is? 'Talking.' Come on, V, you're all over this guy. Have some self-respect."

Uh-oh . . .

"Excuse me?" In five seconds flat, Van is out of the booth and in Caleb's face. His eyes widen in fear, like a Chihuahua that's just realized it's taken on a pit bull, and I can't help cringing in my seat because Caleb Yates just made a Very Big Mistake.

"I didn't mean—"

"Fact number one: *you* do not control me."

"I know but—"

"Fact number two: *we* are not together."

"That's not—"

"Fact number three: even if we were together, that does not give you the right to tell me who I can and cannot talk to."

"I just want to know what's going on, V! Are you dating this guy or what?"

"Maybe! So what if I am? Maybe I finally got tired of waiting for losers like you to grow the eff up, so now I'm giving Marcos a shot. And if he can't give me what I want, maybe I'll move on to someone else. Maybe I'll start working my way through every guy at this school until I find someone who has his shit together and treats me with the respect I deserve. But whatever I do, you do not get a say in the matter. And if you ever—*ever*—hope to have *any* chance of being one of my many, many, *many* options ever again, then you will stop talking and walk away *right now*."

"But, V—"

"Walk. Away. Caleb."

Half of the cafeteria (including two lunch ladies) are staring at the teen soap opera unfolding at our booth. I can tell Caleb desperately wants to have the last word. But he must know that anything he says in the heat of the moment will only obliterate what's left of his chances to get back with Van, because after an excruciatingly long pause he mumbles a barely audible "sorry" and trudges away with his tail between his legs.

"Oh my god! That was awesome!" Marcos exclaims, erupting in laughter. It's such a relief to hear the pure, undiluted joy in his voice after the last couple days of gloom that I can't help laughing too.

"Okay, settle down," Van commands, sliding back into the booth with a barely concealed grin of triumph.

"Seriously, Silvera, that was *amazing*."

Marcos is right. It was amazing. Once again Van stood up for herself and she didn't give a damn who heard her or what people thought. And once again I find myself wishing I could be more like her.

Then again, maybe it's time to stop wishing and start doing.

I look at my friends, at Van and Marcos laughing with pride, and it strikes me once again how insanely lucky I am to have such people in my life. More than anything I want to be worthy of their friendship. Which means I need to stop doing what's easiest for me and start doing what's best for them. Both of them.

"Thanks for covering for us," I say to Van once our laughter has died down. "Again."

"Don't mention it."

"No, *really*, what you've been doing for Marcos and me has been really incredible. You're seriously the best friend anyone could wish for."

"I know. I'm aware of my awesomeness."

"Right, *but* what I'm trying to say is: if you wanted to stop pretending that you're dating Marcos and start getting lunch off campus again with your other friends, I hope you know that's okay. Marcos and I will be totally fine eating lunch on our own. Right, Marcos?"

Marcos looks at me in surprise. In fact, he's so surprised he almost chokes on his lemonade.

"Are you sure?"

I'm not—not completely—but I can't keep relying on Van to solve all our problems whenever life gets too difficult for me to handle. It's not fair to her. And it's not fair to Marcos.

Ever since he came back into my life, I've treated him like he's my dirty little secret—like something I'm ashamed of—and that has to stop. If I want to be with him then I need to *be* with him, and not just when it's easy or convenient for me. Marcos needs to be able to count on me no matter what. He needs to know I'm in this relationship 100 percent, and that I won't abandon him at the first sign of trouble. And if that eventually means coming out . . . Well, we'll get to *that*.

For now, though, I can at least give him this. It's a baby step, no question, but at least it's a step in the right direction.

"I'm sure," I say. "That is, of course, if it's okay with you?"

"Yeah. It's okay with me. But what if people start to talk?"

"Let them."

Marcos breaks into the most dazzling grin, and I see our whole future in his smile.

"You losers trying to get rid of me?" Van huffs in faux indignation.

"Yeah," I chuckle. "I didn't want to say anything earlier, but you've kind of been cramping our style. Marcos and I could really use some QMMT."

"QMMT?"

"Quality Milo and Marcos Time."

"Wow. Okay. My bad," Van laughs. "I mean, it would've been nice to have this information five minutes ago before I basically announced to the whole school that I was dating Marcos."

"Well, technically you said you were planning on dating everyone," Marcos corrects her. "So I guess now you can get a head start on that."

Van steals a tater tot off Marcos's tray and throws it at his face. "I hate you both so much I love you."

I laugh and something touches my hand under the table. I look down, and Marcos has laced his fingers through mine. He squeezes my hand, and I squeeze back, and the world seems full of possibilities.

I'm still riding that buzz of euphoria hours later when I sit down for dinner with my parents. In fact, I'm so caught up in my thoughts of Marcos and our future together that I completely miss when my mom asks if I have any plans for the weekend. She has to repeat the question twice, at which point I realize she's trying to tell me something.

"Sorry, Mom, what did you say?"

"I said, I hope you don't have any plans Saturday night because your father got us tickets."

"Tickets to what?"

"Honestly, Milo, haven't you heard a word I've been saying? To the Reverend Rapture Revival."

I drop my fork and it clatters against my plate, but my mom keeps talking. "Your father was talking to Mr. Price today, and Mr. Price seemed to really recommend it, so he decided to get us tickets."

My dad is staring at his plate of chicken parmesan as if he isn't part of this conversation. It's only then that I realize he hasn't said a word since we sat down. I don't think he's even looked at me.

I turn back to my mother, trying to understand why I feel like I've just walked into a trap. She shoots me a reassuring smile, but her voice sounds almost too casual as she takes a sip of her iced tea and says, "Won't that be fun?"

31

Repent for the End Is Near(er)!

If my worst nightmare were turned into a bad Broadway musical, it still wouldn't be half as garish or half as bizarre as the Reverend Rapture Revival. Sitting here with my parents in the packed bleachers of the Jackie Robinson Ballpark in Daytona and watching the opening pyrotechnics that are supposed to herald the arrival of the great Reverend himself, I'm shocked that anyone with an ounce of taste could find this melodramatic mishmash of high-tech sparklers and low-tech lasers to be a "holy" let alone entertaining experience. Then again this is Florida, the Birthplace of Bad Taste. I shouldn't be surprised such vulgar showboating is going over like gangbusters.

The crowd is riveted. And rapt. And white. Very, *very* white. Which is kind of ironic given the name of the stadium. Of course, POP leans pretty heavily in the Caucasian direction too, but at least Pastor Foley is aware that's a problem and is always trying to find new ways to make the church more inclusive.

Reverend Rapture, on the other hand, seems to have built his career by going in the opposite direction. In fact, his "church" might be the most exclusive church in America because as far as the Reverend is concerned, the only person guaranteed to get into Heaven is the Reverend. Everyone else is headed straight to the sulfurous pits of Hell, and his rallies are basically an aggrandized excuse for him to tell people so to their faces. You'd think that would limit his fan base but somehow his blistering message of humanity's unworthiness has no problem filling up stadiums across the country.

I scan the packed stands hoping to spot Marcos in the throngs of spectators, but so far, I haven't been able to find him. We saw the Prices briefly when we first entered the stadium, shuffling past vendors hawking Reverend Rapture CDs, DVDs, and T-shirts. But Marcos pretended not to notice me, and neither his parents nor mine made any attempt to say hello. Which is definitely *not* a good sign.

I've spent the last twenty-four hours freaking out about what the Prices might've told my parents. It must have been sufficiently incriminating to warrant them dragging me here. Maybe Mrs. Price clocked something between Marcos and me the night we had dinner? Or maybe Mr. Price realized something wasn't right when he caught us fighting at church? I don't know.

I do know that the only thing giving me a shred of hope right now is the fact that my parents seem be acting as if this is all utterly normal. They haven't accused me of anything or asked any probing questions about Marcos. It's possible they really have no agenda for coming here tonight other than a sincere desire to see the show. But I can't shake the feeling that there's something about this whole evening that feels *premeditated*.

"Oh, that's impressive," my mom coos as the opening fireworks build to a climax. The accompanying music reaches an earsplitting crescendo, and the stadium lights cut out, plunging the whole ballpark into darkness.

The crowd goes silent.

Then a single spotlight shines down on a makeshift stage that's been erected over the pitcher's mound, and the stadium bursts into thunderous applause. For there, standing at his pulpit in all his apocalyptic glory, is the Reverend.

He looks about fifty, with a thick mane of luxurious silver hair that oddly complements his baby blue–sequined suit and showbiz swagger. For all his sins—and they are *numerous*—there is something about the man that's eerily magnetic. When he throws his arms up into the air, the entire audience jumps to their feet. Even my parents (who are not demonstrative people) are forced to rise. As am I. Not that I want to. But if a crowd can get this worked up over some roman candles and a techno rendition of "Carmina Burana," then there's no telling what they'll do to someone who doesn't treat their Glorious Leader with the total adoration he deserves.

"Pray with me!" the Reverend commands, his voice booming over the stadium's loudspeakers.

We bow our heads, and the Reverend launches into an opening prayer that manages to simultaneously castigate us for being unworthy sinners *and* praise us for having the foresight to buy tickets to tonight's show—a clear indication we truly hope to be saved. The crowd gives a collective "Amen!" at which point the Reverend doesn't waste any time getting right to the Fire-and-Brimstone Portion of the evening.

General remarks about the End of Days being near (though an exact date isn't specified) give way to more specific political tirades about the moral character of our country. He reviles the "Godless Democrats in Washington" who want to "drive the Lord from our schools and Christ from our capital as they peddle every known perversion in their evil attempt to destroy the soul of our great nation."

I don't know what alternate reality the Reverend is living in, but to hear him talk, you'd think that all liberals want to do is turn America into a modern-day Sodom and Gomorrah, complete with mandatory abortion and devil worship. It's so utterly preposterous I can't believe anyone who's ever read a newspaper would believe a word he's saying. Yet as I look around, I see rapt faces, nodding along in utter sincerity, as if they were receiving the gospel truth.

It makes my blood boil.

I mean, the whole reason I believe in God—the whole reason I'm proud to call myself a Christian—is because it's an entire belief system dedicated to helping human beings become their best self so they, in turn, can help each other, and make the world a better place. Or at least that's what it *should* be.

The Reverend, though, is just using religion to make outrageous claims so he can whip up hate and tear people apart. When he praises the "real Americans and real Christians who are fighting the war to redeem our country for Jesus" the crowd around me bursts into applause, and I've never felt more alone or more disgusted in all my life.

"Yes, we *shall* overcome!" the Reverend shouts, his voice trembling with passion. "*But* we must be wary! Victory will be ours but only if we are vigilant and heed God's warnings. And it seems to me, friends, that recently God has been sending the people of Florida quite a few warnings."

The hairs on the back of my neck stand up, and the disgust in my stomach turns to dread. Why do I have the feeling I'm not going to like where this is going?

"In fact, just a couple of weeks ago, a meteor—an enormous space rock—fell from the sky and landed on your doorstep."

Oh no.

"Let that sink in. A rock *from the heavens* came hurtling through space and crashed in a fiery explosion right here in your fair city. A rock, I should point out, that no one—not one *single* person—saw coming. These so-called scientists have got about a million satellites zooming over our heads and about another million telescopes pointed straight up at the sky. But not a single one of them—not a *single* one— saw this rock coming. Why is that?"

Please don't say God, please don't say God, please don't say God . . .

"Because *God* was in that rock."

Kill. Me. Now.

"That rock was God's celestial messenger! It was a wake-up call. To turn away from sin! And fornication! And depravity! Because God has been watching the people of Florida. He has seen into your hearts and into your souls and He knows there is sin within! And He has come to *stomp* it out!"

(More thunderous applause.)

"Now some of you might be thinking, 'Reverend, how do you

know all this?' Well, folks, sometimes God works in mysterious ways. And sometimes He makes Himself *crystal* clear. This rock of God, where did it fall? Did it fall in the ocean? Or in some empty field? No! God's rock fell on a school. But not just any school!"

No, no, no, no, no, no, no, no, no, no—

"This school was hosting a dance—a dance for *certain people* whom the 'politically correct' call the LGBT, but for whom the Bible has a much different name."

The crowd boos, and their collective vehemence is so intense I have to resist the urge not to hide under my seat.

"That's right! A school that you pay for with your hard-earned tax dollars! A school where you entrust your children to become decent young men and women! *That* is where God hurled His fiery messenger! Because that is the school that turned its back on God!"

I'm going to be sick.

"That school encouraged men to lie with men, and women to lie with women! It encouraged perversity and unnatural acts! And God said NO! God smote this school—this school that was nothing more than a playground for Satan. He rained down His fiery justice as a warning to others who would dare to follow the Devil into Hell. So I ask you, friends, now that you have seen the power of the Lord, when the Devil comes a-knocking, will you let him into your homes?"

"No!" the crowd shouts.

"Will you let him into your schools?"

"No!"

"Will you let him into your hearts?"

"No!"

"Brothers, sisters, pray with me!"

The crowd bows their heads in silence, but this time I refuse to genuflect. My cheeks are burning, and I'm so filled with rage that I'm shaking. Because for the first time in my life I know what it's like to truly hate someone. And I *hate* the Reverend.

I hate him because he's a fraud and a narcissist and a bully. I hate him because he's whipping up this crowd into a frenzy of self-righteous bigotry. I hate him because even though he hasn't said his name, I know that with every word he utters, he's hurting the one person I care most about in the whole entire world. He's hurting Marcos. And that is unforgivable.

I don't care if it's petty. I don't care if it's un-Christian. I hate him for trying to make someone as amazing as Marcos feel small and dirty and shameful. I hate him for making *me* feel small and dirty and shameful. And for making Orion and every other kid at that dance—and every kid who *wishes* they were at that dance—feel like there's something wrong with them. I hate him because he's turning parents against their kids, and kids against themselves. I hate him for smashing up people's hearts and then gloating over the broken pieces. I hate him for the lives he's ruined.

But mostly I hate him because right now a part of me can't help wondering, *What if he's right?*

It makes me sick to consider it. It feels like a betrayal to even entertain the possibility. But at the same time, *a lot* of really weird stuff has happened since Marcos came back into my life. The sinkhole on the first day of school. The blackout after Ashleigh's party. The hailstorm at the beach.

The meteor.

Each time I told myself it was just a coincidence. That it's *all* been a coincidence. But at the center of every impossible thing that's happened, I also know that there has been one consistent and common denominator—one thing that connects every single episode—and that is Marcos and me.

We are the only two people in all of Florida who have been directly involved with all four incidents, and I'd be lying if I said I hadn't noticed the connection before. The night of the meteor, I felt like we were being warned. But I pushed those fears aside. All of them. The nagging thoughts. The doubts. The guilt.

I assumed I was being paranoid, that I was just looking for excuses to sabotage my relationship with Marcos. It never occurred to me that all these freak occurrences could actually *mean* something. That they could be messages.

It's inconceivable and yet . . .

What if these coincidences aren't coincidences? What if they really are signs from God?

No.

I refuse to believe it. The Reverend can't be right. I mean, yes, I believe in God. And, yes, I believe there are certain rules He expects us to live by. But how can my feelings for Marcos be so wrong—so sacrilegious—that God Himself has finally decided to come out of retirement and make Himself known after several *thousand* years just to break us up? It's absurd. More than absurd, it's *impossible*.

The only problem is I can't think of any other explanation.

Thunder booms in the distance and my entire body shivers. At first, I think it's just another of the Reverend's over-the-top sound effects, but then I look up and see the storm clouds gathering on the horizon. Is this another sign?

My stomach does a somersault, and I feel the fish I had for dinner trying to swim its way back up my throat. I'm starting to have trouble breathing, and my shirt is soaked with sweat even though there's a sharp breeze whipping through the ballpark.

I think I'm having a panic attack.

Thankfully, the Reverend announces it's time for an intermission and, as the crowd leaps to their feet in an earsplitting ovation, I barrel past my startled parents and make a run for it. More than anything I want to get out of this stadium and as far away from the Reverend as humanly possible. But I can't. If I disappear now, it'll only raise more questions later. Still, I need to be alone. I need to *think*.

I race to the nearest men's room and I lock myself in the first empty stall. My hands are trembling, and my knees are weak, but at least I'm alone. For one satisfying minute the only sound I hear is my own hysterical breathing. Then the bathroom fills with laughter and chatter and flushing, and I have to work twice as hard to block it all out.

Stay calm, Milo. You can do this. You cannot fall apart. Just get through tonight and you'll never have to do anything like this ever again. Just keep it together and breathe, Milo. Just. Breathe.

I put my head between my knees and wait for my heart to stop racing. Ten minutes pass. Then another ten. Through the concrete walls I hear the deafening swell of organ music. The second half of the show is starting. There's a flurry of flushing, and a few seconds later the men's room is blissfully still.

I know I have to go back to my seat, but I can't bear the thought of listening to any more of the Reverend's sermon. There's no way I won't be sick. But if I don't go back, my parents will know something's wrong, and I can't give them any more reasons to be suspicious.

I wipe down my brow with toilet paper and take a deep breath. When I'm finally ready, or as ready as I can be, I open the stall door—and come face-to-face with Marcos.

He's standing by the sink, hands in his suit pockets, staring at me with a sad smile on his face. He must have been waiting for me.

"Hey," he says.

"Hey."

"You're freaking out, aren't you?"

"Aren't *you*?"

Our voices carry, so I take a few steps closer and drop to a whisper in case there's anyone outside who might be listening. I'm terrified of being caught with Marcos. And in a men's room no less.

"You need to go back to your seat," I hiss. "What are you even doing here?"

"I saw you practically knock your dad over. I wanted to make sure you're okay."

"Well, I'm *not*."

"Yeah. I can see that. Tell me what's wrong."

"What's *wrong*?" Is he really asking me that? Did he not just hear everything the Reverend said? "What if he's *right*?"

"Who?"

"The Reverend! What if God *has* been sending us messages, and everything that's happened over the last month really *is* our fault?"

"You can't be serious."

Marcos is looking at me like I've lost what's left of my mind. And maybe I have. But I also can't ignore the evidence. Not anymore.

"Think about it. The sinkhole, the blackout, the hailstorm, the meteor? We were together for all of them."

"We're also together every day at school and nothing happens."

"But we don't do anything. We don't touch."

"We hold hands at lunch."

"Only for a few seconds."

"So, what, God has a five-second rule?"

"Maybe!"

"Milo—"

"How else do you explain everything?" I shout, my voice rising in desperation. I know I'm being irrational and illogical, but so far rationality and logic have gotten me squat. Maybe some good old-fashioned hysteria is exactly what's called for. "Every time we're together something terrible happens. If that's not God, what is it?"

"Look," Marcos sighs, using that tone he adopts when he's trying to be as patient with me as he can, "I know things have been strange and a lot of weird crap has happened, but it's just a *coincidence*. God isn't real. And even if He were, do you really think He spends his time screwing with the weather just to punish horny teenagers? Think about how *ridiculous* that sounds. I mean, yeah, maybe if we were the *only* two gay people in *all* of Florida and God wanted to make an example of us, *maybe* there *might* be an *infinitesimal* chance the Reverend could be right. But we're not. There are hundreds if not thousands of people like us all over the state. All over the country!"

"I know."

"So why would God be picking on us?"

"Maybe I'm the worst."

The words hang in the air like the terrible confession they are. And for the first time since I've known him, Marcos looks angry. Truly and terribly angry. He takes a step forward, and for a second, I think he's going to yell at me. Instead, he grabs me by my shoulders and forces me to look at him.

"Don't ever say that. Do you hear me? There is nothing wrong with you. With either of us. We have as much right to be in love as anyone else on this stupid planet, and I refuse to let some pompous, bigoted, tax-evading asshole tell me otherwise!"

Wait. What did he just say?

"Are you listening to me?"

"In love?"

"What?"

"You said . . . You said we have just as much right as anyone else to be *in love*."

"Oh." Marcos stares at the floor and nervously fixes his hair. He's embarrassed, and for a second, I'm sure he's going to deny what he said.

"Yeah, okay, I love you, all right?" he says, finally looking up at me and releasing an exasperated sigh. "But it's *not* a big deal. You don't need to freak out or anything. I know you need to take things slow and you're not ready for—"

"I love you too."

The words are out of my mouth, and I don't regret them. Because they're true. They've been true for the last three years. And regardless of sinkholes or meteors, I'm done pretending they're not.

"You do?" he asks, his facing breaking into a grin.

"Yeah."

"You're not just saying it because I said it?"

I throw my arms around him, and he holds me against his chest, practically crushing me in his embrace. *We're in love.* I want to live inside this moment. I want time to stop. In this sliver of happiness, it's almost possible to believe that Marcos and I are the only two people in the universe—that *this* is our happy ending.

Then the bleating horns of the Reverend's gaudy extravaganza scream through the men's room walls and reality reassembles itself around us.

"What do we do now?" I ask, my heart sinking with despair.

Marcos, though, is ready with his answer. "I'm going to prove to you once and for all that God doesn't care if two boys fall in love."

"How are you going to do that?"

Marcos smiles. He's got that look in his eyes—the same look he gave me right before he asked me to that wonderful/disastrous/life-changing dance. He's about to suggest something reckless. And dangerous. And impossible.

And I know before he says another word that whatever it is, I'm going to say yes.

"Are you sure you want to do this?" Marcos asks for the third time as we step out onto the infield.

At his makeshift pulpit over the pitcher's mound, the Reverend is excoriating the crowd to confess their sins and be reborn in Christ's love. Anyone who wants can come down from the bleachers and kneel before the Reverend where he will—with an over-the-top showmanship that would make Elmer Gantry blush—drive out their demons and set them on the righteous path. He calls it the Gathering of the Saved and it's one of the reasons he can charge fifty bucks per ticket. He's offering instant absolution to anyone willing to pay for it.

There are already about thirty-five people kneeling in a semicircle around the stage, but the Reverend is still haranguing the stadium, demanding more sinners come forward. He probably has a quota he likes to hit for maximum effect.

I look over my shoulder, back at the stands, and see my parents watching us. I still haven't answered Marcos's question, so when he asks again if I'm sure I want to do this, I take his hand and nod. How can I not? Only yesterday I vowed to start stepping up and prioritizing our relationship. And as a master plan this one certainly checks all the boxes.

Come out to our parents? Check.

Prove God doesn't punish gay people with freak acts of nature? Check.

Show the Reverend what we think of him and his agenda? Check.

I can't believe what I'm about to do. I can't believe the boy who spent the last seventeen years hiding from the world is about to make himself the center of attention in the most public way possible. But then I never thought I'd have someone like Marcos in my life. He almost makes it easy to be brave. Because everything I'm about to do I'm doing for us—so we have a future. And that is absolutely worth fighting for.

Marcos and I stop directly in front of the Reverend's pulpit. There are about seventy-five people kneeling on the grass now, heads bowed in prayer. The wind has picked up, giving the ceremony an apocalyptic flair, especially when combined with the ominous thunderclouds looming overhead. The Reverend certainly has all the ingredients to put on one heck of a show. I just hope he's ready to share the spotlight.

Marcos turns to me, squeezes my hand, and asks one last time if I'm ready.

I nod. And we kiss.

We kiss in the infield of the Jackie Robinson Ballpark.

We kiss as what feels like the world's largest spotlight glares down on us in all our teenage glory.

We kiss in front of four thousand shocked Christians, two very surprised sets of parents, and one apoplectic reverend.

The stadium unleashes a collective gasp. In fairness, though, I can't be sure if it's in response to our kiss or to what happens immediately after. Which is a lightning bolt.

A lightning bolt that strikes the Reverend's wooden stage and starts a fire that quickly consumes the infield before spreading toward the bleachers.

"Oh my god," Marcos gasps, grabbing my hand and pulling me in the direction of the fleeing crowd. "Milo, run!"

Ten minutes later Marcos and I stand in the parking lot surrounded by thousands of speechless spectators and watch as the Jackie Robinson Ballpark burns to the ground.

PART IV

32

Good News, Bad News

The good news is no one is hurt in the fire. The bad news is my life is over.

I don't think I have words to describe what I'm feeling in the aftermath of the revival. Shock, definitely. Horror, totally. Complete emotional, spiritual, and metaphysical dread? Check, check, and triple check. But there's also something else. Something new. Something I don't think I've ever quite fully experienced before.

If I had to give it a name, I think I'd call it hopelessness.

The drive home from the (now nonexistent) Jackie Robinson Ballpark is the longest and most excruciating drive of my life. I've never seen my parents so quiet. I keep hoping they'll break down and yell at me because I know the longer this silence lasts, the worse things are going to be for me. But by the time we pull into our garage, they still haven't said a word.

We pass into the house like mourners arriving at a funeral. Instinctively, I start to head to my room, but when the staircase creaks under the weight of my first step, my father's voice booms behind me.

"Not so fast. Living room. Now."

I do as he says. I sit on the sofa. Before anyone has a chance to speak, though, our landline rings and my parents dash to the kitchen to answer it, leaving me alone to stare at the carpet in soul-crushing dread.

What have I done?

I thought my life got knocked off course when a meteor slammed into it. But this? This feels so much worse. Because there is *no* coming back from this. Not for me. And certainly not for Marcos.

Oh God . . . Marcos . . .

Of all the horrible things that happened tonight—having to sit through the Reverend's hate-filled sermon; watching a ballpark named after a beloved sports legend burn to the ground; seeing my parents pull away from me in disgust—the worst, the absolute *worst*, was the look on Marcos's face after the fire.

If my parents had the look of people who'd been betrayed by their only son, Marcos looked like someone who'd been betrayed by the whole entire universe. Before we stepped out onto that field, he had been so sure of himself. So confident. He'd looked like someone who could take on the world and win. But after the ballpark went up in flames, he didn't look sure of anything. Marcos looked scared. Not of the fire or the Reverend or even of his parents.

Marcos looked scared of the truth.

And the truth is that no matter how impossible it may seem, or how illogical it sounds, God *is* punishing us. There's no other way to explain what happened. A righteous if bombastic minister was attempting to bring lost souls into grace, and Marcos and I thumbed our noses at him and at every other believer sitting in those stands.

We acted out. We defied God. And God finally had enough.

Can you blame Him? He's basically been warning us for the last month to change our ways, but did we listen? No. We've been too horny and stubborn to see the truth. But our eyes are open now. Mine and Marcos's.

Right before the Prices whisked Marcos away, he looked at me from the back of his father's minivan. It was just for a second, but it was enough. Marcos was defeated. Broken. Done.

And so am I.

I have no idea how much time passes waiting on the sofa, but when I finally look up, my parents are standing over me, their faces long and exhausted with disappointment. Especially my mom. Some people look beautiful when they cry. Usually in movies, where they somehow manage to look both tragic and glamorous. My mom is not such a crier. When she cries, her eyes grow red, her skin turns blotchy, and her whimpers sound like a drowning dog. It's physically hard to look at her.

My dad, on the other hand, looks simultaneously weary and offended—like a firefighter who's spent the day putting out burning buildings only to come home and find his son playing with matches.

"That was the Prices," he informs me. "They want you to stay away from Marcos. You're not to see him or call him or have any contact with him. Is that clear?"

I nod. What else can I do? The events of tonight have made it crystal clear what happens when Marcos and I are together.

"Well?" my dad barks impatiently. "Is there anything you'd care to say for yourself?"

The question throws me. I've been so preoccupied with worrying about what my parents will say to me—about me—that it didn't even occur to me that I'd be given the chance to explain myself. I'm not even sure I *can* explain, but I know I might not get an opportunity like this again, so rather than waste it with evasions or excuses, I tell them the truth.

I tell them about Marcos and Bible camp, and the first day of school and the sinkhole, and Ashleigh's party and the blackout, and the beach and the hail, and our first date and the meteor. I'm not sure how long I talk. A couple of times I have to stop and catch my breath because I'm crying so hard, and by the time I finish, my face is covered in tears. I guess if I've inherited anything from my mom, it's that I too am not a beautiful crier.

"I'm sorry," I sputter when I've finally run out of things to say. Then I say it again. Over and over. "I'm sorry, I'm sorry, *I'm sorry.*"

I keep saying it because maybe, if I say it enough, I'll be able to ward off whatever horrible thing is about to happen. Because something horrible *is* going to happen. My parents' heartbreak is palpable. It permeates every inch of the room. They're both staring at me like I'm someone they no longer recognize. Like I'm some dangerous animal they've let into their home. Like I'm something to be afraid of.

I'd give anything for them not to look at me like that.

"Please still love me," I say.

My father sighs, and my mother stifles a sob. They both look as if they've aged twenty years, and I'm the cause. This is what my secrets and my selfishness have done. This is the price of my sins. I've broken my family.

"It's late," my dad sighs. "Go on up and get to bed."

I nod and make my way to the stairs even though I'm all too aware that my parents still haven't said a word about what they're thinking or what they're planning to do about me. Maybe that will come tomorrow. Maybe they need time to process everything that's happened.

Or maybe they don't say anything because there's nothing to say. Because there are no words that could ever redeem me for what I've done.

I undress for bed and, as I do, I realize I still have my phone. In all the insanity of tonight, my parents forgot to confiscate it. I immediately check to see if I have any messages from Marcos, though I know it's impossible even before my phone confirms it. My next impulse is to call him. To make sure he's okay.

But I don't.

I can't risk getting Marcos into any more trouble with his parents. They've told me to keep away and for now I have to do what they say. Even if it breaks my heart.

Besides, I don't need to talk to Marcos to know he's definitely *not* okay. However bad things are for me—however hopeless I feel in this moment—I know things are a hundred times worse for him. I mean, his dad grounded him for a month because he thought he was sneaking around with Van. What's the punishment going to be for hooking up with a boy?

I try to tell myself that Mrs. Price will be sympathetic. After all, she's got a gay brother. And she seemed so warm and reasonable that night we all had dinner. I know she loves her son.

But I also know Mr. Price has a way of steamrolling his wife to get what he wants. And if Mr. Price has his way, then Marcos's life is about to become a living hell.

33

Bad News, Worse News

"Milo," my mother calls, knocking on my bedroom door. "We're going to be late for church."

I look at my phone and see it's almost nine. I must have slept through my alarm. Which doesn't surprise me. I spent all night worrying about Marcos and dreading what his father might do to him. Every time I closed my eyes, images of Marcos being carted off to a military school or thrown out on the street flashed across my mind. It was only when the sun started coming up that I was finally able to nod off for a few hours.

"Milo?"

I drag myself out of bed and open my door, but my mom is already making her way downstairs. I take a quick shower and dress, and when I head to the kitchen, I find a plate of sausage and scrambled eggs waiting on the table.

"Eat quick. We leave in ten minutes." My mother is in the middle of washing dishes, but she dries her hands and leaves the kitchen as soon as I sit. She still can't look at me. She can't even bear to be in the same room as me.

I'd hoped when I woke up this morning that a part of me might feel some sense of relief that I'd finally told my parents the truth about myself. But I don't. My problems are still mine. I still feel the weight of them crushing down on me. Only now they're also crushing my parents.

I stare at the breakfast growing cold in front of me and wonder if this is what I can expect going forward: to be fed and housed and taken to church, but only out of obligation. Not love.

I've forfeited the right to love.

For the first time since I can remember, I'm dreading church. I know the Prices will be there, and I honestly don't know how I'll face them. But at least I'll get to see Marcos. Obviously, we won't be allowed to speak to each other, but if I could just confirm with my own eyes that he's all right—if I could just have *that*—then maybe the rest of my life wouldn't be utterly unbearable.

Of course, I'm so on edge, I'm pretty sure that if I do see Marcos I'm either going to burst into tears or faint. For that reason alone, I'm surprised my parents are so insistent we go to service. Then again, if there was ever a time that the Connolly family needed the spiritual guidance of their community, it's today. Maybe, also, there's something to be said for the comfort of routine. Of being able to pretend, if only for an hour, that nothing has changed. That I didn't just upend our entire family. That we're okay.

"Just so you know," my father says as we pull into the POP parking lot, "it's all over the news."

I assume he means the fire. Of course everyone's going to be talking about that. How often does a beloved ballpark burn to the ground? But as we make our way across the parking lot, I notice that heads are turning all around us to catch a glimpse of us.

No, correction: heads are turning to catch a glimpse of *me*. And then it hits me. "It's all over the news" doesn't just mean the fire.

I stop in my tracks a few feet from the church entrance. Families I've known for years—people I've prayed next to all my life—are staring at me with an unconcealed mixture of shock and revulsion. Of course they've heard the news. Some of them were probably even there in person to witness my Epic Coming-Out Fail.

How did I not see this coming?

"You wanted people to know," my father whispers in my ear. "Well, they know."

He puts his hand on my back and, with a little pressure, guides me into the church like Daniel being dragged into the lion's den. I do my best to ignore the whispering but, once inside, the scandalized stares of disgust are so much harder to escape that I can't help thinking I'd be better off with lions.

We take our seats in our pew, which is (unsurprisingly) emptier than usual, and wait for service to start. Despite the forced smiles on my parents' faces, I can tell they're as uncomfortable as I am. In fact, I'm so uncomfortable, it takes me a full minute to realize there's something different about the way we're seated today.

Normally, my mother likes to sit between my father and me. She calls it her Love Sandwich. Today, though, I'm the one in the middle. And from the defensive looks that flare across my parents' faces whenever anyone gets too close, I know it's not an accident. My parents are deliberately shielding me from the rest of the congregation.

They're protecting me.

I barely have time to digest the meaning of this simple act of kindness when the organ strikes up, and we're on our feet, fumbling our way through the opening hymn. The song ends, and Reverend Foley takes his place at the pulpit. We wait for his customary pronouncement of "Let us pray" to signal it's time to bow our heads and move forward with the service, but Foley is silent.

He stares out at his flock, quietly taking in the whole of his congregation, almost as if he's reminding himself that there are actual people within these walls. Then he turns his gaze to my family and smiles.

It's a small smile, nothing flashy, but it's enough to signal to the entire congregation that, yes, he's heard the news and, yes, he's still glad we came.

My parents visibly relax. I do too. That is, until Foley's gaze wanders from our pew to the Prices' pew—which is empty.

Foley catches himself and blushes. He didn't intend to draw so obvious a connection between our two families, but it's impossible not to. We're linked in shame for all eternity.

"Let us pray," he announces a little too quickly.

The congregation bows their heads, but my eyes stay glued on the Prices' empty pew. I've been so distracted by my parents and by my own worries, I hadn't even noticed that Marcos and his family weren't here.

Where are they?

After my night of sleepless dreams, all I can think is that my worst nightmares are coming true. That at this very moment, the Prices are disowning their son or shipping him off to God knows where.

What other explanation is there?

I mean, if the Prices of all people are skipping church, then . . .

Anything is possible.

As soon as I get home, I slip my phone out from its hiding place under my bed and check for messages. I know it's stupid to think that Marcos might still have access to his phone, that his parents haven't confiscated it along with his laptop and any other device he might use to contact me, but that doesn't stop me from hoping for a miracle.

I know he and I can't be together. I know any chance of a relationship between us is over and that my one priority going forward has to be getting right with God and my parents. But I also know I'm going out of my mind with worry.

If God would just give me a sign that Marcos is okay—or is *going* to be okay—then I swear I'd stay away from him and not even think about him for the rest of my life. I would. I mean it. I would make that deal right here and now *if* I knew Marcos was safe.

But I don't have any messages from Marcos. All I have are ten missed calls and three increasingly distraught voice mails from Van.

> Message one (Sunday, 12:05 a.m.): "Hey, it's me. Um, I know it's super late, but I just saw the news. Can you call me back when you get this? I just want to make sure you and Marcos are all right. I'll be up all night so—yeah—call me."

> Message two (Sunday, 7:32 a.m.): "Hey, me again. I realize things are probably crazy right now. Your parents

must be freaking out, and I am so, so sorry this is happening to you. But please, dude, call me back when you get this. I just want to make sure you're okay. Also, please know I am here for you if you need anything. Anything at all. Okay? Okay. Call me."

Message three (Sunday, 11:01 a.m.): "Hey, I don't know if you're getting my messages or if your parents have confiscated your phone. If they have and they're listening to this then, Mr. and Mrs. Connolly, please don't be upset with Milo. He's an amazing person, and I know he's got to be going through hell right now, so please just be there for him and try to understand him and tell him everything is going to be okay because it will be okay. Okay?

"Okay. So. That's all I have to say to your parents. If you are getting my messages, then call me back! Also, do yourself a favor and don't go online. I don't want to freak you out, but apparently a bunch of people were filming the revival last night, so there's a ton of footage of you and Marcos all over the internet.

"People are kind of losing their shit over it. So maybe stay offline for a while. Like forever. Kidding. Sort of. Um. Okay. If you get this, call me back. And if you can't call me back, I'll meet you and Marcos in the parking lot tomorrow morning before school. We'll go inside together. I won't leave your sides. It'll be all right. I promise. Okay. Bye, loser. I love you."

I don't call Van back. I don't go online. I don't even go downstairs when my mother calls me for lunch. My stress-activated off switch has been flipped, and all I want is to crawl into bed and sleep for the next one thousand years.

I know I should be freaking out. I know by tomorrow morning there won't be a single person at Crick or in the entire city of Port Orange who hasn't heard about Marcos and me. But my body and my brain have reached their limit.

I close my eyes and, the second my head hits my pillow, I'm out.

34

The Van Strategy

As promised, Van is waiting for me in the parking lot before school. I deliberately time my arrival so that we can just make it from my car to first period trigonometry before the tardy bell rings. That gives us zero time for any meaningful discussion, but it also means zero time for anyone to mess with me. And let's be real: people are going to mess with me. I didn't just creep out of the closet over the weekend. I exploded. With flames. I'm literally a flaming homosexual.

"Have you seen Marcos?" I ask. It's the first question out of my mouth as soon as Van releases me from her viselike hug.

"No. Not yet. I've been waiting here for the last half hour, and I haven't seen his parents drop him off."

I think about the Prices' empty pew, and a sinking feeling opens up in the pit of my stomach.

"But," Van adds quickly, "my friend Arianna—from the soccer team—she lives a couple houses down from the Prices, so I asked her to keep her eyes open, and she told me she saw Marcos putting out the trash this morning. So *that's* good. I mean, at least we know he's alive and his parents haven't done anything crazy like ship him off to Siberia."

She's right. There is something strangely comforting in the thought of Marcos doing something so mundane as chores. Maybe things aren't as bad in the Price household as I'd let myself imagine. Though if that were the case, why isn't he here?

"Maybe his parents are letting him skip school today?" Van suggests, reading my mind or maybe just the panic on my face. "You know, letting him lie low? He hasn't been answering any of my calls, but I'll keep texting him and try to find out what I can. Okay?"

The first warning bell rings before I can answer, and Van takes my hand. "You ready?"

"Not really."

Van pulls me into another hug—this one even tighter than before—and I force myself to smile.

Then it's time to face the music.

As we slide into our desks in the back of the trigonometry classroom, it doesn't take a genius to realize my secret is out. Half of my classmates break into knowing smirks while the other half look genuinely confused as to why I would come to school today. Any human being with an ounce of self-preservation would be home right now furiously googling boarding schools on the other side of the planet.

Thankfully, the second Ms. Müller calls for order, the class falls in line. Müller's one of those old-school disciplinarians who openly mourn for the days when teachers were permitted to "smack some sense into a student." Normally, her no-nonsense brand of teaching earns her the distinction of being the least-beloved instructor at Crick, but today her ability to silence a room with a glare makes her my guardian angel.

I spend the next hour obsessing about Marcos, trying to convince myself that his absence from school today might somehow possibly be a good thing. I mean, with him at home, there's no risk of us running into each other and inadvertently doing anything that might cause God to unleash another one of His monumental disasters. So that's good.

And who knows? Maybe Van's right. Maybe the Prices are actually trying to be protective parents by letting their son stay home until things blow over. Maybe in a few days, once everything settles down, Marcos will be back like nothing ever happened.

After all, this wouldn't be the first time Marcos "disappeared" and I drove myself to distraction suspecting people of nefarious motives when the reality turned out to be something totally simple and totally explainable. I can't let myself spiral like I did at camp. I have to hold it together. After all, there's still a chance that things might not be as bleak as they seem.

Of course, the only way I'll know that for sure is if I get to talk to Marcos. Which means, despite everything I've just said, I really, really, *really* hope he *is* at school today. It might increase our chances of being taken out by a typhoon or volcano or whatever else God decides to throw at us, but at least I would know that Marcos is okay.

First period ends, and I have no idea where the time has gone. What I do know is that I want to get out of this class before anyone decides to say something to me, but Van motions for me to stay in my seat.

"Wait until everyone else leaves," she whispers, staring down my classmates until we're the last two people left in the classroom. She must have a strategy for getting me through this day, and I suspect a large part of that strategy involves me interacting with my classmates as little as humanly possible.

Once we're in the hallway, though, there's no getting away from the catcalls and whispers. Van looks ferocious enough to kill anyone who gets too close, and a couple of times I'm actually afraid she's going to throw a punch, but for the most part people are keeping their distance.

Van walks me all the way to the Spanish classroom, even though it's on the other side of the campus and doing so will make her late for gym. I'm already dreading what will happen once she's not around to protect me. Without her I'm going to be a total sitting duck.

But instead of depositing me at my desk and leaving me to the mercy of my fellow classmates, Van marches me over to her former *Crucible* costar and says, "Okay, stick with Ashleigh. You've got Critical Thinking together after this, so Ashleigh will walk you there and then she'll walk you to the parking lot for lunch. We're going off campus today. No discussion."

My mind is struggling to keep up with everything she just said. I have so many questions, but the only one I can think to ask is, "What about Marcos?"

"If he's here, we'll stick him in the back of your trunk and sneak him off campus."

"What? That's crazy."

"Yeah, so is life, get used to it."

Before I can argue, Van kisses my cheek and races out of the room just as the tardy bell rings. Then I turn to Ashleigh, who flashes me a comforting smile and clears her backpack off the neighboring desk so I can sit beside her.

I'm so overwhelmed by everything that's happening that it takes my brain a second to realize the obvious. That Van has enlisted Ashleigh in her mission to get me through the day. She must have spent yesterday afternoon calling friends and coordinating schedules to make sure I always have someone to watch my back. Which might be the most thoughtful thing anyone has ever done for me.

In fact, I don't know who I'm more touched by. Van for putting this much effort into protecting me. Or Ashleigh for enlisting herself as bodyguard despite the fact she barely knows me.

Actually, that's a no-brainer. Van wins. Hands down. As grateful as I am to Ashleigh, I'm pretty sure I can see her mentally composing her next college application essay, *A Day in the Life of a Saint, or How I Saved Crick's Resident Homosexual from a World of Hurt and Sorrow* by Ashleigh Audrey Woods.

Ashleigh gets me through second and third period and then to the parking lot without any major incidents. Despite her attempts to distract me with small talk about her plans for college and (later) world domination, it's getting harder to ignore all the whispering and not-so-covert looks. I even catch a few teachers staring at me with a combination of confused pity and morbid curiosity, which is somehow *worse*.

Seriously, how am I ever supposed to look my instructors in the face again when I know that for the rest of the year, they'll all be thinking the exact same thing: *This is the boy whose kisses burn down ballparks.*

The only thing keeping me from totally losing my mind as I stare at the clock in my car is the hope that any second Van will show up with Marcos. And, yes, I know I'm thinking a lot about Marcos, especially considering how we have to break up not only for our own safety but apparently for the safety of literally everyone around us. I haven't forgotten that fact. But if God wants us to split up then He should at least give Marcos and me the opportunity to do it in person. So we can say all the things we need to say to each other. I mean, that's only fair, right? We're at least owed *that*.

"Hey, let me in," Van calls out as she knocks on my windshield. I unlock the doors and, as she slides inside, it only takes a quick glimpse at her pinched face to know something's wrong.

"Marcos wasn't in second or third period," she answers before I can ask. "He's not at school today."

The sinking feeling returns in the pit of my stomach. I've tried to hold on to some sliver of hope, but I don't have the strength anymore. It's impossible to convince myself that Marcos's absence is in any way an act of protection or benevolence. Even if his parents had given him the choice to stay home, he wouldn't take it. I know he wouldn't. He'd be too worried about me. Which means the only reason he's *not* here right now is because his parents are keeping him home. Like a prisoner.

How can the Prices do this?

I mean, keeping Marcos away from church is one thing, but keeping him away from school? From his education? From his friends?

Isn't it enough our relationship is over and we're never going to see each other again? What else does Marcos have to lose all because of one mistake? *Because of me?*

I push my door open, and Van asks if I'm okay, but I can't answer. I'm too busy being sick all over the parking lot.

The rest of the day is pretty much a blur. I sleepwalk through my classes, my mind on autopilot. Van sticks by my side when she can and, when she can't, she passes me off to various friends.

"I expect Milo back in *one* piece," she instructs Caleb before handing me off like a delicate crystal vase. "If I see *one* scratch on him, *you're* a dead man. Got it?"

"For sure." Caleb's very public shaming on Friday seems to have prompted him to be on his best behavior today. No doubt he's trying to score some much needed points with Van after their epic fallout, but I'm hardly in a position to question anyone's motivation or refuse their assistance. Even if some of Caleb's attempts at solidarity are a wee bit cringeworthy.

"Hey, man, just so you know, I totally get it," he assures me as he escorts me to World Lit. "Van made me watch *Y tu mamá también* last year and, between you and me, if Diego Luna asked, I would 100 percent go gay for that dude."

Even with Caleb's transition into Woke Samaritan, fourth and fifth period are almost unbearable. Those are the classes I have with Marcos, and in his absence his empty desks are just painful reminders of everything I've lost.

Everything we've both lost.

It takes all that's left of my strength not to break down and cry—to completely and utterly lose it—but I manage. Not because I'm trying to stay strong or because I don't want to give my classmates the satisfaction of watching me fall apart, but because it's simply too soon for tears.

This is just the beginning of My New Hell. And if I start crying now, I don't honestly think I'll ever be able to stop.

By the end of the day, I've been shoved once, tripped once, and called a slur twice. All in all, I suppose things could've gone worse. Then again, when you're measuring success by the fact that you didn't get beaten to a pulp, it's hard to muster much gratitude.

Van and Caleb walk me to the parking lot after our last class. I'm so exhausted, I just want to go home and bury myself in the oblivion of sleep. But as I'm fishing my keys out of my pocket, Van stops me in my tracks with, "We should go check on Marcos."

"*What?*"

"We should swing by his house. Make sure he's okay."

Swing by his house? Is she joking? That's the *last* thing we should do.

"We can't," I say, fumbling to unlock my car, desperate to get away from this conversation.

"Why not? You could stay in the car, so the Prices don't see you. And I could go up to their front door and knock. If his parents answer, I'll make some excuse about bringing Marcos his homework. And if Marcos answers, you could—"

"Van, we can't!" I shout, my voice shaking with fear.

"Whoa. Calm down."

But I can't be calm. I'm terrified for Marcos.

"We have to leave him *alone*," I hiss. "The Prices aren't idiots. They must have figured out by now that you were lying about being his girlfriend. They know you were covering for me."

"Okay, yeah. That's a problem. But—"

"But *nothing*. They're already keeping Marcos home just to stop him from seeing me. What do you think they'll do if we show up *at their house*? Do you want to make things *worse*?"

The Prices have been pushed to their breaking point. Anything we do now to upset them will *only* get Marcos in deeper trouble. That's a fact. So as much as I want to see him—to see with my own eyes that he's okay—I have to think about what he needs. And what he needs more than anything in the world is to *never* see me again.

I know to Van that might seem cruel or cowardly, but there's no other choice. It's the only way Marcos will have any chance of repairing his relationship with his parents. It's the only way he'll be *safe*.

"Okay," Van relents, holding up her hands in surrender. "Maybe you're right. Maybe we should hold off going over. *For now*. But if I don't hear from Marcos in the next couple days, I will go over there and get some answers."

I'm too exhausted to argue. Instead, I mumble a quick "whatever" and slide into the front seat of my car. Before I can key the ignition, though, Van leans through my window and pulls me into another all-consuming hug. I know I should hug her back. I know I should thank her for everything she did for me today, but I am seriously thirty seconds away from completely falling apart.

"I'll see you tomorrow," she says. "Call me if you need anything, okay?"

I nod.

"And, Milo?"

"Yeah?"

"It's not going to be like this every day. I promise. Things will get better."

"Yeah," I say.

Yeah right.

35

America's Most (Un)Wanted

The house is empty when I get home. All I want to do is crawl into bed, but my parents have made an appointment for me to go into POP later this afternoon to "have a little chat" with Reverend Foley. Right before I left for school this morning, they sat me down and explained how they thought it would be a "good idea" if I got some "counseling." Maybe it would "help" me.

I knew I wasn't being offered a choice. Still, I agreed to go as if I thought it was the greatest idea in the universe. Given what I've put my parents through, it's the least I could do. And who knows? Maybe they're right. Maybe Foley really can help me. I wish to God someone could. Because right now, I need someone to show me how to go on with my life when the one thing I want more than anything in the world is the one thing I know I can never have.

Despite everything I said to Van about keeping our distance from Marcos, the urge to call him—to hear his voice—is eating me alive. In fact, I'm so tempted to dial his number, I bury my phone in the back of my closet just to be safe. Then I rush downstairs and turn on the TV. I need noise—a distraction—anything so that I'm not sitting in the silence of my empty house thinking about Marcos.

My dad warned me about the fire being "all over the news," but even so, I flip through the channels, praying I won't find anything. I know it's only been two days, but if the revival is already yesterday's headline—a momentary blip on the local news radar—then maybe there's a chance Van is right—maybe people will start to forget about the fire, and things actually *will* get better.

A story on Channel 7 about Tropical Storm Gabriel brewing out in the Atlantic briefly fills me with hope. A potential hurricane is just the kind of thing to get everyone's attention away from Marcos and me. But as soon as the weather segment ends, I hear, "Coming up next, new information about the fire that destroyed the Jackie Robinson Ballpark—*and* the people involved."

I sweat through the commercial break, wondering what new and awful revelation the kids at school are going to be able to weaponize against me tomorrow. When the news returns, there's a concise and mostly accurate recap of the events from Saturday night. There's also some shaky iPhone footage of Marcos and me kissing in the middle of the baseball diamond.

I can't take my eyes off the screen.

Not because I'm seeing myself on TV for the first time or because I'm kissing another boy on the local news, but because the Milo I'm looking at is *happy*. Deliriously and achingly happy. Even through the grainy footage that much is unmistakably clear. I can hardly believe we're the same person. Because the Milo I am in this moment is pretty certain he's never known a single day of happiness in his whole entire life. And yet there it is. Proof. Of the person I was. Of the person I wanted to be.

Then there's Marcos. If I look happy in the footage, he looks like someone who's just gotten everything he's ever wished for. Like someone whose every dream has finally come true. And my heart breaks all over again to know how quickly that dream soured into a nightmare.

"Channel Seven has new information about one of the boys involved in Saturday's fire," the anchorwoman says. It's Juliana Martinez, Central Florida's Favorite Newscaster (according to Juliana Martinez). And from the way her eyes shine, I know with soul-crushing certainty that whatever she's about to divulge, it's juicy.

"Sources have now confirmed that one of the boys is also the student whose car was struck by a meteorite last month at Atlantis High School."

I feel the floor drop out from under me. No wonder Marcos wasn't at school today. The Prices must have known this was coming.

"Despite the coincidence, authorities are saying the two incidents are not connected. Nor is either boy being charged with any crime. Instead, the city's fire and rescue department is calling both incidents an Act of God."

I can't listen anymore. *An Act of God.* Why did she have to say that?

I mean, yes, *I* know they're Acts of God, but why did Central Florida's Favorite Newscaster have to tell the *world*? Everyone at my school and church is already pissed off enough. They don't need to know God hates us too.

Despite Van's warning to stay offline, I rush upstairs and flip open my laptop. I need to know how bad the situation is and how far the news has spread. Sure enough, there are already over five hundred articles on Google related to Saturday's fire. Some of the more reputable news outlets have harmless enough titles like "Lightning Storm Causes Freak Fire" or "A Fiery Sermon Brings Actual Fire." But the conservative-leaning websites have more inflammatory headlines like "Shameful Sodomites Incur God's Wrath," "Transgressive Teens Insult God Then Pay the Price," and (my personal favorite) "God Hates Gays and We Have the Video to Prove It."

And it's true. They do.

There are videos of Marcos and me *all* over the internet. We're not just in the *Daytona Beach News-Journal* or the *Orlando Sentinel*. The *Washington Post* has picked up the story. And the *Chicago Tribune*. Even the *New York Times*.

We're *everywhere*.

36

Locked Out of Heaven

"Thanks so much for coming by," Foley says with a welcoming smile as I step into his office. I've just spent the last hour online, watching video after video of supposed Christians calling Marcos and me every name in the book while simultaneously wishing us some very creative deaths, so Foley's cheerful tone strikes me as being a little at odds with my current predicament. I don't know why he's so chipper. Or why he's acting like this is some impromptu visit made out of the goodness of my heart when we both know my parents are waiting outside and this is a Highly Orchestrated Homosexual Intervention.

"Thanks for taking the time to see me," I mumble as Foley escorts me to the chair opposite his desk.

"Of course. I imagine things have been a little stressful lately."

A little stressful? Is he trying to win an award for Understatement of the Century?

"Yes, sir."

"Well, hopefully we can do something about that. Before we begin, though, I feel I should tell you that I spoke with Marcos Price earlier today and—"

"You saw Marcos?" The words are out of my mouth before I can stop them, and the intensity of my question visibly takes Foley aback.

"Uh . . . yes. His parents brought him by for a chat a little while ago. He's quite the forthright and passionate young man, isn't he? And certainly not shy about sharing his opinions."

Foley chuckles, but I'm not in a laughing mood. After the last forty-eight hours, I'm just relieved to know that someone other than Arianna has seen Marcos and that he's okay. Or at least okay enough that Foley doesn't seem too concerned about his well-being.

I wonder if Marcos said anything about when he'll be back at school. If his parents are bringing him to church again, then maybe that means he'll be back at Crick soon too.

My body floods with hope. But then, almost on cue, I remember my parents, who at this moment are sitting on the other side of the door praying for me to "get better," and I force myself to swallow down that hope along with all my questions about Marcos. This isn't the time or place for thoughts like that. I'm here for one reason and one reason only.

I'm here to be fixed.

"Obviously, I can't divulge too much about our conversation," Foley continues, "but to save us some time and perhaps spare us some awkwardness, I can say that Marcos gave me a pretty full account of everything that's been going on the last couple weeks. He was also pretty adamant that he regrets nothing."

He doesn't?

"And so, I'm curious if the feeling is mutual. That is to say, before I make any assumptions about *why* you're here, I'd like you to tell me in your own words how *you* feel I might be able to serve you?"

I open my mouth to answer, but after everything that's happened, I honestly don't know what to stay. I know I care about Marcos more than I have ever cared about anyone in my whole entire life. But I also know those feelings are wrong. And that God is punishing us for them.

I know a month ago nobody knew my name, and now my face is all over the internet. I know my parents are barely speaking to me and that I feel like I'm losing my mind. Mostly, though, I know I'd give anything—*anything*—for my life to just go back to the way it was.

"Is that what you want, Milo?"

"What?"

"For everything to go back to the way it was?"

Oops . . . I must have said that last part out loud.

"Milo?"

"Yes," I whisper. Because it's true. I just want to go back to the beginning of the school year when everything made sense. When my parents could still bear to look at me and my biggest fear was not being able to get curly fries with Van.

"I just want things to go back to normal."

"What things?" Foley asks.

"Me. I want to be normal."

And with that simple, ugly confession an enormous sob erupts from my chest. My entire body shakes but I don't even try to hold in my tears because if there's one thing I've learned about despair over the last couple days, it's that when you surrender to it, it becomes one less thing you have to fight against. And right now, I am so *tired* of fighting.

I'm so tired . . .

I'm not sure how long I cry. It feels like hours. But when I pull myself together, Foley is sitting patiently in his chair. Still in the same position. Still smiling.

"Sorry," I croak, grabbing some tissues off his desk.

"It's quite all right. You're going through a lot. And sitting on emotions isn't healthy."

"I bet Marcos didn't cry."

Foley chuckles. "No, he didn't."

I take a deep breath, trying to steady myself. Then I force myself to ask the question I have to ask. The question that will determine the rest of my life.

"Can you fix me?"

It's my last remaining hope. If Foley can take away these feelings, then maybe there's still a chance I can get my old life back. Maybe through prayer or exorcism or I-don't-know-what, I can be the Milo everyone expects me to be. The Milo I *need* to be. I have to believe that's still possible.

"Do you want to be fixed?"

"I don't want my parents to hate me."

Foley sighs, and his face suddenly seems so much older than its forty-odd years. "Milo, I want you to listen to me very carefully. It's part of my job to assist the members of my congregation whenever they're in need. And I want you to know that I will do whatever I can to help you and your family through this difficult time. But before I do anything, I want you to think long and hard about what it is you truly want."

"I want to be normal."

"Well, if you manage that, you'll certainly be the first person who is."

"You *know* what I mean."

"I do," he sighs, clearly disappointed I didn't appreciate his joke. "And another pastor in my position would probably tell you that you're right to want to change. Officially, our faith has a very specific stance when it comes to what you're dealing with. I'm not unaware of how I'm expected to handle this.

"But I also know *you*. I know you're a good person. You're kind and thoughtful with the children in the day care. You're an exemplary student. And your parents love you a great deal. They wouldn't be so worried about you right now if they didn't love you as much as they do.

"As for your feelings about Marcos . . . Well, we all fall short at times of some of the expectations our faith holds us to. That simply makes you human. Like the rest of us. Which is rather a lucky thing for me. If everyone was perfect, I'd be out of a job."

He waits for me to laugh, but I can't get on board with the Reverend Foley Comedy Hour.

"Wow. I'm really striking out, huh?" he chuckles again. "Okay. Here's the bottom line, Milo. This thing that's brought you here today, this thing that's got you so upset? It's a part of you. And maybe in a week or a month or a year, you'll wake up and realize you no longer feel that way. Or, more likely, it will be a part of you for the rest of your life, and you will live and love according to that feeling. But whatever the case, you and only you will know what is truly right for you. And neither I nor your parents nor anyone else can help you to become someone you're not. Do you understand?"

I do even though I don't believe him.

He's making everything sound so easy, like it's simply a matter of live and let live, when I know for a fact it's not. Sure, it's easy enough for him to say, "Just be yourself." He doesn't have to go home to my parents' disappointed faces. He doesn't have the internet calling him a "degenerate pervert." He doesn't have God literally looking over his shoulder and making his life a living hell.

But I give him what he wants. I smile and nod.

Deep down, though, I know the truth. He's only confirming what I've always suspected. That I, Milo Connolly, am beyond help.

37

The Parting of the Ways

When I finish my conversation with Foley, he asks to speak with my parents in private. I can only imagine what I must look like after my last crying jag, so while my mom and dad receive the dismal news that their only son is utterly irredeemable, I head to the bathroom to clean myself up.

The church's administrative offices are surprisingly busy for a Monday, so to avoid the not-so-subtle looks of pity from the staff, I keep my eyes to the ground as I wind my way through the halls. Even after I almost collide with someone abruptly exiting the pantry, I don't look up. That is until an all-too-familiar voice stops me in my tracks.

"Connolly?"

I can't hardly trust my eyes. For the last two days, all I've wanted is to see Marcos, and now here he is. Standing in front of me. His eyes wide with amazement.

"What are you doing here?" he asks, casting a nervous glance down the hallway then quickly pulling me into the deserted pantry.

"My parents made an appointment for me to talk with Foley," I manage to whisper despite my shock. "What are you doing here?"

"Same."

My heart is racing. I don't know what to do. Half of my instincts are telling me to run back to my parents and Foley and forget I even saw Marcos. But the other half knows we might not get a chance like this again. And there is so much I need to say—so much I need to know.

"Why weren't you at school today?" I ask once I trust myself to speak again.

"My dad. He's being a total control freak. He doesn't want me out of his sight for a second, so he made me come to work with him. Apparently, I can't be trusted."

"Are you okay?"

"Not really. Things are pretty much shit right now. Are you okay?"

"Not really."

Marcos nods in sympathy, a sad smile curling on his lips. Then he takes a step closer, his hand instinctively reaching for my face, and I take a step back.

"What's the matter?"

The last time we touched, four thousand people almost died. I'm not taking any chances.

"Nothing," I cover. "I thought I heard someone coming."

Marcos casts a nervous glance at the pantry door. "I'm just supposed to be grabbing a snack, but we should have a couple minutes before my dad comes looking for me," he says. Though whether he's trying to reassure me or himself, I don't know.

"What are your parents going to do?" I ask. "You know, about . . . ?"

"Us?"

There is no "us" anymore. There can't be. But I don't say anything.

"I don't know," Marcos sighs. And for the first time, I notice how tired his eyes are. From the bags alone, it's clear he hasn't been sleeping. "My dad wanted to send me off to one of those conversion therapy camps where they 'pray the gay away,' but my mom said absolutely not. So now my life is kind of in limbo until they figure out what they want to do with me. Though I've heard the phrase 'grounded for life' about fifty times."

A chill shoots down my spine at the thought of Marcos being carted off to one of those terrible camps. Thank God Mrs. Price intervened. Still, I can't believe things have gotten so bleak that a place like *that* is even an option.

I open my mouth to tell Marcos how sorry I am—for everything—but the words are so inadequate, there's no point. Instead, all I can say is, "At least your mom seems to be on your side."

Marcos shakes his head and exhales a long, exasperated sigh. "She just wants to pretend like the whole thing never happened. Like I never came out. She keeps saying 'it's a phase,' and if we ignore it, it'll go away."

"Well, that's good."

"How is that good? It's *not* a phase."

"No, I know. I just meant . . . It's good she's not totally freaking out."

"Maybe," Marcos grumbles, his voice choked with bitterness. "But I can tell you one thing, I am not going back in the closet. For either of them. If they want to punish me for acting out and embarrassing them in front of all their friends, *fine*, they can punish me. But I'm not going to let them tell me who I can be or who I can love. Not any-more. And if they can't accept that—if they can't accept me—I don't care. I'll leave home. I'll run away if I have to."

Run away? Is he serious? I know things are rough. But surely run-ning away would only make things a million times worse.

"Where would you go?" I ask, trying to hide my anxiety.

"My uncle Eddie's. He's on tour with his band right now, but once he gets back to Miami, I'm sure he'd let me stay with him."

He doesn't actually sound so sure. In fact, from the way his eyes stare into mine with aching uncertainty, I can tell he's desperate for me to reassure him. To tell him this is a brilliant plan and that he's right to run off to his uncle's. But I can't do that. I mean, his parents are still his parents. Until he's eighteen, the Prices can legally drag him back home no matter where he runs off to. And even if they don't force him to come home, if they just decide to wash their hands of him or disown him, what will he do for money? How will he pay for college? What happens to his future?

"Well, it's an option," I say, trying not to encourage or discour-age him.

"Yeah. Exactly. An option." Marcos nods, but the way his energy deflates, I can tell it's an option he's not keen on implementing any-time soon. "Not that I think it'll come to that. I mean, this morning my parents were talking about homeschooling me for the rest of the year—which would be so embarrassingly *lame*—but I guess, if I had to, I could live with that."

"Yeah," I agree. "That doesn't sound so bad."

"Except they still wouldn't let me see you."

Marcos stares into my eyes, and his longing is so intense, I have to look away.

I know he's just experienced the worst few days of his life. I know that all he needs right now is for his boyfriend—for me—to hold him and tell him that everything will be okay. That we'll find some way to be together no matter what our parents throw at us. But I can't give him that. I can't give him *anything*. God has made that painfully clear. And who are we to defy God?

"Maybe it's for the best," I say, my voice barely a whisper.

Marcos stares at me, his eyes narrowing in confusion. "What do you mean?"

"I mean . . . maybe your parents are right." The words catch in my throat, but I force myself to keep going. "Maybe we should stay away from each other."

Marcos shakes his head, but his eyes stay fixed on me. "No. Absolutely not. What are you even saying? I know things have been a little crazy these last couple days—"

"A little?"

"Okay. *A lot*. But we knew there would be consequences if we came out. Yeah, the fire complicated things but, at the end of the day, we wanted our parents to know the truth about us and now they do. We got what we wanted. I mean, yeah, they're freaking out, and we're going to have to deal with their BS for a while, but we knew that was coming. I mean, what did you think would happen when we decided to make out in the middle of a Christian rally?"

The truth is I didn't think. I was so caught up in the moment, in wanting to prove my love to Marcos, I honestly didn't give two thoughts to what might happen once we'd staged our little teenage rebellion.

"That was a mistake," I say.

"A mistake?" Marcos takes a step toward me, his hand once again reaching out for me, and once again I pull away. If he touches me, if I let myself start to feel all the things I'm trying to bury inside of me, I'll never be able to say goodbye. And this has to be goodbye.

We have no choice.

Marcos stares at me in silence. I can feel the disbelief emanating off him. Then it switches—ice-cold shock boiling over into a simmering pain—and all I can see is the red-hot fire of his disappointment burning across his face.

"Wow. Okay. *Wow.* So, what? You're going to be straight now? To make your parents happy?"

I nod. Because that's exactly what I'm going to do. Or if I can't be straight, I'll be nothing. I'll seal myself up so tight in my shell no one will ever be able to find me again. Not even God.

"Well, good luck with that," Marcos scoffs. His voice is bitter, but when I finally force myself to look at him, he's wiping tears from his cheeks. "I hope you're really happy living a lie for the rest of your life."

His voice cracks and it breaks my heart. I can feel my resolve crumbling and without thinking, I say, "I'm sorry. Maybe we can still be friends."

"Friends?" The anguish in his voice is almost too much to bear. "We are not going to be *friends*, Milo. I loved you and you said you

loved me, and I thought that mattered more than anything else. And now you're telling me it was a *mistake*?"

I don't want to hurt him anymore. I've already hurt him enough. But all I can do is nod.

"You know what?" he says, his voice suddenly sharp and even. "Maybe you're right. Maybe this was a mistake. Because let's be honest. No matter how much space or time I gave you to figure out your shit and decide what you want, it was always going to end like this. Wasn't it?

"If it came to your parents or us, or your religion or us, you were never going to choose us. Because what we had has never been enough for you. Our love has never been enough for you. And it has been *everything* to me. Don't you understand that?

"I have given you every part of me—*every part*—and all you've done in return is give me *scraps*. Over and over and over again. And I'm sick of it. I am *so* sick of it, Milo. I deserve better. I deserve so much more than anything you have ever given me. Starting with a boyfriend who isn't ashamed to love me—who isn't ashamed of *me*. But you are *never* going to give me that. So I am done. Do you understand? I'm done trying to make this work. I'm done settling for scraps. I'm done letting you hurt me. *I am done!*"

Marcos pushes past me and barges out of the pantry before I can open my mouth.

All I want to do is chase after him. To tell him he's wrong. To tell him that everything I'm doing I'm doing precisely because I love him. Because I'm trying to protect him—from his parents, from God, from an entire effing *universe* that is hell-bent on destroying us.

But I don't.

Because I also know that everything he said is true. He deserves so much more than I could ever give him. And maybe—now that I'm out of his life—he finally has a chance of finding it.

38

Cheer Up, the Worst Is Yet to Come

Marcos isn't at school on Tuesday. Or Wednesday. Or Thursday.

I tell myself that it's for the best.

I tell myself that the longer we're apart, the easier it'll be for us to forget each other and move on with our lives.

I tell myself that, no matter how much it hurts right now, I did what I had to do. For Marcos. For me. For our families.

I don't believe any of it.

All week long, I've replayed our conversation over and over in my mind and, every time, I come to the same conclusion. That I have made the Greatest Mistake of My Life.

Not that I was wrong to end things. I had to do that. But the way I did it?

I keep picturing the look on Marcos's face—the sheer agony in his eyes—when I called our love a mistake. I didn't just break his heart. I crushed his soul.

And I will never forgive myself for that.

Maybe that's why I almost don't mind the unending parade of abuse and indignities inflicted on me by my classmates this week. In the last four days alone, I've been called homo (10 times), fairy (6 times), faggot (6 times), flaming faggot (3 times), flaming fairy (2 times), flaming fairy faggot (6 times), and Barbra Streisand (1 time but extra points for originality).

The "highlight" of the week, though, comes Friday morning when I'm stopped in the hallway on my way to Spanish by Jared Resnick and some of the other knuckle-draggers from the Crick football team.

"Hey, Connolly, quick question," Jared says, blocking my path in a way that feels both totally casual and completely menacing.

I have no idea what's coming but I'm already cringing at the use of my last name. It reminds me of Marcos. Only instead of being a sign of affection, it's clear from the smirk on Jared's face that it's anything but.

"I'm just curious," he continues, stifling a laugh. "How long would I have to kiss you in order for you to burn something down for me?"

His entourage shakes with laughter, like they've just heard the funniest joke of the year. Then again, considering that their skill set is limited to tackling anyone holding a ball, it probably is.

"I just thought since you kiss dudes and then stuff explodes," Jared clarifies, "maybe I could give you a little action and then you could do me a solid and set Ms. Müller's classroom on fire before the midterm next month? It would be a *big* help."

The knuckle-draggers howl with laughter, and Jared high-fives them like he's just scored the winning touchdown. Then he turns to me like he expects me to high-five him too.

"What, no love? Come on, short fry! Help a guy out. Tell you what, what if I pay you? Does that sweeten the pot? Seriously, I do not want to take that test, so what'll it cost me? Ten? Twenty? Fifty?"

The offer to reimburse me for my homosexually activated, pyrokinetic powers elicits another round of laughter not only from the Neanderthals but from everyone else in the hallway. My cheeks burn crimson, and I know there's no way I'm getting out of this conversation with an ounce of my dignity intact. Maybe that's why I get the idea to do what I do next. After all, if I'm going down, I might as well go down in flames.

That—and only that—is the sole thought going through my head as I lean forward, grab Jared's face between my hands, and pull him into a full-on kiss.

"What the hell!" he shouts, shoving me away.

The entire hallway falls silent. For once even the knuckle-draggers aren't laughing. Instead, their faces are a perfect mirror of Jared's: complete and mortifying shock.

I know there will be consequences. I know I'll have to pay for what I've done. But in this moment, I'm riding high on adrenaline and self-destruction because for once in my life I, Milo Connolly, am not the one who's afraid.

I give Jared my most condescending smirk and saunter away. I know everyone is watching me, so just as I'm about to turn the corner, I look back at Jared and his friends and shout my parting shot.

"On the house!"

Despite the thrill of standing up for myself for the first (and probably last) time in my life, I spend the rest of the overcast morning worrying that God is going to misunderstand the nature of the kiss and assume I'm back to my wicked, sodomical ways. Tropical Storm Gabriel was upgraded to a hurricane this morning, and I wouldn't put it past the Almighty to punish me for my latest affront by sending Gabe my way. Though the more I think about it, the more I'm convinced I'm probably in the clear. I'm pretty sure God doesn't mind if two boys kiss—as long as neither one enjoys it.

"Dude, that's *awesome*," Van congratulates me at lunch. "I'm so proud of you."

"Yeah, man, good job," Caleb agrees, popping a curly fry in his mouth. "Jared can be such an ass. I legit regret joining the Falcons. I thought those dudes would be super chill to hang with, but they are all, like, total assholes."

"I told you."

"You did, babe."

This is the third time this week Caleb has joined Van and me at Holloway's, but today is the first day I notice them holding hands. It's an unexpected though not undesirable development. Against all likelihood, Caleb has really stepped up these last couple days. And even though I don't know for sure if that's the reason Van has decided to give him a second chance (or, more accurately, a 272nd chance), it's nice to see her looking so happy.

And Van could use some happiness. She wasn't exactly smiling three days ago when I told her about my encounter with Marcos. I believe her exact words were, "Are you insane? Why would you break up?" I wasn't able to give her much of a reason because I immediately started crying, and she hasn't brought up the subject since. Though she does keep threatening to drive over to the Prices and give them a piece of her mind if Marcos isn't at school on Monday.

"So, tell the truth," Van says, leaning in conspiratorially as she licks the barbecue sauce off her fingers. "Is Jared a good kisser?"

"Actually, his breath smelled like cigarettes and breakfast burritos."

"Hot."

"Wait," Caleb says, sitting up in concern. "I eat breakfast burritos. Do they really make your breath smell bad?"

Van laughs, which makes him more nervous. "Seriously, V, what do I smell like?"

"I don't know. Like nothing."

"Nothing? How can I smell like nothing?"

"I don't know, Caleb. I've never really noticed any particular smell."

"Hey, I'm just looking for some constructive feedback, you know? To see how I measure up. Figure out what needs improvement. I'm a work in progress."

"Dude, you're *fine*."

"Fine?"

"Normal."

"Wow. Way to use your words," Caleb teases. "You know, you better watch out. M-Lo here gives out free kisses now. And I bet *he'd* be more than happy to tell me all about my breath if I ask."

Caleb gives me a playful wink as Van pelts him with a curly fry. And for the first time since the fire, I catch myself laughing. It's a small laugh, but I've honestly never needed one more. The fact that Caleb, whom I would barely call an acquaintance before today, can joke about us kissing like it's the most blasé thing in the world makes me feel like maybe—just maybe—there's a chance I might survive high school after all.

If I stick with people like Van and Caleb and Ashleigh, and I keep a low profile and stay out of trouble, then maybe the rest of this year will be—well, I won't say *good*. Good is far too much to hope for. But *bearable*.

Yeah.

I'd settle for bearable.

For the next few hours, I try to convince myself that this low-key future free from constant terror and unrelenting regret is a genuine possibility. After all, it's not inconceivable that my classmates will get tired of harassing me. Maybe after a few weeks of torment, everyone will move on and forget I exist. Maybe if I'm really, really, *really* lucky, this school year will end exactly as it began. With my name prompting the one and only one response it was ever meant to elicit. Milo *who*?

That's the dream. But as I step out into the parking lot at the end of the day, it only takes one look at my car—or rather what's left of my car—to know with crushing certainty that no one is *ever* going to let me forget what I did or who I am.

"Holy crap," Van says, rushing to my side with Caleb in tow. "What happened?"

All four tires have been removed from my little Toyota. And across the hood, in blazing red letters for all the world to see, someone has painted one single word.

FAGGOT.

"Whoa," Caleb exclaims. "That is seriously messed up."

And he's right. It is messed up. My *life* is seriously messed up. And the worst part is I have no one to blame but myself.

No, correction: there is one other person I can blame. He's currently smirking at me from across the parking lot, his smug face beaming with pride.

"On the house!" Jared shouts.

Something inside me snaps—something primal and angry and desperate to fight back against all the forces of the world that seem determined to grind me down—and before I know what I'm doing, I'm hurtling across the parking lot. I don't have the faintest idea what I'm going to do when I get to Jared, but I know I'm going to make him pay. Of course, he's much bigger than me, and I have zero upper-body strength. I doubt he'll even feel it if I punch him. Instead, I decide to use my current speed to my advantage and knock him down with the sheer force of my velocity.

There's just one problem with that plan. I'm running so quickly that when Jared steps out of my way at the last minute, I don't have time to course correct. I slam straight into his pickup, knocking the side-view mirror off the door and the wind out of myself.

Then I'm on the asphalt with Jared's sneering face looming over me.

All I can do is pray that whatever comes next doesn't hurt as much as I think it will. Then again, if Jared kills me, at least that solves the problem of having to finish high school. I close my eyes, welcoming death. But before Jared can throw his first punch, Caleb is on top of him, wrestling him to the ground and clobbering him.

Van rushes to my side and helps me up, but from the shocked expression on her face, I can't tell if she's impressed with Caleb's heroics or horrified by the violence. If I had to guess, I'd say it's a little of both. Thankfully, the fight is over almost as soon as it begins. Within seconds, teachers are separating Caleb from Jared and dragging them both toward the principal's office. Caleb's got a bloody nose and a torn shirt, but he's grinning from ear to ear. In fact, just before he's escorted inside, he flashes us a cheerful thumbs-up and proudly shouts, "I think I'm off the team!"

Van shakes her head, but she can't stop herself from smiling. Caleb may be a disaster, but he's her disaster.

"Are you all right?" she asks, turning her attention back to me.

I'm not exactly sure how I'm supposed to answer that. By no stretch of the imagination am I even remotely close to "being all right." Nor am I *ever* going to be all right. But that's not what she wants to hear.

"I'm fine," I say, ignoring the dull ache in my shoulder from where I collided with Jared's truck.

"Are you sure? It looked like you went down pretty hard and—"

"I said I'm fine," I snap, turning away from her concerned gaze and staring out at the massive storm clouds gathering on the horizon.

"Okay . . . well . . . If you're all right, then we should probably go to the principal's office too. We need to report what happened. What Jared did to your car is vandalism, which is illegal. He should be arrested. Or at the very least expelled."

"Can you just drive me home?"

Van stares at me like she must have misheard, and I can't help feeling guilty when she realizes she hasn't. I know she wants me to be as angry and indignant as she is. I know she wants me to fight back and stand up for myself. But I can't. I just don't see the point anymore. Even if Jared gets expelled, I know with every fiber of my being that tomorrow there will just be someone else to take his place. And then someone after that. And someone after that. And someone after that . . .

My future is an endless and unrelenting line of people ready and waiting to hurt me until the day I die, and that is never going to change.

"*Please*," I beg her, the tears welling up in my eyes. "Take me home."

By the time we reach my house, I've recovered enough to face my parents. Van offers to come inside and help explain what happened to my car, but I tell her not to bother. I've grown so accustomed to giving my parents bad news that at this point I'm pretty much an expert. Besides, I've got to start learning how to clean up my own messes one of these days.

"How about you spend the night, then?" she counters as it starts to rain. "You could grab your things and come over to my place. Watch some *Golden Girls*."

"Maybe some other time," I say, avoiding her eyes as I open the door. I love Van, but the thought of being around other people—even my best friend—is too much right now. All I want to do is crawl into bed and close my eyes.

Hopefully forever.

When my mother calls me for dinner, I pull the sheets over my head and pretend to be asleep. A few minutes later my bedroom door opens, and I hear her in the doorway, debating with herself whether to wake me. Then the door clicks shut, and her footsteps fade down the hallway.

She must have decided I've earned a rest after what happened with Jared. Or maybe she's just too exhausted herself to deal with me tonight. I don't blame her. Or my father. All I do is find new and inventive ways to make their lives more difficult. All I do is hurt them.

As I drift off to sleep again, I wonder how much longer my parents will put up with me before they finally reach their limit. Before they decide they've had enough. Before they realize that I'm simply not worth it.

39

With Friends like These

"Is Milo home?"

Even half asleep I can hear Van's voice downstairs and I know something's wrong. She never stops by unannounced. And she certainly never comes inside.

I glance at my phone and see it's almost four. I've been asleep for nearly twenty-four hours. Outside, the wind tears through the trees and the rain batters against my window. Hurricane Gabriel must be getting close.

Is that why Van sounds so agitated?

No. That doesn't make sense.

If we were in any real danger, my parents would've woken me up hours ago and driven us inland to my aunt and uncle's house in Maitland. The fact that we've stayed put must mean either Gabriel is expected to swerve north or that it's still only a Category 2. And as my dad is fond of saying: real Floridians don't evacuate for anything under a Category 3.

Still, Van shouldn't be out in this weather. Maybe my mom got nervous that I haven't left my bed in a day and called Van to come check on me. I can hear them discussing something in urgent whispers, but I can't make out the words.

Despite my exhaustion, I force myself out of bed then trudge down the hall. Something important must be happening to have warranted a cease-fire in the Connolly-Silvera Feud and, as I approach the stairs, I'm able to catch a glimpse of Van down in our foyer. She's drenched from head to foot, shaking off her denim jacket, as my mom hands her a towel.

"Do you want some hot tea? Or something to warm yourself up?"

"No, thank you, Mrs. Connolly. I just need to see Milo."

My mom instinctively looks up in the direction of my room and jumps when she sees me hovering at the top of the stairs like a ghost. Then forcing a smile, she squeezes Van's shoulder and says, "Sure, sweetie, go on up. I'm sure Milo would be glad to see you."

Van thanks my mom and hurries up the stairs. Before I can ask what's going on, though, she grabs me by the arm, drags me down the hall, and bundles me into my room, slamming the door behind her. I know Van's a "theater person," but in this moment her flair for the dramatic is wearing on my last nerve. I mean, what could seriously be so important that she had to drive all the way over to my house in the middle of a hurricane?

"Marcos is moving back to Orlando."

Oh. That's actually pretty important.

In fact, I'm suddenly very grateful that Van waited until we were alone in my room to deliver her news because my legs are shaking so badly, I have to sit on my bed to keep myself from collapsing.

This can't be happening. I thought the Prices were just going to home-school Marcos. I didn't think they'd be so desperate to keep their son away from me that they'd flee the city.

"Milo?"

Maybe this is a dream. Yes, that's it. This is a dream. I'm asleep. And tomorrow I'll wake up and realize that none of this is real. It's just a nightmare. In fact, if I concentrate hard enough, I'm sure I can force myself to wake up and—

"Milo, did you hear me?" Van snaps. "The Prices are *moving.* I just drove by their house and there's a U-Haul parked in the driveway. I spoke with Marcos's dad—who's a real piece of work—and he said they were leaving for Orlando *tomorrow.*"

Tomorrow?

I should've seen this coming.

Ever since the night of the fire, I've been praying that my life would go back to the way it was. Before the world turned upside down. Before Marcos. And now it has. God is finally answering my prayers. He's literally putting things back to the way they were. Marcos in Orlando. Me alone. I'm getting *exactly* what I wanted.

So why does it feel like the end of the world?

"Milo, stop spacing out and pay attention!" Van shouts. "We have to do something!"

"Do something?"

"Yes!"

"Like what?"

"I don't know. *Something.* Maybe we can talk the Prices out of moving. Explain to them that they're overreacting."

"You really think Mr. Price will listen to anything you or I have to say?"

Van groans in frustration. She knows I'm right. She knows there's nothing we can do. Tomorrow Marcos will return to his old life. His old school. His old church. It won't be easy for him. His father won't make it easy for him. But maybe, in the end, it's for the best. At least this way Marcos can have a fresh start away from all the things that hurt him. Away from me.

"Don't you at least want to say goodbye?" Van asks, her voice shaking in exasperation. "And give Marcos a chance to say goodbye?"

"Marcos and I have said everything we need to say to each other."

"That's *bullshit*."

"It's not. Marcos doesn't ever want to see me again. I broke his heart."

"Yeah," she sighs. "You did. So don't you think you owe it to him to fix it?"

"Fix it?" She can't possibly think—

"I'm not saying you should try to get back together," she clarifies. "But, dude, he's your friend. He's your friend and you hurt him. And—sorry for the tough love here—but maybe instead of moping around your house and feeling sorry for yourself—it's time you grow a pair and go make things right with Marcos. Now. Before it's too late. You owe him that much *at least*."

She's right. I do owe him that. That and so much more. The only trouble is I have no idea how I would even begin to make things right. Marcos doesn't need another apology from me. I've been giving him nothing but apologies for as long as we've been together and he's sick of them. I'm sick of them. So what do I have to offer?

"Look, you still care about him, don't you?" Van asks, taking my hand in hers and forcing me to look at her. "And he still cares about you."

"I don't know what Marcos feels anymore."

"Oh my god, dude, stop with the pity party. Of course he cares about you. Marcos has been in love with you since the first day he laid eyes on you at that stupid camp."

"He has?" I didn't know that. I mean, I knew he liked me. But love?

"Yes, you idiot."

"How do you know?"

"He told me."

"When?"

"At camp!"

At camp? But that can't be right. That would mean . . .

"Do you honestly think I didn't know about you guys until the night of the meteor?" she asks incredulously. "I've known about you guys for *years*."

Of course she has. Her comment about me "finally" coming out; her constant attempts to get Marcos and me to hang out when he first moved to town; her indignation when I tried to date Margot: it all makes sense now.

"How did you know?" I ask.

For the first time in our entire friendship, Van looks frightened.

"Marcos told me. The day before he left camp to go to his grandfather's funeral."

I don't understand. She *knew*? All this time? And she's never said a word?

"He knew I was your best friend," she says, trying to keep her voice from trembling. "He knew I knew you better than anyone else in the world—probably even better than you knew yourself—so the day before he was supposed to leave camp, he came and found me after lunch and told me what had been going on between you guys. He wanted to know whether or not I thought he should tell you how he felt."

No, no, no . . . I don't like where this is going.

"He told me he loved you, and that he thought you *might* be in love with him, but he couldn't be sure. You were so weird and Jesus-y back then. And you guys had only known each other for two weeks. He wasn't sure how you'd respond. He asked if I thought he should tell you and—"

"What did you say?" But I know what she said. Because her guilt is written on her face. And because I know what happened next.

"I told him no."

"You *what*?"

"I didn't think you were ready! I didn't even know if you'd figured out you liked guys yet. Or if you'd ever figure it out!"

"How could you do that?" I shout, my fists shaking in rage.

"I was trying to protect you!"

"Protect me?"

"Yes, like I've *always* done. If Marcos had been planning to stick around *maybe* I would've handled things differently. Maybe I might've told him, 'Sure, go for it.' But he wasn't, okay? He was leaving the *next* day, and you were never going to see him again. I didn't think it was fair for him to dump all his feelings on you and then disappear. I didn't think you could handle it. I figured you'd either have some religious crisis or an emotional breakdown, and either way I'd be the one left picking up the pieces. Which, for the record, is still exactly what happened anyway. So, yeah, I told Marcos to back off. I told him you weren't ready and that he needed to leave you alone. I told him *no*."

I'm so livid I can barely hear the rest of Van's explanation.

She knew.

She knew about Marcos and me, and she deliberately kept us apart. That's what Marcos wanted to tell me the night of our first date when I asked him why he left camp without saying goodbye. It also explains why Van has gone out of her way to help us these last few weeks. All this time I thought it was pure, unselfish friendship. But it wasn't. It was guilt.

"Milo?" Van is staring at me with tears in her eyes. I think she asked me a question, but if so, I didn't hear it.

"What?"

"I said I'm sorry. And I want you to know I'll do *whatever* it takes to make things right."

"You should go."

"Milo, please, listen—"

"I said go!"

I'm shaking so hard that I'm afraid if she says one more word, I'll do or say something I can never take back. I know she's my best friend, I know she didn't mean to hurt me, I know she only did what she thought was best for me, but right now all I see when I look at her is betrayal.

I know that's unfair. I know that what happened—or what didn't happen—between Marcos and me three years ago isn't entirely her fault. Marcos could've ignored her advice. He could've told me how he felt. Or I could've told him. It's not Van's fault neither of us had the courage to be honest about our feelings. And yet, we were so close. *So close.* If Van's advice hadn't gotten in our way, then maybe Marcos and I would have found our way to each other sooner. Maybe our lives would be different. Maybe *everything* would be different!

And I can't forgive her for that. At least not right now.

"Okay," Van relents, letting out a defeated sigh. "I'm going."

Good. I can't wait for her to leave. Because the second she's gone, I know I can completely fall apart. And this time there will be no putting me back together.

"Look, I understand if you hate me," Van says, stopping in the doorway. "Trust me, right now, I hate myself. But Marcos is going away, and you might never see each other ever again. Do you really want him to leave thinking you don't care what happens to him? Would you seriously do that to him? To *Marcos*?

"He's got to be scared out of his mind right now and, more than anything, he needs to know that he isn't alone. You can't let him leave without giving him that. You have to tell him how you feel—how you *really* feel—before it's too late. You missed your chance to say goodbye before, and that was partially my fault, but if you miss your chance again, that's on you. And trust me, you will *never* forgive yourself."

40

Blow, Gabriel, Blow

Stupid Van. Why does she always have to be right?

Ever since she left my house, her words have been stuck in my head on an endless loop. *If you miss your chance again, that's on you. If you miss your chance again, that's on you. If you miss your chance again, that's on you.* Now I'm getting clobbered by the rain as I bicycle through an *effing* hurricane.

I should've called an Uber. It'd be a million times safer. Not to mention drier. But I didn't want my parents to hear me leaving or Marcos's parents to see me coming. Also, if I get to his house and I decide I want to turn right back around—*which I may very well do*—then at least I won't have a judgmental Uber driver looking at me like I'm crazy. Which, to be clear, I definitely am.

Thankfully, Marcos only lives fifteen minutes away by bike, and the roads are remarkably clear on account of the hurricane, which has just been upgraded to a Category 3. The wind is so intense I've already seen three plastic lawn flamingos take flight and disappear into the horizon. As for the rain, don't even get me started. By the time I turn onto Marcos's street, I'm drenched. My clothes are twenty pounds heavier, my shoes are sponges, and I'm pretty sure even my soul is damp.

If you miss your chance again, that's on you . . .

When I arrive at the Prices' house, there's a big orange moving van in the driveway and a *For Sale* sign in the yard. Looks like Van was telling the truth. Not that I doubted her but seeing the actual confirmation with my own eyes is almost more than I can bear. Marcos really is leaving. I'm about to lose the most important person in my life. And I can't let him go without making things right.

Surely God can't object to *that*. I mean, He's won. Marcos is moving away. It's over between us. All I want is the chance to apologize for how much I hurt him and to make sure he'll be okay before we close this chapter of our lives once and for all. That's got to be allowed.

In fact, the more I think about it, the more I'm certain God *wants* me to do this. If He didn't, He could've struck me with lightning or blown my bike into the path of an oncoming semi. But He didn't. So I'm going to take His lack of smiting to assume I have His celestial approval.

I ditch my bike on the side of the road and race across the yard to the old spruce tree growing in the middle of the Prices' lawn. It's shaggy enough to provide camouflage for my approach but also close enough to the house to give me a clear view into the windows.

Mr. and Mrs. Price are in the kitchen. I can't hear what they're saying, but from their animated expressions they're clearly in the middle of a very heated argument. Marcos's mom, in particular, looks more frustrated than I've ever seen her before. I almost want to get closer and find out what has her so enraged, but time is of the essence. I need to find Marcos before my own parents realize I'm gone.

The rest of the windows on this side of the house are dark, so when the Prices aren't looking, I make a dash for the backyard, where

I'm pretty certain the bedrooms are. I've no idea what I'll do if the Prices catch me prowling around their house and, honestly, I don't care. The one perk of hitting rock bottom is that you literally have nothing to lose.

I dart around the back of the house, and my instincts (for once) are on the money. There, through the window directly in front of me, is Marcos. He's grabbing clothes out of his closet and indignantly shoving them into a suitcase. The rest of his room is bare. I don't know if that's part of his punishment or if it's because all his stuff is already in the U-Haul, but either way the emptiness breaks my heart.

If you miss your chance again, that's on you . . .

Part of my brain is screaming at me to turn around and go home because it knows how much this is going to hurt. But the other part knows I will never forgive myself if I chicken out now. Maybe in the Eyes of the Lord, Marcos and I don't deserve to be together, but we do deserve the chance to say goodbye.

It's probably the last thing we'll ever say to each other.

"Connolly?"

Crap! Marcos spotted me. I was hoping for a little more time to work out exactly what I wanted to say. But I guess you can't linger outside someone's window like a sopping Peeping Tom and not expect to get caught.

"What are you doing?" he shouts over the rain as he slides open his window. "Are you crazy? There's a hurricane!"

"I know! I had to see you!"

"You're going to get yourself killed, you psycho. Get inside. Quick. Before my parents see you!"

He doesn't have to ask twice. I hoist myself up to the sill, and Marcos grabs ahold of my shoulders to help me over the ledge. His hands are firm and strong, and their touch fills my body with an all-too-familiar ache.

Without thinking I throw my arms around him as soon as I'm inside. He tenses and, for a second, I'm certain he's going to push me away. Then I feel his entire body relent, and he pulls me closer.

I guess I'm not the only one who missed the way our bodies fit together.

"Are you okay?" he asks, his voice a whisper, as if he's afraid to speak. "What are you doing here?"

"Van told me you were moving back to Orlando."

"Yeah," he sighs, still not breaking our embrace despite the fact I must be drenching him with my waterlogged clothes. "My dad sprung it on my mom and me last night. Didn't even give us a choice. When Foley told him he couldn't 'pray the gay out of me,' my dad basically turned in his notice on the spot. Then he called his old boss at the Salvation Army and managed to get his job back. My mom is furious. He totally blindsided her."

"I thought they were just going to homeschool you."

"They still might. Nothing's off the table. My dad's even started talking about one of those conversion therapy camps again."

"He *what*?"

I can't believe what I'm hearing. I can't believe I deluded myself that Marcos might actually be better off in Orlando. What was I thinking? He's not leaving town to embark on some "fresh start." He's being dragged away to be punished. To be broken.

"I'm sorry," I say, finally breaking our embrace so I can see his face. "I'm so, so sorry, Marcos."

"Whatever. My dad can threaten me all he wants, but if he thinks he can scare me straight, he has another thing coming. I plan to be just as gay in Orlando as I've been in Port Orange. Gayer even. I'll be so gay he'll see rainbows every time he looks at me."

Marcos's bravery has always been and will always be one of the most incredible things about him and, in this moment, I am in awe of it. He will never back down, and he will never apologize, not for being who he is. I don't know where he finds the courage. But if he can be this fearless in the face of everything that's happening, then the least I can do is have the guts to own up to all the pain and misery I've caused him.

"I'm sorry for how I ended things," I say, the tears welling up in my eyes. "It was cruel and cowardly, and you deserved so much better from me. You've always deserved better from me. And I'm sorry I said our love was a mistake. Because it wasn't. Our love was the best thing that has ever happened to me. And I'm so sorry I wasn't worthy of it."

Marcos stares at me in silence, his face blank and inscrutable. Then I see the first tear escape from his eye, and his whole face crumbles.

"Thank you for saying that," he whispers, pulling me into his arms and burying me against his chest. And for the next minute the only sounds we hear are the raging storm outside and the desperate beating of our two hearts.

"What time do you leave tomorrow?" I ask once I trust myself to speak.

"I don't know," he sighs. "Sometime after breakfast."

His words are like a sledgehammer to my soul. I thought I'd

accepted the reality of losing Marcos, but standing here in his empty room, trying and failing to let go of the one person I want to hold on to more than anything in the world, I realize I haven't begun to fathom what my life will be like without him.

"I don't want you to go," I say, holding on to him as if my arms alone might be enough to keep him by my side forever.

"I don't want to go either. I keep hoping my mom will finally put her foot down and stand up to my dad. She could stop all of this if she wanted. If she loved me, if she *really* loved me . . ."

"She *does* love you," I say. "She's just scared."

"She's not the only one."

Marcos clutches me so tight that it's hard to know where he stops and I begin. What is certain, though, is that he's terrified. Absolutely and completely terrified. Even if his father doesn't send him off to some evangelical brainwashing camp, Mr. Price will still keep punishing his son. He'll still make his life a living hell.

Marcos knows it. For all his bluster and all his vows of rainbow-filled defiance, the boy in my arms is nothing more than a frightened teen facing an impossible future. A future he has no way of escaping.

Unless . . .

"What about your plan?" I ask, pulling out of our embrace.

"My plan?"

"To go to your uncle's house. You said he'd help you if things got bad, right?"

"Yeah. Probably. But he's on tour until November."

"Okay, so, we'll go somewhere else until November."

"We?" he asks, his eyes narrowing in confusion.

"Yeah. If you're running away, I'm going with you."

I didn't start this day planning to flee my hometown with my ex-boyfriend, but as soon as the words are out of my mouth I know they're true. I'll go anywhere with Marcos. For as long as he needs me.

Besides, there's nothing left for me here.

"Run away? You and me?"

"Why not?"

"Because we're in the middle of a hurricane!" Marcos exclaims, gesturing to the storm outside his window as if talking to a stubborn child. I can tell he's tempted, though, because a second later he adds, "I mean . . . Where would we even go?"

Good question. Van's house is out. I know Ms. Silvera would let us crash for a few weeks, but it's also the first place my parents would look.

"I don't know," I confess. "We'll figure it out."

"We'll figure it out? That's your plan? *We'll figure it out?*"

"Yeah," I say with a calmness that surprises me. "We'll figure it out. You and me. Because whatever happens next, whatever you decide you want to do or wherever you want to go, I am here for you. I'm not leaving your side. Not now. Not ever. You and I are in this together. I promise. Just tell me what you want to do."

Marcos is silent. He looks at his bedroom door, then back to me, and when he does his eyes are filled with sadness. I know his heart is breaking, and for one terrible second, I'm afraid he's going to give in to that despair. Then, throwing his head back in a defiant laugh, he says, "Screw it. Let's run away."

My body floods with relief and recklessness. I pull Marcos into my arms and squeeze him so hard I almost knock the wind out of him.

"Jeez, Connolly, let a boy breathe. If you break my ribs, you're going to have to carry me out of here."

This is really happening. We're running away. We might not have the best plan—or *any* plan for that matter—but at least we have each other. And somehow, in this moment, that feels like everything.

Then the doorbell rings.

Even this far back in the house we can hear it, and it sends a shiver down my spine. Call it a teenage premonition or just plain paranoia, but I know in my soul that whoever is at the door, it's not good news. Neither is the buzzing phone in my pocket. I'm pretty sure that whatever luck I've been coasting on for the last half hour has just run out—a suspicion that's confirmed when I see the words "Mom Calling" flash across the screen.

Crap! She must have noticed I snuck out. I hit "ignore" and, when I do, I see I have three missed calls and seven texts. All from my parents. All demanding to know where I am.

Marcos cracks open his door, and from the hallway we hear two sets of agitated voices heading our way. "He's not picking up his phone," my mom sighs. "But he's got to be here."

Oh no . . .

"We need to go!" I whisper.

Marcos doesn't need me to tell him twice. He locks his door, grabs his wallet and suitcase, and hurries to the window. "Where's your car?"

Oops! I've been so caught up in the excitement of running away, I'd completely forgotten how I got here. "Um . . . actually? I rode my bike."

"Your *bike*?"

"I didn't know we were planning a getaway!"

"It's okay," Marcos says, sliding his window open. "I think I have an idea."

"Marcos?" Mrs. Price calls out, knocking on the door. "We need to speak with you." The doorknob rattles, and a second later Mr. Price is pounding on the door.

"Marc? Open this door! Do you hear me? Marc! I'm going to give you until the count of three and then—"

We don't hear the end of that threat. We're already out the window, our feet splashing in the muddy ground.

"Jesus Christ, it's really coming down!" Marcos yells over the downpour.

Maybe it's my imagination, but I'd swear the storm has gotten significantly worse since I've been with Marcos. The rain batters down on us like it's trying to force us back inside, and the wind seems determined to flay our skin off.

"So what's your plan?" I shout.

Marcos nods toward the moving van in his driveway.

"Can you drive stick?" he asks.

"No. Can you?"

"No. Guess we'll have to figure it out."

I want to protest that learning how to drive an unfamiliar vehicle in the middle of a hurricane sounds like the quickest way to turn our getaway into a double suicide, but Marcos is sprinting across the lawn before I can get the words out. I hurry after him, and by the time I reach the van, he's already seated behind the steering wheel—staring at the empty ignition.

"No keys."

Great. Now what? Does Marcos know how to hot-wire a U-Haul? That would be *incredibly* sexy if he did, but I'm not going to hold my breath.

"Hang on." Marcos flips down the sun guard and the keys fall into his lap. "Ha! Knew it! Thank God my dad is so predictable."

"I thought you didn't believe in God?"

Marcos gives me a withering look, but whatever sarcastic response he's preparing will have to wait. The front door to his house swings open and our parents stumble out into the rain.

"Drive!"

Marcos keys the ignition, and with one violent lurch our clunky escape vehicle rumbles backward out of the driveway.

"Marcos, stop!" his mother yells, her face stricken with panic.

But Marcos is on a mission. After a few unsuccessful gear shifts, the engine roars to life. Then we're tearing down the rain-flooded road literally leaving our parents in our wake.

"We did it!" I shout as Marcos's house recedes in the distance.

But I've celebrated too soon. In the side-view mirror, I see my dad and Mr. Price scrambling into my dad's pickup. And from the way Marcos keeps struggling to shift into fourth gear, I know we're not going to get very far before they catch up.

"Can't you go any faster?"

"I'm trying!"

The pickup is gaining on us. Short of divine intervention, there's no way we'll even make it out of this subdivision before our dads over-take us. Then what'll they do? Force us off the road? Call the police?

A deafening BANG shakes our van, and for a split second I

think it's a gunshot. Then a bolt of lightning strikes the massive oak tree sitting near the intersection up ahead. It's simultaneously the most awe-inspiring and terrifying thing I've ever seen—beauty and destruction all rolled into one. The air turns pungent, like chlorine, and for a moment everything is still.

Then the tree starts to topple over into the road.

"Hold on!" Marcos shouts.

He floors the gas, finally shifting into fourth gear, and I brace for impact. I'm 100 percent certain we're about to end up crushed under a tree, but it's too late to back down now. I take Marcos's hand as we hurtle through the intersection and, half a second later, the tree collapses behind us.

OH. MY. GOD.

We made it. We actually made it. I can't believe it! I mean, that was something out of a James Bond film!

I'm so ecstatic to be alive that it takes me a second to remember our dads. I lean out my window to get a better view and am just in time to see my father slam on his brakes. The pickup skids toward the intersection—tires screeching—then smacks into the fallen oak with an unpleasant CRUNCH.

"Holy crap," I gasp.

I watch my dad and Mr. Price stumble out of the wreck. They're not hurt, which is a relief. They're also in no position to come after us, which means Marcos and I are in the clear.

"Wow," Marcos exclaims. I turn back to him and see what I can only describe as the World's Goofiest Grin spread across his face. "We just had a high-speed chase *with our dads!*"

"I know."

"We're like Bonnie and Clyde!"

"I know!"

"Jesus, Connolly, what is going on?"

Before I can even attempt to answer, laughter erupts out of me. I'm not sure if I'm giddy from excitement or just drunk on adrenaline, but I'm laughing so hard that for a second I worry I might be hysterical.

What is *going on?*

And, more importantly, what on earth do we do now?

41

Milo and Marcos at the End of the World

Turns out the Mariner's Inn located off A1A in Daytona isn't such a bad place to wait out the end of the world. The rooms are small but clean. There's free HBO. And their rates are pretty reasonable. Especially during a hurricane. In fact, the old woman who greets us behind the check-in desk practically offers to pay us *not* to stay at her hotel.

"You boys know we're about to get clobbered by a hurricane, right? Latest reports say we're up to a Category Four."

We assure her that we do, in fact, know this (even though we don't) and that we're not concerned in the slightest (even though we are). It's a risky move hiding out in a beachside hotel that's directly in the path of an oncoming hurricane, but we figure it's the last place our parents will look for us.

Also, we're out of options.

The old woman begrudgingly takes our money and gives us two keys to room 307, which comes with double beds and an ocean view. Marcos, though, is more interested in the TV. As soon as we're settled in, he flips on the news.

Every channel is devoting full-time coverage to Hurricane

Gabriel, which contrary to what the hotel manager told us is *not* a Category 4. It's a Category 5. Which makes it one of the largest storms to hit Central Florida in the last fifty years.

"That's not good," Marcos gulps.

No, it's not. In fact, any sensible human being with half a brain ought to be heading inland as fast as their U-Haul can carry them. But Marcos and I clearly took leave of our senses long ago. Besides, even if we wanted to head to higher ground, it's too late now. Channel 7 shows an aerial shot of the interstate and with the entire East Coast evacuating it is nothing but bumper-to-bumper traffic stretching all the way into the horizon. At this point, we're safer in our room than on the roads.

"They're probably making it sound worse than it is," Marcos says, trying to put on a brave face.

I'm about to remind him that we don't exactly have the best track record when it comes to Mother Nature, but then something on the TV catches my eye. It's Juliana Martinez, Central Florida's Favorite Newscaster. She's seated behind her usual desk in the studio, only this time she's flanked by two large photos of two teenage boys who look all too familiar.

Marcos follows my gaze then grabs the remote to turn up the volume.

"Port Orange police are seeking any information about the current whereabouts of seventeen-year-old Spruce Crick seniors Milo Tate Connolly and Marcos Alvarez Price. The two high school students were reported missing earlier this afternoon after stealing a U-Haul rental van. Anyone with information about the boys is asked to notify the police by calling the missing persons number on the screen below."

"I don't believe it," Marcos scoffs. "They called the police?"

"We did steal a van full of furniture," I remind him as I pull out my phone and see eleven missed calls and thirty new texts from my parents.

"Yeah, and I bet my dad's more concerned about the van than me."

"You do have some very nice furniture."

"Is that why you ran away with me, Connolly? For my furniture?"

"No," I say. Then, before I can stop myself, "I ran away with you because I couldn't imagine my life without you."

At any other point in my short but complicated existence, I would be mortified to admit something so nakedly honest. But after everything that Marcos and I have been through, and considering everything ahead of us, there doesn't seem much point in living my life by half-truths or half measures anymore.

"Oh," Marcos says, his eyes staring into me with uncertainty.

I wish he looked happier about my confession. Though I understand that I have no right to expect such a response. After all, he only agreed to run away with me—not get back together.

"It's okay if you don't feel the same," I say. "After everything I've done, I completely get it. But you should know you are the most important person in my life, and I will always be here for you. Even if it's just as your friend."

Marcos runs his hand through his damp hair and releases a sigh. Whether it's from exhaustion, relief, or annoyance, though, I honestly can't tell. His face isn't giving anything away.

"I've been pretty upset with you," he says, his voice unable to hide the pain I've caused him.

I nod. What other answer can he give me? It's all I deserve.

"But . . ."

But? My heart flutters at the possibility in that one little word.

"I've also missed you," he says. "A lot. I've missed . . . *us*."

"I've missed us too."

Marcos smiles and when his eyes meet mine, they don't look uncertain anymore. They look relieved. Almost hopeful. Without a word, he climbs off his bed and sits beside me on mine. Gently, almost tentatively, he takes my hand, and all I can think is how ridiculously lucky I am. After all we've been through, after all I've put him through, I can't believe he's giving me another chance.

Marcos leans in to kiss me, and my entire body shivers in anticipation. Just as our lips are about to touch, though, an earthshaking BOOM of thunder rattles the hotel. The TV goes out—the screen snapping to black—and I pull away from Marcos as if I've been struck.

"What's the matter?" he asks, his smile instantly fading.

I'm not sure what to tell him. All I know is that my heart is racing and not in a romantic way. In fact, it's definitely in an "Oh my god, what have we done?" kind of way because it's just now hitting me that *OH MY GOD, WHAT HAVE WE DONE?*

Yes, we've managed to outrun our parents but there's still one person we can *never* outrun. And I imagine He is probably feeling pretty pissed off right now.

"I'm just thinking about the meteor," I say, trying not to let my panic consume me. But every bit of confidence I had is quickly draining from my body as the reality of our situation sets in. "And the sinkhole. And the blackout. And the hailstorm."

"What about them?"

"You *know* what."

Marcos shakes his head. "You've got to be joking? How many times do I have to tell you those were accidents? Coincidences. We didn't cause them to happen."

The wind howls outside our room like an enormous beast. "Didn't we?"

"Come on, you can't seriously still think God is punishing us?"

"We almost got hit by lightning running away from our dads. A tree almost fell on us."

"Almost doesn't count."

"Okay then, what about the fire?"

"What about it?"

"I saw your face, Marcos. After the ballpark burned down, I saw what you were thinking, and you were thinking the *exact* same thing that I was. That *we* did this. We *made* this happen."

"Yeah, okay, maybe I thought that for a *millisecond*. But then I read that article in the paper the next day where the fire chief explained that the fire was caused by all that wildly unsafe electrical equipment that the Reverend had outside during a thunderstorm. That's what attracted the lightning. That's what caused the fire. Not God. Science."

Huh. Okay. I didn't actually see that interview. I guess I was too busy doom scrolling through all those videos where an endless stream of angry Christians explained all the very un-Christian things they wanted to do to us. Still, that article doesn't let us off the hook. God could be punishing us *through* science. There are no rules against that.

Also, it's just too much of a coincidence! I mean, one coincidence? Sure, maybe it's all in my head. Two coincidences? Less likely but okay. *Five* coincidences? At some point you just have to accept that there is method to the madness.

"Let me guess," Marcos scoffs, when he sees me eyeing the storm outside our window. "The hurricane is our fault too?"

"Maybe. I don't know *what* to believe anymore. When you and I are together, I know I'm happier than I have ever been in my whole entire life. But I also know every time we're together something terrible happens. And I'm afraid terrible things are going to keep happening as long as we're together."

"I don't understand," Marcos says, clearly struggling to keep the frustration out of his voice. "You said our love *wasn't* a mistake."

"I know. And I still believe that."

"But you also think if we touch, God will punish us?"

"I don't know. Maybe."

"So where does that leave us?"

Marcos's question hangs in the air, and I have no answer.

I know I want to be with him, but I'm also pretty sure we're one kiss away from God losing what's left of His Almighty Patience and smiting not just us but the whole effing planet.

As if to prove my point, another crash of thunder shakes our room. The lights flicker, and a chill shoots down my spine straight into my soul.

"Are you okay?" Marcos asks when I can't stop my teeth from chattering. My skin is breaking out in goose bumps and my hands are trembling. "Jesus, you're turning blue. You need to get out of those damp clothes. Maybe warm up in the shower."

I'm touched that Marcos can be so concerned about my well-being considering I've just told him that any chance of us resurrecting the romantic side of our relationship will have to wait in a permanent holding pattern for the foreseeable future. It's yet another example of why I don't deserve him, and why I can't live without him.

I trudge into the bathroom, peeling off my clothes, and step into the powder-blue tub with its nautical-themed shower curtain. The water comes down hot and hard, and within seconds my skin is scoured pink and fresh and clean.

So where does that leave us?

Marcos's question circles my brain like the water in the drain. Did I really run away from everyone and everything I've ever known just to stare at him from across a hotel room because I'm too afraid to touch him? Granted, so far the consequences of us touching have been *disastrous*. Every second we're together we're tempting fate. And yet we've come this far. Despite astronomical odds, Marcos and I are together. We might only have a few weeks or days or hours before our parents or the police track us down, but right here and now we have each other. And if nothing else that's a kind of miracle.

So what am I going to do about it?

Maybe it's the fact that I'm clean and warm for the first time in what feels like days that fills me with this sudden sense of optimism. Or maybe after everything I've been through this week/month/last three years I'm just fresh out of fucks. But when I step out of the shower, I know exactly what I have to do.

I return to the bedroom and find Marcos lighting the candles that the hotel manager gave us in case the power goes out.

"The lights keep flickering," he explains. "I figure better safe than sorry."

"Good idea," I say, my face breaking into a smile.

I know the candles are purely functional. They're in case of an emergency, not romance. Still, I can't help blushing at the unintentional ambience. Especially since I'm standing here in nothing but a towel while Marcos has stripped down to a T-shirt and boxers.

"Are you feeling better?" he asks, noticing my grin.

"Yeah, thanks."

"Good," he says. "You *look* better."

Marcos flashes me a hesitant smile, and I know in that moment it's now or never. "I have something I need to tell you."

Marcos stops lighting candles, and from the look of resignation that falls across his face, I can tell he's bracing for the worst. "Okay?"

"Okay. So. As you know, this last month has pretty much been the strangest month of my entire life. I genuinely have no idea what's happening. I mean, like you said, there have been all these 'coincidences.' And now Florida is about to be wiped off the map by literally the biggest storm of the century. I know it seems impossible, but all I can think—the *only* thing that makes any sense to me—is that someone or something really doesn't want us to be together."

"You mean God?"

"Yeah. I guess I do. I can't really think of anyone else who could pull all of this off. Can you? I mean, we have to at least consider it. For all we know, God is up there right now testing us, and this hurricane is our final warning. This could be our last chance to do the right thing and call things off. I honestly don't know."

The wind is screaming now. The beast outside our window is howling to get in.

"But what I *do* know is that I don't care. I don't care what God or my parents or the whole stupid universe thinks. I care about you. Because you are the best thing that has ever happened to me. You make me braver and better than I ever thought I could be. And I am so lucky to have you in my life because when I am with you, I know exactly who I am and where I belong. And I am done feeling guilty for that. So if this really is our last chance, if I really do have to make a choice between you and my parents, or you and God, or you and the whole stupid planet, then I choose you. From now until the end of time. I choose *you*."

Thunder crashes outside our window, like the sky is splitting open, and all at once our room plunges into darkness. I can just make out Marcos's face in the candlelight. Even in the chaos he hasn't taken his eyes off me.

"I choose you too," he says, stepping forward and taking my face in his hands. Then his lips are on mine and all I can taste is heaven.

I fall back onto one of the beds, pulling Marcos on top of me. The weight of his body against mine makes me ache with desire. Every inch of my skin is desperate for his touch. He kisses my neck and shoulders, and wherever his lips caress me, my body erupts with pleasure, like every piece of me is being set free.

Is this it? I wonder. *Is this what it is to feel alive? To know completely and without question exactly what you want? And to get it?*

Marcos's kisses work their way down my chest and over my stomach. He stops when he gets to my towel and cautiously fingers the cloth around my waist. "Is this okay?"

My answer is to tear his shirt off over his head and then reach for his boxers. Together we slide them off and toss them to the floor with my towel. Then Marcos is on top of me, his kisses leaving me breathless, as I surrender to skin and muscle and heat.

Outside the wind howls.

I can feel the hotel shaking—like the whole building is yearning to break free from its foundation.

There's an earth-shattering crash. Then another. I don't know if it's thunder or falling trees or a nearby building collapsing. And I don't care.

Marcos and I make love as the sky tears itself apart.

We make love as the city crumbles around us.

We make love as the world ends.

42

The End

"Is this death?" Marcos asks.

It's a fair question. For one thing, the Earth is gone. Like completely gone. There's some floating debris in the distance that looks like it might be a bit of Alaska, but as far as I can tell that's pretty much it.

For another thing, I'm pretty certain the laws of physics have gone out the window. Not that we have a window. Or a room. Or even a hotel. We do have our bed, though. At present it's floating through the endless vastness of space while Marcos and I snuggle under the covers. Logically, we shouldn't be able to breathe. And even if we could, we definitely should have frozen to death by now (especially considering we're naked). But like I said, physics seems to be taking the day off.

There's also a third and final clue that we may no longer be in the Land of the Living. I feel great. Like totally 100 percent at peace with myself and the universe. Which is definitely something I've never felt before. Of course, this utter sense of contentment could stem from the fact that I'm curled up in Marcos's arms, breathing him in while he runs his fingers through my hair.

If this isn't paradise, I don't know what is.

I should probably be freaking out that the entire world ended and that everyone and everything I've ever known is gone. But for whatever reason, I'm calm. Perhaps it's because all of this is just a bit too surreal for my brain to process. Or perhaps it's because there's nothing I can do about it. Whatever the case, I'm perfectly content to drift through space in nothing but a cheap hotel bed for the rest of eternity. I have Marcos, after all, and that's enough.

But just to test his hypothesis I give his arm a pinch.

"Ow!"

"Guess we're not dead."

"I think that's the test for dreaming," he says, wrapping me tighter in his embrace so I can't wriggle away and pinch him again.

His arms are so comfortable, and this bed is so warm, I can't help thinking maybe he's right. Maybe we are dead. And this is Heaven. Maybe Heaven is just spending eternity in bed with the one person you love the most in the whole entire universe.

That's a nice thought, I think as I close my eyes. Then I fall asleep to the music of the cosmos.

"At least we can get dressed now."

At some point while we were sleeping our clothes returned. As did the second double bed, the TV, and the rest of our hotel room. Our window still looks out onto the vast nothingness of space, so we're still adrift. Only now we're adrift within four walls, a ceiling, and a floor.

Marcos hops out of bed and slips on his underwear. In my opinion the return of our clothes is *not* an improvement. I've gotten quite used to seeing Marcos naked and frankly I prefer him that way. Who knew the end of the world would make me such a horndog?

I reach out and try to pull off his boxers, but Marcos swats my hand away. "Come on, don't you want to see what else might be back?"

"Nope." I honestly don't care if I get out of bed ever again.

"But why do you think the room returned?"

"Because it missed us?"

Marcos tries the TV, but it just plays static. Then he picks up the landline on the nightstand, but even from my bed I can tell it's dead from the lack of dial tone.

"Hmm . . . ," he says, setting down the receiver. It's funny to see Marcos so inquisitive. He circles the room like a puppy inspecting its new home and trying to figure out the dimensions of its world.

"What do you think will happen if I open the door?" he asks. He's got his shirt and jeans on now, and he's eyeing our door like it's a present on Christmas morning.

"I think you'll be sucked out into space and we'll both die, so come back to bed and kiss me. My lips are cold."

I stretch out my arms and flash him my winningest smile. He looks from me to the door then back to me again and breaks into the naughtiest grin. Then he jumps into bed, tearing off his clothes, and once again we're making love.

I swear a boy could get used to this.

"That was definitely a seagull."

This morning we wake to the sound of birdsong. At least I think it's morning. It's hard to tell when all concepts of time have literally exploded. But that's definitely a gull outside our window. We can see it circling the hotel—the entire hotel—which must also have come back last night while we slept. There's even a patch of beach outside, though instead of sloping off into the ocean, the sand just peters off into the blackness of space.

This time it's impossible not to be a little curious. When Marcos gets dressed after successfully fighting off my amorous advances, I do the same.

"I don't know why I'm so nervous," he says when we're both standing at the door, his hand hesitating over the knob. I know what he means. I wasn't scared to be floating naked through space, but somehow the simple act of opening a door and stepping outside has got my stomach in knots.

"Let's do it together," I say, placing my hand over his.

"Okay."

"On the count of three. One, two, three . . ."

We turn the knob and, as the door creaks open, we find ourselves staring at the Mariner Inn's very normal, very conventional hallway. Which is kind of anticlimactic. Then again, we weren't sucked out into space, so I'm not complaining.

Marcos and I step out into the corridor, gingerly treading on the carpet as if afraid the weight of our feet might somehow bring the whole hotel crashing down.

"Everything looks the same," I whisper.

"Yeah." Marcos looks disappointed. I'm about to suggest we head back to bed so I can cheer him up when he stops in his tracks and sniffs the air. "Do you smell that?"

For a moment I think our noses must be playing tricks on us. After all, it's been several days since we've eaten (I think), so it wouldn't surprise me if we were hallucinating. But we follow the scent down the stairs and into the lobby, where our curiosity is rewarded with a fresh pot of coffee that sits percolating on the check-in counter.

"Weird," I say when I notice a tray full of clean mugs next to a sign that reads *Free Continental Breakfast*.

Marcos shrugs and helps himself. He gulps down his coffee in one long swallow then smacks his lips in satisfaction. "Oh man, I didn't realize how much I needed that."

"I wonder who made it." There doesn't seem to be any sign of the manager who checked us in last night. Or however long ago that was.

"Hello?" I call while Marcos pours himself a second cup. "Is anybody here?" I try ringing the bell on the counter, but if there's anyone else in the hotel, they're keeping to themselves.

"Come on," Marcos says, draining his mug, "let's go outside."

He takes my hand and pulls me to the exit. For a second, I have the inexplicable fear that if we step outside, we'll be sucked into space. Instead, what hits us as we stride out onto the beach isn't the chilly indifference of a subzero universe, but the gentle glow of the sun.

"Wow," Marcos says, digging his toes in the sand. "It's warm."

It *is* warm. In fact, aside from the missing ocean and the fact that instead of a blue sky overhead we've got a million stars, it's almost a perfect beach day.

"Let's go sit by the shore."

I'm about to correct Marcos that the "shore" he's referring to is technically the End of the Known World, but it's too nice a day (or is it night?) to be pedantic.

Marcos plops down in the sand a few feet away from where the beach dissolves into open space. I'm pretty certain nothing would happen if we stepped off the edge, but at the same time there's no point in pushing our luck.

I sit beside Marcos, lacing my fingers through his, and he smiles at me like I'm his favorite person in the whole entire universe. Okay, technically, I'm the *only* other person in the whole entire universe, but I still feel proud of the accomplishment.

"I've been thinking things over," he says, gazing out at the stars. "And I don't think it was God or the universe that was trying to keep us apart."

"You don't?"

"No. I actually think the universe wanted us to be together. And all the bad things that kept happening to keep us apart, I think they were just manifestations of our own fear and anxiety getting in the way."

"So . . . you're saying God didn't cause the sinkhole and the hailstorm and the blackout. I did. With my constant freaking out and meltdowns?"

"Hey, I was freaking out too," Marcos laughs, "I just managed to hide it better."

"Interesting theory," I say, resting my head on his shoulder. "So, in this scenario, how did our fear make all of those crazy things happen? I mean, are we wizards? Or demigods? Are our parents secretly aliens?"

"No, I think we were just two boys who were afraid to fall in love."

"And that's all?"

"Maybe it's enough."

Marcos lies back in the sand and stares up at the sky. As I curl up next to him, it occurs to me he might be on to something. I mean, look at me. Cuddling on the beach with my boyfriend? That's something I could *never* do in a million years if other people were around. As brave as I feel when I'm alone with Marcos, I know there's a part of me that's terrified of what other people will say about us. My parents, my classmates, even strangers. And maybe someday that won't be the case. Maybe someday I'll be brave enough to walk down the street holding Marcos's hand and not give a damn what anyone thinks. But right now . . . ?

Maybe Marcos is right. Maybe we did make this happen. Maybe the only way we could ever feel safe in the world was if we knew we were the only people in it. And maybe, for whatever reason, God or the universe gave us our wish.

That would explain why Marcos and I are the only two people here. Of course, that would mean that not only is God surprisingly cool with gay people, He's also really rooting for Marcos and me. Which isn't a totally impossible idea. I mean, God could be a big ol' softie. Why not? It's better than the alternative.

And when you think about it—I mean really, *really* think about it— maybe a God who roots for love is the only God worth believing in.

"Where do you think all the people are?"

I've been wondering the same thing ever since we left the hotel this morning. Overnight, more of the Earth returned, and today we woke to find the ocean outside our window, its waves crashing against the shore in a constant, steady rhythm. Even more exciting was the discovery that Daytona is back—or at least a big enough chunk of it to make us feel like we're surrounded by an actual city again.

Marcos's first instinct, of course, was to go exploring, and after a little convincing (and a lot of kisses) I agreed. Sure, the constant napping and sex, followed by more napping and sex, has been everything a teenage boy could ever wish for. But we're both starting to go a little stir-crazy from being cooped up in our room all day. So after grabbing our daily coffee, which continues to be waiting for us hot and fresh every morning, we set off down A1A, walking southward toward Port Orange.

Depending on how much of the world has returned, Marcos thinks we might be able to walk all the way home. Not that we're in any hurry. We leisurely stroll by an alternating assortment of stucco hotels, souvenir shops, and chain restaurants. All empty. All silent. Occasionally a seagull screeches overhead, but that's the only sign of life we've encountered so far.

I can't help thinking that the old Milo would be seriously spooked by the eerie emptiness of these streets. But even with the city's new postapocalyptic vibe, things don't strike me as being ominous so much as they just feel empty. Abandoned. Lonely.

"If the Earth is coming back," Marcos says, stopping to peer inside a deserted Denny's, "maybe that means the people will too?"

That seems like a logical conclusion. If they don't, Marcos and I will end up having an entire planet to ourselves. Which sounds fun in theory but in practicality it might be a bit of a waste. Don't get me wrong. I would happily spend eternity exploring the treasures of the natural world with Marcos. It's just . . .

"I miss Van."

"Yeah," he says, taking my hand. "Me too."

As amazing as these last few days (or weeks, or months) have been, and as disgustingly happy as Marcos has made me in our own personal paradise, part of me hasn't been able to stop thinking about Van. Because if this is Heaven, or the Afterlife, or just our Happy Ending, then Van should be here. No question. As angry as I was at her, I know in my heart she only did what she did because she wanted to protect me. Because she's my best friend. And I can't imagine a universe without her.

The same goes for my parents. I've put off thinking about them for as long as I can, but I can't keep ignoring the very real possibility that I might never see them again. And that thought fills me with tremendous sadness. I know I broke their hearts. I know they're disappointed. I know things can never be the same between us. But that doesn't mean I want them out of my life forever.

And maybe they don't have to be.

Marcos squeezes my hand, and when I look in his eyes, I can tell he's thinking the exact same thing. If we really did bring about the end of the world, if we really do have that power, then maybe we also have the power to fix it?

I mean, what was it that Van said about living holistically? That life doesn't have to be either/or. That one choice doesn't have to cancel out another. It's possible, she said, for a person to hold on to more than one dream. You just have to have the courage to want it.

Well, okay then. I want it.

Yes, this world that Marcos and I somehow created might be the safest place for our love. There's no one here to tease or torment us. There's no one here to keep us apart. But it's also not real. And as frightening as it may be, I know Marcos and I deserve a world as real as our love. So if God or the universe or whoever's out there really is listening, if we really do get a choice in the matter, then I know what we have to choose.

"Marcos?"

"Yeah?"

"I'm ready to go back."

43

The Day after the End of the World

"Oh, thank God, he's awake!"

Something's beeping. Why is there beeping? And why is it so dark?

No, wait, my eyes are closed. I'm pretty sure I can feel daylight around me. I just need to open my eyes. Which for some reason seems like a lot of work.

Why am I so tired?

More than tired, I'm exhausted. I think I'll keep my eyes closed a little longer. Just for a bit. Then when I'm feeling better, I'll take another stab at this whole "opening my eyes" thing.

Except now my head hurts. There's a dull throbbing in the back of my skull that's *really* annoying now that I've noticed it. I need some aspirin. In fact, my whole body feels sore. Like I was hit by a truck.

Wait, was I hit by a truck?

No. That doesn't sound right. I'm pretty sure I'd remember a truck.

But why is my mouth so dry? I'd kill for a glass of water. A glass of water and *two* aspirins. Yeah, that would be awesome. Also, can someone *please* stop that beeping?

"Milo?"

The urgency in my mother's voice jolts me awake. I open my eyes, and the glare of the sunlight streaming through the windows is so bright it hurts.

"Mom . . . ?" My voice comes out like sandpaper. *Why is my throat so dry?*

"Hey, buddy," my dad says, leaning over me. "How are you feeling?"

Umm . . . confused? Yeah, confused is definitely the operative word right now. The last thing I remember is wandering down A1A with Marcos and deciding we should put the world back together. Now I'm lying in a hospital room, and my body feels like a thousand elephants just got done trampling me.

"What happened?"

"It's okay," my mom says, fluttering to my side when I try to sit up. "Just rest. You're going to be fine. All the doctors say you were incredibly lucky." Then to my dad she whispers, "Where is Dr. Lim?"

"I pressed the button."

"Well, press it again."

"Dana, I *am* pressing it. You are welcome to press it yourself if you want."

Hang on. What did my mom say? *All* the doctors? *Lucky?* What's going on?

That last question I managed to croak out loud despite my throat feeling like I've swallowed a sandcastle.

"You were trapped beneath some rubble," my dad explains, "when the hotel collapsed. You were under there for about six, seven hours before the rescue team could get to you. But you're okay. The doctors have been taking excellent care of you. Everyone says you're going to make a full recovery."

Rubble? Hotel? Does he mean the Mariner's Inn? I have a vague memory of the hurricane outside our window and—

"Marcos!" I gasp, my body flooding with terror. "Where's Marcos?"

I remember everything now. The wind howling. The thunder shaking the walls. The roof collapsing. And Marcos screaming for me to get down.

"He's fine," my dad assures me, pushing me back against the bed as my heart rate skyrockets. "He's in the room next door. Don't worry."

I want to leap out of bed and see with my own eyes that Marcos is all right, but I'm so exhausted I know I barely have the strength to make it to the door.

"He's okay?" I ask.

"He's okay."

"You promise?"

"Cross my heart and swear to Jesus."

I lie back down, sheer exhaustion forcing me to accept my father at his word.

"We're just so relieved you're okay," my mom says once I'm breathing calmly. "You had us so worried."

"I'm sorry, I didn't mean to scare you."

"That's okay, buddy."

"And I'm sorry I ran away."

"Don't worry about it," my mom whispers, pulling my sheet up over my chest and tucking me in. "We're just so glad to have you back. Your father and I love you very much."

Mom squeezes my hand, and for the first time since I've woken up, I notice how gaunt she looks. Her and my father. They must have been here for hours, waiting for me to wake up. My heart breaks looking into their tired, bloodshot eyes because even though they don't say it, I know I've put them through hell.

"I love you too," I say. Because despite everything that's happened, despite everything I've put them through, they're still here, standing beside me. Loving me. And I would do anything to hold on to that love.

Well, almost anything.

It's true I never want to hurt my parents again, but I also won't lie to them. Not anymore. Those days have to be over. They have to know who I am—who I really am.

"I also love Marcos," I say.

I know this probably isn't the ideal time for this conversation, but I also know there will *never* be an ideal time. I might as well start being honest with them now. It's the only way they can ever be honest with me. If they're going to love me then they need to love all of me. And if they can't do that, if they can't accept me for who I am, then it's best I find out now before we hurt each other any more.

"I'm gay," I continue, when neither of them says a word. "And that's not something that's ever going to change. Because I don't want it to change. Marcos makes me happier than I have ever been in my whole entire life, and I can't imagine a world without him. And I need you both to know that."

My parents turn to each other and do that thing they sometimes do where they manage to have an entire conversation with just a look. My dad shakes his head, but I'm not sure if that means *No, I can't accept this* or *No point fighting this*. My mom's expression is equally inscrutable. All I can do is pray I haven't lost them.

"Well," my father says after what feels like an eternity. "You're almost an adult. I suppose it's time you start making your own decisions. It's your life, after all."

My mother gives an almost imperceptible nod.

As responses go, it's not exactly the wholehearted acceptance I was hoping for. But it's also not the total condemnation I was dreading either. It's honest. And true. And in this moment, I know it's the best they can give me.

And for now that's enough.

The next time I wake I hear voices. They're not exactly shouting but they're loud enough to bleed through my wall from the room next door. It's the Prices.

I sit up in bed, anxiety coursing through my veins, and immediately feel light-headed. It takes a moment for me to steady myself and trust my legs, but once I'm certain I'm not going to faint, I slip out of my bed. My parents are curled up asleep in two uncomfortable-looking chairs, dead to the world, so as quietly as I can I drag my IV drip (and myself) toward the door.

I still feel like those elephants did a pretty thorough job of trampling my body. There isn't a part of me that's not sore or aching, but my concern for Marcos outweighs any pain. I don't know what's going down in his room, but I'm not going to sit around and wait to find out. And I'm not going to let him go through it alone. I made a promise.

I carefully inch my way into the empty hallway and the Prices' voices grow louder.

"Will you let me handle this?" I hear Mr. Price snap as I approach the door to Marcos's room. Through the window I can see Marcos sitting up in his bed. His right arm is in a cast and there's a slight cut running down the left side of his face, but in this moment I'm so relieved to see him, I can't help thinking he looks like the most magnificent creature in the universe. Even if he is scowling at his father.

Mr. Price is pacing the room. He seems agitated. Which might have something to do with Mrs. Price, who's standing next to her son's bed and glaring at her husband, her arms folded across her chest in the same pose of defiance that I've seen so often from Marcos.

"No, Connor," she says. "I've let you handle things for far too long. You have no idea what Marcos needs. Or what this family needs."

"Excuse me? Everything I'm doing, I'm doing for this family."

"No, you're doing what's best for you. Like you always do. And I won't go along with it. Not anymore. If you want to move back to Orlando because you can't face reality, be my guest. I won't stop you. But I'm staying here, in our house, and Marcos is staying with me."

"That is not—"

"Connor, look at me and hear me," Mrs. Price says, her voice sharp as glass. "This is not a negotiation. This is not up for debate. This is what's happening."

Then, stepping forward so she's face-to-face with her husband, she says the words I know Marcos has been waiting seventeen years to hear.

"I am putting my foot *down*."

Mr. Price doesn't answer. His eyes smolder with indignation. Instead of lashing out, though, he shakes his head with an exasperated sigh, throws his hands up in the air, and heads for the door.

I jump back as it swings open, but there's nowhere for me to hide. Mr. Price stops in his tracks and, from the look of unconcealed horror on his face, I have no doubt that I am now and forever will be his Least Favorite Person in the World.

Part of me wants to say something, to try to salvage the situation. I want to tell Mr. Price that, whether he wants to admit it or not, he and his son are way more alike than he cares to admit. After all, they both defied their fathers to be with the person they loved. If anything, Mr. Price should be proud of his son for following in his footsteps.

Before I can say anything, though, Mrs. Price must spot me in the hallway because I hear her call out, "Milo? Is that you? Please come join us."

Mr. Price scoffs as if he can't believe the level of indignity that's being heaped upon him. Then he shakes his head and storms away, though whether it's to get some fresh air and cool down or to drive off to Orlando, I honestly have no idea.

I slip into Marcos's room just in time to see his mother releasing him from a hug. They both smile when they see me, though Mrs. Price's smile is far more hesitant. I might not be her Least Favorite Person in the World, but I suspect I'm also pretty far from being her favorite.

"How are you feeling?" she asks. I can't tell if her stiffness is residual anger at her husband or just general awkwardness at meeting the boy who encouraged her son to run away in the middle of a hurricane. Probably a little of both.

"Um, good. Thanks."

She nods. Though in the silence that follows, I get the impression she isn't quite sure what else to say. "Well," she finally sighs. "I imagine you boys have a lot to discuss. I'll let you have some privacy."

I'm a little surprised she's okay with leaving the two of us alone and unsupervised considering our past behavior, but after what just went down with her husband, maybe she needs a moment to collect herself.

Mrs. Price pats her son's shoulder and heads for the door. She's just about to leave when Marcos calls out to her from his bed.

"Mom?" Mrs. Price stops but doesn't turn around. "Thank you."

Mrs. Price looks back to her son and, when she does, her eyes are wet with tears. She nods and smiles, then slips out of the room.

"Is your mom okay?" I ask.

"Yeah," Marcos says, wiping a tear from his own eye. "I think so."

"Are *you* okay?"

"I'd be better if my boyfriend kissed me."

I don't need any more encouragement than that. I press my lips to his, and their touch is the best medicine I've had all day. Well, second best.

"Marcos!" I shout, no longer able to conceal my excitement. "You're not moving to Orlando!"

"I know!" he laughs.

We're both grinning like idiots, giddy from the joy of watching Jacinta Price finally put her foot down.

"I can't believe your mom changed her mind. That's amazing!"

"Yeah, it is, isn't it?" Then looking a little sheepish, he adds, "I think me almost dying kind of scared her into doing some serious soul-searching."

"I'm so happy for you."

"Thanks, I'm pretty happy too." Though a second later his smile falters. "I mean, I don't know what this means for my parents' marriage but, honestly, I think they'll be a lot happier if they end up taking some time apart. I know I can certainly use some space from my dad."

I nod and take Marcos's hand. "Maybe someday he'll change."

"Yeah. Maybe." He doesn't sound convinced. "Right now, though, I'm just thankful my mom came around."

"Me too." Though I can't help wondering what exactly this means for us as a couple. Especially considering how reserved she was around me a minute ago. "Is your mom going to be okay with you and me being, you know, *together*?"

"She's not *thrilled*," Marcos says, grimacing. "It's probably going to take her some time to come around to the idea of her son dating boys."

"Uh, correction, *one* boy."

"Right. One boy. But, yeah, she's not forbidding it. I mean, she left us alone together in a room with a bed so that's something. And earlier she mentioned inviting my uncle and his partner to come visit when they finish up with their tour, so I really think she's *trying*."

"Definitely."

Marcos beams, and seeing him so happy makes my heart full. He's like a new person. Or rather, he's like the person he always should've been if his life hadn't been so shrouded in sadness. But now that awful chapter is over. For both of us. I'm so overjoyed I could—

"Don't cry," Marcos says.

Wow. He knows me so well.

And he's right. There's no reason to be sad. Well, correction: there might be one reason. School probably won't be a picnic. We'll still have Jared Resnick and his knuckle-draggers to deal with. But that's exactly what we'll do. Deal with it. Together.

But before I let myself get too carried away with dreams about our future, there's still one question I'd like answered. It's a question that's been nagging me ever since I woke up.

"Marcos?"

"Yeah?"

"After the hurricane, what happened?"

Snatches of images—a bed, a coffeepot, a beach stretching into the stars—have been flickering through my dreams. I think they're memories. They seem so real. But the more time that passes, the hazier everything gets.

"What do you mean?"

"I mean, did the world . . . *end*?"

"You mean, like, metaphorically?"

"No, I mean . . ." But I'm not sure what I mean or even how to finish that sentence. "You didn't have a dream? About the world exploding? And the two of us floating through space? In a bed?"

Marcos looks like he's contemplating whether to fetch a doctor and have my head examined. "No," he says carefully, "but then again I wasn't the one who was knocked unconscious."

"You weren't?"

"No. Didn't your parents tell you? I was awake the whole time. I tried to get you to come around a couple times, but you were out cold. It was actually pretty scary."

His voice drops to a whisper when he says that last part, and I realize now how lucky I was to have been knocked out for our whole ordeal. It must have been terrifying for him to be trapped under all that debris with me, not sure if I was alive or dead, or if anyone was coming to rescue us.

I reach out for Marcos's hand and pull him into a kiss. It's all I can think to do to thank him for watching over me. Both in the real world and in my dreams.

"What's that smell?" he asks, suddenly pulling back from our embrace.

At first, I'm not sure what he means, but then I catch the faint scent of something familiar in the air. An aroma I can't quite place.

"Hey, losers."

Van smirks at us from the doorway, concealing something behind her back as a mischievous grin spreads across her face. "I heard this was the room where I could find the two idiots who thought it would be a good idea to hide out at the beach *during a hurricane.*"

"Yeah," I sigh, cringing with embarrassment. "I guess it wasn't our best idea."

"Actually, no, that's the sad part. It *was* your best idea. That's the level of incompetence I'm dealing with here."

"Ouch."

"Yeah. Also, just so you know, the second you're fully recovered, I am going to beat you both within an inch of your lives for being so goddamn *stupid*." Her voice chokes with emotion and a second later she's rushing to the bed and pulling Marcos and me into a hug so tight it nearly cracks my ribs. "Don't you *ever* do something like that again," she demands. "Do you hear me?"

"We won't," I say.

"We promise."

I hold her tight, or as tight as I can given my condition. Eventually, she nods and pulls away, wiping her eyes with the backs of her hands.

"Here," she says, tossing me a brown, grease-stained to-go bag from Holloway's. "I brought you this even though you totally don't deserve it. And, yes, there might be a few missing. But after what you both put me through, I think I've earned it."

God bless Van. Only she would know how to make a good day even better.

I pull a fistful of curly fries out of the bag and, in yet another tiny miracle, they're still hot. I shove the whole handful in my mouth, ravenous with hunger, and let out a mortifying moan of undiluted pleasure.

"Happy?" Marcos chuckles as he takes some fries for himself.

"Pretty happy."

And why shouldn't I be? My boyfriend and best friend are by my side. The sun is shining. And even though I still can't identify all twenty-seven ingredients in Holloway's special seasoning, there are two things I can definitely taste.

Salt and hope.

Acknowledgments

If you liked this book, the following is an account of all the talented and generous people who helped to make it happen. Conversely, if you hated this book, the following is a list of all the people who probably should've tried harder to stop me.

First and foremost, this book would not exist if ten years ago Kirby and Leuinda Fields hadn't given me a copy of Andrew Smith's *Grasshopper Jungle*. It was the first YA novel that I read as an adult, and it sparked an immediate passion/obsession for the genre that eventually led me, after years of working in the theater, to attempt my first novel.

Early in the writing process, when I had little idea what I was doing and zero faith in my abilities, I received invaluable feedback and ridiculous amounts of encouragement from my first two readers, Lauren Uzdienski and Kirby Fields, as well as from the talented writers in my writing group: Chris Cragin-Day, Mashuq Deen, Don Nguyen, Stella Fawn Ragsdale, Vickie Ramirez, Christina Telesca, and Pia Wilson.

It was Deen who also graciously introduced me to my agent, Tanusri Prasanna, who has been an enthusiastic advocate of *Milo and Marcos* from the very beginning and who didn't let a global pandemic stop her from finding a home for this book.

Of course, I owe a debt of gratitude to everyone at HarperTeen, especially my editor, Carolina Ortiz, who not only took a chance on a debut author but who also helped shape the story with her thoughtful notes and insightful questions. Additionally, a big thanks is owed to all the copy editors and proofreaders who had to deal with my creative spelling and grammar, including Veronica Ambrose, Vincent Cusenza, Lisa Lester Kelly, Daniel Seidel, and Kathryn Silsand.

I also want to give a special shout-out to Carolina Rodríguez Fuenmayor for the amazingly dreamy and awesomely apocalyptic cover art; Chris Kwon for the exciting cover design; and Erika Holzinger for fact-checking my details about the Florida public school system.

Last but not least, I'd be incredibly remiss if I didn't thank my parents. When I was little, they instilled a love of stories in me by reading me books before bed and by entertaining me on long car rides with stories that they would make up on the spot. Most of those impromptu stories took place in outer space and, more often than not, involved fantastical aliens called Kissy-Woos. Kissy-Woos (for the uninformed) are flying lips that travel in a swarm and can kiss a person to death.

I mention this because, if you happen to think my book is just plain weird, now you know where I get it from and who's to blame.